PENGUIN BOOKS

THE BASTARD OF ISTANBUL

'Unquestionably an ambitious book, exuberant and teeming' *Guardian*

'Heartbreaking . . . the beauty of Islam pervades Shafak's book' *Vogue*

'A tender and spirited novel . . . Steeped in the sights, colours and smells of Turkey's capital, it grapples with the country's dark legacies' *NPR Books*

'Wonderfully magical, breathtaking . . . [it] will have you gasping with disbelief' *Sunday Express*

'A beautiful book, the finest I have read' *Irish Times*

'A supernatural personal history . . . In this new book [Elif Shafak] has taken on a subject of deep moral consequence' *The New York Times*

'With compassion and a deftly humorous touch, Shafak fashions a woman's world that is at once micro and macro, using everyday material – recipes, lullabies, superstitions – to illuminate a broader reality' *Metro*

'A brave and passionate novel' Paul Theroux

'Tremendous exuberance' Margaret Forster

'An astonishingly rich and lively story . . . handled with an enchantingly light touch' *Kirkus Reviews*

'Overflows with a kitchen sink's worth of zany characters . . . an entertaining and insightful ensemble novel that posits the universality of family, culture and coincidence' *Publishers Weekly*

The
Bastard
of Istanbul

—————

ELIF SHAFAK

PENGUIN BOOKS

PENGUIN BOOKS

UK | USA | Canada | Ireland | Australia
India | New Zealand | South Africa

Penguin Books is part of the Penguin Random House group of companies
whose addresses can be found at global.penguinrandomhouse.com.

First published in the United States of America by Viking Penguin,
a member of Penguin Group (USA) Inc. 2007
First published in Great Britain by Viking 2007
Published in Penguin Books 2008
Reissued in this edition 2015

001

Printed in Great Britain by Clays Ltd, St Ives plc

A CIP catalogue record for this book is available from the British Library

ISBN: 978-0-241-97290-8

www.greenpenguin.co.uk

MIX
Paper from
responsible sources
FSC® C018179
www.fsc.org

Penguin Random House is committed to a
sustainable future for our business, our readers
and our planet. This book is made from Forest
Stewardship Council® certified paper.

ONE

Cinnamon

Whatever falls from the sky above, thou shall not curse it. That includes the rain.

No matter what might pour down, no matter how heavy the cloudburst or how icy the sleet, you should never ever utter profanities against whatever the heavens might have in store for us. Everybody knows this. And that includes Zeliha.

Yet, there she was on this first Friday of July, walking on a sidewalk that flowed next to hopelessly clogged traffic; rushing to an appointment she was now late for, swearing like a trooper, hissing one profanity after another at the broken pavement stones, at her high heels, at the man stalking her, at each and every driver who honked frantically when it was an urban fact that clamor had no effect on unclogging traffic, at the whole Ottoman dynasty for once upon a time conquering the city of Constantinople, and then sticking by its mistake, and yes, at the rain . . . this damn summer rain.

Rain is an agony here. In other parts of the world, a downpour will in all likelihood come as a boon for nearly everyone and everything—good for the crops, good for the fauna and the flora, and with an extra splash of romanticism, good for lovers. Not so in Istanbul though. Rain, for us, isn't necessarily about getting wet. It's not about getting dirty even. If anything, it's about getting angry. It's mud and chaos and rage, as if we didn't have enough of each already. And struggle. It's always about struggle. Like kittens thrown into a bucketful of water, all ten million of us put up a futile fight against the drops. It can't be said that we are completely alone in this scuffle, for the streets too are in on it, with their antediluvian names stenciled on tin placards, and the tombstones of so many saints scattered in all directions, the piles of garbage that wait on almost every corner, the hideously huge construction pits soon to be turned into glitzy, modern buildings, and the seagulls. . . . It angers us all when the sky opens and spits on our heads.

But then, as the final drops reach the ground and many more perch unsteadily on the now dustless leaves, at that unprotected moment, when you are not quite sure that it has finally ceased raining, and neither is the rain itself, in that very interstice, everything becomes serene. For one long minute, the sky seems to apologize for the mess she has left us in. And we, with driblets still in our hair, slush in our cuffs, and dreariness in our gaze, stare back at the sky, now a lighter shade of cerulean and clearer than ever. We look up and can't help smiling back. We forgive her; we always do.

At the moment, however, it was still pouring and Zeliha had little, if any, forgiveness in her heart. She did not have an umbrella, for she had promised herself that if she was enough of an imbecile to throw a bunch of money to yet another street vendor for yet another umbrella, only to forget it here and there as soon as the sun came back, then she deserved to be soaked to the bone. Besides, it was too late now anyway. She was already sopping wet. That was the one thing about the rain that likened it to sorrow: You did your best to remain untouched, safe and dry, but if and when you failed, there came a point in which you started seeing the problem less in terms of drops than as an incessant gush, and thereby you decide you might as well get drenched.

Rain dripped from her dark curls onto her broad shoulders. Like all the women in the Kazancı family, Zeliha had been born with frizzy raven-black hair, but unlike the others, she liked to keep it that way. From time to time her eyes of jade green, normally wide open, and filled with fiery intelligence, squinted into two lines of untainted indifference inherent only to three groups of people: the hopelessly naïve, the hopelessly withdrawn, and the hopelessly full of hope. She being none of these, it was hard to make sense of this indifference, even if it was such a flickering one. One minute it was here, canopying her soul to drugged insensibility, the next minute it was gone, leaving her alone in her body.

Thus she felt on that first Friday of July desensitized as if anesthetized, a powerfully corrosive mood for someone so zestful as she. Could this be why she had had absolutely no interest in fighting the city today, or the rain for that matter? While the yo-yo indifference went up and down with a rhythm all its own, the pendulum of her mood swayed between two opposite poles: from frozen to fuming.

As Zeliha rushed by, the street vendors selling umbrellas and raincoats and plastic scarves in glowing colors eyed her in amusement. She managed to ignore their gaze, just as she managed to ignore the gaze of all the men who stared at her body with hunger. The vendors looked disapprovingly at her shiny nose ring too, as if therein lay a clue as to her deviance from modesty, and thereby the sign of her *lustfulness*. She was especially proud of her piercing because she had done it herself. It had hurt but the piercing was here to stay and so was her style. Be it the harassment of men or the reproach of other women, the impossibility of walking on broken cobblestones or hopping into the ferryboats, and even her mother's constant nagging . . . there was no power on earth that could prevent Zeliha, who was taller than most women in this city, from donning miniskirts of glaring colors, tight-fitting blouses that displayed her ample breasts, satiny nylon stockings, and yes, those towering high heels.

Now, as she stepped on another loose cobblestone, and watched the puddle of sludge underneath splash dark stains on her lavender skirt, Zeliha unleashed another long chain of curses. She was the only woman in the whole family and one of the few among all Turkish women who used such foul language so unreservedly, vociferously, and knowledgeably; thus, whenever she started swearing, she kept going as if to compensate for all the rest. This time was no different. As she ran, Zeliha swore at the municipal administration, past and present, because ever since she was a little girl, never a rainy day had passed with these cobblestones primed and fixed. Before she was done swearing, however, she abruptly paused, lifted her chin as if suspecting someone had called her name, but rather than looking around for an acquaintance, she instead pouted at the smoky sky. She squinted, sighed a conflicted sigh, and then unleashed another profanity, only this time against the rain. Now, according to the unwritten and unbreakable rules of Petite-Ma, her grandmother, *that* was sheer blasphemy. You might not be fond of the rain, you certainly did not have to be, but under no circumstances should you cuss at anything that came from the skies, because nothing poured from above on its own and behind it all there was Allah the Almighty.

Surely Zeliha knew the unwritten and unbreakable rules of Petite-Ma, but on this first Friday of July she felt spoiled enough not to care. Besides, whatever had been uttered had been uttered, just like whatever had been done in life had been done and was now gone. Zeliha had no time for regrets. She was late for her appointment with the gynecologist. Not a negligible risk, indeed, given that the moment you notice being late for an appointment with the gynecologist, you might decide not to go there at all.

A yellow cab with bumper stickers all over its back fender pulled up short. The driver, a rough-looking, swarthy man who had a Zapata mustache and a gold front tooth, and who might very well have been a molester when off duty, had all the windows down and a local rock station blasting Madonna's "Like a Virgin" full bore. There was a sharp mismatch between the man's utterly traditional look and his contrastingly unconventional musical preferences. He braked brusquely, cocked his head out of the window, and after whistling at Zeliha, barked, "I'll have some of that!" His next words were muffled by Zeliha's.

"What's wrong with you, creep? Can't a woman walk in peace in this city?"

"But why walk when I could give you a ride?" the driver asked. "You wouldn't want that sexy body to get wet, would you?"

As Madonna cried in the background "*My fear is fading fast, been saving it all for you,*" Zeliha began to swear, thus breaking another unwritten and unbreakable rule, this time not one of Petite-Ma's but one of Female Prudence. *Never cuss at your harasser.*

The Golden Rule of Prudence for an Istanbulite Woman: When harassed on the street, never respond, since a woman who responds, let alone swears back at her harasser, shall only fire up the enthusiasm of the latter!

Zeliha was no stranger to this rule, and she knew better than to violate it, but this first Friday of July was like no other, and there was now another self unleashed in her, one far more carefree and brash, and frighteningly furious. It was this other Zeliha that inhabited most of her inner space and took charge of things now, making decisions in the name of both. That must be why she continued to curse at the top of her voice. As she drowned out Madonna, the pedestrians and umbrella vendors gathered to see what kind of trouble was brewing. In the turmoil, the stalker behind her flinched, knowing better than to mess with a madwoman. But the cabdriver was neither as prudent nor as timid, for he welcomed all the fuss with a grin. Zeliha noticed how surprisingly white and flawless the man's teeth were, and could not help wondering if they were porcelain capped. Little by little, she once again felt that wave of adrenaline escalate in her belly, churning her stomach, accelerating her pulse, making her sense that she, rather than any other woman in her whole family, might someday kill a man.

Fortunately for Zeliha, it was then that the driver of a Toyota behind the cab lost patience and honked. As if awakened from a bad dream, Zeliha came to her senses and shivered at her grim situation. Her proclivity to violence scared her, as it always had. In an instant she was quiet and veered aside, trying to inch her way through the crowd. Yet in her haste, Zeliha's right heel became stuck under a loose cobblestone. Infuriated, she pulled her foot out of the puddle under the stone. While her foot and shoe came loose, the heel of her shoe broke, thus reminding her of a particular rule she should have never put out of her mind in the first place.

The Silver Rule of Prudence for an Istanbulite Woman: When harassed on the street, do not lose nerve, since a woman who loses her nerve in the face of harassment, and thus reacts excessively, will only make matters worse for herself!

The cabdriver laughed, the horn of the Toyota behind blared yet again, the rain hastened on, and several pedestrians tsk-tsked in unison, though it was hard to tell what exactly they were reprimanding. Amid all the tumult, Zeliha caught sight of an iridescent bumper sticker glittering on the back of the cab: DON'T CALL ME WRETCHED! it declared. THE WRETCHED TOO HAVE A HEART. As she stood there blankly staring at these words, suddenly she felt tired beyond herself—so tired and taken aback that one would suppose it wasn't the everyday problems of an Istanbulite that she was dealing with. Rather it was some sort of cryptic code that a faraway mind had specifically designed for her to decipher and that she in her mortality had never managed to crack. Soon, the cab and the Toyota left and the pedestrians went their separate ways, leaving Zeliha there, holding the broken heel of her shoe as tenderly and despondently as if she were carrying a dead bird.

Now, among the things included in Zeliha's chaotic universe, there might be dead birds, but certainly not tenderness and despondency. She would have none of those. She straightened up and did her awkward best to walk with one heel. Soon she was hurrying amid a crowd with umbrellas, exposing her stunning legs, limping her way like a note out of tune. She was a thread of lavender, a most unbefitting hue fallen into a tapestry of browns, grays, and more browns and grays. Though hers was a discordant color, the crowd was cavernous enough to swallow her disharmony and bring her back into its cadence. The crowd was not a conglomeration of hundreds of breathing, sweating, and aching bodies, but one single breathing, sweating, and aching body under the rain. Rain or sun made little difference. Walking in Istanbul meant walking in tandem with the crowd.

As Zeliha passed by dozens of rough-looking fishermen silently standing side by side along the old Galata Bridge, each holding an umbrella in one hand and a spinning rod in the other, she envied them for their capacity for stillness, this ability to wait for hours for fish that did not exist, or if they did, turned out to be so tiny that in the end they could only be used as bait for another fish that would never get caught. How amazing was this ability to achieve plenty by achieving little, to go home empty-handed yet still satisfied at the end of the day! In this world, serenity generated luck and luck generated felicity, or so suspected Zeliha. Suspect was all she could do on this particular matter, for she had never before tasted that kind of serenity, and she didn't think she ever could. At least not today. Definitely not today.

Despite her hurry, as she wound her way through the Grand Bazaar, Zeliha slowed down. She had no time for shopping but would go inside for just a quick glance, she assured herself, as she surveyed the storefronts. She lit a cigarette and as the smoke curled from her mouth, she felt better, almost relaxed. A woman who smoked on the streets was not highly regarded in Istanbul, but who cared? Zeliha shrugged. Hadn't she already waged a war against the entire society? With that she moved toward the older section of the bazaar.

There were vendors here who knew her on a first-name basis, especially the jewelers. Zeliha had a soft spot for glittery accessories of all sorts. Crystal hairpins, rhinestone brooches, lustrous earrings, pearly boutonnieres, zebra-stripe scarves, satin satchels, chiffon shawls, silk pom-poms, and shoes, always with high heels. Never a day had she passed by this bazaar without ducking into at least several stores, bargaining with the vendors, and ending up paying far less than the amount proposed for things she had not planned to purchase in the first place. But today she drifted by a few stalls and peeped into some windows. That was it.

Zeliha lingered in front of a stand full of jars and pots and flasks full of herbs and spices of every color and kind. She remembered one of her three sisters asking her this morning to get some cinnamon, though she couldn't remember which one had asked. She was the youngest of four girls who could not agree on anything but retained an identical conviction of always being right, and feeling each had nothing to learn from the others but lots to teach. It felt as bad as missing the lottery by a single number: Whichever way you might try to consider the situation, you could not rid yourself of feeling subjected to an injustice that was beyond correction. All the same, Zeliha purchased some cinnamon, not the crushed powder, but sticks. The vendor offered her tea and a cigarette and a chat, and she rejected none. While she sat there talking, her eyes nonchalantly scanned the shelves, until they locked onto a glass tea set. That too was among the list of the things she could not resist buying: tea glasses with gilded stars and thin, delicate spoons and brittle saucers with gilded belts around their bellies. There already must be at least thirty different glass tea sets at home, all bought by her. But there was no harm in buying another set, for they broke so easily. "So damn fragile . . . " muttered Zeliha under her breath. She was the only one among all the Kazancı females capable of getting infuriated at tea glasses when they broke. Meanwhile, seventy-seven-year-old Petite-Ma, for her part, had developed a completely different approach.

"There goes another evil eye!" Petite-Ma exclaimed each time a tea glass fractured and fell apart. "Did you hear that ominous sound? Crack! Oh it echoed in my heart! That was somebody's evil eye, so jealous and malicious. May Allah protect us all!"

Whenever a glass broke or a mirror cracked, Petite-Ma heaved a sigh of relief. After all, given the fact that you could not completely wipe out wicked people from the surface of this madly spinning world, it was far better to have their evil eye ram into a frontier of glass than penetrate deep inside God's innocent souls and ruin their lives.

Twenty minutes later when Zeliha rushed into a chic office in one of the most well-off quarters of the city, she had a broken heel in one hand and a new set of tea glasses in the other. Once inside the door, she was dismayed to remember that she had left the wrapped cinnamon sticks at the Grand Bazaar.

In the waiting room there were three women, each with terrible hair, and a man with almost none. Given the way they sat, Zeliha instantly noted and cynically deduced, the youngest was the least worried of all, languidly leafing through the pictures of a women's magazine, too lazy to read the articles, probably here to renew her prescription for birth control pills; the plump blonde next to the window, who seemed to be in her early thirties and whose black roots begged to be dyed, was swaying on her feet nervously, her mind apparently elsewhere, probably here for a routine checkup and annual Pap smear. The third one, who was wearing a head scarf and had come along with her husband, seemed to be the least composed of them all, the corners of her mouth turned down, her eyebrows knit. Zeliha guessed she was having trouble getting pregnant. Now *that*, Zeliha assumed, could be bothersome, depending on one's perspective. She personally did not see infertility as the worst thing that could happen to a woman.

"Hellooo you!" chirped the receptionist, forcing herself into a goofy, phony smile so well practiced it looked neither goofy nor phony. "Are you our three o'clock appointment?"

The receptionist seemed to be having a hard time pronouncing the letter *r*, and as if to compensate she went to extraordinary lengths by accentuating the sound, raising her voice, and offering an extra smile on top of that whenever her tongue bumped into that ominous letter. To save her the burden, Zeliha nodded instantly and perhaps too heartily.

"And what exactly are you here for, Miss Three-o'clock-Appointment?"

Zeliha managed to ignore the absurdity of the question. By now she knew too well that it was precisely this unconditional and all-embracing female cheerfulness that she sorely lacked in life. Some women were devoted *smilers*; they smiled with a Spartan sense of duty. How could one ever learn to do so naturally something so unnatural, Zeliha wondered. But leaving aside the question that tugged at the edges of her mind, she responded: "An abortion."

The word hovered in the air, and they all waited for it to sink. The receptionist's eyes grew small, then large, while the smile on her face disappeared. Zeliha couldn't help feeling relieved. After all, unconditional and all-embracing female cheerfulness brought out a vindictive streak in her.

"I have an appointment. . . . " Zeliha said, tucking a ringlet behind her ears while letting the rest of her hair fall around her face and over her shoulders like a thick, black burka. She lifted her chin, thus accentuating her aquiline nose, and felt the need to repeat, a notch louder than she had intended, or maybe not. "Because I need to have an abortion."

Torn between impartially registering the new patient and giving a scolding eye to such intrepidness, the receptionist stood still, a huge, leather-covered notebook lying open in front of her. A few more seconds passed before she finally started scribbling. In the meantime Zeliha muttered:

"I'm sorry that I'm late." The clock on the wall indicated that she was forty-six minutes late, and as her gaze rested on it, for a second, she looked as if she were drifting away. "It's because of the rain. . . ."

That was a little unfair to the rain, since the traffic, the broken cobblestones, the municipality, the stalker, and the cabdriver, not to mention the stop for shopping, should also have been held accountable for her delay, but Zeliha decided to bring up none of those. She might have violated The Golden Rule of Prudence for an Istanbulite Woman, she might also have violated The Silver Rule of Prudence for an Istanbulite Woman, but she held her ground to abide by the Copper Rule.

The Copper Rule of Prudence for an Istanbulite Woman: When harassed on the street, you'd better forget about the incident as soon as you are on your way again, since to recall the incident all day long will only further wrack your nerves!

Zeliha was smart enough to know that even if she had brought up the harassment now, other women, far from being supportive, would have the tendency to pass judgment on a harassed *sister* in cases like these. So she kept the answer short and the rain remained the only thing to blame.

"Your age, miss?" the receptionist wanted to know.

Now *that* was an annoying question, and utterly unnecessary. Zeliha squinted at the receptionist as if she were some sort of a semidarkness one needed to adjust her eyes to better see. All of a sudden, she remembered the sad truth about herself: her age. Like too many women used to acting above and beyond their years, she was disturbed by the fact that, after all, she was far younger than she'd like to be.

"I am," she conceded, "nineteen years old." As soon as the words came out of her mouth, she blushed, as if caught naked in front of all these people.

"We'd need the consent of your husband, of course," the receptionist continued, no longer in a chirpy voice, and wasted no time in proceeding on to another question, the answer of which she already suspected. "May I ask you, are you married, miss?"

From the corner of her eye Zeliha noticed the plump blonde on her right and the head-scarved woman on her left wriggle uncomfortably. As the inquisitive gaze of every person in the room weighed heavier upon her, Zeliha's grimace evolved into a beatific smile. Not that she was enjoying the tortuous moment, but the indifference deep underneath had just whispered to her not to mind other people's opinions since they would make no difference at the end of the day. Lately she had decided to purge certain words from her vocabulary and now that she recalled that decision, why not start with the word *shame*. Still, she didn't have the nerve to utter aloud what by now everyone in the room had fully understood. There was no husband to consent to this abortion. There was no father. Instead of a *BA-BA*★ there was only a VO-ID.

Fortunately for Zeliha, the fact that there was no husband turned out to be an advantage in formalities. Apparently she didn't need to get anyone's written approval. The bureaucratic regulations were less keen to rescue babies born out of wedlock than those born to married couples. A fatherless baby in Istanbul was just another bastard, and a bastard just another sagging tooth in the city's jaw, ready to fall out at any time.

"Your birthplace?" the receptionist continued drearily.

"Istanbul!"

★ *Baba* means *Father* in Turkish.

"Istanbul?"

Zeliha shrugged as if to say, where else could it be? Where else on earth but here? She belonged to this city! Wasn't that visible on her face? After all, Zeliha considered herself a true Istanbulite, and as if to reprimand the receptionist for failing to see such an apparent fact, she turned back on her broken heel and invited herself to the chair next to the head-scarved woman. It was only then that she took notice of the latter's husband, who was sitting still, almost paralyzed with embarrassment. Rather than passing judgment on Zeliha, the man seemed to be wallowing in the discomfort of being the only male here, in such a blatantly feminine zone. For a second Zeliha felt sorry for him. It occurred to her to ask the man to step onto the balcony and have a smoke with her, for she was sure he smoked. But that could be misinterpreted. An unmarried woman could not ask such questions of married men, and a married man would display hostility toward another woman when next to his wife. Why was it difficult to become friends with men? Why did it always have to be like that? Why couldn't you just step out onto the balcony and have a smoke and exchange a few words, and then go your separate ways? Zeliha sat there silently for one long moment, not because she was dog-tired, which she was, or because she was fed up with all the attention, which she was as well, but because she wanted to be next to the open window; she was hungry for the sounds of the street. A street vendor's husky voice infiltrated the room: "Tangerines . . . Fragrant, fresh tangerines . . ."

"Good, keep shouting," Zeliha muttered to herself. She didn't like silence. As a matter of fact, she abhorred silence. It was okay that people stared at her on the street, in the bazaar, at the doctor's waiting room, here and there, day and night; it was all right that they watched and gawked, and eyeballed at length again as if seeing her for the first time. One way or another she could always fight back their gaze. What she could not possibly fight back was their silence.

"Tangerinist . . . Tangerinist . . . How much costs a kilo?" a woman yelled from an open window on the upper floor of a building across the street. It had always amused Zeliha to see how easily, almost effortlessly, the denizens of this city were capable of inventing unlikely names for ordinary professions. You could add an -*ist* to almost every single thing sold in the market, and the next thing you knew, you had yet another name to be included in the elongated list of urban professions. Thus, depending on what was put on sale, one could easily be called a "tangerinist," "waterist," or "bagelist," or . . . "abortionist."

By now Zeliha had no doubt. Not that she needed one to know what she already was sure about, but she had also had a test done at the newly opened clinic in their vicinity. On the day of the "grand opening" the people at the clinic had given a showy reception for a bunch of selected guests, and had lined up all the bouquets and garlands right outside at the entrance so that the passersby on the street could be informed about the occasion as well. When Zeliha had visited the clinic the very next day, most of these flowers had already faded, but the flyers were as colorful as before. FREE PREGNANCY TEST WITH EACH BLOOD SUGAR TEST! it said in phosphorescent capital letters. The correlation between the two was unknown to Zeliha, but she had taken the test all the same. When the results arrived, her blood sugar turned out to be normal and she turned out to be pregnant.

"Miss, you can come in now!" called the receptionist as she stood in the doorway, fighting another *r*, this time one that was hard to avoid in her profession. "The doctor . . . he is waiting for you."

Grabbing her box of tea glasses and the broken heel, Zeliha jumped to her feet. She felt all the heads in the room turn toward her, recording her every gesture. Normally, she would have walked as rapidly as she could. At the moment, however, her moves were visibly slow, almost languorous. Just when she was about to leave the room, she paused, and as if pushed by a button, she turned around, knowing exactly whom to look at. There, at the center of her gaze, was a most embittered face. The head-scarved woman grimaced, her brown eyes shadowed by resentment, her lips moving and cursing the doctor and this nineteen-year-old about to abort the child Allah should have bestowed not on a slapdash girl but on her.

The doctor was a burly man who communicated strength through his erect posture. Unlike his receptionist, there was no judgment in his stare, no unwise questions on his tongue. He seemed to welcome Zeliha in every way. He made her sign some papers, and then more papers in case anything went wrong either during or after the procedure. Next to him, Zeliha felt her nerve slacken and her skin thin out, which was too bad because whenever her nerves slackened and her skin thinned out, she became as fragile as a tea glass, and whenever she became as fragile as a tea glass, she couldn't help but come close to tears. And *that* was one thing she truly hated. Harboring profound contempt for weepy women ever since she was a little girl, Zeliha had promised herself never to turn into one of those walking miseries who scattered tears and nitpicky complaints everywhere they went and of which there were far too many around her. She had forbidden herself to cry. To this day, she had on the whole managed pretty well to stick to her promise. When and if tears welled up in her eyes, she simply held her breath and remembered her promise. So on this first Friday of July she once again did what she had always done to stifle the tears: She took a deep breath and thrust her chin upward as an indication of strength. This time, however, something went awfully wrong and the breath she had held came out as a sob.

The doctor did not look surprised. He was used to it. The women always cried.

"There, there," he said, trying to console Zeliha while putting on a pair of medical gloves. "It's going to be all right, don't you worry. It's only a slumber. You'll sleep, you'll dream, before you finish your dream, we'll wake you up and you'll go home. After that, you'll remember nothing."

When Zeliha cried like this all of her expressions became discernible and her cheeks sunk in, thus accentuating the most telling feature of hers: her nose! That remarkably aquiline nose of hers, which she, like her siblings, had inherited from their father; hers, unlike her siblings, was sharpened further on the ridge and elongated a bit more on the edges.

The doctor patted her shoulder, handed her a tissue, and then handed her the whole box. He always had a spare box of tissues ready by his desk. Drug companies distributed these tissue boxes free of charge. Along with pens and notebooks and other things that carried their company names, they made tissues for women patients who could not stop crying.

"Figs . . . Delicious figs . . . Good ripe figs!"

Was it the same vendor or a new one? What did his customers call him . . . ? Figist . . . ?! Zeliha thought to herself, as she laid still on a table in a room unnervingly white and immaculate. Neither the accoutrements nor even the knives scared her as much as this absolute whiteness. There was something in the color white that resembled silence. Both were emptied of life.

In her endeavor to sway away from the color of silence, Zeliha grew distracted by a black spot on the ceiling. The more she fixed her stare on it, the more the spot resembled a black spider. First it was still, but then it started to crawl. The spider grew bigger and bigger as the injection started to spread in Zeliha's veins. In a few seconds she was so heavy she could not move a finger. As she tried to resist being carried away by the anesthetized slumber, she started to sob again.

"Are you sure this is what you want? Perhaps you would like to mull it over," said the doctor in a velvety voice as if Zeliha was a pile of dust and he was afraid of brushing her away with the wind of his words if he spoke louder. "If you'd like to reconsider this decision, it is not too late."

But it was. Zeliha knew it had to be done now, on this first

Friday of July. Today or never. "There is nothing to consider. I cannot have her," she heard herself blurt out.

The doctor nodded. As if waiting for this gesture, all of a sudden the Friday prayer poured into the room from the nearby mosque. In seconds another mosque joined in and then another and another. Zeliha's face contorted in discomfort. She hated it when a prayer originally designed to be called out in the pureness of the human voice was dehumanized into an electro-voice roaring over the city from microphones and cabinet speakers. Soon the clamor was so deafening she suspected there was something wrong with the loudspeaker system of each and every mosque in the vicinity. Either that or her ears had become extremely sensitive.

"It will be over in a minute. . . . Don't worry."

It was the doctor speaking. Zeliha looked at him quizzically. Was her contempt for the electro-prayer so obvious on her face? Not that she minded. Among all the Kazancı women she was the only one who was openly irreligious. As a child it used to please her to imagine Allah as her best friend, which was not a bad thing of course, except that her other best friend was a garrulous, freckled girl who had made smoking a habit at the age of eight. The girl happened to be the daughter of their cleaning lady, a chubby Kurdish woman with a mustache she did not always bother to shave. Back in those days, the cleaning lady used to come to their house twice a week, bringing her daughter along on each visit. Zeliha and the girl became good friends after a while, even cutting their index fingers to mix their blood and become lifelong blood-sisters. For a week the two girls went around with bloody bandages wrapped around their fingers as a sign of their sisterhood. Back in those days, whenever Zeliha prayed it would be this bloody bandage she'd be thinking about—if only Allah too could become a blood-sister . . . *her* blood-sister. . . .

Pardon me, she would instantly apologize and then repeat again and again because whenever you apologized to Allah you had to do it thrice: *Pardon me, pardon me, pardon me.*

It was wrong, she knew. Allah could not and should not be personified. Allah did not have fingers, or blood for that matter. One had to refrain from attributing human qualities to him—that's to say, Him—which was not easy since every one of his—that's to say, His—ninety-nine names happened to be qualities also pertinent to human beings. He could see it all but had no eyes; He could hear it all but had no ears; He could reach out everywhere but had no hands. . . . Out of all this information an eight-year-old Zeliha had drawn the conclusion that Allah could resemble us, but we could not resemble Him. Or was it vice versa? Anyway, one had to learn to think about him—that's to say, Him—without thinking of Him as him.

The chances are she would not have minded this as much if one afternoon she had not spotted a bloody bandage around her elder sister Feride's index finger. It looked like the Kurdish girl made her a blood-sister too. Zeliha felt betrayed. Only then it dawned on her that her real objection to Allah was not his—that's to say, His—not having any blood but rather having too many blood-sisters, too many to care for so as to end up not caring for anyone.

The episode of friendship had not lasted long after that. The *konak* being so big and dilapidated and Mom being so grumpy and mulish, the cleaning lady quit after a while, taking her daughter away. Having been left without a best friend, whose friendship, indeed, had been rather dubious, Zeliha felt a subtle resentment, but she hadn't quite known toward whom—to the cleaning lady for quitting, to her mom for making her quit, to her best friend for playing two sides, to her elder sister for stealing her blood-sister, or to Allah. The others being utterly out of her reach, she chose Allah to be resentful toward. Having felt like an infidel at such an early age, she saw no reason why she shouldn't do so as an adult.

Another call to prayer from another mosque joined in. The prayers multiplied in echoes, as if drawing circles within circles. Oddly enough, at this moment in the doctor's office, she worried about being late for dinner. She wondered what would be served at the table this evening, and which one of her three sisters had done the cooking. Each of her sisters was good with a particular recipe, so depending on the cook of the day she could pray for a different dish. She craved stuffed green peppers—a particularly tricky dish since every one of her sisters made it so differently. *Stuffed . . . green . . . peppers . . .* Her breathing slowed while the spider started to descend. Still trying to stare at the ceiling, Zeliha felt as if she and the people in the room were not occupying the same space. She stepped into the kingdom of Morpheus.

It was too bright here, almost glossy. Slowly and cautiously, she walked along a bridge teeming with cars and pedestrians, and motionless fishermen with worms wiggling at the ends of their spinning rods. As she navigated among them, every cobblestone she stepped on turned out to be loose, and to her awe, there was only void underneath. Soon she'd realize in horror that what was below was also above, and it was raining cobblestones from the blue skies. When a cobblestone fell from the sky, a cobblestone lessened from the pavement below. Above the sky and under the ground, there was the same thing: VO-ID.

As cobblestones rained from above, enlarging further the cavity underneath, she panicked, afraid of being swallowed by the hungry abyss. "Stop!" she cried out as the stones kept rolling under her feet. "Stop!" she commanded the vehicles speeding toward her and then running her over. "Stop!" she begged the pedestrians shouldering her aside.

"Please stop!"

When Zeliha woke up she was alone, nauseous, and in an unfamiliar room. How on earth she could have walked here was a puzzle she had no desire to solve. She felt nothing, neither pain nor sorrow. So, she concluded, in the end the indifference must have won the race. It wasn't only her baby but her senses too that had been aborted on that pure white table in the next room. Perhaps there was a silver lining somewhere. Perhaps now she could go fishing, and finally manage to stand still for hours on end without feeling frustrated or left behind, as if life were a swift hare she could only watch from a distance but never possibly catch.

"There you are, finally back!" The receptionist was standing by the door, arms akimbo. "Goodness gracious! What a fright! How you scared us! Do you have any idea how you shrieked? It was so awful!"

Zeliha laid still, without blinking.

"The pedestrians on the street must have thought we were slaughtering you or something. . . . I only wonder why the police did not show up at our door!"

Because it is the Istanbul police you are talking about, not some brawny cop in an American movie, Zeliha thought to herself as she finally allowed herself a blink. Still not quite understanding why she had annoyed the receptionist but seeing no point in annoying her any further, she offered the first excuse that came to her mind: "Maybe I screamed because it hurt. . . ."

But that excuse, no matter how compelling, was instantly crushed: "It could not possibly, miss, for the doctor . . . has not performed the operation. We have not even laid a hand on you!"

"What do you mean . . . ?" Zeliha faltered, trying less to find out the answer than to comprehend the weight of her own question. "You mean . . . you have not . . ."

"No, we haven't." The receptionist sighed, holding her head as if at the onset of a migraine. "There was absolutely no way the doctor could do anything with you screaming at the top of your voice. You did not pass out, woman, no way; first you were blathering, and then you started yelling and cursing. I've never seen anything like it in fifteen years. It must have taken the morphine twice as long to take effect on you."

Zeliha suspected some exaggeration behind this statement but did not feel like arguing. Two hours into her visit to the gynecologist she had come to realize that herein a patient was expected to talk only when asked to.

"And when you finally blacked out it was so hard to believe that you wouldn't start shrieking again, the doctor said, let's wait till her mind is clear. If she wants to have this abortion for sure, she can still go for it afterward. We brought you here and let you sleep. And sleep indeed you did!"

"You mean there was no . . ." The word she had so daringly uttered in front of strangers just this afternoon felt unutterable now. Zeliha touched her belly while her eyes appealed for a consolation the receptionist was the last person on earth to grant. "So she is still here. . . ."

"Well, you do not know yet if it is a she!" the receptionist said, her voice matter-of-fact.

But Zeliha knew. She simply did.

Once on the street, despite the gathering darkness, it felt like early morning. The rain had ceased and life looked beautiful, almost manageable. Though the traffic was still a mess and the streets full of sludge, the crisp smell of the after-rain gave the whole city a sacred air. Here and there children stomped in mud puddles, taking delight in committing simple sins. If there ever was a right time to sin, it must have been at this fleeting instant. One of those rare moments when it felt like Allah not only watched over us but also cared for us; one of those moments when He felt close.

It almost felt as if Istanbul had become a blissful metropolis, romantically picturesque, just like Paris, thought Zeliha; not that she had ever been to Paris. A seagull flew close crying a coded message she was almost on the verge of deciphering. For half a minute Zeliha believed she was on the cutting edge of a new beginning. "Why did you not let me do it, Allah?" she heard herself mutter, but as soon as the words came out of her mouth, she apologized in panic to the atheist in herself.

Pardon me, pardon me, pardon me.

Far and under the rainbow Zeliha limped back home, clutching the box of tea glasses and the broken heel, somehow feeling less dispirited than she had felt in weeks.

So on that first Friday of July around eight p.m. Zeliha came home, to the slightly decrepit, high-ceilinged Ottoman *konak* that looked out of place amid five times as tall modern apartment buildings on both sides. She trudged up the curved staircase and found all the Kazancı females gathered upstairs around the wide dinner table, occupied with their meal, obviously having felt no reason to wait for her.

"Hello stranger! Come on in, join our supper," Banu exclaimed, craning her neck over an oven-fried crispy chicken wing. "The prophet Mohammed advises us to share our food with strangers."

Her lips were glossy, so were her cheeks, as if she had taken extra time to wipe the chicken grease all over her face, including on those shiny, fawn eyes of hers. Twelve years older and thirty pounds heavier than Zeliha, she looked less like her sister than like her mother. If she was to be believed, Banu had a bizarre digestive system that stored everything ingested, which could have been a more credible claim had she not also argued that even if it were pure water that she consumed, her body would still evolve it into fat, and thereby she could not possibly be held accountable for her weight or be asked to go on a diet.

"Guess what's on today's menu?" Banu continued merrily, as she wagged a finger at Zeliha before she clutched another chicken wing. "Stuffed green peppers!"

"This must be my lucky day!" Zeliha said.

Today's menu looked splendidly familiar. In addition to a huge chicken, there was yogurt soup, *karnıyarık, pilaki, kadın budu köfte* from the day before, *turşu,* newly made *çörek,* a jar of *ayran,* and, yes, stuffed green peppers. Zeliha instantly pulled up a chair, her hunger prevailing over her lack of enthusiasm for attending a family dinner on such a hard day's eve.

"Where were you, missy?" grumbled her mother, Gülsüm, who might have been Ivan the Terrible in another life. She squared her shoulders, lifted her chin, knitted her eyebrows, and then turned her contorted face toward Zeliha's, as if by doing so she could read her youngest daughter's mind.

So there they stood, Gülsüm and Zeliha, mother and daughter, scowling at each other, each ready to quarrel but reluctant to start the fight. It was Zeliha who first averted her eyes. Knowing too well what a big mistake it would be to display her temper in front of her mother, she forced herself to smile and attempted an answer, albeit an indirect one.

"There were good discounts at the bazaar today. I bought a set of tea glasses. They are absolutely gorgeous! They have gilded stars and little spoons that match."

"Alas, they break so easily," murmured Cevriye, the second eldest of the Kazancı sisters and a Turkish national history teacher at a private high school. She always ate healthy, balanced meals and wore her hair in a perfectly pinned chignon that twisted at the nape of her neck without letting even a tangle of hair loose.

"You've been to the bazaar? Why didn't you get any cinnamon sticks?! I told you this morning we were going to have rice pudding today and there was no cinnamon left at home to sprinkle on it." Banu frowned in between two bites of bread, but this problem occupied her for no more than a split second. Her theory of bread, which she was fond of pronouncing regularly and putting into practice all the time, was that if not given a proper amount at each and every sitting, the stomach would not "know" it was full and would thereby ask for more food. For the stomach to fully *comprehend* its fullness, one had to eat decent portions of bread with everything. Thus, Banu would have bread with potatoes, bread with rice, bread with pasta, bread with *börek,* and at those times when she wanted to give her stomach a far clearer message, she would have bread with bread. Dinner without bread was a sheer sin, which Allah might forgive, but Banu definitely would not.

Zeliha pursed her lips and stood silent, only now remembering the fate of the cinnamon sticks. Avoiding the question, she put a stuffed pepper on her plate. Each time she could easily tell if it was Banu or Cevriye or Feride who had prepared the peppers. If it was Banu, they turned out to be full of stuff they'd have otherwise sorely lacked, including peanuts and cashews and almonds. If it was Feride, they would be full of rice, each green pepper so ballooned it was impossible to eat without breaking. When her tendency to overstuff the peppers was added to her love for seasonings of all sorts, Feride's *dolmas* burst with herbs and spices. Depending on the combination, this turned out either exceptionally well or simply awful. When it was Cevriye who had cooked the dish, however, it was always sweeter, because she added powdered sugar to every edible thing no matter what, as if to compensate for the sourness in her universe. And today it happened to be she who had made the *dolmas*.

"I was at the doctor's. . . . " Zeliha murmured, carefully stripping the *dolma* of its pale green cloak.

"Doctors!" Feride grimaced and lifted her fork in the air as if it were a baton she would use to indicate a faraway mountain range on a map and her audience was not her own family but students in a geography class. Feride had a problem with making eye contact. She was more comfortable talking to objects. Accordingly, she addressed her words to Zeliha's plate: "Haven't you seen the newspaper this morning? They operate on a nine-year-old child for appendicitis and then forget a pair of scissors inside. Do you have any idea how many doctors in this country should be put into jail for medical malpractice?"

Among all the Kazancı women, Feride was the one best acquainted with medical procedures. In the last six years, she had been diagnosed with eight different illnesses, each of which sounded more alien than the one before. Whether it was the doctors who could not make up their minds or Feride herself industriously working on new infirmities, one could never tell. After a while it didn't really matter one way or another. Sanity was a promised land, the Shangri-la she had been deported from as a teenager, and to which she intended to return to one day. On the way there she rested at sundry stopovers that came with erratic names and dreary treatments.

Even as a little girl, there was something bizarre about Feride. A most difficult student at school, she had shown no interest in anything other than physical geography classes, and in the geography classes had shown no interest in anything other than a few subjects, starting with the layers of the atmosphere. Her favorite topics were how the ozone was broken down in the stratosphere, and the connection between surface ocean currents and atmospheric patterns. She had learned all the information she could gather on high-latitude stratospheric circulation, the characteristics of the mesosphere, valley winds and sea breezes, solar cycles and tropical latitudes, and the shape and size of the earth. Everything she had memorized at school she would then volley in the house, peppering every conversation with atmospheric information. Each time she displayed her knowledge on physical geography, she would speak with unprecedented zeal, floating high above the clouds, jumping from one atmospheric layer to the next. Then, a year after her graduation, Feride had started to display signs of eccentricity and detachment.

Although Feride's interest in physical geography had never petered out in the fullness of time, it inspired yet another area of interest that she profoundly enjoyed: accidents and disasters. Every day she read the third page of the tabloids. Car accidents, serial killings, hurricanes, earthquakes, fires and floods, terminal illnesses, contagious diseases, and unknown viruses. . . . Feride would peruse them all. Her selective memory would absorb local, national, and international calamities only to convey them to others out of the blue.

It never took her long to darken any conversation, as from birth she was inclined to see misery in each and every story, and to fabricate some when there was none.

But the news she conveyed did not upset the others, as they had renounced believing in her long ago. Her family had figured out one way of dealing with insanity, and that was to confuse it with a lack of credibility.

Feride was first diagnosed with a "stress ulcer," a diagnosis no one in the family took seriously because "stress" had become some sort of catchphrase. As soon as it was introduced into Turkish culture, "stress" had been so euphorically welcomed by the Istanbulites that there had emerged countless patients of stress in the city. Feride had traveled nonstop from one stress-related illness to another, surprised to discover the vastness of the land since there seemed to be virtually nothing that could not be related to stress. After that, she had loitered around obsessive-compulsive disorder, disassociative amnesia, and psychotic depression. Managing to poison herself, she was once diagnosed with Bittersweet Nightshade, the name she most relished among her infirmities.

At each stage of her journey to insanity, Feride changed her hair color and style, so that after a while the doctors, in their endeavor to follow the changes in her psychology, started to keep a hair chart. Short, midlength, very long, and once entirely shaven; spiked, flattened, flipped, and braided; subjected to tons of hairspray, gel, wax, or styling cream; accessorized with barrettes, gems, or ribbons; cropped in punk style, pinned up in ballerina buns, highlighted and dyed in every possible hue, each one of her hairstyles had been a fleeting episode while her illness had remained firm and fixed.

After a lengthy sojourn in "major depressive disorder," Feride had moved to "borderline"—a term construed quite arbitrarily by different members of the Kazancı family. Her mother interpreted the word "border" as a problem to be associated with police, customs officers, and illegality, thereby finding a "felon foreigner" in the persona of Feride. She thus became even more suspicious of this crazy daughter whom she had not trusted in the first place. In stark contrast, for Feride's sisters, the concept of "border" mainly invoked the idea of edge, and the idea of edge invoked the image of a deadly cliff. For quite a while they treated her with utmost care, as if she were a walking somnambulist on a wall meters high and could fall down any time. However, the word "border" invoked the trim of latticework for Petite-Ma, and she studied her granddaughter with deep interest and sympathy.

Feride had recently emigrated into another diagnosis nobody could even pronounce, let alone dare to interpret: "hebephrenic schizophrenia." Ever since then, she remained faithful to her new nomenclature, as if finally content to achieve the nominal clarification she sorely needed. Whatever the diagnosis, she lived according to the rules of her own fantasyland, outside of which she had never set foot.

But on this first Friday of July, Zeliha paid no attention to her sister's renowned distaste for doctors. As she started to eat, she realized how hungry she had been all day long. Almost mechanically, she ate a piece of *çörek,* poured herself a glass of *ayran,* forked another green *dolma* onto her plate, and revealed the piece of information growing inside her: "I went to a gynecologist today. . . ."

"Gynecologist!" Feride repeated instantly, but she made no specific comment. Gynecologists were the one group among all the physicians she had had the least experience with.

"I went to a gynecologist today to have an abortion." Zeliha completed her sentence without looking at anyone.

Banu dropped her chicken wing and looked down at her feet as if they had something to do with this; Cevriye pursed her lips hard; Feride shrieked and then oddly unleashed a whoop of laughter; their mother tensely rubbed her forehead, feeling the first aura of a terrible headache approaching; and Petite-Ma . . . well, Petite-Ma just continued to eat her yogurt soup. It might be because she had gone quite deaf in the course of the recent months. It might also be because she was suffering from the early stages of dementia. Perhaps it was simply because she thought there was nothing to fuss about. With Petite-Ma you never knew.

"How could you slaughter your baby?" Cevriye asked in awe.

"It is not a *baby*!" Zeliha shrugged. "At this stage, I'd rather call it a *droplet*. That'd be more scientific!"

"Scientific! You are not scientific, you are cold-blooded!" Cevriye burst into tears. "Cold-blooded! That's what you are!"

"Well, I have good news then. I have not killed . . . it—*her*—whatever!" Zeliha turned toward her sister calmly. "Not that I did not want to. I did! I tried to have the *droplet* aborted but somehow it did not happen."

"What do you mean?" asked Banu.

Zeliha put on a brave face. "Allah sent me a message," she said tonelessly, knowing it was the wrong thing to say to a family like hers but saying it anyway. "So there I am lying anesthetized with a doctor and a nurse on each side. In a few minutes the operation will begin and the baby will be gone. Forever! But then just when I am about to go unconscious on that operating table, I hear the afternoon prayer from a nearby mosque. . . . The prayer is soft, like a piece of velvet. It envelops my whole body. Then, as soon as the prayer is over, I hear a murmur as if somebody is whispering in my ear: 'Thou shall not kill this child!' "

Cevriye flinched, Feride nervously coughed into her table napkin, Banu swallowed hard, and Gülsüm frowned. Only Petite-Ma remained far off in a better land, having now finished her soup, obediently waiting for her next dish to arrive.

"And then . . . " Zeliha carried on with her story, "this mysterious voice commands: 'Oooo Zeliha! Oooo you the culprit of the righteous Kazancı family! Let this child live! You don't know it yet, but this child will be a leader. This baby will be a monarch!' "

"He cannot!" the teacher Cevriye broke in, missing no opportunity to show her expertise. "There aren't monarchs anymore, we are a modern nation."

"'Oooo you sinner, this child will rule over others!'" Zeliha continued, pretending not to have heard the lesson. "'Not only this country, not only the entire Middle East and the Balkans, but the whole world will know her name. This child of yours will lead the masses, and bring peace and justice to humankind!'"

Zeliha paused and let out a breath.

"Anyhow, good news everybody! The baby is still with me! Before long, we'll put another plate at this table."

"A bastard!" Gülsüm exclaimed. "You want to bring into this family a child out of wedlock. A bastard!"

The word's effect spread out, like a pebble thrown into still water.

"Shame on you! You've always brought disgrace on this family." Gülsüm's face contorted in anger. "Look at your nose piercing. . . . All that makeup and the revoltingly short skirts, and oh, those high heels! This is what happens when you dress up . . . like a whore! You should thank Allah night and day; you should be grateful that there are no men around in this family. They'd have killed you."

It wasn't quite true. Not the part about the killing perhaps, but the part about there being no men in the family. There were. Somewhere. But it was also true that there were far fewer men than women in the Kazancı family. Like an evil spell put on the whole lineage, generations after generations of Kazancı men had died young and unexpectedly. Petite-Ma's husband, Rıza Selim Kazancı, for instance, had all of a sudden dropped dead at sixty, unable to breathe. Then in the next generation, Levent Kazancı had died of a heart attack before he had reached his fifty-first birthday, following the patterns of his father and his father's father. It looked as if the life span of the men in the family got shorter and shorter with each generation.

There was a great-uncle who had run away with a Russian prostitute, only to be robbed by her of all his money and frozen to death in St. Petersburg; another kinsman had gone to his last resting place after being hit by a car while trying to cross the autobahn heavily intoxicated; various nephews had died as early as their twenties, one of them drowning while swimming drunk under the full moon, another one hit in the chest by a bullet fired by a hooligan enjoying himself after his soccer team had won the cup, yet another nephew having fallen into a six-foot-deep ditch dug out by the municipality to renovate the street gutters. Then there was a second cousin, Ziya, who had shot himself, for no apparent reason.

Generation after generation, as if complying with an unwritten rule, the men in the Kazancı family tree had died young. The greatest age any had reached in the current generation was forty-one. Determined not to repeat the pattern, another great-uncle had taken utmost care to lead a healthy life, strictly refraining from overeating, sex with prostitutes, contacts with hooligans, alcohol and other sorts of intoxicants, and had ended up crushed by a concrete chunk falling from a construction site he happened to pass by. Then there was Celal, a distant cousin, who was the love of Cevriye's life and the husband she lost in a brawl. For reasons still unclear, Celal had been sentenced to two years on charges of bribery. During this time Celal's presence in the family had been confined to the infrequent letters he had been sending from jail, so vague and distant that when the news of his death had arrived, for everyone other than his wife, it had felt like losing a third arm, one that you never had. He departed this life in a fight, not by a blow or a punch, but by stepping on a high-voltage electricity cable while trying to find a better spot to watch two other prisoners exchange blows. After losing the love of her life, Cevriye sold their house and joined the Kazancı domicile as a humorless history teacher with a Spartan sense of discipline and self-control. Just as she waged battle against plagiarism at school, she took it upon herself to crusade against impulsiveness, disruption, and spontaneity at home.

Then there was Sabahattin, the tenderhearted, good-natured, but equally self-effacing husband of Banu. Though he was not a blood relative and looked exceptionally hale and hearty, though the two were still married on paper, except for a brief period following their honeymoon, Banu had spent more time in her family's *konak* than at home with her husband. So noticeable was their physical distance that when Banu had announced being heavy with twin boys everyone had joked about the technical impossibility of the pregnancy. Yet the ominous fate awaiting every Kazancı man had struck the twins at an early age. Upon losing her toddler boys to childhood illnesses, Banu permanently moved into her family house, only to sporadically visit her husband in the years that followed. Every now and then she went to see if he was doing okay, more like a concerned stranger than a loving spouse.

Then, of course, there was Mustafa, the only son in the current generation, a precious gem bequeathed by Allah amid four daughters. The result of Levent Kazancı's fixation on having a boy to bear his surname had been that the four Kazancı sisters had each grown up feeling like unwelcome visitors. The first three children were all girls. Banu, Cevriye, and Feride had each felt like an introduction before the real thing, an accidental prelude in their parents' sex life, so determinedly were they oriented toward a male child. As for the fifth child, Zeliha, she knew she had been conceived with the hope that fortune could be generous twice in a row. After finally having a boy, her parents had wanted to see if they were lucky enough to make another one.

Mustafa was precious from the day he was born. A series of measures had been taken to protect him from the grim fate awaiting all the men in the family tree. As a baby he was bundled in evil-eye beads and amulets; as a toddler he was kept under constant surveillance, and until age eight his hair was kept long like a girl's so as to deceive Azrail, the angel of death. Whenever someone needed to address the child, "girl" they would say, "girl, come here!" Though a good student, most of Mustafa's high school life was ruined by his inability to socialize. A king in his house, the boy seemed to refuse to be one among many in the classroom. So unpopular had he become over time that when Gülsüm wanted to throw a party for Mustafa and his friends to celebrate their graduation, there was no one to invite.

So arrogantly antisocial outside his house, so indisputably cherished as the king at home, and with the passing of each birthday so ominously close to the doom suffered by all the Kazancı men, after a while it seemed like a good idea to send Mustafa abroad. Within a month, Petite-Ma's jewels were sold for the money required and the eighteen-year-old son of the Kazancı family left Istanbul for Arizona, where he became an undergraduate student in agricultural and biosystems engineering and would hopefully survive to see his old age.

Hence, when on that first Friday of July, Gülsüm chided Zeliha, asking her to be grateful for the lack of men in the family, there was *some* truth somewhere in that statement. In response Zeliha said nothing. Instead she went to the kitchen to find and feed the only male in the house—a silver tabby cat with an insatiable hunger, an unusual fondness for water, and plentiful social-stress symptoms, which could at best be interpreted as independent, and at worst, as neurotic. His name was Pasha the Third.

In the Kazancı *konak* generations of cats had succeeded each other, like human beings; all had been loved and without exception swept away solely by old age, unlike human beings. Though each cat had retained its distinct character, overall two competing genes ran through the feline lineage in the house. On the one hand, there was the "noble" gene coming from a longhaired, flat-nosed, powder white Persian cat Petite-Ma had brought with her as a young bride in the late 1920s ("the cat must be what little dowry she has," the women in the neighborhood had mocked). On the other hand, there was the "street" gene coming from an unidentified but apparently tawny street cat the white Persian had managed to copulate with in one of her runaways. Generation after generation, as if taking turns, one of the two genetic traits had prevailed in the feline inhabitants born under this roof. After a while the Kazancıs had stopped bothering to find alternative names, instead just following the feline genealogy. If the kitten looked like a descendant of the aristocratic line, white and furry and flat-nosed, they would name it successively, Pasha the First, Pasha the Second, Pasha the Third. . . . If it were from the street cat's lineage, they would name it Sultan—a more superior name, signaling the belief that street cats were self-governing free spirits, in no need of flattering anyone.

To this day the nominal distinction, without exception, had been reflected in the personalities of the cats under this roof. Those of the nobility turned out to be the aloof, needy, quiet types, constantly licking themselves, wiping out all traces of human contact whenever someone patted them; those of the second group had been the more curious and vigorous types who delighted in bizarre luxuries, such as eating chocolates.

Pasha the Third characteristically embodied the features of his lineage, always walking with a pompous rhythm, as if tiptoeing through broken glass. He had two favorite occupations, which he put into practice on every occasion: gnawing electrical cords and observing birds and butterflies, too lazy to chase them. Of the latter he could get tired, but of the former, never. Almost every electrical cord in the house had been once or thrice chewed, scraped, dented, and damaged by him. Pasha the Third had managed to survive to a ripe old age despite the numerous electric shocks he had received.

"There, Pasha, good boy." Zeliha fed him chunks of feta cheese, his favorite. She then put on an apron and toiled through a hill of pots and pans and plates. When she had finished the dishes and calmed herself, she shuffled back to the dinner table, where she found the word *bastard* still hanging in the air, and her mother still frowning.

They all sat there motionless until someone remembered the dessert. A sweet, soothing smell filled the room as Cevriye poured rice pudding from a huge cauldron into tiny bowls. While Cevriye kept doling with practiced ease, Feride followed her, sprinkling shredded coconut on top of each bowl.

"It would have been much better with cinnamon," whined Banu. "You shouldn't have forgotten to buy cinnamon. . . ."

Leaning back in her chair, Zeliha lifted her nose and inhaled as if taking a drag on an invisible cigarette. As she breathed out her fatigue bit by bit, she felt the yo-yo indifference slacken off again. Her spirits sank under the weight of all that had and had not happened on this prolonged and hellish day. She scanned the dinner table, feeling more and more guilt-ridden at the sight of each bowl of rice pudding now canopied by coconut flakes. Then, without turning her gaze, she murmured in a voice so gracefully soft, it didn't sound like her at all.

"I am sorry. . . . " she said. "I am so sorry."

TWO

Garbanzo Beans

Supermarkets are perilous places filled with traps for the despondent and the dazzled, or so thought Rose as she headed to the aisle of diaper refills, this time determined not to purchase anything other than what she *really* needed. Besides, this was not the right moment to putter around. Having left her little girl inside the car in the parking lot, she now felt ill at ease. Sometimes she did things she instantly regretted but could not possibly take back, and if truth be told, such incidents had multiplied alarmingly over the last few months—three and a half months to be exact. Three and a half months of hell on earth as she resisted, fought over, cried about, refused to accept, begged not to, and finally yielded to her marriage coming to an end. Matrimony might be a fleeting folly that tricked you into believing that it would be forever, but it was harder to appreciate the humor when you were not the one who ended it. The fact that marriage had to tarry before it irretrievably lapsed gave the false impression that there was still hope until you understood it was not hope for the better that you were living for, but hope that the suffering finally would end for both so that each could go his or her own way. And go her own way was precisely what Rose had decided to do from now on. If all this was tantamount to some sort of a tunnel of anguish God was compelling her to crawl through, she would emerge from it no longer recognizable as that weak woman she once had been.

As a sign of her resoluteness Rose tried to force a chuckle but it didn't make it past her throat. Instead she sighed, a sigh that sounded more troubled than intended only because she had reached an aisle she'd rather not visit: Sweets and Chocolate Bars. As she scuttled by the Carb Watchers Gourmet Sugar-Free Vanilla Crème Flavor Dark Chocolate, she halted abruptly. She got herself one, two . . . five bars. Not that she was carb-watching, but she liked the sound of it, or more precisely, she liked the *possibility* of being watchful of something, *anything*. After being repeatedly accused of being a slipshod housewife and a terrible mother, Rose was eager to prove the contrary in any way she could.

In a flash she swerved the cart, but found herself in another aisle of junk food. Where the hell were the diapers? Her eyes caught sight of a pile of toasted coconut marshmallows and the next thing she knew there were one, two . . . six packages in the cart. *Don't Rose, don't. . . . Just this afternoon you gobbled a whole quart of Cherry Garcia ice cream. . . . You've already gained so much weight. . . .* If this was an inner warning, it didn't come through loud enough. Nevertheless, it activated a guilt button somewhere in Rose's subconscious and a picture of herself popped up in her mind. For a fleeting second, she stood staring at her reflection in an imaginary mirror, although she had so deftly avoided the real mirror behind the organic baby lettuces. With a sinking heart she eyed her widened hips and buttocks but still managed to smile at her high cheekbones, gold blond hair, misty blue eyes, and those perfect ears of hers! The ear was such a trustworthy part of the human body. No matter how much weight you gained, your ears remained exactly the same, always loyal.

Unfortunately, that was not the case with the rest of the human body. Rose's physical form was anything but loyal. So volatile was her body she could not even classify it, the way *Healthy Living Magazine* categorized the body types of their female readers. If she belonged to the "pear-shaped" group, for instance, she would have wider hips than shoulders. If "apple shaped," she would be prone to gain weight in the stomach and chest. Having the qualities of both pears and apples, Rose didn't quite know what category to fit in, unless there was another group left unmentioned, the "mango shaped," thick all over and thicker in the bottom. *What the hell,* she thought to herself. She would shed the extra pounds. Now that this hell-of-a-divorce season was over, she was going to become a new woman. *Definitely,* she thought. "Definitely" was the word Rose used in lieu of "yes." Instead of "no" she used "definitely not."

Buoyed at the thought of surprising her ex-husband and his large extended family with the new woman she would soon become, Rose scanned the aisle. Her hands reached out to sweets and toffees—Sweet 'N Low Sugar Free Butter Toffee, Starburst Fruit Chews, black licorice twists—and as soon as she had tossed these into the cart, she hurried as if running from someone chasing her. But surrendering to her sweet tooth must have had a triggering effect on her guilty conscience because in next to no time she was struggling with a deeper sense of remorse. How could she have left her baby girl inside the car all alone? Every day you heard on KVOA about a toddler abducted in front of her home or a mother charged with reckless endangerment. . . . Last week a Tucson woman had set her house on fire and almost killed her two kids sleeping inside. If anything close to that ever happened to her, thought Rose, her mother-in-law would be thrilled. Shushan-the-Omnipotent-Matriarch would instantly file suit for the custody of her granddaughter.

Immersed in these grim scenarios, Rose couldn't help shuddering. It was true she had been slightly off recently, forgetting things that were second nature, but nobody, not a single soul in his right mind, could justly accuse her of being a bad mother! Definitely not! She was going to prove that both to her ex-husband and to that mammoth Armenian family of his. Her ex-husband's family was from another country where people bore a surname she couldn't spell and secrets she couldn't decipher. Rose had always felt like an outsider there, always aware of being an *odar*—this gluey word that had stuck on her from the very first day.

How terrible it was to still be mentally and emotionally attached to someone from whom you have been physically separated. When the dust had settled, out of that one year and eight months of marriage, all that was left for Rose was pure resentment and a baby.

"This is all I am left with. . . ." Rose muttered to herself. That, indeed, was the most common side effect of postmarital chronic bitterness: It made you talk to yourself. No matter how much dialogue you imagined, you were never out of words. Over the past weeks Rose had repeatedly argued in her imagination with each and every member of the Tchakhmakhchian family, defending herself with determination, winning every time, fluently articulating all the things she had failed to voice during the divorce and had been lamenting ever since.

There they were! Latex-free superabsorbent diapers. As she placed them in the cart, she noticed a middle-aged man with graying hair and a goatee smiling at her. The truth is, Rose liked to have her motherhood observed, and now that she had an audience, she couldn't help but break into a grin. Happily, she reached up to get a huge box of lightly scented wipes with aloe vera and vitamin E. Thank God *some* people appreciated her motherhood. Piloted by her yearning for further recognition, she walked up and down the aisle of baby products, each time finding something she had no intention of purchasing earlier but now saw no reason why not to: three bottles of antibacterial diaper-rash lotion, a baby bath safety ducky that warned when the water in the tub was too hot, a set of six plastic door guards to protect little fingers, a Max the Monkey car litterbag, and a water-filled freezable chewy butterfly teether.

She put them all in the cart. Who could possibly call her an irresponsible mom? How could they accuse her of paying no heed to her baby girl's needs? Had she not given up her college education when the baby was born? Had she not been working hard to sustain this marriage? Every now and then Rose liked to imagine her best self still going to college, still a virgin, and yes, still slim. Recently she had found a job at the university cafeteria, which might help the first dream to come true, though it wouldn't help the other two.

As she stepped into the next aisle Rose's face contorted. International Food. She stole a nervous glance at the jars of eggplant dips and cans of salted grape leaves. No more *patlijan!* No more *sarmas!* No more weird ethnic food! Even the sight of that hideous *khavourma* twisted her stomach into knots. From now on she would cook whatever she wanted. She would cook real Kentucky dishes for her daughter! For one long minute Rose stood there racking her brain to find an example of the perfect meal. Her face perked up as she thought of hamburgers. Definitely! she assured herself. What's more, fried eggs and maple-syrup-soaked pancakes and hot dogs with onions and mutton barbecue, yes especially mutton barbecue. . . . And instead of that squelchy yogurt drink that she was sick of seeing at every meal, they would drink apple cider! From now on she would choose their daily menu from Southern cuisine, hot spicy chili or smoked bacon . . . or . . . garbanzo beans. She would serve these dishes without complaining. All she needed was a man who would sit across from her at the end of the day. A man who would truly love her, and her cooking. Definitely, that was what Rose needed: a lover with no ethnic luggage, no hard-to-pronounce names, and no crowded family; a fresh new lover who would appreciate garbanzo beans.

There was a time when she and Barsam had loved each other. A time when Barsam did not even notice, and certainly did not mind, whatever food she placed on the table, for his gaze would be elsewhere, locked into hers, immersed in love. Rose's cheeks warmed at the recollection of these prurient moments but instantly chilled as she remembered the very next phase. Alas, in next to no time that horrendous family of his had entered onto the stage only to dominate it forever, and ever since then their affection for each other had worn thin. If that Tchakhmakhchian gang had not poked their aquiline noses into her marriage, Rose thought, her husband would still be by her side. "*Why did you constantly snoop into our marriage?*" she asked Shushan, whom she now imagined sitting in her armchair, counting the stitches in her knitting, making yet another baby blanket for her granddaughter. But her mother-in-law did not respond. Frustrated, Rose repeated the question. That, indeed, was the second most common side effect of postmarital chronic resentment: It made you not only talk to yourself, but also made you obstinate with others. Even if you might be dangerously close to the breaking point, you would never bend. "*Why didn't you ever leave us alone?*" Rose posed the same question one by one to her husband's three sisters—Auntie Surpun, Auntie Zarouhi, and Auntie Varsenig—while she glared at the jars of baba-ghanoush on the grocery shelves.

Rose left the ethnic foods section, making a sharp, swift U-turn into the next aisle. Inspired by her anger and melancholy, she moved down the aisle of Canned Food and Dry Beans from one end to the other, almost bumping into a young man standing there. He was eyeing the shelf where different brands of garbanzo beans were lined up. *That guy surely wasn't there a second ago!* thought Rose. He seemed to have simply materialized, as if zoomed down from the sky. He had fair skin, a slim, well-proportioned body, hazel eyes, and a pointed nose, which made him look attentive and studious. His sable hair was short. Rose suspected that she had seen him before, but where and when she couldn't remember.

"They are good, aren't they?" Rose asked. "Unfortunately not everyone is sensible enough to appreciate them. . . ."

Yanked out of his meditation, the young man flinched, turned toward the rosy-faced, plumpish woman who had mushroomed by his side, and still clutching in each hand a can of garbanzo beans, blushed. Having been caught by surprise, he could not easily get his masculine guard back.

"I am sorry. . . . " he said, and tilted his head to the right, a nervous tic, which Rose interpreted as a sign of shyness.

She smiled to show the young man that she pardoned him and then looked at his face without so much as a blink, making him even more nervous. Besides the suave-bunny expression that she now wore, Rose had three other animal-like looks inspired by Mother Nature, which she interchangeably employed for all her dealings with the opposite sex: her staunch-canine expression, one that she chose when she wanted to convey complete dedication; her impish-feline expression, which she used when she wanted to seduce; and her pugnacious-coyote expression, which she wore whenever she was criticized.

"Oh, I know you!" All of a sudden Rose beamed an ear-to-ear grin, satisfied with her memory. "I was racking my brain wondering where I'd seen you before. Now I know! You're from the U of A, right? I'll bet you like chicken quesadillas!"

The young man glanced up the aisle, as if he were considering running away at any moment but couldn't figure out toward which direction.

"I work part-time at the Cactus Grill"—Rose tried her best to help him comprehend—"the big restaurant on the second floor inside the Student Union, remember? I am usually behind the counter where the hot food is served—you know, omelettes and quesadillas. It's a part-time job, of course; it doesn't pay much but what are you gonna do? This is just for the time being. What I really want is to become a primary schoolteacher."

The young man was now quizzically studying Rose's face as if to memorize every detail for future reference.

"Anyway, that is where I must have seen you before," Rose concluded. She narrowed her eyes and moistened her bottom lip, switching to her feline expression. "I dropped out when I had a baby last year, but now I'm trying to go back to college. . . ."

"Oh, really?" the guy said, but then instantly shut his mouth. If Rose had had any previous experience with foreigners she would have detected the *foreigner's introduction reflex*—the fear of engaging in a conversation and not expressing the right words at the right time or with the correct pronunciation.

However, ever since she was a teenager Rose harbored a propensity to assume everything around her was either for or about or against her. Accordingly, she interpreted the silence as a sign of her own inability to make a decent introduction. To compensate for the error, she reached out her hand.

"Oh, I am sorry. I forgot to introduce myself. My name is Rose."

"Mustafa . . ." The young man swallowed, his Adam's apple moving up and down.

"Where are you from?" Rose asked.

"Istanbul," he answered curtly.

Rose raised her eyebrows and a trace of panic crossed her face. If Mustafa had any previous experience with provincials, he could detect the *provincial's information reflex*—the fear of not having enough knowledge of geography or world history. Rose was trying to recall where on earth Istanbul was. Was it the capital of Egypt or perhaps somewhere in India . . . ? She frowned in confusion.

However, ever since he was a teenager Mustafa harbored a fright of losing his grip on time and his appeal for women. So he interpreted the gesture as a sign of having bored Rose by failing to come up with anything interesting to say, and to compensate for the lack, he hastened to cut off the conversation.

"Nice meeting you, Rose," he said, drawling his vowels with a mellow but obvious accent. "I have to go now. . . ."

Very quickly he put back both cans of garbanzo beans, stared at his watch, grabbed his basket, and walked off. Before he disappeared, Rose heard him mumble "bye-bye" and then, as if echoing himself, another "bye-bye." Then he was gone.

Having thus lost this mysterious companion, Rose suddenly realized how much time she had squandered in the supermarket. She grabbed a few cans of garbanzo beans, including the ones Mustafa had left behind, and hurried to the checkout. She passed through the aisle of journals and books, and it was there that she caught sight of something she sorely needed: *The Great World Atlas*. Underneath the title it said: *A World Atlas of Flags, Facts, and Maps/Helping Parents, Students, Teachers, and Travelers Worldwide*. She grabbed the book, pinpointed "Istanbul" in the index, and once having found the relevant page, looked at the map to see where it was.

Outside in the parking lot she found the ultramarine 1984 Jeep Cherokee heating up under the Arizona sun while her baby girl slept inside.

"Armanoush, wake up sweetheart, Mama's back!"

The baby moved but did not open her eyes, not even when Rose rained kisses all over her face. Her soft brown hair was tied with a golden ribbon almost as big as her head and she was wearing a fluffy green outfit adorned with salmon stripes and purplish buttons. She looked like a dwarf Christmas tree decorated by someone in a state of frenzy.

"Are you hungry? Mama is gonna cook you real American food tonight!" Rose exclaimed as she put the plastic bags in the backseat, reserving a package of coconut marshmallows for the road. She checked her hair in the rearview mirror, put on a cassette that was her favorite these days, and grabbed a handful of marshmallows before she started the engine.

"Did you know that the guy I've just met in the supermarket is from Turkey?!" Rose said, as she winked at her daughter in the rearview mirror. Everything about her baby seemed just about right: her button nose, her round hands, her feet, everything except her name. Her husband's family had wanted to name the baby girl after her grandmother's mother. How deeply Rose lamented not having named her something less outlandish, like Annie or Katie or Cyndie, instead of accepting the name her mother-in-law had come up with. A child was supposed to have a childlike name and "Armanoush" was anything but that. The name sounded so . . . so mature and cold, appropriate for a grown-up, perhaps. Did Rose have to wait until her baby girl had reached forty to use her name without it pricking her tongue? Rose rolled her eyes and ate another marshmallow. Then and there she had a revelation: She could call her daughter "Amy" from now on, and as part of the baptism ceremony, she sent the baby a kiss.

At the next intersection they waited for the light to turn green. Rose drummed on the steering wheel, accompanying Gloria Estefan.

No modern love for me, it's all a hustle
What's done is done, now it's my turn to have fun . . .

Mustafa placed the few items he had selected in front of the cashier: Kalamata olives, frozen spinach and feta pizza, a can of mushroom soup, a can of cream of chicken soup, and a can of chicken noodle soup. Until he came to the United States, he had never had to cook in his life. Every time he labored in the small kitchen in his two-bedroom student apartment, he felt like a dethroned king living in exile. Long gone were the days when he was served and fed by a devoted grandmother, mother, and four sisters. Now, dishwashing, room-cleaning, ironing, and especially shopping were a huge burden for him. It wouldn't be as difficult if he could only rid himself of the feeling that someone else should be doing these things for him. He was no more used to doing chores than he was to being alone.

Mustafa had a housemate, an undergrad student from Indonesia who spoke very little, worked hard, and listened to odd tapes, such as *Sounds of Mountain Streams* or *Songs of the Whales,* in order to go to sleep every night. Mustafa had hoped that if he had a housemate, he would feel less lonely in Arizona, but the result had been quite the opposite. At night, alone in his bed and thousands of miles away from his family, he couldn't fight back the voices inside his head. Voices that questioned and blamed him for who he was. He slept poorly. He spent many nights watching old comedies or surfing on the Internet. It helped. The thoughts stopped at those times. Yet they would return with daylight. Walking from home to the campus, between classes or during lunchtime, Mustafa would catch himself thinking about Istanbul. How he wished he could remove his memory, restart the program, until all of the files were deleted and gone.

Arizona was to have spared Mustafa the bad omen that fell upon every man in the Kazancı family. But he didn't believe in such things. Drifting away from all those superstitions, evil-eye beads, coffee-cup readings, and fortune-telling ceremonies in his family was less a conscious choice than an involuntary reflex. He thought they were all part of a dark and complicated world peculiar to women.

Women were a mystery anyway. Having grown up with so many women, it was odd that he had felt so estranged from them all of his life.

Mustafa had grown up as the only boy in a family where the men died too soon and too unexpectedly. He experienced growing sexual desires while surrounded by sisters who were taboo to a fantasy life. Nevertheless, he slipped into unspeakable thoughts about women. At first Mustafa fell for girls who rejected him. Terrified that he would be rejected, ridiculed, and reviled, he turned to yearning for the female body from a distance. This year he had looked angrily at the photos of top models in glossy American magazines, as if to absorb the excruciating fact that no woman this perfect would ever desire him.

Mustafa would never forget the fierce look on Zeliha's face when she called him "a precious phallus." The embarrassment of that moment still burned through him today. He knew Zeliha could see behind his forced masculinity to the real story of his upbringing. She recognized that he had been pampered and spoon-fed by an oppressed mother, intimidated and beaten by an oppressive father. "In the end you have become both narcissistic and insecure," she had said. Could things have been different between Zeliha and him? Why did he feel so rejected and unloved with so many sisters around and a doting mother by his side?

Zeliha always mocked Mustafa and his mother always admired him. He wanted to be just an ordinary man, good and fallible at the same time. All he needed was compassion and a chance to be a better person. If only he had a woman who loved him, everything would be different. Mustafa knew he had to make it in America not because he wanted to attain a better future but because he had to dispose of his past.

"How you doin'?" The young woman at the cash register smiled at him.

That was one thing Mustafa still had not gotten used to. In America everyone asked everyone how they were doing, even complete strangers. He understood that it was a way of greeting more than a real question. But then he didn't know how to greet back with the same graceless ease.

"I am fine, thank you," he said. "How are you?"

The girl smiled. "Where are you from?"

One day, Mustafa thought, I will speak in such a way that no one will ask this rude question because they will not believe, even for a minute, that they are talking to a foreigner. He picked up his plastic bag and walked outside.

———

A Mexican American couple crossed the sidewalk, she pushing a baby in a stroller, he holding the hand of a toddler. They walked unhurriedly while Rose watched them with envy. Now that her marriage was over, every couple she saw seemed blissfully content.

"You know what? I wish your grandma-the-witch could have seen me flirting with that Turk. Can you imagine her horror? I cannot think of a worse nightmare for the proud Tchakhmakhchian family! Proud and puffed up . . . proud and . . ."

Rose didn't finish her sentence because she was distracted by a most puckish thought. The light turned green, the cars that were lined up in front of her lurched forward, and the van behind her honked. But Rose remained motionless. The fantasy was so delicious she could not move. Her mind wallowed in many images, while her eyes beamed a ray of pure rage at an oblique angle. That, indeed, was the third most common side effect of postmarital chronic resentment: It not only made you talk to yourself and be obstinate with others, but it also made you quite irrational. Once a woman felt justifiable resentment, the world turned upside down, and unreason appeared perfectly reasonable.

Oh sweet vengeance. Recovery was a long-term plan, an investment that paid off over time. But retaliation was quick to act. Rose's first instinct was to do something, anything, to exasperate her ex–mother-in-law. And there existed on the surface of the earth only one thing that could annoy the women of the Tchakhmakhchian family even more than an *odar*: a Turk!

How interesting it would be to flirt with her ex-husband's archenemy. *But where would you find a Turkish man in the midst of the Arizona desert? They didn't grow on cacti, did they?* Rose chuckled as her facial expression changed from recognition to one of intense gratitude. What a lovely coincidence that fortune had just introduced her to a Turk. Or was it not a coincidence?

Singing along with the song, Rose moved forward. But instead of going straight on her route she veered to the left, made a full U-turn, and once in the other lane, sped in the opposite direction.

Primitive love, I want what it used to be,

In next to no time the ultramarine 1984 Jeep Cherokee had reached Fry's Supermarket's parking lot.

I don't have to think, right now you've got me at the brink
This is good-bye for all the times I cried . . .

The car moved in a semicircle, then maneuvered crosswise, thus reaching the main exit of the supermarket. Just when Rose was about to lose any hope of finding the young man, she spotted him patiently waiting at the bus stop with a flimsy plastic bag next to him.

"Hey, Mostapha!" Rose yelled, cocking her head from the half-open window. "Wanna ride?"

"Sure, thanks." Mustafa nodded and made a frail attempt to correct her pronunciation: "It's Mus-ta-fa. . . ."

Inside the car, Rose smiled. "Mustapha, meet my daughter, Armanoush. . . . But I call her Amy! Amy this is Mustapha, Mustapha this is Amy. . . ."

While the young man beamed at the sleepy baby, Rose studied his face for signs of recognition but couldn't find any. So, she decided to give him another hint, this time a more revealing one: "My daughter's full name is Amy Tchakhmakhchian."

If the words had inspired any negative recognition, Mustafa's face didn't show it. So Rose felt the need to repeat, just in case it hadn't been understood the first time: "Armanoush Tchakh-makh-chi-an!"

It was only then that the young man's hazel eyes flickered, though not exactly in the way Rose had anticipated.

"Chak-mak-chi-an . . . Çak-mak-çı . . . ! Hey, that sounds like Turkish!" he exclaimed happily.

"Well, as a matter of fact, it's *Armenian*," Rose said. Suddenly she felt insecure. "Her father—I mean, my ex-husband—" She swallowed hard as if trying to get rid of some sour taste. "He was, I mean, he *is*, Armenian."

"Oh yeah?" he said nonchalantly.

He didn't get it, did he? Rose wondered to herself as she chewed the inside of her mouth. Then, as if breathing out a suppressed hiccup long welling up in her throat, she let out a whoop of laughter. *But he is cute . . . very cute. . . . He will be my sweet vengeance!* she thought.

"Listen," Rose said. "I don't know if you like Mexican art but there is a group exhibition opening tomorrow night. If you don't have other plans we could go to it and grab a bite afterward."

"Mexican art . . . ?" Mustafa paused.

"People who have seen it elsewhere say it's really good," Rose said. "So what do you say. . . . Would you like to come with me?"

"Mexican art . . . !" Mustafa echoed with confidence. "Sure, why not?"

"Awesome." Rose cheered up. "It's so nice to meet you, Mostapha," she said, distorting his name again. But this time Mustafa felt no need to correct her.

THREE

Sugar

"Is it true? Please somebody tell me it is not true!" Uncle Dikran Stamboulian exclaimed as he banged the door open and dashed into the living room, searching for his nephew or nieces or anyone willing to console him. His dark eyes were slightly bulged with excitement. He had a full, drooping mustache that turned up slightly at the ends, making him look like he was smiling even when seriously enraged.

"Please calm down and have a seat, Uncle," Auntie Surpun, the youngest of the Tchakhmakhchian sisters, muttered without directly looking at him. Being the only one in the family who had unreservedly supported Barsam's marriage to Rose, she now felt culpable. Such self-reproach was not something she was used to. A professor of humanities at the University of California at Berkeley, Surpun Tchakhmakhchian was a self-confident feminist scholar who believed that every problem in this world was negotiable by calm dialogue and reason. There were times this particular conviction had made her feel alone in a family as temperamental as hers.

Dikran Stamboulian did as he was told and scuffled toward an empty chair, chewing on the ends of his mustache. The whole family was gathered around an antique mahogany table full of food, although nobody seemed to be eating anything. Auntie Varsenig's twin babies slept peacefully on the sofa. Distant cousin Kevork Karaoglanian was here too, having flown from Minneapolis for a social event organized by the Armenian Youth Community in the Bay Area. Over the past three months Kevork had dutifully attended every event organized by the group—a benefit concert, Annual Picnic, Christmas Party, Friday Night Light Party, Annual Winter Gala, Sunday Brunch, and a rafting race to benefit ecotourism in Yerevan. Uncle Dikran suspected the reason his handsome nephew came to San Francisco so frequently was not only because he was committed to these organizational events, but also because he had a yet-to-be-revealed affection for a girl he had met in the group.

Dikran Stamboulian gazed longingly at the food set out on the table, and reached for a jar of yogurt drink, Americanized with too many ice cubes. In multihued clay bowls of different sizes were many of his favorite dishes: *fassoulye pilaki, kadın budu köfte, karnıyarık,* newly made *churek,* and to Uncle Dikran's delight, *bastırma.* Though he was still fuming, his heart warmed at the sight of *bastırma* and entirely melted when he saw his favorite dish next to it: *burma.*

Despite the fact that he had always been under the strict dietary surveillance of his wife, every year Uncle Dikran had added another layer of flab to his infamous belly, like a tree trunk adding a growth ring with the passing of each year. Now he was a squat and portly man who did not mind drawing attention to either fact. Two years ago he had been offered a role in a pasta commercial. He had played a jolly cook whose spirits could not be dampened, even when he was dumped by his fiancée, since he still owned his kitchen and could cook spaghetti casserole. In truth, just as in the commercial, Uncle Dikran was such an exceptionally good-humored man that whenever one of his many acquaintances wanted to illustrate the cliché of fat people being far more cheery fellows than others, they would cite his name. Except today Uncle Dikran didn't look like his usual self.

"Where is Barsam?" Uncle Dikran asked as he reached for a *köfte* from the pile. "Does he know what his wife is up to?"

"Ex-wife!" Auntie Zarouhi corrected. As a new-to-the-job elementary school teacher grappling with unruly kids all day long, she couldn't help correcting any mistake she heard.

"Yeah, ex! Except she doesn't acknowledge that! That woman is nuts, I tell you. She is doing this on purpose. If Rose is not doing this just to upset us, let my name not be Dikran anymore. Find me another name!"

"You don't need another name," Auntie Varsenig consoled her uncle. "No doubt she is doing this deliberately. . . ."

"We have to rescue Armanoush," interrupted Grandma Shushan, the matriarch of the family. She left the table and scuffled toward her armchair. Though a wonderful cook, she had never had a big appetite and lately, her daughters feared, had somehow developed a way to stay alive by eating no more than a teacupful a day. She was a short, bony woman who possessed an exceptional strength to handle situations even more dire than this, and whose delicate face radiated an aura of competence. Her refusal to admit defeat no matter what, her unflagging conviction that life was always a struggle but if you were an Armenian it was three times as grueling, and her ability to win over everyone she came across had over the years bewildered many in her family.

"Nothing is as important as the well-being of the child," Grandma Shushan muttered as she caressed the silver pendant of Saint Anthony that she always wore. The patron saint of lost articles had helped her numerous times in the past to cope with the losses in her life.

With that Grandma Shushan took up her knitting needles and sat down. The first skeins of a cerulean baby's blanket dangled from the needles with the initials *A. K.* woven on the border. There was silence for a moment as everyone in the room watched her hands move gracefully with the needles. Grandma Shushan's knitting affected the family like group therapy. The sure and even cadence of each stitch soothed everyone watching, making them feel that as long as Grandma Shushan kept knitting, there was nothing to fear and in the end, everything would be all right.

"You are right. Poor little Armanoush," said Uncle Dikran, who as a rule took Shushan's side in every family dispute, knowing better than to disagree with the omnipotent materfamilias. Uncle Dikran dropped his voice as he asked, "What's going to become of that innocent lamb?"

Before anyone could respond, there was a jingling at the doorstep and the door was opened with a key. Barsam walked in, his face pale, his eyes staring worriedly behind wire-rimmed glasses.

"Hah! Look who's here!" said Uncle Dikran. "Mr. Barsam, your daughter is going to be raised by a Turk and here you are doing nothing about it. . . . *Amot!*"

"What can I do?" lamented Barsam Tchakhmakhchian, turning to his uncle. He moved his eyes to a huge reproduction of Martiros Saryan's *Still Life with Masks* on the wall, as if the answer he needed was hidden somewhere in the painting. But he must have failed to encounter any solace there because when he spoke again his voice sounded as inconsolable as before. "I have no right to interfere. Rose is her mother."

"*Aman!* What a mother!" Dikran Stamboulian laughed. For a man of his size he had an oddly shrill laugh—a detail he was usually conscious of and able to control, except when he was under stress.

"What will that innocent lamb tell her friends when she grows up? My father is Barsam Tchakhmakhchian, my great-uncle is Dikran Stamboulian, his father is Varvant Istanboulian, my name is Armanoush Tchakhmakhchian, all my family tree has been Something Somethingian, and I am the grandchild of genocide survivors who lost all their relatives at the hands of Turkish butchers in 1915, but I myself have been brainwashed to deny the genocide because

I was raised by some Turk named Mustafa! What kind of a joke is that? . . . Ah, *marnim khalasim!*"

Dikran Stamboulian paused and looked closely at his nephew to see the effect of his words. Barsam stood stone still.

"Go, Barsam!" Uncle Dikran exclaimed louder this time. "Fly to Tucson tonight and stop this comedy before it's too late. Talk with your wife. *Haydeh!*"

"Ex-wife!" Auntie Zarouhi corrected him, as she served herself a piece of *burma*. "Ah, I shouldn't be eating this. It has so much sugar in it. So many calories. Why don't you try artificial sweeteners, Mom?"

"Because nothing artificial enters my kitchen," Shushan Tchakhmakhchian replied. "Eat freely until you have diabetes in old age. Everything has a season."

"Right, I guess I am still in my sugar season." Auntie Zarouhi winked at her, but dared to eat only half a *burma*. Still chewing, she turned to her brother: "What is Rose doing in Arizona, anyway?"

"She has found a job there," said Barsam tonelessly.

"Yeah, what a job!" Auntie Varsenig tapped the ridge of her nose. "What the hell does she think she is doing, stuffing enchiladas as if she didn't have a penny to her name? She is doing that on purpose, you know. She wants the whole world to blame us, thinking we are not giving her any child support. A brave single mom fighting against all odds! That's the role she is trying to play!"

"Armanoush will be just fine," Barsam muttered, trying not to sound hopeless. "Rose stayed in Arizona because she wants to go back to college. Working at the Student Union is a temporary thing. What she really wants is to become a grade school teacher. She wants to spend her time with kids. There is nothing bad in that. As long as she is OK and takes good care of Armanoush, what difference does it make who she is dating?"

"You are right, but you are also wrong," Auntie Surpun spoke as she drew her legs under her in her chair and resettled, her eyes suddenly hardening with a trace of cynicism. "In an ideal world, you could say, well, that's her life, none of our business. If you have no appreciation of history and ancestry, no memory and responsibility, and if you live solely in the present, you certainly can claim that. But the past lives within the present, and our ancestors breathe through our children and you know that. . . . As long as Rose has your daughter, you have every right to intervene in her life. Especially when she starts dating a Turk!"

Never quite comfortable with philosophical speeches, and preferring straight talk over intellectual jargon, Auntie Varsenig interjected: "Barsam dear, show me a Turk who speaks Armenian, will you?"

Instead of an answer, Barsam gave his elder sister a sidelong look.

Auntie Varsenig continued, "Tell me how many Turks ever learned Armenian. None! Why did our mothers learn their language and not vice versa? Isn't it clear who has dominated whom? Only a handful of Turks come from Central Asia, right? And then the next thing you know they are everywhere! What happened to the millions of Armenians who were already there? Assimilated! Massacred! Orphaned! Deported! And then forgotten! How can you give your flesh-and-blood daughter to those who are responsible for our being so few and in so much pain today? Mesrop Mashtots would turn in his grave!"

Shaking his head, Barsam remained silent. To ease the distress of his nephew, Uncle Dikran began telling a story.

"An Arab goes to a barber for a haircut. After the haircut, he tries to pay but the barber says, 'No way, I cannot accept your money. This is a community service.' The Arab is pleasantly surprised and leaves the shop. The next morning when the barber opens his shop, he finds a 'Thank you' card and a basket of dates waiting at his door."

One of the twins sleeping on the sofa fidgeted but stopped short of crying.

"The very next day a Turk goes to the same barber for a haircut. After the haircut, he tries to pay but the barber once again says, 'I cannot accept your money. This is a community service.' The Turk is pleasantly surprised and leaves the shop. The next morning when the barber opens his shop, he finds a 'Thank you' card and a box of *lokum* waiting at his door."

Awakened by her sister's movement, the other twin started to cry. Auntie Varsenig ran to her side and managed to shush her with only the touch of her fingers.

"Then the next day an Armenian enters for a haircut. After the haircut, he tries to pay the barber and the barber objects—'Sorry, I cannot accept your money. This is a community service.' The Armenian is pleasantly surprised and leaves the shop. The next morning when the barber opens his shop . . . guess what he finds?"

"A package of *burma*?" Kevork suggested.

"No! He found a dozen Armenians waiting for a free haircut!"

"Are you trying to tell us that we are penny-pinching people?" Kevork asked.

"No, you ignorant young man," Uncle Dikran said. "All I am trying to tell you is that we care for one another. If we see something good, we immediately share it with our friends and relatives. It is because of this collective spirit that the Armenian people have managed to survive."

"But they also say, 'When two Armenians come together, they create three different churches,'" said Cousin Kevork, taking a firm stand.

"*Das' mader's mom'ri, noren koh chi m'nats.*" Dikran Stamboulian grunted, switching to Armenian as he always did when he tried to teach a young person a lesson, but failed.

Able to comprehend only house-Armenian but not newspaper-Armenian, Kevork chuckled, a bit too nervously perhaps, as he tried to conceal the fact that he had understood the first half of the sentence but failed to get the rest.

"*Oğlani kizdirmayasin.*" Grandma Shushan raised an eyebrow, speaking Turkish, as she always did when she wanted to directly convey a message to an elder in the room without the younger ones understanding.

Having gotten the message, Uncle Dikran heaved a sigh, like a boy scolded by his mother, and went back to his *burma* for consolation. A silence ensued. Everyone and everything—the three men, the three generations of women, the myriad rugs decorating the floor, the antique silver in the cupboard, the samovar on the chiffonier, the videocassette in the VCR (*The Color of Pomegranates*), as well as the multiple paintings and the icon of The Prayer of Saint Anna and the poster of Mount Ararat canopied under pure white snow—fell silent for a brief moment as the room acquired a rare luminosity under the drowsy light of a streetlamp just lit outside. The ghosts of the past were with them.

A car pulled over and parked in front of the house, its headlights panning the interior of the room, illuminating the letters on the wall in a gilded frame: AMEN, I SAY TO YOU, WHATEVER YOU BIND ON EARTH, SHALL BE BOUND IN HEAVEN, AND WHATEVER YOU LOOSE ON EARTH SHALL BE LOOSED IN HEAVEN.—ST. MATTHEW 18:18. Another trolley passed by chiming its bells, transporting noisy children and tourists from Russian Hill to Aquatic Park, the Maritime Museum, and Fisherman's Wharf. The rush-hour sounds of San Francisco poured into the room, pulling them out of their reverie.

"Rose is not a bad person at heart," Barsam ventured. "It was not easy for her to get used to our ways. She was a shy girl from Kentucky when we first met."

"They say the road to hell is paved with good intentions," Uncle Dikran snapped.

But Barsam ignored him, and continued. "Can you imagine? They don't even sell alcohol there! Forbidden! Did you know that the most exciting event in Elizabethtown, Kentucky, is this annual festival when people dress up as the Founding Fathers?" Barsam flipped his hands upward either to make a point or to call God's attention in a desperate prayer. "And then they walk downtown to meet General George Armstrong Custer!"

"That is why you shouldn't have married her in the first place." Uncle Dikran cackled quietly. By now all the anger had drained out of him, replaced by the knowledge that he couldn't possibly manage to remain upset with his favorite nephew any longer.

"What I am trying to say is that Rose had no multicultural background," Barsam remarked. "The only child of a kind Southern couple operating the same hardware store forever, she lives a small-town life, and before she knows it, she finds herself amid this extended and tightly knit Armenian Catholic family in the diaspora. A huge family with a very traumatic past! How can you expect her to cope with all of this so easily?"

"Well, it wasn't easy for us either," Auntie Varsenig objected, pointing the tines of her fork at her brother before spearing them into another *köfte*. Unlike her mother she had a good appetite, and given the amount of food she ate every day, plus the fact that she had recently given birth to twins, it was nothing short of a miracle that she could stay so thin. "When you come to think that the only food she knew how to cook was that horrendous mutton barbecue on buns! Each time we came to your house, she would put on that dirty apron and cook mutton."

Everyone but Barsam laughed.

"Oh, but I should be fair," Auntie Varsenig continued, pleased with her audience's response. "She would change the sauce every now and then. Sometimes we would get mutton barbecue with Spicy Tex-Mex sauce, and other times mutton barbecue with Creamy Ranch sauce. . . . Your wife's kitchen was a land of variety!"

"Ex-wife!" Auntie Zarouhi corrected again.

"But you guys gave her a hard time too," Barsam said, without looking at anyone in particular. "Mind you, the very first word she learned in Armenian was *odar*."

"But she is an *odar*." Uncle Dikran lurched forward, slapping his nephew on the back. "If she is an *odar*, why not call her an *odar*?"

Shaken by the slap more than the question, Barsam dared to add: "Some in this family have even called her Thorn."

"What is wrong with that?" Auntie Varsenig took it personally, in between her final two bites of *churek*. "That woman should have her name changed from Rose to Thorn. Rose is not appropriate for her. Such a sweet name for that much bitterness. If her poor papa and mama had had the faintest idea as to what sort of a woman she would turn out to be, believe me, my dear brother, they would have named her Thorn!"

"That's enough joking!"

It was Shushan Tchakhmakhchian. The exclamation had sounded neither like a reproach nor like a warning, but somehow had both effects on everyone in the room. By now the dusk had turned to night and the light inside shifted. Grandma Shushan stood up and turned on the crystal chandelier.

"We should save Armanoush from harm, that is the only thing that matters," Shushan Tchakhmakhchian said softly, the many lines on her face and the thin, purplish veins in her hands all the more apparent under the harsh white light. "That innocent lamb needs us, just like we need her."

Her face faded from determination to resignation as she slowly bobbed her head and added: "Only an Armenian can understand what it means to be so drastically reduced in numbers. We've shrunk like a pruned tree. . . . Rose can date and even marry whomever she wants, but her daughter is Armenian and she should be raised as an Armenian."

Then she leaned forward and with a smile said to her eldest daughter: "Give me that half on your plate, will you? Diabetes or no diabetes, how could one decline *burma*?"

FOUR

Roasted Hazelnuts

Asya Kazancı didn't know what it was that made some people so fond of birthdays, but she personally detested them. She always had.

Perhaps her disapproval had something to do with the fact that ever since she was a little girl, each year on her birthday she was made to eat exactly the same cake—a triple-layer caramelized apple cake (extremely sugary) with whipped lemon cream frosting (extremely sour). How her aunts could expect to please her with this cake, she had no idea, since all they heard from her on the matter was a litany of protests. Perhaps they simply forgot. Perhaps each time they erased all recollections of last year's birthday. That was possible. The Kazancıs were a family inclined to never forget other people's stories but to blank when it came to their own.

Thus on each birthday Asya Kazancı had eaten the same cake and at the same time had discovered a new fact about herself. At the age of three, for instance, she had found that she could get almost anything she wanted, provided she went into tantrums. Three years later on her sixth birthday, however, she realized she'd better stop the tantrums since with each episode, although her demands were met, her childhood was prolonged. When she reached the age of eight, she learned something that until then she had had only a sense of but did not know for sure: that she was a bastard. Looking back, she thought she shouldn't be given the credit for this particular information since if it weren't for Grandma Gülsüm, it would have taken her much longer to discover it.

It so happened that the two were alone in the living room on that day. Grandma Gülsüm was immersed in watering her plants, and Asya in watching her as she colored in a clown in a children's coloring book.

"Why do you talk to your plants?" Asya wanted to know.

"Plants bloom if you talk to them."

"Really?" Asya beamed.

"Really. If you tell them soil is their mother and water is their father, they buoy up and blossom."

Asking no more, Asya went back to her coloring. She made the clown's costume orange and his teeth green. Just when she was about to color his shoes a bright crimson, she stopped, and began to mimic her grandmother. "Sweetie, sweetie! Soil is your mom, water is your daddy."

Grandma Gülsüm pretended not to have noticed. Emboldened by her indifference, Asya increased the dose of her chant.

It was the African violet's turn to be watered, Grandma Gülsüm's favorite. She cooed to the flower, "How are you, sweetie?" Asya cooed mockingly, "How are you, sweetie?"

Grandma Gülsüm frowned and pursed her lips. "How beautifully purple you are!" she said.

"How beautifully purple you are!"

It was then that Grandma Gülsüm's mouth tightened and she murmured, "Bastard." She uttered the word so calmly, Asya did not immediately understand that her grandmother was addressing her, not the flower.

Asya didn't learn the meaning of the word until one year later, sometime close to her ninth birthday, when she was called a bastard by a kid at school. Then, at age ten, she discovered that unlike all the other girls in her classroom, she had no male role model in her household. It would take her another three years to comprehend that this could have a lasting effect on her personality. On her fourteenth, fifteenth, and sixteenth birthdays, she uncovered respectively three other truths about her life: that other families weren't like hers and some families could be *normal*; that in her ancestry there were too many women and too many secrets about men who disappeared too early and too peculiarly; and that no matter how hard she strived, she was never going to be a beautiful woman.

By the time Asya Kazancı reached seventeen she had further comprehended that she no more belonged to Istanbul than did the ROAD UNDER CONSTRUCTION or BUILDING UNDER RESTORATION signs temporarily put up by the municipality, or the fog that fell over the city on gloomy nights, only to be dispersed at the crack of dawn, leading nowhere, accumulating into nothing.

The very next year, exactly two days before her eighteenth birthday, Asya plundered the pillbox in the house and swallowed all the capsules she found there. She opened her eyes in a bed surrounded by all her aunts and Petite-Ma and Grandmother Gülsüm, having been forced to drink muddy, smelly herbal teas as if it wasn't bad enough that they had made her vomit up everything she had had in her stomach. She began her eighteenth year discerning a further fact to be added to her previous discoveries: that in this weird world, suicide was a privilege as rare as rubies, and with a family like hers, she sure wouldn't be one of the privileged.

It's hard to know if there was a connection between this deduction and what ensued next, but her obsession with music started more or less in those days. It wasn't an abstract, encompassing love for music in general, not even a fondness for selected musical genres, but rather a fixation on one and only one singer: Johnny Cash.

She knew everything about him: the myriad details of his trajectory from Arkansas to Memphis, his drinking buddies and marriages and ups and downs, his pictures, gestures, and, of course, his lyrics. Making the lyrics of "Thirteen" her lifelong motto at the age of eighteen, Asya had decided she too was born in the soul of misery and was going to bring trouble wherever she went.

Today, on her nineteenth birthday, she felt more mature, having made yet another mental note of another reality of her life: that she had now reached the age at which her mother had given birth to her. Having made this discovery, she didn't quite know what to do with it. All she knew was that from now on she could not possibly be treated like a kid.

So she grumbled, "I warn you! I do not want a birthday cake this year!"

Shoulders squared, arms akimbo, she forgot for a second that whenever she stood like this, her big breasts came to the fore. If she had noticed it, she surely would have gone back to her hunchback position, since she abhorred her ample bosom, which she detected as yet another genetic burden from her mother.

Sometimes she likened herself to the cryptic Qur'anic creature *Dabbet-ul Arz,* the ogre destined to emerge on the Day of Judgment, with each one of its organs taken from a different animal found in nature. Just like that hybrid creature, she carried a body composed of disconnected parts inherited from the women in her family. She was tall, much taller than most women in Istanbul, just like her mother, Zeliha, whom she also called "Auntie"; she had the bony, thin-veined fingers of Auntie Cevriye, the annoyingly pointed chin of Auntie Feride, and the elephantine ears of Auntie Banu. She had a most blatantly aquiline nose, of which there were only two others in world history—Sultan Mehmed the Conqueror's and Auntie Zeliha's. Sultan Mehmed had conquered Constantinople—whether you liked it or not, a fact significant enough to overlook the shape of his nose. As for Auntie Zeliha, so imposing was her personality and so captivating her body that no one would see her nose—or any other part of her, for that matter—as a source of imperfection. But having no imperial achievements on her curriculum vitae and possessing a natural incapability for charming people, Asya thought, what on earth could she do about her nose?

Among what she inherited from her relatives, there were some pleasant qualities too. For one thing, her hair! She had frizzy, sable, wild hair—theoretically, like every other woman in the family, but in practice, only like Auntie Zeliha. The disciplined high school teacher in Auntie Cevriye, for instance, kept her hair in a tight chignon while Auntie Banu was disqualified from any comparison, since she wore a head scarf almost all the time. Auntie Feride frantically changed her hair color and style depending on her mood. Grandma Gülsüm was a cotton-head, as her hair had gone snowy and she refused to dye it, claiming it wouldn't be appropriate for an old woman. Yet Petite-Ma was a devoted redhead. Her ever-worsening Alzheimer's might have caused Petite-Ma to forget a plethora of things, including her children's names, but to this day she had never forgotten to dye her hair with henna.

Finally in her list of positive genetic features, Asya Kazancı included her almond-shaped fawn eyes (from Auntie Banu), a high forehead (from Auntie Cevriye), and a temperament that rendered her prone to explode too quickly but that also, in an odd way, kept her alive (from Auntie Feride). Nevertheless, she hated to see that with the passing of each year she more and more resembled *them*. Except for one thing: their proclivity for irrationality. The Kazancı women were categorically irrational. Some time ago, so that she would not act like *them,* Asya had promised herself she'd never swerve from the path of her own rational, analytical mind.

By the time of her nineteenth birthday, Asya was a young woman so profoundly stimulated by the need to assert her individuality that she had become capable of the most peculiar rebellions. Thus, if she repeated her cake objection, this time even more fervently, there was a deeper reason behind her fury: "No more stupid cakes for me!"

"Too late, miss. It's already done," Auntie Banu said, darting a glance at Asya over a newly opened Eight of Pentacles. Unless the next three cards did not turn out to be exceptionally promising, the tarot deck on the table was heading in the direction of a bad omen. "But pretend not to know anything about it or your poor mama will be upset. It must be a surprise!"

"How could something so predictable be a surprise?" Asya grumbled. By now she knew too well that being a member of the Kazancı family meant, among other things, professing the alchemy of absurdity, continually converting nonsense into some sort of logic with which you could convince everyone, and with a little push, even yourself.

"I am the one who is supposed to predict and portend in this house, not you." Auntie Banu winked.

It was true, at least to a certain extent. Having worked upon and fleshed out her talent for clairvoyance over the years, Auntie Banu had started seeing customers at home and making money from it. It took a fortune-teller no longer than a flash to become legendary in Istanbul. If luck was on your side, it sufficed to successfully read someone's future, and the next thing you knew, that person would become your top customer. And with the help of the wind and the seagulls, she would spread the word so quickly throughout the city that in no more than a week there would be a line of customers waiting at the door. So had Auntie Banu made her way up the ladder of the art of clairvoyance, becoming more famous with each rung. Her customers came from all around the city, virgins and widows, lasses and toothless grannies, the poor and the affluent, each immersed in their own qualms and all dying to learn what Fortuna, that fickle feminine force, had in store for them. They arrived with gobs of questions and left the house with additional ones. Some paid large sums of money to express their gratitude or in the expectation that they could bribe Fortuna, but there were also some who did not shell out a penny. Diverse as they were, the customers had one basic thing in common: All were women. The day she had baptized herself a soothsayer, Auntie Banu had taken an oath never to receive male customers.

Several things about Auntie Banu had undergone a radical trans- formation in the meantime, starting with her appearance. At the beginning of her career as a clairvoyant, she had paraded around the house in flamboyantly embroidered scarlet shawls carelessly flung around her shoulders. Soon, however, the shawls were replaced by cashmere scarves and scarves by pashmina stoles and stoles by loosely tied silk turbans, always in hues of red. After that, Auntie Banu had suddenly announced the decision that she had secretly been con- templating for only Allah knows how long: to withdraw from ev- erything material and mundane, and to dedicate herself totally to the service of God. Toward this end, she had solemnly declared that she was ready to go through a phase of penitence and abandon all worldly vanities, just like the dervishes had done in the past.

"You are not a dervish," her sisters cynically chorused in uni- son, determined to dissuade her from such sacrilege, unheard of within the annals of the Kazancı family. And then all three of them started to raise objections, each in the most officious voice she could muster.

"Mind you, the dervishes used to clad themselves in coarse sacks or woolen garbs, not cashmere scarves," interjected Auntie Cevriye, the most maudlin of all.

Auntie Banu swallowed uneasily, uncomfortable in her clothes, uncomfortable in her body.

"Dervishes used to sleep on hay, not on queen-size feather mat- tresses," Auntie Feride joined in, the most moonstruck of all.

Auntie Banu stood silent, gazing across the room to avoid eye contact with her interrogators. What could she do, her back pain went through the roof if she didn't sleep on a special bed.

"Besides, the dervishes had no *nefs*. Look at you!" It was Auntie Zeliha, the most offbeat of all.

Eager to defend herself, Auntie Banu launched a counterattack.

"Neither do I. Not any longer. Those days are over." Then she added in her new mystical voice, "I will go into battle with my *nefs* and I shall prevail!!!"

In the Kazancı family whenever someone had the nerve to do something unusual, the others always reacted in the same way, following the old course of action, which could be summarized as: "Go ahead. See if we care." Accordingly, no one took Auntie Banu seriously. Upon noticing the general skepticism, she headed to her room and slammed the door, never to open it again for the next forty days except for quick visits to the kitchen and toilet. Other than that the only time she left the door ajar was to attach a cardboard sign that said: ALL *SELF* ABANDON YE WHO ENTER HERE!

Initially, Banu attempted to take with her Pasha the Third, who at the time was going through his last days on earth. She must have thought he could keep her company in her lonesome penitence, not that the dervishes kept pets. But no matter how antisocial he could be at times, the life of a hermit was too much for Pasha the Third, he having too many stakes in worldly vanities, starting with feta cheese and electrical cords. After no more than an hour inside Auntie Banu's cell, Pasha the Third launched a series of high-pitched meows and scratched the door so forcefully he was immediately let out. After losing her only company, Auntie Banu sunk into her lonesomeness and stopped talking, mute and deaf to everyone. She also stopped taking showers, combing her hair, and even watching her favorite soap opera, *The Malediction of the Ivy of Infatuation*—a Brazilian drama in which a kindhearted supermodel suffered all sorts of betrayals by those she loved most.

But the true shock came when Auntie Banu, always a woman of immense appetite, stopped eating anything but bread and water. She had been notoriously fond of carbohydrates, especially bread, but no one ever thought that she could *survive* on bread. To tempt her into indulgence, her three sisters did their best, cooking many dishes, filling the house with the scents of sweet desserts, deep-fried fish, and roasted meat, often heavily buttered to enhance the smell.

Auntie Banu did not waver. If anything, she more resolutely clung to her devotion, as well as to her dry bread. For forty days and nights she remained unreachable under the same roof. Washing the dishes, doing the laundry, watching TV, gossiping with neighbors—everyday life routines became profanities she wanted to have nothing to do with. During the days that followed, every time the sisters checked to see how she was doing, they found her reciting the Holy Qur'an. So intense was her blissful abyss, she became alien to those who had known her all her life. Then on the morning of day forty-one, while everyone else was eating grilled *sucuk* and fried eggs at the breakfast table, Banu shuffled out of her room, beaming a radiant smile, with an uncanny sparkle in her eyes and a cherry red scarf on her head.

"What's that sorry thing on your head?" was the first reaction of Grandma Gülsüm, who having not softened a wee bit after all these years still maintained her Ivan the Terrible resemblance.

"From this moment on I am going to cover my head as my faith requires."

"What kind of nonsense is that?" Grandma Gülsüm frowned. "Turkish women took off the veil ninety years ago. No daughter of mine is going to betray the rights the great commander-in-chief Atatürk bestowed on the women of this country."

"Yeah, women were given the right to vote in 1934," Auntie Cevriye echoed. "In case you didn't know, history moves forward, not backward. Take that thing off immediately!"

But Auntie Banu did not.

She remained head-scarved, and having passed the test of the three Ps—penitence, prostration, and piety—declared herself a soothsayer.

Just like her appearance, her techniques of clairvoyance underwent profound change throughout her psychic trajectory. At first she solely used coffee cups to read the future of her customers, but in the fullness of time she gradually employed new as well as highly unconventional techniques, including tarot cards, dried beans, silver coins, rosary beads, doorbells, imitation pearls, real pearls, ocean pebbles—anything, as long as it would bring news from the paranormal world. Sometimes she chatted passionately with her shoulders whereupon, she claimed, sat two invisible *djinn,* dangling their feet. The good one on the right shoulder and the bad one on the left shoulder. Though she knew the name of each, in order not to utter them aloud, she simply called them Mrs. Sweet and Mr. Bitter, respectively.

"If there is a bad *djinni* on your left shoulder, why don't you throw him down?" Asya asked her aunt once.

"Because there are times when we all need the company of the bad," was the answer.

Asya tried a frown and then rolled her eyes, gaining no effect with either gesture other than a childish face. She whistled a tune from a Johnny Cash song, which she liked to recall on various encounters with her aunts: *"Why me Lord, what have I ever done . . ."*

"What are you whistling?" Auntie Banu asked suspiciously. She didn't know any English and was deeply distrustful of any language that made her miss something obvious.

"I was singing a song that says as my eldest aunt you are supposed to be a role model for me and teach me right from wrong. But here you are giving me lessons on the necessity of evil."

"Well, let me tell you something," Auntie Banu decreed, looking at her niece intently. "There are things so awful in this world that the good-hearted people, may Allah bless them all, have absolutely no idea of. And that's perfectly fine, I tell you; it is all right that they know nothing about such things because it proves what good-hearted people they are. Otherwise they wouldn't be good, would they?"

Asya couldn't help but nod. After all, she had a feeling Johnny Cash would be of the same opinion.

"But if you ever step into a mine of malice, it won't be one of these people you will ask help from."

"And you think I will ask help from a malicious *djinni!*" Asya exclaimed.

"Perhaps you will." Auntie Banu shook her head. "Let's just hope you'll never have to."

That was that. Never again did they talk about the limitations of the good and the necessity of the unscrupulous.

At or around that time Auntie Banu once again remodeled her clairvoyant reading techniques, and switched to hazelnuts, roasted hazelnuts more often than not. Her family suspected that the origin of this novelty, as with most other novelties, might have been pure coincidence. Most likely Auntie Banu had been caught gobbling hazelnuts by a client and offered the best explanation that had come to her mind: that she could read them. This was the belief shared by all in the family. Everyone else had a different interpretation. Being the holy lady that she was, rumor had it in Istanbul, she did not demand any money from her needy customers and instead asked them to bring her only a handful of hazelnuts. The hazelnut became a symbol of her bigheartedness. In any case, the oddity of her technique only served to further augment her already bloated fame. "Mother Hazelnut" they started to call her, or even "Sheikh Hazelnut," oblivious to the fact that women in their limitedness could not assume this respected title.

Bad *djinni,* roasted hazelnuts . . . though Asya Kazancı had in time gotten used to these and other eccentricities, there was one thing about her eldest aunt she seemed to be having a hard time accepting: her name. It was just impossible to accept that "Auntie Banu" could metamorphose into one "Sheikh Hazelnut," so whenever there were customers inside the house or tarot cards opened on the table, she simply avoided her. That is why, although Asya had perfectly heard the last words uttered by her aunt, she pretended not to. And she would have remained blissfully ignorant had Auntie Feride not walked into the living room at that moment, carrying a huge, flat plate upon which glistened the birthday cake.

"What are you doing here?" Auntie Feride frowned at Asya. "You are not supposed to be here; you've got a ballet class now."

Now *that* was another shackle around Asya's ankles. Like numerous middle-class Turkish mothers aspiring to see their children excel in all the things the children of upper classes supposedly did, her upper–middle class family compelled her to perform activities she had absolutely no interest in.

"This is a nuthouse," Asya muttered to herself. These four words had become her mantra these days and she repeated it freely. Then she raised her voice a notch, and said, "Don't worry. Actually, I was about to leave."

"What's the use of it now?" Auntie Feride snapped, pointing at the plate. "This was supposed to be a surprise!"

"She doesn't want a cake this year," Auntie Banu intervened from her corner as she flipped the first of the three waiting tarot cards. It was The High Priestess. The symbol of unconscious awareness— an opening to imagination and hidden talents but also to the unknown. She pursed her lips and turned the next card: The Tower. A symbol of tumultuous changes, emotional eruptions, and sudden downfall. Auntie Banu looked pensive for a minute. Then she flipped the third card. It looked like they were going to have a visitor soon, a most unexpected visitor from beyond the ocean.

"What do you mean she doesn't want a cake? It's her birthday for heaven's sake!" Auntie Feride exclaimed with her lips puckered and an irate glimmer in her eyes. But then another thought must have come to her because she turned toward Asya and squinted. "Are you afraid that someone poisoned the cake?"

Asya looked at her in astonishment. After all this time and so much direct experience, she had still not been able to develop a strategy, that golden strategy, to stay calm and cool in the face of Auntie Feride's outbreaks. After faithfully sojourning in "hebephrenic schizophrenia" for years, Auntie Feride had recently moved into paranoia. The harder they tried to bring her back to reality, the more she became paranoid and suspicious of them.

"Is she afraid of someone poisoning the cake? Of course she is not, you harmless eccentric!"

All the heads in the room turned toward the door where Auntie Zeliha stood, corduroy jacket over her shoulders, high heels on her feet, with a quizzical expression that made her look heartbreakingly beautiful. She must have sneaked into the room and then stood silently listening to the conversation, unless she had developed a talent for materializing at will. Unlike most Turkish women who might have enjoyed short skirts and high heels in their youth, Zeliha had not lengthened the former and shortened the latter as she got older. Her style of dress was as flamboyant as it had ever been. The years had only added to her beauty while taking their toll on each of her sisters. As if she knew the effect of her presence, Auntie Zeliha remained in the doorway, eyeing her manicured fingernails. She cared deeply about her hands because she used them in her work. Having no liking for bureaucratic institutions or any chain of command, and possessing too much exasperation and anger inside, she had realized at an early age that she would have to choose a profession where she could be both independent and inventive—and also, if possible, inflict a bit of pain.

Ten years ago Auntie Zeliha had opened a tattoo parlor, where she had started to develop a collection of original designs. In addition to the classics of the art—crimson roses, iridescent butterflies, hearts pumped with love—and the usual compilation of hairy insects, fierce wolves, and giant spiders, she had introduced her own designs inspired by one basic principle: contradiction. There were faces half-masculine half-feminine, bodies half-animal half-human, trees half-blossomed half-dry. . . . However, her designs were not popular. The customers wanted to make a statement through their tattoos, not to add yet another ambiguity to their already uncertain lives. Their tattoos had to express a simple emotion, not an abstract thought. Learning her lesson well, Zeliha had then launched a new series, a compound collection of images, which she entitled "the management of abiding heartache."

Every tattoo in this special collection was designed to address one person only: the ex-love. The dumped and the despondent, the hurt and the irate brought a picture of the ex-love they wanted to banish from their lives forever but somehow could not stop loving. Auntie Zeliha then studied the picture and ransacked her brain until she found which particular animal that person resembled. The rest was relatively easy. She would draw that animal and then tattoo the design on the desolate customer's body. The whole practice adhered to the ancient shamanistic practice of simultaneously internalizing and externalizing one's totems. To strengthen vis-à-vis your antagonist you had to accept, welcome, and then transform it. The ex-love was interiorized—injected *into* the body, and yet at the same time exteriorized—left *outside* the skin. Once the ex-lover was located in this threshold between inside and outside, and deftly transformed into an animal, the power structure between the dumped and the dumper changed. Now the tattooed lover felt superior, as if the key to the ex-love's soul was in his or her hands. As soon as this stage was reached and the ex-love lost his or her appeal, those suffering from abiding heartache could finally let go of their obsession, for love loves power. That is why we can suicidally fall in love with others but can rarely reciprocate the love of those suicidally in love with us.

Istanbul being a city of broken hearts, it didn't take Auntie Zeliha long to expand the business, becoming legendary particularly among bohemian circles.

Now Asya averted her eyes so as not to have to stare any longer at her mother, the mother whom she had never called "mom" and had perhaps hoped to keep at a distance by "auntifying." A surge of self-pity engulfed her. What an unpardonable injustice on the part of Allah to create a daughter far less beautiful than her own mother.

"Don't you understand why Asya doesn't want any cake this year?" Auntie Zeliha said when she had finished with the inspection of her manicure. "She's just afraid of gaining weight!"

Though she knew too well what a big mistake it was to display her temper in front of her mother, Asya yelled furiously: "That's not true!"

Auntie Zeliha surrendered with a puckish twinkle in her eyes, "All right, sweetie, if you say so."

Only then did Asya notice the tray Auntie Feride was carrying. There was a big ball of meat and a bigger ball of dough. They were going to have *mantı* for dinner tonight.

"How many times do I need to tell you I do not like *mantı*?" Asya bellowed. "You know I've stopped eating meat." Her voice sounded strange to her, hoarse and alien.

"I told you she was afraid of gaining weight." Auntie Zeliha shook her head and brushed away a strand of black hair that had fallen across her face.

"Haven't you ever heard of the word *vegetarian*?" Asya shook her head too but resisted brushing away a strand of hair, for fear of imitating her mother's gestures.

"Of course I have," Auntie Zeliha said, squaring her shoulders. "But do not forget, my dear," she continued in a softer voice that she knew would prove more persuasive, "that you are a Kazancı, not a vegetarian!"

Asya swallowed hard, her mouth suddenly dry.

"And we Kazancıs love red meat! The redder, the greasier, the better! If you don't believe me, ask Sultan the Fifth, isn't that so, Sultan?" Auntie Zeliha tilted her head toward the overweight cat lying on his velvet cushion by the balcony door. He turned toward Auntie Zeliha with squinted, misty eyes as if he had fully understood and approved the statement.

Reshuffling the deck of tarot cards, Auntie Banu chided from her corner, "There are people in this country so desperately poor that they wouldn't even know what red meat tastes like, if it weren't for the alms benevolent Muslims give them during the Feast of Sacrifice. That is the only time they can have a decent meal. Go and ask those destitute souls what it really means to be vegetarian. You should be grateful for every morsel of meat put on your plate, because it is a symbol of opulence."

"This is a nuthouse! We are all nuts, each and every one of us." Asya repeated her mantra, only this time her voice was drenched in defeat. "I am going out, ladies. You can eat whatever you want. I am already late for my ballet class!"

No one noticed that she had snorted the word *ballet* as if it were some sputum she had to spit out but was simultaneously disgusted at not being able to control the urge to do so.

FIVE

Vanilla

Café Kundera was a small coffee shop on a narrow, snaky street on the European side of Istanbul. It was the only bistro in the city where you wasted no energy on conversation and tipped the waiters to be treated badly. How and why it was named after the famous author, nobody knew for sure—a lack of knowledge magnified by the fact that there was nothing, literally *nothing,* inside the place reminiscent of either Milan Kundera or any one of his novels.

On four sides there were hundreds of frames that came in all sizes and shapes, a myriad of photographs, paintings, and sketches, so many that one could easily doubt if there really were walls behind them. The whole place gave the impression of being erected on frames instead of bricks. In all the frames without exception shone the image of a road. Wide motorways in America, endless highways in Australia, busy autobahns in Germany, glitzy boulevards in Paris, crammed side streets in Rome, narrow paths in Machu Picchu, forgotten caravan routes in North Africa, and maps of the ancient trade routes along the Silk Road, following the foot-steps of Marco Polo—there were road pictures from all around the world. The customers were perfectly happy with the decor. They thought it was a useful alternative to useless chats that led nowhere. Whenever they didn't feel like chatting, they would pick a frame, depending on the angle of the table where they sat and on where exactly they wished to be zoomed on that specific day. Then they would fasten a bleary gaze on the chosen picture, little by little tak-ing off to that faraway land, craving to be somewhere in there, any-where but here. The next day they could travel elsewhere.

No matter how far away the pictures could take you, one thing was certain: None of them had anything to do with Milan Kun-dera. When the place was newly opened, one theory ran, the au-thor had happened to be in Istanbul, and on his way to elsewhere he had fortuitously stopped by for a cappuccino. The cappuccino wasn't so good and he hated the vanilla biscuit they brought with it, but he had soon ordered another one and even done some writ-ing, since nobody had disturbed or even recognized him. On that day, the place was baptized under his name. Yet another theory claimed that the owner of the café was an avid reader of Kundera; having devoured all his books and had each one autographed, he had decided to dedicate the place to his favorite author. This could have been the more plausible contention had the owner of the café not been a middle-aged musician and singer who always looked tanned and athletic, and who had such deep dislike for the printed word that he did not even bother to read the lyrics of the songs his band played on Friday nights.

The real reason why the bistro was named after Kundera, ran the counterargument, was because this spot in space was nothing but a figment of his flawed imagination. The café was a fictive place with fictive people as the regulars. Sometime ago Kundera had, as part of a new book project, started to write about this place, thus breathing life and chaos into it, but before long he had gotten dis-tracted by far more important projects—invitations, panels, and literary prizes—and amid the hectic pace he had eventually forgotten this dingy hole in Istanbul, the existence of which he was solely responsible for. Ever since then, the customers and waiters in Café Kundera had been struggling with a sense of void, digging away at disconsolate futuristic scenarios, grimacing over Turkish coffee served in espresso cups, waiting for a purpose in some highbrow drama wherein they would play the leading role. Among all the theories on the genesis of the café's name, this last explanation was the most widely championed. Still, every now and then, someone new to the place or in need of drawing attention would come forward with another theory, and for an ephemeral lull the other customers would believe him, toying with the new theory, until they got bored and sunk back to their marshes of moroseness.

Today, when the Dipsomaniac Cartoonist started toying with a new theory on the café's name, all of his friends—even his wife—felt obliged to listen to him attentively, as a sign of their support for his finally summoning the courage to do what everyone had forever been begging him to do: join Alcoholics Anonymous.

There was, however, a second reason why everyone at the table was more sympathetic toward him than usual. Today he had for the second time been indicted for insulting the prime minister in his cartoons, and if on the day of the hearing the judge agreed with the charge, he could get up to three years in prison. The Dipsomaniac Cartoonist was famous for a series of political cartoons in which he depicted the entire cabinet as a flock of sheep and the prime minister as a wolf in sheep's clothing. Now that he had been forbidden from using this metaphor, he was planning to draw the cabinet as a pack of wolves and the prime minister as a jackal in wolf's clothing. Should this caricature too be taken away from him, he had thought of an exit strategy: penguins! He was determined to sketch all the members of the parliament as penguins in tuxedos.

"Here is my new theory!" the Dipsomaniac Cartoonist said, unaware of the compassion he had evoked and a bit surprised to see this much interest on the part of his audience—and even his wife.

He was a large man with a patrician nose, high cheekbones, intense blue eyes, and a grim set to his mouth. He had long been familiar to misery and melancholy. However, after secretly falling in love with a most unattainable woman, his gloom had doubled.

Looking at him, it was hard to imagine that he made a living from humor, and that behind that sullen face of his streamed the funniest jokes. Though he was always a notorious drinker, lately his problems with alcohol had skyrocketed. He started waking up in questionable places he'd never been before. But the final straw came when early one morning he found himself in the courtyard of a mosque lying on the flat stone where the dead were washed, apparently having passed out there while trying to mastermind his own funeral. When he managed to open his eyes at dawn, a young *imam,* on his way to recite the morning prayer, was standing next to him, shocked to encounter a stranger snoring on the stone of the dead. After that, the Dipsomaniac Cartoonist's friends—and even his wife—were so alarmed they urged him to get professional help and to make something more of his life. Finally today he had attended a meeting of Alcoholics Anonymous and pledged to stop imbibing. Hence, everybody at the table—even his wife—considerately leaned back to listen to whatever his theory might be.

"This café is called what it is called because the word *Kundera* is a code. The gist of the issue is not what the name is but what the name is symptomatic of!"

"And what would that be?" asked the Nonnationalist Scenarist of Ultranationalist Movies, a short, gaunt man with a beard dyed ash gray ever since the day he concluded young women preferred mature men. He was the writer and creator of a popular TV series, *Timur the Lionheart,* which featured a hefty, robust national hero capable of mashing entire battalions of enemies into a bloody puree. When asked about his tacky TV show and movies, he would defend himself by arguing that he was a nationalist by profession but a true nihilist by choice. Today he showed up with another girlfriend— a comely, eye-catching woman but without much depth. This he didn't confess to her, but within male circles they had a specific name for shallow females like her: "appetizers"—not the main course, of course, but good to snack on. Bolting cashews from the bowl on the table, he guffawed as he put his arm around his new girlfriend: "Come on, tell us what that code is!"

"Boredom," the Dipsomaniac Cartoonist said with a puff of smoke. Coils of smoke ascended from all sides as people smoked like chimneys all around, and his wispy puff lazily joined the thick, gray cloud hovering over the table.

The only one who didn't smoke at the table was the Closeted-Gay Columnist. He detested the smell of smoke. Every day when he went home he immediately took off his clothes to get rid of the stinky odors of Café Kundera. Still, he did not object when others smoked. Neither did he stop going to the café. He came here regularly both because he enjoyed being part of this motley group and also because he was secretly attracted to the Dipsomaniac Cartoonist.

Not that the Closeted-Gay Columnist wanted to have anything physical with the cartoonist. Even the thought of him naked was enough to send shivers down his spine. This wasn't about sex, he assured himself, but about kindred spirits. Besides, there were two big obstacles that blocked his way. First, the Dipsomaniac Cartoonist was strictly heterosexual and the chances of him changing seemed slim. Second, he had a crush on that morose girl Asya—a fact that everyone but she had noticed by this time.

So the Closeted-Gay Columnist did not harbor any hopes about having an affair with the Dipsomaniac Cartoonist. He just wanted to be close to him. Every now and then he felt a sudden shudder when the cartoonist, while reaching for a glass or an ashtray, accidentally touched his hand or shoulder. Still, in the itch to assure everyone that he had absolutely no interest in him, or in any man for that matter, there were times the columnist treated the cartoonist distantly, denigrating his opinions out of the blue. It was a complicated story.

"Boredom," the Dipsomaniac Cartoonist remarked when he had knocked back his café latte. "Boredom is the summary of our lives. Day after day we wallow in ennui. Why? Because we cannot abandon this rabbit hole for fear of a traumatic encounter with our own culture. Western politicians presume there is a cultural gap between Eastern Civilization and Western Civilization. If it were that simple! The real civilization gap is between the Turks and *the* Turks. We are a bunch of cultured urbanites surrounded by hill-billies and bumpkins on all sides. They have conquered the whole city."

He threw the windows a sidelong look, as if afraid that a throng of folks might ram them with their clubs and cannonballs.

"The streets belong to them, the plazas belong to them, the ferries belong to them. Every open area is theirs. Perhaps in a few years this café will be the only place left for us. Our last liberated zone. We rush here every day to seek refuge from them. Oh yes, *them*! God save me from my own people!"

"You are talking poetry," said the Exceptionally Untalented Poet. Since he was an exceptionally untalented poet, he had the habit of likening everything to poetry.

"We are stuck. We are stuck between the East and the West. Between the past and the future. On the one hand there are the secular modernists, so proud of the regime they constructed, you cannot breathe a critical word. They've got the army and half of the state on their side. On the other hand there are the conventional traditionalists, so infatuated with the Ottoman past, you cannot breathe a critical word. They've got the general public and the re-maining half of the state on their side. What is left for us?"

He put the cigarette back between his pale, chapped lips, where it remained throughout his continued grievance. "The Modernists tell us to move forward, but we have no faith in their idea of prog-ress. The Traditionalists tell us to move backward, but we do not want to return to their ideal order either. Sandwiched between the two sides, we march two steps forward and one step backward, just like the Ottoman army band did! But we don't even play an instrument! Where can we possibly escape to? We are not even a minority. I wish we were an ethnic minority or an indigenous people under the protection of the UN Charter. Then we could have at least some basic rights. But nihilists, pessimists, and anarchists are not regarded as a minority, although we are an extinct species. Our number is lessening every day. How long can we survive?"

The question hung heavily above their heads, somewhere below the cloud of smoke. The cartoonist's wife, who was a jittery woman with full, somber eyes and too much umbrage welled inside, and who happened to be a better cartoonist than her husband but far less appreciated, gnashed her teeth, torn between picking on her partner of twelve years, as she would like to do, and supporting his frenzy no matter what, as an ideal wife would do. They sincerely disliked each other and yet all these years they both had clutched at their marriage, she with the hope of revenge, he out of hope that it would get better. Today they spoke with words and gestures stolen from each other. Even their caricatures were analogous now. They drew deformed bodies and invented twisted dialogues involving depressed people dropped into sad and sarcastic situations.

"You know what we are? The scum of this country. A sorry soggy pulp, nothing more than that! Everyone but us is obsessed with entering the EU, making profits, buying stocks, trading up their cars, and trading up their girlfriends. . . ."

The Nonnationalist Scenarist of Ultranationalist Movies fidgeted nervously.

"This is where Kundera enters into the picture," the Dipsomaniac Cartoonist continued without noticing the gaffe. "The whole idea of lightness permeates our lives in the form of a meaningless emptiness. Our existence is kitsch, a beautiful lie, which helps us to defy the reality of death and mortality. It is precisely this—"

But his words were cut off by the jingling of the bells as the door of Café Kundera opened with a blast and a young woman walked in, looking tired beyond her age and pissed off.

"Yo, Asya!" the scenarist yelled, as if she were the much-awaited savior who would terminate this daft conversation. "Over here! We're here!"

Asya Kazancı offered a half smile and her forehead furrowed with an expression that said, *Oh well, I can join you folks briefly, what difference does it make anyway, life sucks either way.* Slowly, as if saddled with invisible sacks of inertia, she approached the table, gave everyone a toneless greeting, took a seat, and started to roll a cigarette.

"What are you doing here at this hour? Aren't you supposed to be at ballet now?" asked the Dipsomaniac Cartoonist, forgetting his soliloquy. His eyes flickered with consideration—a sign that was noticed by all but his wife.

"But that's exactly where I am: in my ballet class. And right now"—Asya stuffed the rolling paper with tobacco—"I am doing one of the most difficult jumps, meeting my calves in the air between forty-five and ninety degrees—*cabriole!*"

"Wow!" The cartoonist smiled.

"Then I make a turning jump," Asya continued. "Right foot front, demi plié, jump up!" She grabbed the leather tobacco pouch and held it in the air. "Turn a hundred and eighty degrees"—she ordered as she rotated the pouch, sprinkling some tobacco on the table—"and land on left foot!" The pouch perched next to the bowl of cashews. "Then repeat the whole thing one more time to go back to the starting position. *Emboîté!*"

"Ballet is like writing poetry with your body," muttered the Exceptionally Untalented Poet.

A sullen torpor set in. Someplace far away churned the sounds of the city, an amalgam of sirens, horns, shouts, and laughter accompanied by the squeaks of the seagulls. A few new customers came in, a few customers left. One of the waiters fell with a trayful of glasses. Another waiter fetched a broom and as he swept the glass off the floor, the customers watched nonchalantly. Here the waiters changed frequently. The working hours were long and the pay not great. Still, no waiter had resigned to this day; instead they would get themselves fired. That's how it was in the Café Kundera; once you stepped inside, you remained fastened to it until the place spat you out.

In the following half hour some people at Asya Kazancı's table ordered coffee, the rest ordered beer. In the second round, the former drank beer and the latter drank coffee. And so it went. Only the cartoonist stuck to café lattes and nibbled the vanilla biscuits that came with them, although by this time his frustration was becoming visible. In any case, nothing was done in harmony, and yet in that dissonance there lay an unusual cadence. This is what Asya liked most about the café: its comatose indolence and farcical disharmony. This place was out of time and space. Istanbul was in a constant hurry and yet at Café Kundera only lethargy prevailed. People outside the café stuck to one another to disguise their loneliness, pretending to be far more intimate than they really were, whereas in here it was the opposite, everyone pretending to be far more detached than they really were. This spot was the negation of the whole city. Asya took a drag on her cigarette, fully appreciating the inaction until the cartoonist looked at his watch and turned toward her. "It's seven forty, dear. Your class is over."

"Oh, do you have to go? Your family is so outmoded," the scenarist's girlfriend blurted out. "Why are they making you take ballet classes when obviously you aren't into it?"

That was the problem with all these butterfly-life-spanned girlfriends the scenarist brought with him. Driven by an impulse to become friends with everyone in the group, they asked too many personal questions and made too many personal comments, miserably failing to acknowledge that it was precisely the opposite, the lack of any serious and sincere interest in each other's privacy, that drew the group members to one another.

"How can you cope with all those aunts?" the scenarist's girlfriend continued, failing to read Asya's face. "Gosh, so many women playing the role of mother all under the same roof. . . . I couldn't stand it a minute."

Now that was too much. There were unwritten rules in a group as eclectic as this and they were not to be violated. Asya sniffed. She did not like women, which would have been easier to deal with had she not been one of them. Whenever she met a new woman she did one of two things: either waited to see when she would hate her or hated her right away.

"I don't have a family in the normal sense of the word." Asya gave her a condescending gaze, hoping this would stop whatever the other was planning to say next. Yet in the endeavor she caught sight of a shiny silver frame on the wall right above the latter's right shoulder. It was the picture of a road to the Red Lagoon in Bolivia. How nice it would be to be on that road right now! She finished her coffee, stubbed out her cigarette, and began to roll another one as she mumbled, "We are a pack of female animals forced to live together. I don't call that a family."

"But that's exactly what a family is about, my dear," objected the Exceptionally Untalented Poet. At times like this he remembered that he was the eldest of the group, not only in terms of age years but also in terms of *mistakes* years. Married and divorced three times, he had watched as one by one all of his ex-wives left Istanbul to get as far away from him as possible. From each marriage he had children whom he visited only once in a long while, but always proudly claimed ownership of. "Remember"—he wagged a paternal finger toward Asya—"all happy families resemble one another, but each unhappy family is unhappy in its own way."

"It is so easy for Tolstoy to sputter that nonsense," the Dipsomaniac Cartoonist's wife shrugged. "The guy had a wife who took care of every little detail, raised the dozens of kids they had, and worked like a dog so that his majesty the great Tolstoy could concentrate and write novels!"

"What do you want?" the Dipsomaniac Cartoonist asked.

"Recognition! That's what I want. I want the whole world to admit that if given the opportunity, Tolstoy's wife could be a better writer than him."

"Why? Just because she was a woman?"

"Because she was a very talented woman oppressed by a very talented man," his wife snapped.

"Oh," said the Dipsomaniac Cartoonist. Perturbed, he called the waiter and to everyone's chagrin, he ordered a beer. Yet when it was served he must have felt some sort of guilt, for all of a sudden he switched the topic, embarking on a speech on the benefits of alcohol.

"This country owes its freedom to this little bottle which I can so freely hold in my hand." The cartoonist raised his voice over an ambulance siren squealing outside. "Neither social reforms, nor political regulations. Not even the War of Independence. It is this very bottle that differentiates Turkey from all other Muslim countries. This beer here"—he raised the bottle as if to toast—"is the symbol of freedom and civil society."

"Oh, come on. Since when is being a rotten drunkard a symbol of freedom?" the scenarist reprimanded sharply. The others did not join in. Debating was a waste of energy. Instead, they chose a frame on the wall and focused on a road picture.

"Since the day alcohol was forbidden and denigrated in all the Muslim Middle East. Since forever." The Dipsomaniac Cartoonist grunted. "Think about Ottoman history. All those taverns, all those *mezes* to accompany each glass. . . . It looks like the guys were having a good time. We as a nation relish alcohol, why don't we accept that? This is a society that likes to imbibe eleven months a year and then panic, repent, and fast in Ramadan, only to go back to drinking when the holy month is over. If there never was *sharia* in this country, if the fundamentalists never succeeded as they did elsewhere, I tell you, we owe it to this twisted tradition. It is thanks to alcohol that there is something resembling democracy in Turkey."

"Well, why don't we drink, then?" the Dipsomaniac Cartoonist's wife gave a tired smile. "And what better reason do we have to drink than Mr. Tiptoe? What was his name—Cecche?"

"Cecchetti," Asya corrected her, still lamenting the day she had been intoxicated enough to give the group a speech on ballet history, and in passing mentioned the name Cecchetti. They loved him. Ever since that day, now and again someone at the table would propose a toast to him, the dancer who introduced the pointe walk on the toes.

"So if it weren't for him ballet dancers wouldn't be able to walk on their toes, huh?" Someone would chuckle each time.

"What was he thinking?" Someone else would add, and then everybody would have a laugh.

Every day they met at the Café Kundera. The Exceptionally Untalented Poet, the Nonnationalist Scenarist of Ultranationalist Movies and whomever his girlfriend might be at that moment, the Dipsomaniac Cartoonist, the Dipsomaniac Cartoonist's wife, the Closeted-Gay Columnist, and Asya Kazancı. There was tension buried far below the surface, waiting for talk of the day to pump it out. In the meantime, things flowed swimmingly. Some days they brought other people along, friends or colleagues or consummate strangers; some days they came alone. The group was a self-regulating organism wherein individual differences were displayed but could never take over, as if the organism had a life outside and beyond the personalities composing it.

Among them Asya Kazancı found inner peace. Café Kundera was her sanctuary. In the Kazancı domicile she always had to correct her ways, striving for a perfection that was beyond her comprehension, whereas here in Café Kundera no one forced you to change since human beings were thought to be essentially imperfect and uncorrectable.

It is true, they were not the ideal friends her aunts would have chosen for her. Some in the group were old enough to be Asya's mother or father. Being the youngest, she enjoyed watching their childishness. It was rather comforting to see that nothing really improved in life over the years; if you were a sullen teenager, you ended up being a sullen adult. The pattern was with us to stay. True, it sounded a bit glum, but at least, Asya consoled herself, it proved that one didn't have to become something else, something more, like her aunts kept nagging her about day and night. Since nothing was going to change in time and this sullenness was here forever, she could continue to be her same sullen self.

"Today is my birthday," announced Asya, surprising herself since she hadn't had any intention of declaring that.

"Oh yeah?" someone asked.

"What a coincidence! It is also my youngest daughter's birthday today," exclaimed the Exceptionally Untalented Poet.

"Oh yeah?" Now it was Asya's turn.

"So you were born on the same day as my daughter! Gemini." The poet shook his fluffy head with glee, theatrically.

"Pisces," Asya corrected.

And that was that. Nobody tried to hug her or suffocate her with kisses, just like nobody thought about ordering a cake. Instead the poet recited an awful poem for her, the cartoonist drank three bottles of beer in her honor, and the cartoonist's wife drew her caricature on a napkin—a surly young woman with electrified hair, huge tits, and a sharp nose under a pair of piercingly astute eyes. The others bought her another coffee and at the end did not let her pay her share of the bill. It was as simple as that. Not that they hadn't taken Asya's birthday seriously. To the contrary, they had taken it so seriously that soon they were excogitating aloud the notion of time and mortality, only to travel from there to the questions of when they were going to die and whether there really was an afterlife. "There *is* an afterlife and it's going to be worse than here," was the general opinion in the group. "So enjoy whatever time you have left."

Some mulled it over, others stopped midword and fled into this or that road picture on the wall. They took their time, as if no one was waiting for them outside, as if there was no outside, their grimaces gradually evolving into beatific smiles of indifference. Having no energy, no passion, no need for further conversation, they sunk deeper into the murky waters of apathy, wondering why on earth this place was named Café Kundera.

At nine o'clock that night, after finishing a square meal and with the lights turned off, amid singing and clapping, Asya Kazancı blew out the candles on the triple-layer caramelized apple cake (extremely sugary) with whipped lemon cream frosting (extremely sour). She was able to blow out only a third of them. The rest of the candles were doused by her aunts, grandmother, and Petite-Ma, all of them blowing from all sides.

"How was your ballet class today?" Auntie Feride asked as she turned the lights back on.

"It was good." Asya smiled. "My back hurts a little because of all the stretching the teacher compels us to do, but, still, I can't complain. I learned many new moves. . . ."

"Oh yeah?" came a suspicious voice. It was Auntie Zeliha. "Like what?"

"Well . . . " Asya replied as she took her first bite of the cake. "Let's see. I learned the petit jeté, which is a little jump, and the pirouette and the glissade."

"You know, this is like killing two birds with one stone," Auntie Feride remarked. "We pay for her ballet class, but she ends up learning both ballet and French. We save a whole lot of money!"

Everyone nodded—everyone except Auntie Zeliha. With a skeptical glint in the abyss of her jade green eyes, she drew her face up close to her daughter's and said in an almost inaudible voice, "Show us!"

"Are you crazy?" Asya flinched. "I can't do those things right in the middle of our living room! I need to be in the studio and working with a teacher. We warm up and stretch first, and concentrate. And there is always music. . . . *Glissade* means to glide, did you know that? How am I possibly going to glide here on the carpet?! One cannot start doing ballet just like that!"

A saturnine smile etched along Auntie Zeliha's lips as she ran her fingers through her dark hair. She said nothing further, seeming to be more interested in eating her cake than in quarreling with her daughter. But her smile was enough to infuriate Asya. She pushed her own plate away, pulled her chair back, and stood up.

At nine fifteen that evening, in the living room of a once fashionably opulent but now long outmoded and dilapidated *konak* in Istanbul, Asya Kazancı was doing ballet on a Turkish carpet, her face romantically poised, her arms stretched out, her hands softly curved so that her middle fingers touched her thumbs, while her mind swirled with rage and resentment.

SIX

Pistachios

Armanoush Tchakhmakhchian watched the cashier at A Clean Well-Lighted Place for Books pile the twelve novels she had just purchased one by one into a canvas backpack while they waited for her credit card to be processed. When finally given the receipt, she signed the paper, trying to avoid looking at the total. Once again she had spent all her monthly savings on books! She was a true bookworm, not a promising feature at all given that it had zero value in the eyes of boys and thus served to only further upset her mother about the prospects of her getting married to a moneyed husband. Just this morning on the phone her mother had made her promise not to whisper a word about novels when she went out tonight. Armanoush felt a surge of angst rise in her stomach as she thought about her upcoming date. After a year of not going out with anyone—a solemn tribute to her twenty-one years of chronic singleness marked with disastrous pseudodates—finally today Armanoush Tchakhmakhchian was going to give love a try again.

If her passion for books had been one fundamental reason behind her recurring inability to sustain a standard relationship with the opposite sex, there were two additional factors that had fanned the flames of her failure. First and foremost, Armanoush was beautiful—too beautiful. With a well-proportioned body, delicate face, dark blond, wavy hair, huge gray blue eyes, and a sharp nose with a slight ridge that might seem a defect on others but on her only added an air of self-confidence, her physical attractiveness when combined with her brains intimidated young men. Not that they preferred ugly women, or that they had no appreciation for intelligence. But they didn't quite know where exactly to pigeonhole her: among the group of women they were dying to sleep with (the darlings), or among the group they sought advice from (the buddies), or among the group they wished to marry eventually (the fiancée-types). Since she was sublime enough to be all at once, she ended up being none.

The second factor was far more complicated but equally beyond her control: her relatives. The Tchakhmakhchian family in San Francisco and her mother in Arizona had antagonistically different views when it came to the question of who would be the right man for Armanoush. Since she had been spending almost five months here (summer vacation, spring break, and frequent visits over the weekends) and the remaining seven months in Arizona almost every year since she was a toddler, Armanoush had had the chance to learn firsthand what each side expected from her and how utterly irreconcilable those expectations were. Whatever made one side happy was bound to distress the other. In order not to upset anyone, Armanoush had tried to date Armenian boys in San Francisco and anyone but them when she was in Arizona. But fate must have been pulling her leg, because in San Francisco she had been attracted only to non-Armenians, whereas all three of the young men she had had a crush on while in Arizona turned out to be Armenian Americans, much to her mother's disappointment.

Lugging her anxieties together with the heavy backpack, she crossed Opera Plaza while the wind whistled and wailed uncanny tunes to her ears. She caught sight of a young couple inside Max's Opera Café who were either disappointed with the piled-high corned beef sandwiches in front of them, or else had just had a quarrel. *Thank God I'm single,* Armanoush half jokingly thought to herself before she turned toward Turk Street. Years ago when she was still in her teens, Armanoush had shown the city to an Armenian American girl from New York. Upon reaching this street the girl's face had crumpled. *"Turk Street! Aren't they everywhere?"*

Armanoush recalled her own surprise at the girl's reaction. She had tried to explain to her that the street was named after Frank Turk, an attorney who had served as second alcalde and was important in the city's history.

"Whatever." Her friend had broken off the lecture, showing not too much interest in urban history. "All the same, aren't they everywhere?"

Yes indeed, they were everywhere, so much so that one of them was married to her mom. But this last bit of information Armanoush had kept to herself.

She avoided talking about her stepfather with her Armenian friends. She did not talk about him with non-Armenians either. Not even with those who had absolutely no interest in life outside of their own and therefore couldn't care less about the history of the Armenian-Turkish conflict. All the same, wise enough to know that secrets could spread quicker than dust in the wind, Armanoush maintained her silence. When you didn't tell anyone the extraordinary, everyone assumed the normal, Armanoush discovered at an early age. Since her mother was an *odar,* what could have been more normal for her than to get married to another *odar?* This being the general assumption on the part of her friends, Armanoush's stepfather was thought to be an American, presumably from the Midwest.

On Turk Street she passed by a gay-friendly bed-and-breakfast, a Middle Eastern grocery store, and a small Thai market, and strolled next to pedestrians from all walks of life until she finally got on the trolley to Russian Hill. Leaning her forehead on the dusty window, she reflected on the "other I" in Borges's *Labyrinths* as she watched the wispy fog drift up off the horizon. Armanoush too had another self, one that she kept at bay no matter where she went.

She liked being in this city, its vim and vigor pulsating in her body. Ever since she was a toddler she had enjoyed coming here and living with her dad and Grandma Shushan. Unlike her mom, her dad had not married again. Armanoush knew he had had girl-friends in the past but none had been introduced to her, either be-cause the affairs weren't serious enough or her dad had been afraid of upsetting her in some way. Probably it was the latter. That would be more typical of Barsam Tchakhmakhchian. He was the most un-selfish soul and the most *genderless* man, Armanoush believed, that existed on the face of the earth, and to this day she couldn't help marveling at how he could have ever ended up with a woman as self-absorbed as Rose. Not that Armanoush didn't love her mother; she did, in her own way, but there were times in which she felt suf-focated by her mother's dissatisfied love. At those times she escaped to San Francisco right into the arms of the Tchakhmakhchian fam-ily, where a satisfied but equally demanding love would be await-ing her.

Once off the trolley she began to hurry. Matt Hassinger would be picking her up at seven thirty. She had less than an hour and a half to get ready, which basically meant to take a shower and don a dress, perhaps the turquoise one everyone said looked so good on her. That would be all. No makeup, no jewelry. She was not going to doll herself up for this date and she certainly wasn't going to ex-pect much from it. If it worked out well, that would be nice. But if it didn't, she would be prepared for that too. Thus inching her way under the fog canopying the city, at ten past six in the evening Ar-manoush reached her grandmother's two-bathroom condominium in Russian Hill, a lively neighborhood built on one of the steepest hills in San Francisco.

"Hello, sweetheart, welcome home!"

Surprisingly, it was not her grandmother but Auntie Surpun

who opened the door. "I missed you," she twittered lovingly. "What have you done all day long? How was your day?"

"It was OK," Armanoush said placidly, wondering what her youngest aunt was doing here on a Tuesday evening.

Auntie Surpun lived in Berkeley, where she had been teaching forever, at least ever since Armanoush was a child. She drove to San Francisco on the weekends but it was highly unusual of her to show up during the week. But the question would cease to concern Armanoush once she proceeded to give an account of her day. She remarked heartily, with a beaming face, "I bought myself some new books."

"Books!? Did she say 'books' again?" a familiar voice yelled from inside.

That sounded like Auntie Varsenig! Armanoush hung up her raincoat, flattened her wind-ruffled hair, and wondered in the meantime what Auntie Varsenig was doing here as well. Her twin daughters were coming back this evening from Los Angeles, where they had been participating in a basketball tournament. Auntie Varsenig was so excited about the competition that she hadn't been able to sleep properly for the last three days, constantly chatting on the phone with either of her daughters or their coach. And yet on the day the team was returning, instead of arriving at the airport hours early, as was her habit, here she was at grandma's house setting the dinner table.

"Yes, I did say 'books,'" Armanoush said, shouldering her canvas backpack as she walked into the spacious living room.

"Don't you listen to her. She's just getting old and grumpy," Auntie Surpun chirped from behind her as she followed her into the living room. "We are all so proud of you, sweetheart."

"We *are* proud of her, but she could just as well act her age." Auntie Varsenig shrugged as she placed the last china plate on the table and then gave her niece a hug. "Girls your age are usually busy beautifying themselves, you know. Not that you need to, of course, but if you read and read and read, where is it going to end?"

"You see, unlike in the movies, there is no THE END sign flashing at the end of books. When I've read a book, I don't feel like I've finished anything. So I start a new one." Armanoush winked without knowing how pretty she looked under the sun's fading light in the room. She set her backpack on her grandma's armchair and instantly emptied it, like a kid eager to see a bunch of new toys. Books rained on top of one another: *The Aleph and Other Stories, A Confederacy of Dunces, A Frolic of His Own, The Management of Grief,* Borges's *Collected Fictions, Narcissus and Goldmund, The Mambo Kings Play Songs of Love, Landscape Painted with Tea, Yellow Woman and a Beauty of the Spirit,* and two by Milan Kundera, her favorite author, *The Book of Laughter and Forgetting* and *Life Is Elsewhere.* Some of them were new to her, others she'd read years ago but had been wanting to read again.

All things considered, Armanoush knew, perhaps not rationally but instinctively, that the Tchakhmakhchian family's resistance to her passion for books came from a deeper, darker source than simply from an urge to remind her of the things girls her age were busy with. It was not only because she was a woman but also because she was an Armenian that she was expected to refrain twice as much from becoming a bibliophile. Armanoush had a feeling that beneath Auntie Varsenig's constant objection to her reading lay a more structural, if not primordial, concern: a fear of survival. She simply did not want her to shine too bright, to stand out from the flock. Writers, poets, artists, intellectuals were the first ones within the Armenian *millet* to be eliminated by the late Ottoman government. They had first gotten rid of "the brains" and only then proceeded to extradite the rest—the laypeople. Like too many Armenian families in the diaspora, safe and sound here but never truly at ease, the Tchakhmakhchians were both elated and vexed when a child of theirs read too much, thought too much, and swerved too far away from the ordinary.

Though books were potentially harmful, novels were all the more dangerous. The path of fiction could easily mislead you into the cosmos of stories where everything was fluid, quixotic, and as open to surprises as a moonless night in the desert. Before you knew it you could be so carried away that you could lose touch with reality—that stringent and stolid truth from which no minority should ever veer too far from in order not to end up unguarded when the winds shifted and bad times arrived. It didn't help to be so naïve to think things wouldn't get bad, for they always did. Imagination was a dangerously captivating magic for those compelled to be realistic in life, and words could be poisonous for those destined always to be silenced. If as a child of survivors you still wanted to read and ruminate, you should do so quietly, apprehensively, and introspectively, never turning yourself into a vociferous reader. If you couldn't help harboring higher aspirations in life, you should at least harbor only simple desires, reduced in passion and ambition, as if you had been de-energized and now had only enough strength to be average. With a fate and family like this, Armanoush had to learn to downplay her talents and do her best not to glimmer too brightly.

A sharp, spicy smell wafted from the kitchen and tickled her nostrils, yanking her out of her reverie. "So," Armanoush exclaimed, turning toward the most talkative of her three aunts, "are you going to stay for dinner?"

"Only briefly, honey," Auntie Varsenig murmured. "I need to leave for the airport soon; the twins are coming back today. I just stopped by to bring you guys homemade *mantı* and"—Auntie Varsenig beamed with pride—"guess what? We got *bastırma* from Yerevan!"

"Gosh, I'm not eating *mantı* and I'm definitely not going to eat *bastırma*." Armanoush frowned. "I can't reek of garlic tonight."

"No problem. If you brush your teeth and chew a mint gum there will be no smell whatsoever."

That was Auntie Zarouhi walking in with a plate of *musaqqa,* beautifully garnished with parsley and slices of lemon. She left the plate on the table and opened her arms wide to embrace her niece.

Armanoush embraced her back wondering all the while what was *she* doing here . . . ? But she started to get the picture. What a well-planned "coincidence" it was that the whole Tchakhmakhchian family had materialized at Grandma Shushan's house at the same time Armanoush would be going on her date. Everyone here had shown up with a different pretext but exactly the same purpose: They wanted to see, test, and judge with their own eyes this Matt Hassinger, the lucky young man who would be dating the apple of their eye this evening.

Armanoush looked at her relatives with a stare that bordered on desperate. What could she do? How could she be independent when they were so frighteningly close? How could she convince them that they didn't have to worry so much about her when they had had so much in life to worry about? How could she break free from her genetic heritage, especially when a part of her was so proud of it? How could she fight off the kindness of her loved ones? Could goodness be fought?

"That's not going to help!" Armanoush gasped. "No toothpaste, no chewing gum, not even those awful minty mouthwashes—there is nothing on earth strong enough to suppress the smell of *bastırma*. It takes a week to finally disappear. If you eat *bastırma* you smell and sweat and breathe *bastırma* for days on end. Even your pee smells like *bastırma*!"

"What's peeing got to do with dating?" Armanoush heard a befuddled Auntie Varsenig whisper to Auntie Surpun as soon as she had turned her back.

Still protesting but unwilling to squabble with them, Armanoush headed to the bathroom, only to find Uncle Dikran there, his head inside the cabinet under the sink, his bulky body on hands and knees.

"Uncle?" Armanoush almost let out a shriek.

"Hellooo!" Dikran Stamboulian hooted from the cabinet.

"This house is full of Chekhovian characters," Armanoush muttered to herself.

"If you say so," echoed a voice from under the sink.

"Uncle, what are you doing?"

"Your grandma always complains about the old faucets in the house, you know. So this evening I said to myself, why don't I close the store early, stop by Shushan's house, and repair those damn pipes?"

"Yeah, I can see," Armanoush remarked, suppressing a smile. "Where is she, by the way?"

"She's taking a nap," Dikran said, worming his way out of the cabinet to get the pipe bender and crawling back inside. "Old age—what you gonna do?—body needs sleep! She will be awake before seven thirty, though, don't worry."

Seven thirty! It looked like every person in the family had set a biological alarm for the moment Matt Hassinger would ring the bell.

"Give me the smooth jaw wrench, will you?" came a frustrated voice. "This one doesn't seem to be working."

Armanoush pouted at the bag on the floor, in which glinted over a hundred tools of all sizes. She handed him a chain tong, a pipe reamer, and an HTP300 hydrostatic test pump before she chanced upon the smooth jaw wrench. Inauspiciously, that wrench too turned out to be "not working." Seeing the impossibility of taking a shower with Uncle Dikran the Impossible Plumber on the job, Armanoush moved toward her grandma's bedroom, opened the door slightly, and peeked inside. There she was sleeping lightly but with the blissful placidity found only in elderly women who are surrounded by their children and grandchildren. An elfin woman who had always had a flimsy body and too much to shoulder, she had been shortened and slimmed down by old age. As she had aged she had grown more and more in need of some sleep during the day. At night, however, she was as awake as ever. Old age had not diminished Shushan's insomnia one tiny bit. The past didn't let her rest for too long, her family thought; it allowed her only these fleeting catnaps. Armanoush closed the door and let her sleep.

The table was ready when she returned to the living room. They had also set a plate for her. She wondered how she could possibly be expected to eat if she was going to have a date in less than an hour, but preferred not to ask. To be too reasonable in this family would be a blunder. She could nibble a little so that everyone would be happy. Besides, she liked this cuisine. Her mother in Arizona wanted to keep Armenian cuisine as far from the borders of her kitchen as possible, and profoundly enjoyed vilifying it to her neighbors and friends. She was especially fond of drawing attention to two dishes, which she publicly disparaged on every available occasion: cooked calf's feet and stuffed intestines. Armanoush recalled how Rose once complained to Mrs. Grinnell, the next-door neighbor.

"Gross," Mrs. Grinnell exclaimed with a trace of disgust creeping into her voice. "Do they really eat the intestines?"

"Oh yeah." Rose nodded heartily. "Believe me, they do. They spice it up with garlic and herbs, stuff it with rice, and wolf it down."

The two women unleashed a condescending snicker and would have probably snickered some more if at that moment Armanoush's stepfather had not turned toward them and, with a jaded look on his face, remarked: "What's the big deal? That sounds just like *mumbar*. You should try it sometime, it's really good."

"Is he Armenian too?" Mrs. Grinnell whispered when Mustafa left the room.

"Of course not," Rose said, her voice trailing off. "It's just that they have some things in common."

The doorbell rang shrilly, snatching Armanoush out of her trance and making everyone else jump in panic. It was not even seven o'clock yet. Punctuality, apparently, wasn't one of Matt Hassinger's merits. As if a button had been pressed, all three aunts scampered to the door only to stop short of opening it. Uncle Dikran hit his head on the cupboard he was still working in and Grandma Shushan opened her eyes in fright. Only Armanoush remained calm and composed. In intentionally measured steps she walked to the door under the fixed gaze of her aunts and opened it.

"Daddy!!!" Armanoush fluted with delight. "I thought you had a meeting this evening. How come you're home so early?"

But before she reached the end of her question, Armanoush had already sensed the answer.

Barsam Tchakhmakhchian smiled his soft dimpled smile and hugged his daughter, his eyes glimmering with pride and traces of anxiety. "Yeah, but it didn't work out, we had to reschedule the meeting," he said to Armanoush. As soon as she was beyond earshot, he whispered to his sisters: "Is he here yet?"

The last thirty minutes before Matt Hassinger's arrival were marked with escalating apprehension on the part of everyone but Armanoush. They made her put on several dresses and parade around in each one, until they unilaterally reached a decision: the turquoise dress. The outfit was completed with earrings that matched, a burgundy beaded purse that Auntie Varsenig claimed would add a feminine touch, and a fluffy dark blue cardigan, just in case it got cold. That was one other thing Armanoush knew she should not question. Somehow the world outside the family house had an arctic character in the eyes of the Tchakhmakhchians. "Outside" meant "chilly land," and to visit it, you had to take your cardigan, preferably handwoven. This she partly knew from her childhood, having spent her early years under the downy blankets Grandma knit for her with her initials stitched at the edges. To go to sleep without anything covering your body was simply unthinkable, and going out into the street without a cardigan would be a blunder. Just like a house needed a roof above its head, human beings too needed an additional skin between them and the rest of the world so that they could feel safe and warm.

Once Armanoush agreed to put on her cardigan and the dressing part was over, they came forth with another demand, one that was fundamentally paradoxical but not to the Tchakhmakhchians.

They wanted her to sit with them at the table and eat, so that she could be ready and strong for tonight's dinner.

"But honey you are just nibbling like a bird. Don't tell me you are not even going to taste my *mantı*?" Auntie Varsenig wailed with a scoop in her hand and such severe dismay in her dark brown eyes that it made Armanoush wonder if something far more life-and-death than a bowl of *mantı* was concerned.

"Auntie, I can't." Armanoush exhaled. "You already filled my plate with *khadayıf*. Let me finish this, that's more than enough."

"Well you didn't want to smell of meat and garlic," Auntie Surpun chimed in with a hint of mischief in her voice. "So we served you *ekmek khadayıf*. This way your breath will smell of pistachios."

"Why would anyone want to smell like pistachios?" Grandma Shushan asked amazed, having missed the first episode of the debate, not that it would have made sense to her anyway.

"I do *not* want to smell like pistachios." Armanoush widened her eyes with desperation and turned to her dad, flashing a distress signal, waiting to be saved.

Before Barsam Tchakhmakhchian could utter a word, however, Armanoush's cell phone started to ring a classical melody by Tchaikovsky: "Dance of the Sugar Plum Fairy." She picked it up and pouted at the little screen. Private number. It could be anyone. It could even be Matt Hassinger, calling to give her a weird excuse to cancel the dinner tonight. Armanoush stood there, holding the phone uneasily. On the fourth ring, she answered it, hoping it wasn't her mother.

It was.

"Honey, are they treating you all right?" was the first thing she asked.

"Yes, Mother," Armanoush muttered tonelessly. By now she was kind of used to it. Ever since she was a little girl, whenever she stayed at the Tchakhmakhchian domicile, her mother acted as if her life was in danger.

"Amy, don't tell me you're still at home?"

Armanoush was used to this too, relatively speaking. Since the day her parents had separated, a separation of a different sort had happened between her mother and her own name. She had stopped calling her "Armanoush," as if she needed to rename her daughter to be able to continue loving her. To this day Armanoush had not told anyone in the Tchakhmakhchian family about this shift of nomenclature. Sometimes things had to be kept as secrets, of which she happened to have way too many.

"Why don't you respond?" her mother insisted. "Weren't you going out tonight?"

Armanoush paused, fully aware that everyone in the room was eavesdropping. "Yes, Mother," was all she uttered after an awkward lull.

"You haven't changed your mind, have you?"

"No, Mother. But why do you have a private number?"

"Well, I have my own reasons, just like any mother would. You don't always answer the phone if you know it's me." Rose's voice dwindled desolately only to escalate again. "Is Matt going to meet the family?"

"Yes, Mother."

"Don't! That will be the worst mistake ever. They'll scare the life out of him. Oh your aunts, you don't know them, you are such a good girl you can't see the bad, they'll strike terror into the poor boy with their questions and interrogations."

Armanoush didn't say anything. There were bizarre swishes on the line and she suspected her mother was brushing her hair at the same time as she delivered her tongue-lashing.

"Honey, why don't you say something? Are they all there?" Rose asked. There came another muffled rustle, except it didn't sound like brushing to Armanoush anymore. Rather it sounded like a mushy object dropping into a liquid without a splash, or more precisely, a scoop of pancake mix being poured into a sizzling pan.

"Oh, why do I ask the obvious? Of course they are. All of them, I bet. They still hate me, don't they?"

Armanoush had no answers. She could see Rose in her mind's eye, there in the dim kitchen with light salmon laminate cabinets, which she planned to have refaced but never had the money or the time to do, her hair pulled into a loose bun, the cordless phone glued to her ear, a spatula in her other hand, making a heap of pancakes as if there were an army of children at home, only to eat them all by herself at the end of the day. She could also envision her stepfather, Mustafa Kazancı, sitting at the kitchen table, stirring half-and-half into his coffee as he skimmed through the *Arizona Daily Star*.

Upon graduating from the University of Arizona and getting married to Rose, Mustafa had started working at a mineral company in the region, and as far as Armanoush could tell, he enjoyed the world of rocks and stones more than anything. He wasn't a bad man; if anything he was just a bit dull. He seemed to have no passion whatsoever for anything in life. He hadn't gone back to Istanbul for God knows how long, although he had family there. At times Armanoush had the impression that he wanted to break away from his past, but she could not possibly tell why. A few times she had tried to converse with him about 1915 and what the Turks had done to the Armenians. "I don't know much about those things," Mustafa had replied, shutting her out with a genteel but equally stiff manner. "It's all history. You should talk with historians."

"Amy, are you gonna talk to me?" Rose's voice now sounded irritated.

"Mama, I have to hang up. I'll call you later," Armanoush said. There was an abrupt click accompanied by a swish on the phone, which sounded like her mother had either scooped another dollop of pancake mix into the pan or had broken into a sob. Armanoush preferred to think it was the former.

Utterly pissed off, she returned to the table, resettled in her chair, grabbed her spoon, and avoiding eye contact, started to cram down what was in front of her, except it wasn't what she wanted. It took her a few more spoonfuls to realize the mistake.

"Why am I eating *mantı*!?" Armanoush exclaimed.

"I don't know, honey," Auntie Varsenig exclaimed back, staring at her with fright as if she were a kind of creature new to her. "I put it there in case you wanted to try it. And it looks like you did."

Now Armanoush felt like crying. She asked permission to leave the table and whisked off to the bathroom to brush her teeth, deeply regretting in the meantime this whole silly date. She stood in front of the mirror with a half-squeezed tube of toothpaste in her hand and the look of someone who was about to forswear society forever to become a lonely hermit on some godforsaken mountain. What could a Colgate Total Whitening Paste do to fight the infamous *mantı*? Perhaps she could call Matt Hassinger and cancel the whole thing? All she wanted was to lie in bed saturated in despair and read the novels she had purchased. Read and read until her nose bled and her eyes drooped. That was all she wanted.

"You should have stayed in bed and read your novels," she scolded the familiar face in the mirror.

"Nonsense!" It was Auntie Zarouhi, having just materialized next to her in the mirror. "You are a beautiful young woman who deserves the best man in the world. Now let's see a little feminine glamor. Put on some lipstick, miss!"

She did. It didn't say *feminine glamor* on the bottom of the lipstick tube but close enough: It said CHERRY GLAMOR. Armanoush generously applied the lipstick, only to pat her mouth with a napkin and wipe most of it off. And that was precisely when the doorbell rang. Seven thirty-two! Punctuality seemed to be among Matt Hassinger's merits, after all.

A minute later Armanoush was smiling at a neatly dressed, noticeably excited, and somewhat baffled Matt Hassinger standing at the door. He was three years younger than her—a trivial fact which she hadn't felt the need to tell anyone but was very much evident from his face now. Either because he had done something with his cropped hair or slipped into clothes he wouldn't normally wear, dark brown lambskin blazer and Ralph Lauren honeydew pants,

Matt Hassinger looked like a teenager dressed as an adult. He stepped inside with a huge bouquet of crimson tulips in his left hand, smiled at Armanoush, then noticed the audience in the background and froze. The whole Tchakhmakhchian family had lined up behind Armanoush.

"Come on in, young man," said Auntie Varsenig in her most encouraging voice, which also happened to be her most intimidating one.

Matt Hassinger shook hands with each family member, feeling their inquiring gazes rake his face. He lost his confidence and broke into a sweat. Somebody took the flowers and someone else took his blazer. Looking like a plucked peacock now that his blazer was off, he shuffled toward the living room and threw himself on the first chair he spotted. Everyone else sat close, forming a half-moon around him. They exchanged a few words about the weather, about Matt's education (he was in law school, which could be good and bad), about Matt's family (he was an only child, which could be good and bad), about Matt's parents (they too were lawyers, which could be good and bad), about Matt's level of knowledge on the Armenians (not much, which was bad, but he was eager to learn more, which was good), and then went back to the weather again before an irritating silence fell. For almost five minutes no one had a word to utter but everyone beamed as if they all had something lodged in their throats and found humor in this. From this awkward state they were about to pass into an almost dismal impasse when "Dance of the Sugar Plum Fairy" was heard again. Armanoush checked the screen: private number. She shut off the phone, letting it vibrate. She arched her eyebrows and twisted her lips as a "never mind" gesture to Matt, which neither he nor anyone else understood.

At seven forty-five Armanoush Tchakhmakhchian and Matt Hassinger were finally outside, steadily speeding up along Hyde Street in a Venetian red Suzuki Verona, heading toward a restaurant that Matt had heard much about and assumed would be cute and romantic: Skewed Window.

"I hope you like Asian fusion with a touch of Caribbean influence," Matt chuckled, amused at his own words. "This place was highly recommended."

Now "highly recommended" was not a criterion for Armanoush, mainly because she was always wary of "highly recommended" best sellers. Still, she didn't object, hoping that her cynicism would stand corrected at the end of the night.

That, however, turned out to be far from the case. A popular meeting place for urban intellectuals and artists, Skewed Window was anything but a cute, romantic restaurant. It was a funky warehouse with lofty ceilings, art deco pendant lights, and walls on which glimmered examples of contemporary abstract art. Dressed head-to-toe in black, the waiters scurried around like a colony of ants who had just discovered a pile of granulated sugar. The colony of waiters served artfully crafted dishes with the knowledge that soon you'd be replaced by a new customer, probably someone who would tip better. As for the menu, it was simply incomprehensible. As if the contents weren't perplexing enough, each dish was shaped, trimmed, and garnished so as to allude to a particular abstract expressionist painting.

The Dutch chef of the restaurant had three aspirations in life: to become a philosopher, to become a painter, and to become a restaurant chef. Having badly failed in both philosophy and art during his youth, he saw no reason not to bring his unappreciated talents into his cuisine. Thus, he prided himself on rematerializing the abstract, and reinserting into the human body the work of art that had come out through an artist's desire to externalize his inner emotional state. Here at the Skewed Window, dining was less culinary than philosophical, and the act of eating was deemed to be guided not by the primordial urge to fill your stomach or suppress your hunger but by a sublime dance with catharsis.

After numerous aborted attempts to choose what they were going to eat, Armanoush decided to go for the sesame-crusted ahi tuna tartare with foie gras yakiniku, and Matt decided to try a prime rib-eye with hot mustard cream sauce on a bed of passion fruit vin-aigrette and jicama. Not knowing which wine would match with these dishes but in need of making a good impression, Matt inspected the wine list and after five minutes of bewilderment, he did what he always did when he had absolutely no idea about what to pick: Decide on a wine by looking at its price. A 1997 Cabernet Sauvignon looked perfect, expensive enough but also within his means. Thus having given their order, they tried to read how good their choices were on the face of the waiter who served them, but all they could find there was a blank page of professional politeness.

They talked a little, he about the career he wanted to build, she about the childhood she would like to destroy; he about his future plans, she about the traces of the past; he about his expectations in life, she about family recollections. The Sugar Plum Fairy started to dance just when they were about to embark on another conversational topic. Armanoush fretfully checked the number. It wasn't a familiar number, but it wasn't private either. She answered.

"Amy, where are you?"

Dumbfounded, Armanoush stuttered, "Ma-ma! How did you . . . how come your number is different now?"

"Oh, it's because I'm calling you on Mrs. Grinnell's cell phone," Rose conceded. "I wouldn't have to go to this much trouble if you cared to answer my calls, of course."

Armanoush blinked blankly as she watched the waiter place a peculiar-looking plate of food in front of her, composed of hues of red, beige, and white. Amid a sauce that resembled smudged brush strokes rested three spherical chunks of red, raw tuna and a bright yellow egg yolk, altogether forming a sorry face with hollow eyes. Still holding the cell phone to her ear but not listening to her mother anymore, Armanoush puckered her lips, as she tried to figure out how to eat a face.

"Amy, why aren't you responding to me? Am I not your

mother? Don't you allow me at least half the rights you grant the Tchakhmakhchians?"

"Mom, please," Armanoush said, because this seemed like a question that could only be answered by begging her not to ask it. She hunched her shoulders as if the weight of her body had doubled. Why was it so hard to communicate with her mother?

With a quick excuse and a promise to call her back as soon as she got home, Armanoush hung up and turned off the cell phone. She sneaked a look at Matt to see if he minded the phone call, but upon noticing he was still inspecting his plate, she decided not to worry. Matt's plate was rectangular, not round, and the food on it was divided into two zones separated by a perfectly straight line of mustard cream sauce. It was less the design or the colors that had struck him than the flawlessness of the arrangement. He swallowed hard as if afraid of spoiling the seamless rectangularity.

Their dishes were replicas of two expressionist paintings. Armanoush's plate was based on a painting by Francesco Boretti titled *The Blind Whore*. As for Matt's plate, it was inspired by one of Mark Rothko's paintings and was aptly titled *Untitled*. So absorbed were the two in their plates that neither of them heard the waiter when he asked them if everything was all right.

The rest of the evening was nice but only as far as the word *nice* can go. The food turned out to be delicious and they quickly got used to wolfing down works of art, so much so that when their desserts arrived, Matt had no trouble in messing up the impeccably lined blueberries in *April Blues Bring May Yellows* by Peter Kitchell, and Armanoush did not even hesitate to jab her spoon into the shaky velvety custard representing Jackson Pollock's *Shimmering Substance*. But when it came to conversing they couldn't make half the progress they achieved in eating. Not that Armanoush did not enjoy being with Matt or did not find him attractive. But something was terribly missing, not in the sense of a detail missing from the whole, but in the sense of the whole dissolving into pieces without that missing part. Perhaps it was too much philosophical food. At any rate, Armanoush had understood her limits; she could not possibly fall in love with Matt Hassinger. After making this discovery, she stopped questioning herself, and her interest in him was replaced by sheer sympathy.

On the way back home they stopped the car and walked a little bit along Columbus Avenue, both pensive and silent. The breeze shifted then, and for a fleeting moment Armanoush caught the sharp, salty whiff of the sea, longing to be by the seaside now, aching to run away from this very moment. Once in front of the City Lights bookstore, however, she couldn't help perking up with interest as she spotted one of her favorite books behind the window: *A Tomb for Boris Davidovich.*

"Oh, have you read that book? It's awesome!" she blurted out, and upon hearing a definite "no," she started describing the first story of the book, and then all seven of them. Since she sincerely believed the book could not be fully grasped without mapping the bumpy terrain of Eastern European literature first, during the ensuing ten minutes that was more or less what Armanoush Tchakhmakhchian did, thus breaking the promise she had made to her mother that very morning about not uttering a word about books, at least for just the first date.

Once back in Russian Hill, in front of Grandma Shushan's condo, they stood face to face, aware that the night was over and eager to make the ending better than the preceding evening in the only way they could think of. It was meant to be a *real* kiss, long-awaited and fantasized. Instead it turned out to be a gentle kiss, sealed with compassion on the part of Armanoush and admiration on the part of Matt, as both were miles away from feeling any passion.

"You know I meant to tell you this all night long," Matt stammered, as if saddled with the uncomfortable truth he was about to confess. "You have this incredible smell. . . . It's unusual and exotic. . . . Just like—"

"Like what?" Armanoush's face went pale, as the sight of a plate of steaming *mantı* popped into her mind.

Matt Hassinger put his arm around her and whispered: "Pistachios . . . yes, you smell just like pistachios."

At a quarter past eleven Armanoush fished out a bunch of keys to open the many locks of Grandma Shushan's door, fearing in the meantime encountering the whole family in the living room, talking politics, drinking tea, and eating fruit, awaiting her return.

But inside it was dark and empty. Her dad and grandma had gone to sleep and everyone else had left. On the table there was a plate of two apples and two oranges, all carefully peeled and apparently left for her to eat. Armanoush grabbed one of the apples, now darkened on the outside. Her heart sank. In the eerie serenity of the night she nibbled the apple, feeling sad and tired. Soon she would have to go back to Arizona, but she wasn't sure she could put up with her mother's encapsulating universe. Though she liked it here in San Francisco and perhaps could take a semester off to stay with her father and Grandma Shushan, she also couldn't help feeling that something was absent here, that a part of her identity was missing and without it she couldn't start living her own life. The lackluster date with Matt Hassinger had only served to reinforce this feeling. Now she felt wiser, more cognizant of her situation, but saddened at the cost of this knowledge.

She kicked off her shoes and hurried to her room, taking the fruit with her. There she bundled her hair into a ponytail, stripped off the turquoise dress, and slipped into the silk pajamas she had bought in Chinatown. When she was ready, she closed the door of her room and immediately turned on the computer. It took just a few minutes to reach the only safe haven she could escape into at times like this: Café Constantinopolis.

Café Constantinopolis was a chat room, or as the regulars called it, a cybercafé, initially designed by a bunch of Greek Americans, Sephardim Americans, and Armenian Americans who, other than being New Yorkers, had one fundamental thing in common: They all were the grandchildren of families once based in Istanbul. The Web site opened with a familiar tune: *Istanbul was Constantinople / Now it's Istanbul, not Constantinople . . .*

With that melody appeared the silhouette of the city canopied under the flickering shades of sunset, veils upon veils of amethyst and black and yellow. In the middle of the screen there was a flashing arrow to indicate where to click to enter the chat room. You had to sign in with a password to be able to proceed further. Just like many real cafés this one was in theory open to everyone but in practice reserved for regular customers. Accordingly, although numerous off-the-cuff chatters showed up day in and day out, the core group remained more or less the same. Once you successfully signed in, the silhouette faded at the bottom and pulled apart, the way a velvet theater curtain opens before the act begins. As you entered the cybercafé, you heard bells chiming and then the same melody, only this time distant in the background.

Once inside, Armanoush disregarded the *Armeniansingles, Greeksingles, Weareallsingles* forums and clicked on *Anoush Tree*—a forum where only the regulars and those with intellectual interests met. Armanoush had discovered the group ten months ago and ever since she had been a regular member, joining the discussion on an almost daily basis. Although some members occasionally posted during the daytime, the real discussions always took place at night when the fuss of the daily routine was over. Armanoush liked to imagine this forum as a dingy, smoky bar she habitually stopped by on her way home. Just like that, Café Constantinopolis was a sanctuary where you could forgo your true, humdrum Self at the entrance, like leaving a sopping raincoat in need of drying in the vestibule.

The Anoush Tree section of Café Constantinopolis consisted of seven permanent members, five Armenians and two Greeks. They had not met in person and had never felt the need to. All of them came from different cities and had dissimilar professions and lives. All of them had nicknames. Armanoush's nickname was Madame My-Exiled-Soul. She had chosen this name as a tribute to Zabel

THE BASTARD OF ISTANBUL

Yessaian, the only woman novelist the Young Turks put on their death list in 1915. Zabel was a fascinating personality. Born in Constantinople, she lived much of her life in exile. She had enjoyed a tumultuous life as a novelist and columnist. Armanoush kept a picture of her on her desk, in which Zabel broodingly peered out from under the brim of her hat at some unknown spot beyond the frame.

The others in the Anoush Tree had different nicknames for reasons unasked. Every week they would choose a specific discussion topic. Though the themes varied greatly, they all tended to revolve around their common history and culture—"common" oftentimes meaning "common enemy": the Turks. Nothing brought people together more swiftly and strongly—though transiently and shakily—than a shared enemy.

This week the subject was "The Janissaries." As she scanned through some of the most recent postings Armanoush was happy to see Baron Baghdassarian was online. She didn't know much about him, other than that he was the grandchild of survivors, just like her, and resplendent with rage, unlike her. Sometimes he could be extremely harsh and skeptical. Throughout the last few months, despite the elusiveness of cyberspace or perhaps thanks to it, Armanoush had unknowingly developed a liking for him. A day would be incomplete if she couldn't read his messages. Whatever this thing she felt for him—friendship, fondness, or sheer curiosity—Armanoush knew it was mutual.

People who believe the Ottoman rule was righteous don't know anything about the Janissary's Paradox. The Janissaries were Christian children captured and converted by the Ottoman state with a *chance* to climb the social ladder at the expense of despising their own people and forgetting their own past. The Janissary's Paradox is as relevant today for every minority as it was yesterday. You the child of expatriates! You need to ask yourself this age-old question time and again: What will your position be with regards to this paradox; are you going to accept the role of the Janissary? Will you abandon

your community to make peace with the Turks and let them
whitewash the past so that, as they say, we can all move *forward*?

Glued to the screen, Armanoush took a bite of the remaining apple and chewed nervously. Never before had she felt such admiration for a man—other than her dad, of course, but that was different. There was something in Baron Baghdassarian that both enthralled and scared her; she wasn't afraid of him exactly or the things he so boldly claimed—if anything, she was scared of herself. His words had a far-reaching effect, capable of digging out this other Armanoush that resided inside her but as of yet had not come out, a cryptic being in deep slumber. Somehow Baron Baghdassarian poked that creature with the spear of his words, prodding it until it woke up with a roar and came to light.

Armanoush was still running her brain over this frightening outcome when she glimpsed a long message posted by Lady Peacock/Siramark—an Armenian American wine expert who worked for a California-based winery, frequently traveled to Yerevan, and was known for her amusingly smart comparisons between the United States and Armenia. Today, she had posted a self-scoring test that measured the degree of one's "Armenianness."

1. If you grew up sleeping under handwoven blankets or wearing handwoven cardigans to school
2. If you have been given an Armenian alphabet book on each birthday until the age of six or seven
3. If you have a picture of Mount Ararat hanging in your house, garage, or office
4. If you are used to being loved and cooed at in Armenian, scolded and disciplined in English, and avoided in Turkish
5. If you serve your guests hummus with nacho chips and eggplant dip with rice cakes
6. If you are familiar with the taste of *mantı*, the smell of *sudžuk*, and the curse of *bastırma*

7. If you easily get pestered and aggravated over remarkably trivial
   things but manage to stay composed when there is something
   really grave to worry or panic about
8. If you have had (or are planning to have) a nose job
9. If you have a jar of Nutella in your refrigerator and a *tavla* board
   somewhere in your storeroom
10. If you have a cherished rug on the floor of your living room
11. If you can't help feeling sad when you dance to "Lorke Lorke,"
    even if the melody is bouncy and you don't understand the lyrics
12. If gathering to eat fruit after each dinner is a deeply rooted habit
    at your house and if your dad still peels oranges for you, no
    matter what age you might have reached
13. If your relatives keep shoveling food into your mouth and do not
    accept "I am full" as an answer
14. If the sound of *duduk* sends shivers down your spine and you
    cannot help wondering how a flute made from an apricot tree
    can cry so sadly
15. If deep inside you feel like there is always more about your past
    than you will ever be allowed to learn

Having given a "yes" to every single one of the questions, Armanoush scrolled down to learn her score:

0–3 points: Sorry dude, you must be an outsider.
4–8 points: You sound like an inside-outsider. Chances are you are
    married to an Armenian.
9–12 points: Almost certainly you are an Armenian.
13–15 points: There's no doubt, you are a proud Armenian.

Armanoush smiled at the screen. And in that moment she
grasped what she already knew. It was as if a secret gate had been
unlatched in the depths of her brain, and before her mind could ac-
commodate the thoughts gushing in, a wave of introspection rolled
over her. She had to go there. That was what she sorely needed: a
journey.

Because of her fragmented childhood, she had still not been able to find a sense of continuity and identity. She had to make a journey to her past to be able to start living her own life. As the weight of this new revelation dawned on her, it also motivated her to type a message, seemingly to everyone but in particular to Baron Baghdassarian:

> The Janissary's Paradox is being torn between two clashing states of existence. On the one hand, the remnants of the past pile up—a womb of tenderness and sorrow, a sense of injustice and discrimination. On the other hand glimmers the promised future—a shelter decorated with the trimmings and trappings of success, a sense of safety like you have never had before, the comfort of joining the majority and finally being deemed normal.

> Hello there Madame My-Exiled-Soul! Glad you are back. So nice to hear the poetess in you.

That was Baron Baghdassarian. Armanoush couldn't help re-reading the last part aloud: *so nice to hear the poetess in you*. She lost her train of thought but only momentarily.

> I think I can relate to the Janissary's Paradox. As the only child of resentfully divorced parents coming from different cultural backgrounds,

She paused with the discomfort of revealing her personal story, but the urge to carry on was too strong.

> Being the only daughter of an Armenian father, he himself a child of survivors, and of a mother from Elizabethtown, Kentucky, I do know how it feels to be torn between opposite sides, unable to fully belong anywhere, constantly fluctuating between two states of existence.

To this day she had never written anything so personal and so direct to anyone in the group. Her heart pumping hard, she took a breather. What was Baron Baghdassarian going to think about her now and would he write his true thoughts?

That must be hard. For most Armenians in the diaspora, Hai Dat is the sole psychological anchor that we have in order to sustain an identity. Your situation is different but ultimately we are all Americans and Armenians, that plurality is good as long as we do not lose our anchor.

That was Miserable-Coexistence, a housewife unhappily married to the editor-in-chief of a prominent literary journal in the Bay Area.

Plurality means the state of being more than one. But that was not the case with me. I've never been able to become an Armenian in the first place, Armanoush wrote, realizing she was on the brink of making a confession. I need to find my identity. You know what I've been secretly contemplating? Going to visit my family's house in Turkey. Grandma always talks about this gorgeous house in Istanbul. I'll go and see it with my own eyes. This is a journey into my family's past, as well as into my future. The Janissary's Paradox will haunt me unless I do something to discover my past.

Wait, wait, wait, Lady Peacock/Siramark typed in panic. What the hell do you think you are doing? Are you planning to go to Turkey on your own, did you take leave of your senses?

I can find connections. It's not that difficult.

How so Madame My-Exiled-Soul? Lady Peacock/Siramark insisted. How far do you think you can go with that name on your passport?

Why don't you instead directly walk into a police headquarters in Istanbul and get yourself nicely arrested! broke in Anti-Khavurma, a grad student in Near Eastern Studies at Columbia University.

Armanoush felt this could be the right moment to confess another fundamental truth of her life. Finding the right connections might not be that difficult for me since my mother is now married to a Turk.

There was an unsettling lull. For a full minute no one wrote anything back, so Armanoush continued.

His name is Mustafa, he is a geologist who works for a company in Arizona. He's a nice man, but he is completely disinterested in history and ever since he arrived in the USA, which is like twenty years ago, he has never been back home. He didn't even invite his family to the wedding. Something's fishy there but I don't know what. He just doesn't talk about that. But I know he has a large family in Istanbul. I asked him once what kind of people they were and he said: Oh, they are just ordinary people, like you and me.

He doesn't sound like the most sensitive man on earth—that is, of course, if men can ever have feelings, barged in the Daughter of Sappho, a lesbian bartender who had recently found a job in a shabby reggae bar in Brooklyn.

He sure doesn't, Miserable-Coexistence added. Does he have a heart?

Oh, he does. He loves my mom, and my mom loves him, Armanoush replied. She realized she had for the first time recognized the love between her mother and stepfather, as if seeing them through a stranger's eyes. Anyway, I can stay with his family; after all I am his step-daughter, I guess they will have to accept me as a guest. It's a puzzle to me how I will be received by *ordinary* Turks. A real Turkish family, not one of those Americanized academics.

What are you going to talk about with ordinary Turks? asked Lady Peacock/Siramark. Look, even the well-educated are either nationalist or ignorant. Do you think ordinary people will be interested in accepting historical truths? Do you think they are going to say: *Oh yeah, we are sorry we massacred and deported you guys and then contentedly denied it all.* Why do you want to get yourself in trouble?

I understand that. But you should try to understand me as well.

Armanoush felt a sudden surge of despondency. Disclosing one secret after another had triggered the feeling of being lonely in this huge world—something she always knew about but waited for the right moment to face. You guys were all born into the Armenian community and never had to prove you were one of them. Whereas I have been stuck on this threshold since the day I was born, constantly fluctuating between a proud but traumatized Armenian family and a hysterically anti-Armenian mom. For me to be able to become an Armenian American the way you guys are, I need to find my Armenianness first. If this requires a voyage into the past, so be it, I am going to do that, no matter what the Turks will say or do.

But how will your father and his family let you go to Turkey? That was Alex the Stoic, a Bostonian Greek American who was content with life as long as he was surrounded by sunny weather, tasty food, and pretty women. As a loyal follower of Zeno, he believed that people should do their best not to push their limits and be happy with what they had. Don't you think your family in San Francisco will be worried?

Worried? Armanoush grimaced as the faces of her aunts and grandmother crossed her mind. She knew they would be worried sick.

They should not know anything about this, for their own good. Spring break is coming and I can spend the whole ten days in Istanbul. Dad will think I am in Arizona with my mom. And mom will think I am still here in San Francisco. They never talk to each other. And my stepfather never talks with his family in Istanbul. There's no way this can be revealed. It'll be a secret. Armanoush squinted at the screen as if she were perplexed by the statement she had typed there. If I keep calling my mom on a daily basis and my dad every two or three days, I can keep everything under control.

Nice plan! Once in Istanbul, Lady Peacock/Siramark suggested, you can send reports to the café every day.

Wow, you will be our war reporter, enthused Anti-Khavurma, but there followed an even longer pause as no one joined in the joke.

Armanoush leaned back in her chair. Deep in the stillness of the night she could hear her father's unruffled breathing and her grandmother tossing in her bed. She felt her body slipping sideways, as if part of her craved sitting in this chair all night long to savor what insomnia was like, while part of her wanted to go to bed and fall into a deep slumber. She munched the last bit of her apple, feeling a rush of adrenaline about her dangerous decision.

Armanoush turned off the table lamp, leaving a grainy light radiating from the computer. Just when she was about to exit Café Constantinopolis, however, a line appeared on the screen.

Wherever your inner journey might take you, please take care of yourself dear Madame My-Exiled-Soul, and don't let the Turks treat you badly.

It was Baron Baghdassarian.

SEVEN

Wheat

It had been more than two hours since she had woken up, but Asya Kazancı was still lying in bed under a goose-feather quilt, listening to the myriad sounds only Istanbul is capable of producing while her mind meticulously composed a Personal Manifesto of Nihilism.

> **Article One: If you cannot find a reason to love the life you are living, do not pretend to love the life you are living.**

She gave this statement some thought and decided she liked it well enough to make it the opening line of her manifesto. As she proceeded into the second article, outside on the street somebody slammed on his brakes. In next to no time the driver was heard swearing and shouting at the top of his voice at some pedestrian who had materialized on the road, crossing an intersection diagonally and also on a red light. The driver yelled and yelled until his voice dwindled amid the humming of the city.

Article Two: The overwhelming majority of people never think and those who think never become the overwhelming majority. Choose your side.

Article Three: If you cannot choose, then just exist; be a mushroom or a plant.

"I cannot believe you are still in the same position that I found you in half an hour ago! What the hell are you doing in bed, lazy girl?"

That was Auntie Banu, having ducked her head into the room without feeling the need to knock on the door first. She was wearing an eye-catching head scarf this morning of a hue so dazzlingly red that from a distance it made her head look like a huge, ripe tomato. "We have finished a whole samovar of tea while waiting for you, our Lady Queen. Come on, rise and shine! Can't you smell the grilled *sucuk*? Aren't you hungry?" She slammed the door shut before waiting for an answer.

Asya muttered under her breath as she pulled the quilt up to her nose and turned to the other side.

Article Four: If you have no interest in their answers, then do not ask questions.

There amid the typical bustle of a weekend breakfast, she could hear the water dropping from the tiny faucet of the samovar, the seven eggs feverishly boiling in a stockpot, the slices of *sucuk* sizzling inside the grill pan, and somebody continually flipping through the TV channels, skipping from cartoons to pop music videos and from there, to local and international news. Without needing to sneak a peek, Asya knew that it was Grandma Gülsüm who was in charge of the samovar; just like she could tell it was Auntie Banu who grilled the *sucuk,* her unparalleled appetite having returned now that the forty days of Sufi penitence was over and she had successfully declared herself a clairvoyant. Asya also knew that it was Auntie Feride who flipped through the channels, unable to decide on one, having enough room in the vast land of schizophrenic paranoia to absorb them all, cartoons and pop music and news at the same time, just like she yearned for success in multiple tasks in life and ended up accomplishing none.

Article Five: If you have no reason or ability to accomplish anything, then just practice the art of becoming.

Article Six: If you have no reason or ability to practice the art of becoming, then just be.

"Asya!!!" The door banged open and Auntie Zeliha rammed in, her green eyes glittering like two round pieces of jade. "Do we have to keep sending envoys to your bed to make you join us?"

Article Seven: If you have no reason or ability to be, then just endure.

"Asya!!!"
"What?!!!" Asya's head popped up from under the bedcovers in a curly, raven ball of fury. Jumping to her feet she kicked the pair of lavender slippers beside the bed, missing one of them but managing to catapult the other directly on top of the dresser where it hit the mirror and from there parachuted to the floor. She then pulled up her loose-around-the-waist pajamas in a funny sort of way, which, if truth be told, did not quite support the dramatic effect she wanted to generate.

"For heaven's sake, can't I possibly have a moment's peace on a Sunday morning?"

"Regrettably there exists no *moment* on earth that lasts two hours," Auntie Zeliha pointed out, after watching the distressing trajectory of the slipper. "Why are you getting on my nerves? If this is a teenage rebellion that you are going through, you're too late, miss, you should have been there at least five years ago. Remember, you are already nineteen."

"Yeah, the age you had me out of wedlock," Asya croaked, knowing she shouldn't be so brutal but doing it anyway.

Standing in the doorway, Auntie Zeliha stared at Asya with the disappointment of a visual artist who after drinking and working on a piece of art all night long sleeps with satisfaction, only to wake up later the next morning confronted with the bedlam he has created while intoxicated. Despite the dourness of the discovery, she didn't say anything for a full minute. Then her lips twisted into a morose smile as if she had just realized that the face she had been looking at was in fact her own image in the mirror, so alike and yet completely detached. Her daughter had turned out to be just like her in character, though vastly different in appearance.

As far as the personality went, it was the same skepticism, the same unruliness, the same bitterness she had displayed when she was Asya's age. Before she knew it, she had neatly passed on the role of the maverick of the Kazancı family to her daughter. Fortunately, Asya didn't look world-weary or angst-ridden yet, being too young for all of that. But the temptation to raze the edifice of her own existence was there, softly glittering in her eyes, the sweet lure of self-destruction that only the sophisticated or the saturnine will ever suffer from.

As far as the appearance went, however, Auntie Zeliha could plainly see that Asya barely resembled her. She was not and probably would never become a beautiful woman. Not that there was anything wrong with her body or face or anything. In point of fact, when regarded independently every part of her was in good shape: the right height and weight, the right curly raven hair, the right chin . . . but when added together, there was something flawed in the combination. She wasn't ugly either, not at all. If anything, a mediocre prettiness, one that is good to look at but won't stick in anybody's mind. Her face was so average many who met her for the first time had the impression of having seen her before. She was uniquely ordinary. Rather than "beautiful," "cute" would be the best compliment she could get at this stage, which was perfectly okay, except that here she was painfully going through a phase of her life in which "cuteness" was the last thing she wanted to be associated with. Twenty years down the road she would come to see her body differently. Asya was one of those women who though not pretty in their teens or attractive in their youth, could nevertheless become quite good-looking in their middle age, provided they could endure until then.

Regrettably Asya was not blessed with even a wee bit of faith. She was too mordant to have confidence in the flow of time. She was a burning fire inside without the slightest faith in the righteousness of the divine order. In that respect too, she greatly resembled no one but her mother. With this kind of moral fiber and in this mood, there was no way she could be patient and faithful, waiting for the day life would turn her body to her advantage. At this point in time, Auntie Zeliha could clearly see that the knowledge of her physical dullness, among other things, was pricking at her daughter's young heart. If only she could tell her that the beauties would only attract the worst guys. If only she could make her understand how lucky she was not to be born too beautiful; that in fact both men and women would be more benevolent to her, and that her life would be better off, yes, much better off without the exquisiteness she now so craved.

Still without a word Auntie Zeliha walked toward the dresser, fetched the slipper, and placed the now united pair in front of Asya's naked feet. She stood up before her mutinous daughter, who instantly lifted her chin and straightened her back in the posture of a proud prisoner of war who had surrendered arms but certainly not his dignity.

"Let's go!" Auntie Zeliha commanded. Mutely, mother and daughter convoyed toward the living room.

The folding table was long set for breakfast. Despite her grumpiness Asya couldn't help noticing that when the table was festooned like this, it fit perfectly, almost picturesquely, with the huge, fire-brick rug underneath, glowing in its intricate floral patterns within a handsome coral border. Just like the rug, the table above looked ornamented. There were black olives, red pepper–stuffed green olives, white cheese, braided cheese, goat cheese, boiled eggs, honey-combs, buffalo cream, homemade apricot marmalade, homemade raspberry jam, and olive-oil-soaked minted tomatoes in china bowls. The delectable smell of newly baked *börek* wafted from the kitchen: white cheese, spinach, butter, and parsley melting into one another amid thin layers of phyllo pastry.

Now ninety-six years old, Petite-Ma was sitting at the far end of the table, holding a teacup even thinner than herself. With an engrossed and somewhat befuddled look on her face, she was watching the canary twittering in the cage by the balcony door, as if she had only now noticed the bird. Perhaps she had. Having en-tered the fifth stage of Alzheimer's, she had started to muddle up the most familiar faces and facts of her life.

Last week, for instance, toward the end of the afternoon prayer, as soon as she had bent down and put her forehead on her little rug for the stage of *sajda,* she had forgotten what to do next. The words of the prayer she had to utter had all of a sudden fastened together into an elongated chain of letters and walked away in tandem, like a black, hairy caterpillar with too many feet to count. After a while, the caterpillar had stopped, turned around, and waved at Petite-Ma from a distance, as if surrounded by glass walls, so clearly visible yet unreachable. Lost and confused, Petite-Ma had just sat there facing the *Qibla,* glued on her rug with a prayer scarf on her head and the string of amber prayer beads in her hand, motionless and soundless, until someone noticed the situation and lifted her up.

"What was the rest of it?" Petite-Ma had asked in panic when they made her lie on the sofa and put soft cushions under her head. "In the *sajda* you must say Subhana rabbiyal-ala. You must say it at least thrice. I did. I said it three times. *Subhana rabbiyal-ala, Subhana rabbiyal-ala, Subhana rabbiyal-ala,*" she twirped the words repeatedly, as if in a frenzy. "And then what? What is next?"

As luck would have it, it was Auntie Zeliha who happened to be by her side when Petite-Ma raised this question. Having no practice in *namaz,* or in any religious duty for that matter, she had absolutely no idea what her grandmother might be talking about. But she wanted to help, to soothe the old woman's anguish in any way she could. Thus she fetched the Holy Qur'an, and skimmed through the pages until she came across a resemblance of solace in some verse: "Look what it says. When the call is sounded for prayer on Fridays, hasten to the remembrance of God . . . but when the prayer is ended, disperse abroad in the land and seek of God's grace and remember God, that you may be successful" (62:9–10).

"What do you mean?" Petite-Ma blinked her eyes, now more lost than ever.

"I mean, now that the prayer has ended in one way or another, you can stop thinking about it. That's what it says here, right? Come on Petite-Ma, disperse abroad in the land . . . and have supper with us."

It had worked. Petite-Ma had stopped worrying about the forgotten line and had dined with them peacefully. Nonetheless, incidences like this had lately started to occur with an alarming frequency. Often subdued and withdrawn, there were times in which she forgot the simplest things, including where she was, which day of the week it was, or who these strangers were with whom she sat at the same table. And yet there were also times it was hard to believe she was ill, as her mind seemed as clear as newly polished Venetian glass. This morning it was hard to tell. Too early to tell.

"Good morning, Petite-Ma!" Asya exclaimed as she shuffled her lavender feet toward the table, having finally washed her face and brushed her teeth. She leaned over the old woman and gave her a sloppy kiss on both cheeks.

Ever since she was a little girl, of all the women in her family,

Petite-Ma retained a most special place in Asya's heart. She loved her dearly. Unlike some others in the family, Petite-Ma had always been capable of loving without suffocating. She would never nag or nitpick or sting. Her protectiveness was not possessive. From time to time she secretly put grains of wheat sanctified with prayers into Asya's pockets to save her from the evil eye. Other than crusading against the evil eye, laughing was the thing she did best and most—that is, until the day her illness escalated. Back in the past, she and Asya used to laugh together a lot: Petite-Ma, a lengthy stream of mellifluous chuckles; Asya, a sudden spurt of rich, resonant tones. Nowadays, though deeply worried about her great-grandmother's well-being, Asya was also respectful of the autonomous realm of amnesia that she drifted into, being constantly denied autonomy herself. And the more the old woman digressed from them, the closer she felt to her.

"Good morning my pretty great-granddaughter," Petite-Ma replied, impressing everyone with the clarity of her memory.

Sitting there with a remote control in her hand, Auntie Feride chirped without looking at her. "At last, the grumpy princess is awake." She sounded jovial despite the tinge of harangue in her voice. Just this morning she had dyed her hair, turning it to a light blond, almost ashen. By now Asya knew too well that a radical change in hairstyle was a sign of a radical change in mood. She inspected Auntie Feride for traces of insanity. Other than that she seemed to be absorbed in the TV, watching with delight a terribly untalented pop singer spinning around in a dance too ridiculous to be real, Asya couldn't find any.

"You have to get ready, you know, our guest is arriving today," Auntie Banu said as she entered the living room with the tray of *börek* fresh out of the oven, visibly pleased to have her daily carbohydrates. "We need to get the house ready before she arrives."

Trying to push Sultan the Fifth away from the dripping little faucet with her feet, Asya poured herself tea from the steaming samovar and asked dully: "Why are you all so excited about this

American girl?" She took a sip of the tea, only to make a face and search for sugar. One, two . . . she filled up the tiny glass with four cubes of sugar.

"What do you mean 'why are you all excited'? She is a guest! She is coming all the way from the other side of the globe." Auntie Feride stretched her arm forward in the Nazi salute to indicate where and how far the other side of the globe was. The thought of the globe brought an agitated timbre to her voice, as the map of global atmospheric and oceanic circulation patterns flashed in her mind's eye. The last time Auntie Feride had seen this map on paper, she was in high school. This nobody knew, but she had learned the map by heart down to its tiniest detail, and today it remained engraved in her memory as vividly as the day she had first scruti-nized it.

"Most importantly, she is a visitor sent to us by your uncle," broke in Grandma Gülsüm, who still tenaciously retained her repu-tation of having been Ivan the Terrible in another life.

"My *uncle*? Which uncle? The one I have never seen to this day?" Asya tasted her tea. It was still bitter. She threw in another cube of sugar. "Hello, wake up everyone! The man you are talking about has not visited us even once ever since he stepped on Ameri-can soil. The only thing we have received from him to prove he is still alive are patchy postcards of Arizona landscapes," Asya said, with a venomous look. "Cactus under the sun, cactus at twilight, cactus with purple flowers, cactus with red birds. . . . The guy doesn't even care enough to change his postcard style."

"He also sends his wife's pictures," Auntie Feride added to be fair.

"I couldn't care less about those pictures. Plump blond wife smiling in front of their adobe house, where by the way we have never been invited; plump blond wife smiling in the Grand Can-yon; plump blond wife smiling, wearing a huge Mexican sombrero; plump blond wife smiling with a dead coyote on the porch; plump blond wife smiling, cooking pancakes in the kitchen. . . . Aren't you sick of him sending us every month the poses of this complete stranger? Why is she smiling at us, anyway? We have not even met the woman, for Allah's sake!" Asya gulped her tea, ignoring the fact that it was still scalding hot.

"Journeys are not safe. The roads are full of perils. Airplanes are hijacked, cars crash in accidents . . . even trains tumble. Eight people died in a car accident yesterday on the Aegean Coast," Auntie Feride noted. Unable to make eye contact with anyone, her eyeballs drew nervous circles around the table until they landed on a black olive resting on her plate.

Every time Auntie Feride conveyed ghastly news from the third page of the Turkish tabloids there followed a prickly silence. This time it was no different. In the ensuing silence Grandma Gülsüm grimaced, disturbed to hear her only son being disparaged like this; Auntie Banu tugged on the ends of her head scarf; Auntie Cevriye tried to remember what kind of an animal "coyote" was, but since twenty-four years in the profession of teaching had made her terrific with answers and equally bad with questions, she didn't dare ask anyone; Petite-Ma stopped nibbling the slice of *sucuk* on her plate; and Auntie Feride tried to think of some other accidents she'd read about, but instead of more macabre news, she recalled the bright blue sombrero that Mustafa's American wife was wearing in one of the pictures—if only she could find anything close to that in Istanbul, she sure would like to wear it day and night. In the meantime, no one noticed that Auntie Zeliha's face looked woeful all of a sudden.

"We need to face the truth!" Asya announced with certitude. "All these years you have all doted on Uncle Mustafa as the one and only precious son of this family, and the instant he flew from the nest, he forgot about you. Isn't it obvious that the man doesn't give a hoot about his family? Why should he mean anything for us, then?"

"The boy is busy," Grandma Gülsüm interjected. In truth, she favored her son, of which she had only one, over the daughters, of which she had too many. "It is not easy to be abroad. America is a long way away."

"Yeah, of course it's a long way, especially when you consider the fact that you need to swim the Atlantic Ocean and walk the entire European continent," Asya said, biting into a slice of white cheese to soothe her tea-burned tongue. To her surprise the cheese was really good, soft and salty, the way she liked it. Finding it a bit difficult to gripe and enjoy the food at the same time, she shut up for a second and chewed nervously.

Taking advantage of the momentary lull, Auntie Banu launched into a moral story, as she always did in times of distress. She told them the story of a man who decided to travel the entire globe round and round, in an endeavor to escape his mortality. North and south, east and west, he wandered every which way he could. Once, in one of his numerous trips, he unexpectedly ran into Azrail, the angel of death, in Cairo. Azrail's piercing gaze raked the man with a mysterious expression. He neither said a word nor followed him. The man right away abandoned Cairo, traveling nonstop thereafter until he arrived in a small, sleepy town in China. Thirsty and tired he rushed into the first tavern on his way. There, next to the table to which he was ushered, sat Azrail patiently waiting for him, this time with a relieved expression on his face. "I was so surprised to run into you in Cairo," he rasped to the man, "for your destiny said it was here in China that we two would meet."

Asya knew this story by heart, just like she knew the many other stories repeatedly narrated under this roof. What she didn't understand, and didn't think she ever could, was the thrill her aunts derived from narrating a story of which the punch line was already known. The air in the living room grew snug, all too sheltered, enveloped by the recurrence of the routine, as if life were one long, uninterrupted rehearsal and everyone memorized their speech. During the ensuing minutes, as the women around her jumped from tittle-tattle to tittle-tattle, each story triggering the next, Asya perked up, looking quite unlike the girl she had been earlier this morning. Sometimes she herself was baffled by her own inconsistencies. How could she so begrudge the ones she loved most? It was as if her mood were a yo-yo, bobbing up and down, now incensed, now contented. In this respect too she resembled her mother.

A *simit* vendor's monotonous voice infiltrated from the open window, piercing the ongoing chatter. Auntie Banu rushed to the window and popped her red head outside. "*Simitist! Simitist!* Come this way!" she yelled. "How much are they?"

Not that she didn't know how much a *simit* cost, she sure did. The question was less a query than a rite, performed dutifully. That is why as soon as the question came out of her mouth, she proceeded to the next line, without waiting for the man to answer. "All right, give us eight *simits*."

Every Sunday at breakfast they bought eight *simits,* one for each person in the family, and then one extra, for the missing sibling now far away.

"Oh, they smell superb." Auntie Banu beamed when she returned to the table wearing the *simits* on each arm like a circus acrobat ready to juggle with hoops. She left one in front of everyone, scattering the sesame seeds all over. Visibly relaxed now that she had a stockpile of carbohydrates, Auntie Banu started to cram them down, combining *simit* with *börek,* and *börek* with bread. But soon after, either because she was struck by heartburn or by a sullen thought, she put on a grim expression, like the one she used when telling a customer about an ominous portent flickering in the tarot cards. "It all depends on how you see things." Auntie Banu shot up her eyebrows, betraying the gravity of the statement she was going to announce.

"Once there was; once there wasn't. . . . There lived two basket weavers back in the old Ottoman days. Both were hard workers, but one had faith, the other was always grumpy. One day the sultan came to the village. He said to them: 'I will fill your baskets with wheat, and if you take good care of this wheat, the grains will turn into golden coins.' The first weaver accepted the offer with joy and filled his baskets. The second weaver, who was no less crabby than you, my dear, refused the great sultan's gift. You know what happened in the end?"

"Of course I do," Asya said. "How can I *not* know the end of a story I must have listened to at least a hundred times? But what you don't know is the damage these stories do to a child's creativity. It is because of this ridiculous story that I spent my preschool years sleeping with a wheat straw under my pillow, hoping it would turn into a golden coin the next morning. And then what? I start going to school. One day I tell the other kids how I will soon become rich with my gold-to-be wheat, and the next thing I know, I am the butt of every silly joke in the classroom. You made an idiot out of me."

Of all the shocks and traumas Asya suffered in her childhood, none remained in her memory more bitterly than the wheat incident. It was then that she reheard the word that would keep escorting her in the years to come, always at those moments when she least expected it: "Bastard!" Until that wheat incident in her first year at primary school, Asya had only once heard the word *bastard* but not minded it much, primarily because she didn't know what it meant. The other students were quick to make up for her lack of knowledge. But that part of the story she keenly kept to herself and instead poured another tea, burning hot.

"Listen Asya, you can keep grouching to us as much as you like, but when our guest arrives, you should pipe down and be nice to her. Your English is better than mine and better than anyone else's in the family."

This was not a modest statement on the part of Auntie Banu since it made her look as if she spoke some English when in fact she spoke none. Sure, she had taken English courses back in high school, but whatever she may have learned there, she had forgotten twice as much. Since the art of fortune-telling had no foreign language requirement, she never felt the need to study English. As for Auntie Feride, she had never been interested in learning English in the first place, choosing German at school. But since that coincided with the time she had lost interest in every course other than physical geography, her German had not made much progress either. With Petite-Ma and Grandma Gülsüm as disqualified members, that left only Auntie Zeliha and Auntie Cevriye with enough English to move forward from beginner level to an intermediate stage. That said, there was a stark difference between the two aunts' command of the English language. Auntie Zeliha spoke a daily-life English, woven with slang and idioms and argot, which she practiced almost every day with the foreigners visiting her tattoo parlor; while Auntie Cevriye spoke a grammar-oriented, frozen-in-time, textbook English taught at high schools and at high schools only. Concomitantly, Auntie Cevriye could distinguish simple, complex, and compound sentences, identify adverb, adjective, and noun clauses, even recognize misplaced and dangling modifiers in syntactic structure, but she could not *talk*.

"Therefore, dear, you will be her translator. You will ferry her words to us and our words to her." Auntie Banu narrowed her eyes and furrowed her brow in an attempt to hint at the magnitude of what she was about to announce. "Like a bridge extending over cultures, you will connect the East and the West."

Asya crinkled her nose, as if she had just detected an awful stink in the house that was apparent only to her, and screwed up her lips, as if to say, "You wish!"

In the meantime nobody noticed that Petite-Ma had risen from her chair and approached the piano, which had been unplayed in years. From time to time they used the top of the closed piano as a sideboard for the extra dishes and plates that did not fit on the dinner table.

"It is wonderful that you two girls are the same age," Auntie Banu concluded her soliloquy. "You two will become friends."

Asya stared at Auntie Banu with renewed interest, wondering if she would ever stop seeing her as a kid. When she was little, whenever another child was brought to the house, her aunts would put the two of them together and order: "Play now! Be friends!" Being of the same age group automatically meant getting along well; somehow peers were regarded as the broken pieces of the same puzzle, expected to suddenly make it complete when brought side by side.

"This is going to be so exciting. And when she goes back to her country, you girls can become pen pals," Auntie Cevriye trilled. She was a strong believer in pen-pal friendships. As a comrade-teacher of the Turkish Republican regime it was her belief that every Turkish citizen, no matter how ordinary she might be in society, had a duty to proudly represent the motherland vis-à-vis the whole world. What better opportunity than in an international pen-pal friendship was there to represent one's country?

"You girls will exchange letters to and fro between San Francisco and Istanbul," Auntie Cevriye murmured half to herself. Corresponding with a stranger without an educational purpose being utterly unthinkable for her, she then lectured on the underlying pedagogical reason. "The problem with us Turks is that we are constantly being misinterpreted and misunderstood. The Westerners need to see that we are not like the Arabs at all. This is a modern, secular state."

With Auntie Feride increasing the volume of the TV all of a sudden, they got distracted by a new Turkish pop video. As her eyes slid to the zany singer, Asya noticed that the woman's hairstyle looked familiar, very familiar. Her gaze bounced back and forth between the screen and Auntie Feride, now recognizing where the inspiration for the new hairdo had stemmed from.

"The Americans have mostly been brainwashed by the Greeks and the Armenians, who unfortunately arrived in the United States before the Turks did," Auntie Cevriye continued. "So they are misled into believing that Turkey is the country of the *Midnight Express*. You'll show the American girl what a beautiful country this is, and promote international friendship and cultural understanding."

Asya gasped with a frustrated expression on her face, and she could have more or less remained in that position had her eldest aunt not proven relentless.

"What's more, she will improve your English and perhaps you will teach her Turkish. Won't this be a wonderful friendship?"

Friendship. . . . Speaking of which, Asya rose to her feet and grabbed her half-eaten *simit,* getting ready to leave to see some *real* friends.

"Where are you going, miss? The breakfast is not over yet," Auntie Zeliha said, opening her mouth for the first time since they sat down at the table. Working amid the hustle and bustle of the tattoo store six days a week from twelve to nine, it was she more than anyone else in the family who savored the droopy slowness of Sunday-morning breakfasts.

"There's this Chinese Film Festival," Asya answered, her voice slightly strained from the effort to look serious and sincere. "The professor of one of my courses asked us to go and see a movie this weekend and then write a critical, analytical paper on it."

"What kind of an assignment is that?" Auntie Cevriye cocked an eyebrow, always wary of unconventional pedagogical techniques.

But Auntie Zeliha did not push it any further. "All right, go and see your Chinese movie," she nodded. "But don't be late, miss. I want you back home before five o'clock. We pick up our guest at the airport this evening."

Asya grabbed her hippie bag and hurried toward the door. Just when she was about to step outside, however, she heard a most unexpected sound. Somebody was playing the piano. Timid, rickety notes looking for a melody long lost.

A look of recognition appeared on Asya's face as she whispered to herself: "Petite-Ma!"

———

Petite-Ma was born in Thessaloníki. She was only a little girl when she migrated with her mother, a widow, to Istanbul. It was the year

1923. The time Petite-Ma arrived in this city cannot be confused for it coincided with the proclamation of the modern Turkish Republic.

"You and the Republic have arrived in this city together. I was desperately waiting for both of you," her husband Rıza Selim Kazancı told her amorously years later. "You both ended the old regimes forever, the one in the country and the one in my house. When you came to me, life brightened up."

"When I came to you, you were sad but strong. I brought you joy and you gave me strength," Petite-Ma had said back.

The truth is, Petite-Ma being so pretty and convivial, the number of men who asked for her hand by the time she was sixteen could have made a line from one end of the old Galata Bridge to the other. Among all the candidates who knocked on her door, there was one and only one that she felt sympathy for the moment she set eyes on him from behind the latticework partition: a portly, tall man who went by the name *Rıza*.

He had a thick beard and a thin mustache, full, somber, dark eyes, and was no less than thirty-three years older than her. He had been married before and rumor had it that his wife, a heartless woman, had abandoned him and their boy. After his wife's betrayal, and though left on his own with a toddler, he had for a long time refused to remarry, preferring to live in his family mansion all alone. There he had stayed, inflating his wealth, which he shared with his friends, and his wrath, which he reserved for his enemies. He was a self-made businessman, once a cauldron maker, an artisan, then an entrepreneur wise enough to enter into the flag-making business at the right time and the right place. During the 1920s the new Turkish Republic was still throbbing with fervor, and manual work, though systematically venerated in government propaganda, brought little money. The new regime needed teachers to create patriotic Turks out of their students, financiers to help generate a national bourgeoisie, and flag manufacturers to adorn the entire country with the Turkish flag, but it surely did not need any cauldron makers. This is how Rıza Selim entered into the flag-making business.

Despite earning oodles of money and influential friends in his new business, when choosing a surname in 1925, after the Law of Surnames obliged every Turkish citizen to carry a surname, it was his first craft that Rıza Selim wished to be called after: *Kazancı*.

Though fine-looking and definitely well off, given his age and the trauma of his first marriage (who knows why his wife abandoned him; perhaps the man was a pervert, the women gossiped), Rıza Selim Kazancı was one of the last men on earth Petite-Ma's mother would have liked to see her treasured daughter marry. There sure were *better* candidates than him. But despite her mother's persistent objections, Petite-Ma refused to listen to anyone but her heart. Perhaps it was because there was something in Rıza Selim Kazancı's dark eyes that made Petite-Ma grasp, not intellectually but intuitively, that he was gifted with something barred to many in this world: the ability to love another human being more than you love yourself. Though too young and too inexperienced at the age of sixteen, Petite-Ma was sensible enough to comprehend what an exceptional bliss it could be to be loved and adored by a man with such a gift. Rıza Selim Kazancı's eyes were soft and sparkly, just like his voice; there was something in him that made one feel secure in his company, cherished and protected even amid surrounding turbulence. This man was no deserter.

But that was not the only reason why Petite-Ma was attracted to Rıza Selim Kazancı. The truth is, she was drawn to his story long before being attracted to him. She sensed how badly his soul had been bruised by the desertion of his first wife. She sure could mend those bruises. After all, women enjoy taking care of one another's wreckages. Petite-Ma didn't take long to make up her mind. She was going to marry him and nobody, not even her destiny, could change that.

If Petite-Ma so intuitively believed in Rıza Selim Kazancı, he, in turn, was going to merit that trust until his last breath. This blond, blue-eyed wife, who came to him with a furry, snow white cat instead of a proper dowry, was the delight of his life. Never a day did he refuse to fulfill any demand of hers, no matter how whimsical. That, however, was hardly the case with the then six-year-old boy at home: Levent Kazancı never accepted Petite-Ma as a mother. He resisted and ridiculed her at every opportunity for years to come, ending his childhood with suppressed bitterness, if childhood could ever come to an end when one remained so bitter inside.

At a time when marriage without kids was, if not a sign of an incurable malady, then surely a sacrilege, Petite-Ma and Rıza Selim Kazancı didn't have a child. Not because he was too old but because at the beginning she was too young and disinterested in raising kids, and then when she changed her mind, he was simply too old. Levent Kazancı remained the only child to continue the lineage, a title he wasn't thrilled to hold.

Though saddened and offended by her stepson's acrimony, Petite-Ma was an exuberant, extroverted girl with a wide imagination and an even wider list of requests. There were things in this world far more interesting than nursing babies, such as learning the piano. Before long, a Bentley piano made by Stroud Piano Co., Ltd., in England was gleaming in the best spot in the living room. It was with this piano that Petite-Ma started taking her first lessons from her first piano teacher—a white Russian musician who had escaped the Bolshevik Revolution and settled permanently in Istanbul. Petite-Ma was his best student. She not only had the talent but also the perseverance to make the piano a lifelong companion rather than a fleeting pastime.

Rachmaninoff, Borodin, and Tchaikovsky were her favorites. Whenever she was alone at home, playing just for herself with Pasha the First on her lap, these were the composers whose works she would perform. When she played for guests, however, she'd choose songs from an entirely different repertoire. A Western repertoire: Bach, Beethoven, Mozart, Schumann, and above all, Wagner, on those special occasions when they had government officials and their dainty wives as guests. After supper the men would gather near the fireplace with drinks in their hands to discuss world politics. The late 1920s were the years when national politics could only be either venerated or reaffirmed, the louder the better since the walls had ears. Accordingly, whenever there emerged a need for genuine discussion, the new Turkish Republic's political and cultural elite instantly switched to world politics, which was a mess on its own and thereby always interesting to talk about.

Meanwhile, the ladies clustered at the other end of the house, holding crystal glasses of mint liquor, eyeing one another's clothes. In the ladies section there were two types of women, starkly different from each other: the professionals and the wives.

The professionals were the comrade-women, the epitome of *the new Turkish female*: idealized, glorified, and championed by the reformist elite. These women constituted the new professionals—lawyers, teachers, judges, managers, clerks, academics. . . . Unlike their mothers they were not confined to the house and had the chance to climb the social, economic, and cultural ladder, provided that they shed their sexuality and femininity on the way there. More often than not they wore two-piece suits in browns, blacks, and grays—the colors of chastity, modesty, and partisanship. They had short haircuts, no makeup, no accessories. They moved in defeminized, desexualized bodies. And whenever the wives giggled in that annoyingly feminine way of theirs, the professionals tightened their fingers around the small, leather purses under their arms, as if they had some top-secret information in them and had given their word of honor to protect it no matter what. The wives, conversely, came to these invitations wearing satin evening gowns in whites, pasty pinks, and pastel blues—the hues of ladylikeness, innocence, and vulnerability. They didn't like the professionals very much, whom they regarded more as "comrades" than women, and the professionals didn't like them, whom they regarded more as "concubines" than women. In the end nobody found anyone "woman" enough.

Each time the tension between the comrades and the concubines intensified, Petite-Ma, who identified herself with neither group, secretly gestured to the maid to serve mint liquor in crystal glasses and almond paste sweets on silver plates. This duo, she had discovered, was the only thing that could soothe the nerves of every single Turkish woman in the room, no matter which camp she was in.

Late into the party, Rıza Selim Kazancı would call his wife and ask her to play the piano for the honored guests. Petite-Ma never refused. In addition to Western composers, she played national anthems exuding patriotic fervor. The guests cheered and applauded. Particularly in the year 1933, when the anthem of the Tenth Anniversary was composed, "March of the Republic," she had to play it over and over again. The anthem was everywhere, echoing in their ears when they slept. It was a time when even babies in their cradles were put to sleep with this hearty rhythm.

Consequently, at a time when Turkish women were going through a radical transformation in the public sphere thanks to a series of social reforms, Petite-Ma was savoring her own independence within the private sphere of her home. Though her interest in the piano never diminished, it didn't take Petite-Ma too long to come up with a list of new diversions. Hence in the years to follow, she would learn French, pen never-to-be-published short stories, excel in different techniques of oil painting, doll herself up in shiny shoes and satin ball gowns, drag her husband to dances, throw crazy parties, and never do a day of housework. Whatever his perky wife asked for, Rıza Selim Kazancı complied with fully. He was usually a composed man with a lot of esteem for others and a profound sense of justice. However, like too many made out of a similar mold, he could not be mended once broken. Consequently, there was one topic that brought the bad side out in him: his first wife.

Even years later whenever Petite-Ma happened to ask him anything about his first wife, Rıza Selim Kazancı drifted into silence, his eyes shadowed by an uncharacteristic gloom. "What kind of a woman can abandon her son?" he said, his face crumpling with detestation.

"But don't you want to know what happened to her?" Petite-Ma inched closer and sat on her husband's lap, caressing his chin softly, as if to cajole him into facing the question.

"I have no interest in learning that slut's fate." Rıza Selim Kazancı stiffened, without caring to lower his voice so that Levent wouldn't hear him smear his mother.

"Did she run away with someone else?" Petite-Ma insisted, knowing she was surpassing her limits but confident that she could not fully know what her limits were until she had surpassed them.

"Why are you poking your nose into things that are none of your business?" Rıza Selim Kazancı snapped in reply. "Are you interested in repeating the act or what?"

With that Petite-Ma learned what her limits were.

Except for the moments when the topic of the first wife came up, their life flowed tranquilly in the years that followed. Comfortable and contented. Unusual indeed given that the families around them were anything but. Their contentment was a source of envy for relatives and friends and neighbors. They would meddle in whenever they could. The most suitable topic to pick on was the couple's childlessness. Many tried to persuade Rıza Selim Kazancı to marry another woman before it was too late. Since under the new civil law men could no longer have more than one wife, he would have to divorce this wife of his who, by now everybody suspected, was either barren or bolshie. Rıza Selim Kazancı turned a deaf ear to such counsels.

On the day he died, a totally unexpected death common to generations of Kazancı men, Petite-Ma came to believe in the evil eye for the first time in her life. She was convinced that it was the gaze of the jealous people around them that had pierced through the walls of this otherwise blissful *konak* and killed her husband.

Today she barely remembered any of that. As her creased, bony fingers caressed the old piano, Petite-Ma's days with Rıza Selim

Kazancı flickered from a distance like a dim, ancient lighthouse misguiding her through the stormy waters of Alzheimer's.

On a divan in a renovated apartment facing the Galata Tower, a neighborhood where the streets never slept and the cobblestones knew many secrets, under the rays of the sunset reflecting from the glass windows of decrepit buildings and amid the squeals of the seagulls, Asya Kazancı sat nude and still, like a statuette absorbing the talent of the artist who had carved her out of a block of marble. As her mind drifted into fantasyland, so did the thick smoke she had just inhaled coil inside her body, burning her lungs, elating her spirits until she finally exhaled it slowly, reluctantly.

"What are you pondering, sweetheart?"

"I am working on Article Eight of my Personal Manifesto of Nihilism," Asya replied as she opened her foggy eyes.

Article Eight: If between society and the Self there lies a cavernous ravine and upon it only a wobbly bridge, you might as well burn that bridge and stay on the side of the Self, safe and sound, unless it is the ravine that you are after.

Asya took another drag, and held the smoke in.

"Here, let me feed you," said the Dipsomaniac Cartoonist, taking the joint from her hands. He leaned toward her, his hairy chest pressing against her; she opened her mouth like a blind baby bird ready to be fed. He blew the stream of smoke directly into her mouth; she inhaled it eagerly as if thirstily drinking water.

Article Nine: If the ravine inside enthralls you more than the world outside, you might as well fall in it, fall into yourself.

They repeated the act, he directing the smoke into her mouth, she taking it in again and again, until the last puff of smoke that had disappeared down her throat was released.

"I bet you are feeling better now," cooed the Dipsomaniac Cartoonist, his face reflecting his desire for more sex. "There is no cure better than a good screw and a good joint."

Asya bit the inside of her mouth to fight back the urge to raise objections. Instead, she tilted her head toward the open window and stretched her arms as though she were about to embrace the whole city, with all its chaos and splendor.

He in the meantime was busy perfecting his statement: "Let's see. There is nothing so overrated as a bad fuck and nothing so underrated as a good—"

"Shit." Asya lent a hand.

Nodding heartily, the Dipsomaniac Cartoonist stood up with only his silken boxers on and his slight beer belly exposed. He lolloped toward the CD player to put on a song, which happened to be one of her all-time Johnny Cash favorites: "Hurt." Swinging with the opening rhythm of the song, he walked back, his eyes all glittery: *I hurt myself today / To see if I still feel . . .*

Asya scrunched up her face like she had just been pinched by an invisible needle. "It's such a pity. . . ."

"What is a pity, sweetheart?"

She stared at him with widely opened troubled eyes that seemed to belong to someone three times her age. "It sucks," she groaned. "These managers and organizers, whatever they are called, they organize European tours or Asian tours or even hurrah-perestroika-Soviet Union tours . . . but if you are a music fan in Istanbul you do not fit into any geographical definition. We fall through the cracks. You know, the only reason why we don't have as many concerts as we'd like to is the geostrategic position of Istanbul."

"Yeah, we should all line up along the Bosphorus Bridge and puff as hard as we can to shove this city in the direction of the West.

If that doesn't work, we'll try the other way, see if we can veer to the East." He chuckled. "It's no good to be in between. International politics does not appreciate ambiguity."

But high above the clouds, Asya didn't hear him. She lit another joint and put it between her chapped lips. She drew a deep puff of indifference, ignoring afterward the feeling of his fingers on her skin, his tongue on her tongue.

"There had to be a way to reach Johnny Cash before he passed away. I mean the guy *had* to come to Istanbul, he died without knowing he had die-hard fans here. . . ."

The Dipsomaniac Cartoonist broke into a soft smile. He kissed the little mole on her left cheek, caressed her neck gently, until his hands started moving down to her abundant breasts, cupping them each in his hands. The kiss was brash, unhurried, but also woven with a shade of force, if not ferocity. With shimmering eyes he asked, "When are we meeting again?"

"Whenever we both run into each other in Café Kundera, I guess." Asya shrugged, pulling herself away from him. When she withdrew, he came closer.

"But when are we meeting here in my house?"

"You mean *when are we meeting here in my cathouse*?" Asya spit out, no longer fighting back the urge to backbite. "Because as we both know too well, this is not your home! Home is where your wife of so many years is, whereas this place is your secret cathouse where you can imbibe and get laid without your wife knowing a thing. This is where you screw your *chicks*. The younger, the shallower, the tipsier, the better!"

The Dipsomaniac Cartoonist sighed and grabbed his glass of *rakı*. He drank half in one gulp. His face was marred with a desolation so intense that for a second Asya feared he would either yell at her or start to sob, she could not imagine that much hurt remaining calm. Instead, he muttered in a hoary voice, "You can be so cruel sometimes."

There was an eerie silence in the room, muffled by the screams of the children playing soccer on the street outside. From the pitch of the screams it sounded like one of the boys had just been shown a red card and all the players on his team were now busy arguing with the referee, whoever that was.

"You have such a dark side, Asya," the Dipsomaniac Cartoonist's voice came from a distance. "Because it doesn't show on your sweet face, it is hard to tell at first glance. But it is there. You have a bottomless potential for demolition."

"Well, I do not *demolish* anyone, do I?" Asya felt the need to defend herself. "All I want is to be free and to be myself and all that shit. . . . If only I could be left on my own . . ."

"If only you could be left on your own so that you could destroy yourself faster and earlier. . . . Is that what you want? You are attracted to self-destruction like a moth is attracted to light."

Asya snorted a tense chuckle.

"When you drink you drink to extremes, when you criticize you bulldoze, when you get down you sink and hit the bottom. I honestly don't know how to approach you. You are so full of rage, baby. . . ."

"Perhaps it's because I was born a bastard," remarked Asya, taking another puff. "I don't even know who my father is. I never ask, they never tell. Sometimes when my mother looks at me I think she sees him in my face but never says a word. We all pretend there is no such thing as *father*. Instead there is only *Father*, with a capital *F*. When you have Allah up there in the sky to look after you, who needs a father? Aren't we all His children? Not that my mother buys that crap. I tell you she is more cynical than any woman I've ever known. And that is precisely where the problem is. My mom and I, we are so alike and yet so distant."

She blew a plume of smoke in the direction of the mahogany desk where the Dipsomaniac Cartoonist kept some of his best works, those he was afraid his wife might destroy after one of their frequent fights. He also kept there the first rough sketches of the

Amphibian Politician and *Rhinoceros Politicus,* two new series in which he depicted the members of the Turkish parliament as different animal species. He planned to release this series soon, especially now that the court had agreed to postpone indefinitely his three-year prison sentence for drawing the prime minister as a wolf in sheep's clothing. The main prerequisite of the deferment was that he did not repeat the wrong, which he was determined to do. What was the use of fighting for freedom of expression, he thought, if one didn't fight for freedom of humor first?

At the corner of the desk, beneath the ochre light of a gooseneck art deco table lamp, sat a huge hand-carved wood sculpture of Don Quixote bent over a book, lost in his ruminations. Asya liked this sculpture very much.

"My family is a bunch of clean freaks. Brushing away the dirt and dust of the memories! They always talk about the past, but it is a cleansed version of the past. That's the Kazancıs' technique of coping with problems; if something's nagging you, well, close your eyes, count to ten, wish it never happened, and the next thing you know, it has never happened, hurray! Every day we swallow yet another capsule of mendacity. . . ."

What was it that Don Quixote read, Asya wondered in her pixilated mind. What was written on that open page there? Had the sculptor cared to scribble down a few words? Curiously she bolted from the sofa and got closer to the sculpture. Alas, there were no words on the wooden page. She took a long drag before she went back to her seat and started complaining again.

"It annoys me to see all those home-sweet-homes. Sad facsimiles of happy families. You know at times I envy my Petite-Ma, she is almost a hundred years old now, how I wish I had her disease. Sweet Alzheimer's. Memory withers away."

"That's not good, sweetie."

"It might not be good for the people around you, but it's good for you," Asya insisted.

"Well, usually the two are related."

ELIF SHAFAK

But Asya ignored that. "You know, today Petite-Ma opened her piano after so many years; I heard her play these dissonant sounds. It's depressing. This woman used to play Rachmaninoff, and now she can't even play a silly children's song." She paused for a second, considering what she had just said. Sometimes she talked first, thought later.

"But my point is, she doesn't know that, we do!" Asya exclaimed with a forged zest. "Alzheimer's is not as terrible as it sounds. The past is nothing but a shackle we need to get rid of. Such an excruciating burden. If only I could have no past—you know, if only I could be a nobody, start from point zero and just remain there forever. As light as a feather. No family, no memories and all that shit. . . ."

"Everybody needs a past," the Dipsomaniac Cartoonist took a pull from his glass, his expression hovering somewhere between rue and ire.

"Don't count me in because I sure don't!" Asya now grabbed the Zippo on the coffee table and thumbed it to life, only to instantly snap the lighter closed with a sharp click. She liked the sound and repeated the routine several times, without knowing that she drove the Dipsomaniac Cartoonist slightly mad. Click! Click! Click!

"I'd better go." She handed him the Zippo and looked for her clothes. "My dear family has assigned me an important duty. I have to go to the airport with Mom and welcome my American pen pal."

"You have an American pen pal?"

"Sort of. This girl who materialized out of nowhere. So one day I wake up and there is this letter in the mailbox, guess from where? San Francisco! Some girl named Amy. She says she is my uncle Mustafa's stepdaughter. We didn't even know the man had a stepdaughter! So now it dawns on us that this marriage is his wife's second marriage, you know? He never told us that! My grandma almost had a heart attack finding out that her precious son's wife of

148

twenty years was in fact not a virgin when they got married, no sir, no virgin, but a *divorcée!*"

Asya paused to pay her respects to the song that had just started to play. It was "It Ain't Me, Babe." She whistled the melody and then mouthed the words before she went back to her speech again.

"Anyway, out of the blue this Amy writes a letter saying she is a college student at the University of Arizona, and she is deeply interested in getting to know other cultures and she looks forward to meeting us one day, blah blah blah. And then she lets the cat out of the bag: By the way, I am coming to Istanbul in a week. May I stay with you at your house?"

"Wow!" the Dipsomaniac Cartoonist exclaimed as he threw three ice cubes into his replenished *rakı* glass. "But does she say why she is coming here of all places? Just as a tourist?"

"I dunno," Asya mumbled from the floor on her knees, searching for one of her socks under the divan. "But given that she is a college student, I bet she is doing some research on 'Islam and the oppression of women' or 'patriarchal precedents in the Middle East.' Otherwise why would she want to stay at our nuthouse—you know, full of women—when there are so many hotels in this city, cheap and funky? I am sure she wants to interview each of us about the situation of women in Muslim countries and all that—"

"Shit!" the Dipsomaniac Cartoonist completed the sentence for her.

"Right!" Asya exclaimed triumphantly, having found the lost sock. In a flash, she donned her skirt and shirt and ran a brush through her hair.

"Well, bring her to Café Kundera sometime."

"I'll ask her, but I'm sure she'll want to go to a museum instead." Asya grunted as she put on her leather boots. She glanced around to make sure she hadn't forgotten anything. "Well, I will certainly have to spend some time with her, since my family keeps prodding me about guiding her all over the place so that she can marvel at Istanbul. They want her to sing the praises of this city when she goes back to America."

Despite the open windows the room still smelled heavily of marijuana, *rakı,* and sex. Johnny Cash roared in the background.

Asya grabbed her bag and motioned toward the door. Just when she was about to leave, however, the Dipsomaniac Cartoonist blocked her way. Looking her directly in the eye, he grabbed her shoulders and gently pulled her toward himself. His dark brown eyes had the plum rings and puffy bags common to the alcoholic or the grief-stricken or both.

"Dear Asya," he whispered, his face brightening up with a compassion she'd never seen there before. "Despite all that poison that you harbor inside, and perhaps precisely because of it, you are in some odd way so special and such a kindred soul. And I love you. I fell in love with you the day you first appeared in Café Kundera, with that troubled look on your face. I don't know if this means anything to you but I am going to confess it all the same. Before you leave this apartment you need to understand that this is no cat-house, and I do not bring *chicks* here. I come here to drink and draw and get depressed, get depressed and draw and drink, and sometimes to draw and get depressed and drink. . . . That's it. . . ."

Utterly astounded, Asya clutched the door's handle and stood still for a moment at the threshold. Not knowing where to place her hands, she thrust them into the pockets of her skirt and fingered something there that felt like crumbs. She took her hands out, only to see the tips of her fingers covered with the brownish seeds consecrated by Petite-Ma to protect her against the evil-eye.

"Look at this! Wheat . . . wheat . . ." Asya slurred the word every which way. "Petite-Ma is trying to protect me from evil." She opened her hand and gave him a grain of wheat. No sooner had she done this, however, than she blushed as if having revealed an amorous secret.

Her cheeks still rosy, the bitterness inside her no longer tempered by brashness, Asya opened the door. Stepping out as quickly as she could, she hesitated for a second before she turned back. She looked as if she wanted to say something but instead she gave him a huge hug. Then she sprinted down five flights of stairs and ran as fast as she could from every torment chasing her soul.

EIGHT

Pine Nuts

How come she is still asleep?" Asya asked, her chin pointing in the direction of her bedroom. On the way back from the airport, to her dismay, she had found out that her aunts had placed a second bed right across from hers and turned her only private space under this roof into "the girls' room." They had done so either because they were always looking for new ways of tormenting her or because this room had a better view and they wanted to make a good impression on their guest, or else, they had seen the accommodation as yet another opportunity to bring the girls closer within their PIFCUP—Promoting International Friendship and Cultural Understanding Project. Having absolutely no desire whatsoever to share her private space with a complete stranger, yet unable to protest in front of the guest, Asya had grudgingly consented. But now her tolerance was wearing thin. As if it weren't enough that they put the American girl in her bedroom, the Kazancı women seemed determined not to start supper before the guest of honor joined them. Thus, although the dinner had been put on the table more than an hour ago and everyone had long taken her place around the table, including Sultan the Fifth, nobody had fully dined yet, including Sultan the Fifth. Every twenty minutes or so, somebody got up to warm the lentil soup and reheat the meat dish, carrying the pots back and forth between the kitchen and the living room, while Sultan the Fifth followed the smell each time with beseeching meows. They were in such a state, pasted to their chairs, watching TV on the lowest volume, and talking in whispers. Nonetheless, since they kept picking at this dish or that, everyone but Sultan the Fifth had already eaten more then they normally would have at one sitting.

"Perhaps she is already awake and is just lying in bed because she is too shy or something. Why don't I go in and take a look?" Asya asked.

"Stay put, miss. Let the girl sleep." Auntie Zeliha puckered an eyebrow.

Keeping an eye on the screen, another eye on the remote control, Auntie Feride agreed: "She needs to sleep. It is because of the jet lag. She traversed not only oceanic currents but also different time zones."

"Well, at least some people in this house are given the chance to stay in bed as long as they want," Asya grumbled.

It was precisely then that a sparkling soundtrack started to play in the background and the program everybody had been waiting for flashed on the screen: the Turkish version of *The Apprentice*. In rapt silence they watched the Turkish Donald Trump materialize from behind the bright satin curtains of a spacious office with a wonderful panorama of the Bosphorus Bridge. After a quick, condescending glance at the two teams awaiting his orders, the businessman informed them of their task. Each team was instructed to design a bottle of sparkling water, find a way to manufacture ninety-nine of them, and then sell them all as swiftly and as expensively as possible in one of the most luxurious quarters of the city.

"I don't call that a challenge," Asya said with a whoop. "If they want a real challenge they should send all these contestants to the most religious and conservative neighborhoods in Istanbul and have them sell bottled red wine there."

"Oh, be quiet," Auntie Banu snapped, sighing. She was discontent with the way her niece constantly made fun of religion and religiosity; in that regard she could plainly see who Asya resembled exactly: her mother. If blasphemy, more or less like breast cancer or diabetes, was genetically passed on from mother to daughter, what was the use of trying to correct it? Thus, she sighed again.

Ignoring the anguish she instilled in her aunt, Asya shrugged. "But why not? That would be far more creative than this baseless Turkish imitation of America. You should always amalgamate the technical material borrowed from the West with the particular features of the culture you address. That's what I call a Donald Trump ingeniously *alla turca*. So he should, for instance, ask the contestants to sell packaged pork in a Muslim neighborhood. There you go. Now that's a *challenge*. Let's see those marketing strategies flower."

Before anyone could comment on that, the door of the bedroom opened with a creak and out stepped Armanoush Tchakhmakhchian, a bit diffident, a bit dizzy. She was wearing faded denim jeans and a navy sweatshirt long and loose enough to hide the features of her body. While packing for her flight to Turkey she had thought hard about what kind of clothing to take with her and had ended up choosing her most modest clothes so as not to look strange in a conservative place. It had therefore come as a shock to be welcomed at the Istanbul airport by Auntie Zeliha wearing an outrageously short skirt and even more outrageously high heels. What was even more startling, however, was to meet Auntie Banu afterward in a head scarf and a long dress, and to learn how pious she was, praying five times a day. That the two women, despite the stark contrast in their appearance and obviously in their personalities, were sisters living under the same roof was a puzzle Armanoush figured she would have to work on for a while.

"Welcome, welcome!" Auntie Banu exclaimed cheerily, but instantly ran out of English words.

As they watched her approach, the four aunts at the table fidgeted awkwardly with the discomfort of unfamiliarity, but still wore ear-to-ear smiles on their faces. Curious as to what the stranger smelled like, Sultan the Fifth immediately sprang to his feet and paced a narrowing circle around Armanoush, sniffing her slippers, until he had decided there was nothing of interest there.

"I am very sorry, I don't know how I slept that long," Armanoush stammered in slow-motion English.

"Of course, your body needed that sleep. It's a long flight," Auntie Zeliha said. Though she had a mellow yet blatant accent and tended to stress the wrong syllables, she also sounded pretty comfortable expressing herself in English. "Aren't you hungry? I hope you will enjoy Turkish food."

Capable of recognizing the word *food* in every language possible, Auntie Banu bolted to the kitchen to bring the lentil soup. Almost robotically Sultan the Fifth leaped over his cushion to follow her, meowing and pleading along the way.

As she sat in the chair reserved for her, Armanoush inspected the living room for the first time. Quickly, warily, she looked around, pausing at certain spots: the carved rosewood, glass-door cupboard with gilded coffee cups, tea-glass sets, and several antiques inside; the old piano against the wall; the exquisite rug on the floor; the multiple pieces of latticework glowing on top of the coffee tables, velvet armchairs, and even the TV set; the canary in an ornamented cage swinging by the balcony door; the pictures on the walls—a bucolic oil painting of a countryside too picturesque to be real, a calendar with the photograph of a different cultural and natural site in Turkey for each month; an evil-eye amulet; and a portrait of Atatürk in a tuxedo, waving his fedora toward a crowd not included in the frame. The entire room was pulsating with mementos and vivid hues—blues, maroons, sea greens, turquoises—and blazing with such luminosity that it seemed there was an additional light somewhere other than what radiated from the lamps.

Armanoush then looked at the dishes on the table with growing interest. "What a gorgeous table." She beamed. "These are all my favorite foods. I see you have made hummus, baba ghanoush, *yalancı sarma* . . . and look at this, you have baked *churek*!"

"Aaaah, do you speak Turkish?!" Auntie Banu exclaimed, flabbergasted as she walked back in with a steaming pot in her hands and Sultan the Fifth still tailing her.

Armanoush shook her head, half-amused, half-solemn, as if feeling sorry to let down so much anticipation. "No, no. I do not speak the Turkish language, unfortunately, but I guess I speak the Turkish cuisine."

Unable to get this last bit, Auntie Banu turned to Asya in despair, but the latter seemed to have no interest in fulfilling her role as translator, so fully absorbed was she in the task designated by the Turkish Donald Trump. The competitors were now instructed to dive deep into the textile industry to redesign the yellow and azure uniforms of one of the biggest soccer teams competing in the national league. The design rated highest by the soccer players themselves was going to win the competition. Meanwhile, Asya had been contemplating an alternative plan for this specific task as well, but this time she decided to keep it to herself. She didn't feel like talking anymore. To tell the truth, the American girl had turned out to be far more beautiful than she had expected; not that she was *expecting* anything, but deep inside Asya had thought, and perhaps hoped, that it would be some stupid blonde who they would welcome at the airport.

For some reason unknown to her, Asya wanted to confront the guest, but lacked not so much the reason as the energy. At this point, she'd rather remain aloof and reserved to make clear that she shunned this Turkish hospitality.

"So, tell us," Auntie Feride asked after completing the inspection of the American girl's hairstyle and finding it too plain. "How is America?"

The absurdity of the question was enough to make Asya lose her composure, no matter how resolute she might have been in her decision to remain detached. She gave her aunt a pained look. But if Armanoush too had found the question ludicrous, she didn't show it. She was good with aunts. Aunts were her specialty. Her right cheek slightly gorged with the lump of hummus inside, she replied: "Good, good. It's a big country, you know. Depending on where you live, there are different Americas."

"Ask her how is Mustafa." Grandma Gülsüm demanded, completely dismissing the last pieces of information, which she hadn't understood.

"He is good, working hard," Armanoush said while she simultaneously listened to Auntie Zeliha's melodious voice translate her words. "They have a lovely house and two dogs. It is gorgeous out there in the desert. And the weather in Arizona is always nice, you know, nice and sunny. . . ."

When the soup was eaten and the starters nibbled, Grandma Gülsüm and Auntie Feride made a visit to the kitchen and returned carrying a huge tray each, perfectly synchronized in an Egyptian walk. They put the plates they had shouldered onto the table.

"You have pilaf," Armanoush smiled and leaned forward inspecting the dishes. "There is *turşu* and . . ."

"Wow!" the aunts exclaimed in unison, impressed by their guest's command of Turkish cuisine.

Armanoush suddenly spotted the last pot brought to the table. "Oh, I wish my grandma could see this, now this is a treat, *kaburga*. . . ."

"Wow!" echoed the chorus. Even Asya perked up with a dash of interest.

"Turkish restaurant many in America?" Auntie Cevriye asked.

"Actually, I happen to know this food because it is also part of the Armenian cuisine," Armanoush replied slowly. Being presented to the family as Mustafa's stepdaughter Amy, an American girl from San Francisco, she had initially planned to gradually reveal the secret about the remaining part of her identity, after having built up some degree of mutual trust. But here she was, galloping full speed directly into the nub of the matter.

Now lapsing into a taut yet equally self-confident mood, Armanoush straightened her back and looked from one end of the table to the other to see how everyone was reacting. The blank expressions she encountered on their faces urged her to explain herself better.

"I am Armenian . . . well, Armenian American."

The words were not translated this time. There was no need to. The four aunts smiled simultaneously, each in her own way: one of them politely, the second worriedly, the third curiously, and the last amiably. But the most visible reaction came from Asya. Having now stopped watching *The Apprentice,* she eyed their guest with genuine interest for the first time, realizing that, after all, she might not be here to conduct research on "Islam and women."

"Oh yeah?" Asya finally opened her mouth, and leaned forward putting her elbows on the table. "Tell me, is it true that System of a Down hates us?"

Armanoush blinked, having no idea what she was talking about. A cursory glance was enough to make her understand that she was not alone in her bewilderment; the aunts too looked puzzled.

"It's this rock band that I like very much. The guys are Armenian and there are all these urban legends about how they hate the Turks and they wouldn't want any Turk to enjoy their music, so I was just curious." Asya shrugged, visibly discontent with giving this explanation to such an unknowledgeable bunch of people.

"I don't know anything about them." Armanoush pursed her lips. All of a sudden she felt so tiny here, weedy and vulnerable in the lonesomeness of being a stranger in a strange land. "My family was from Istanbul—I mean, my grandmother." She pointed a finger at Petite-Ma as though she needed an elderly person to better illustrate the story.

"Ask her what their family name is." Grandma Gülsüm elbowed Asya, sounding like she possessed the key to a secret archive in the basement wherein the records of all the Istanbulite families, past and present, were neatly kept.

"Tchakhmakhchian," Armanoush replied when the question was translated to her. "You can call me Amy if you want but my full name is Armanoush Tchakhmakhchian."

Auntie Zeliha's face brightened as she exclaimed in recognition, "I've always found that interesting. The Turks add this suffix -cı to every possible word to generate professions. Look at our family name. It is *Kazan-cı*. We are the "Cauldron Makers." Now I see Armenians do the same thing. *Çakmak . . . Çakmakçı, Çakmakçı-yan.*"

"So that's one more thing in common." Armanoush smiled. There was something in Auntie Zeliha she had liked right away. Was it the way she carried herself, with that eye-catching nose ring, the radically mini miniskirts, and the extra makeup she applied? Or was it her stare? Somehow she had a look that made one trust her to understand without being judgmental.

"Look, I have the address of the house." Armanoush fished out a piece of paper from her pocket. "My grandma Shushan was born in this house. If you could help me with the directions, I'd like to go and visit it sometime."

While Auntie Zeliha peered at the writing on the piece of paper, Asya noticed that something was bothering Auntie Feride. Casting panicky glances at the partly open balcony door, she looked agitated, like someone who had found herself facing a dangerous situation and not knowing which way to run.

Asya leaned sideways and, hunching over the steaming pilaf, muttered to her crazy aunt, "Yo, what's up?"

Auntie Feride too leaned sideways, hunched over the steaming pilaf, and then, with eccentric sparkles in her gray green eyes, she whispered, "I heard stories about Armenians coming back to their old houses to dig out the chests their grandfathers had hidden there before they ran away." She squinted her eyes and raised her voice a notch. "Gold and jewels," she gasped, and paused to give that some thought until she had affably come to an agreement with herself: "Gold and jewels!"

It took Asya a few extra seconds to grasp what her aunt might be talking about.

"You understand what I'm saying, this girl is here to track down a treasure chest," Auntie Feride added excitedly, now poring over the contents of an imaginary chest, her face brightening with the taste of adventure and the glow of rubies.

"You're damn right!" Asya exclaimed. "Didn't I tell you this? When she walked off the airplane, she was carrying a shovel and pushing a wheelbarrow instead of luggage. . . ."

"Oh, shut up!" Auntie Feride snapped, offended. She folded her arms and leaned back.

In the meantime, having detected a far deeper reason behind Armanoush's visit, Auntie Zeliha asked, "So you came here to see your grandmother's house. But why had she left?"

Armanoush was both eager to be asked this question and reluctant to answer. Was it too early to let them know? How much of her story should she reveal? If not now, when? Why should she have to wait, anyway? She sipped her tea. In a listless, almost sapped voice she said, "They were forced to leave." But as soon as she said this, her weariness disappeared. She lifted her chin as she added, "My grandmother's father, Hovhannes Stamboulian, was a poet and a writer. He was an eminent man, who was profoundly respected in the community."

"What does she say?" Auntie Feride nudged Asya's elbow, understanding the first half of the sentence but missing the rest.

"She says her family was a prominent family in Istanbul," Asya whispered to her.

"*Dedim sana altın liralar icin gelmiş olmalı.* . . . I told you she must have come here for golden coins!"

Asya rolled her eyes, less sarcastically than she had intended, before concentrating on Armanoush's story.

"They tell me he was a man of letters who liked to read and contemplate more than anything in this world. My grandmother says I remind her of him. I too like books very much," Armanoush added with a bashful smile.

Some of the listeners smiled back, and when the translation was over, all of the listeners smiled back.

"But unfortunately his name was on the list," Armanoush said tentatively.

"What list?" Auntie Cevriye wanted to know.

"The list of Armenian intellectuals to be eliminated. Political leaders, poets, writers, members of clergy. . . . They were two hundred and thirty-four people total."

"But why's that?" asked Auntie Banu, a question which Armanoush skipped.

"On April 24, a Saturday, at midnight, dozens of Armenian notables living in Istanbul were arrested and forcibly taken to police headquarters. All of them had dressed up properly, spick-and-span as if going to a ceremony. They were wearing immaculate collars and elegant suits. All were men of letters. They were kept in the headquarters without an explanation until finally they were deported either to Ayash or to Chankiri. The ones in the first group were in worse condition than the second. Nobody survived in Ayash. The ones taken to Chankiri were killed gradually. My grandpa was among this group. They took the train from Istanbul to Chankiri under the supervision of Turkish soldiers. They had to walk three miles from the station to the town. Until then they had been treated decently. But during the walk from the station, they were beaten with canes and pickax handles. The legendary musician Komitas went mad as a result of what he saw. Once in Chankiri they were released on one condition: They were banned from leaving the town. So they rented rooms there, living with the natives. Every day, two or three of them would be taken by the soldiers outside the town for a walk and then the soldiers would come back alone. One day the soldiers took my grandpa for a walk too."

Still smiling, Auntie Banu looked left and right, first to her sister then to her niece, to see who was going to translate all this, but to her surprise there was only perplexity on the faces of the two translators.

"Anyway, it is a long story. I won't take your time with all the details. When her father died, my grandma Shushan was three years old. There were four siblings, she being the youngest and the only girl. The family had been left without its patriarch. My grandmother's mother was a widow now. Finding it difficult to stay in Istanbul with the children, she sought refuge in her father's house, which was in Sivas. But as soon as they arrived, the deportations began. The entire family was ordered to leave their house and belongings and march with thousands of others to an unknown destination."

Armanoush studied her audience carefully, and decided to finish the story.

"They marched and marched. My grandmother's mother died on the way and before long the elderly died as well. Having no parents to look after them, the younger children lost each other amid the confusion and chaos. But after months apart, the brothers were miraculously reunited in Lebanon with the help of a Catholic missionary. The only missing sibling among those still alive was my grandmother Shushan. Nobody had heard of the fate of the infant. Nobody knew that she had been taken back to Istanbul and placed in an orphanage."

Out of the corner of her eye, Asya could tell that her mother was now intently looking at her. At first she suspected Auntie Zeliha might be trying to convey to her to censure the story as she translated it. But then she realized that what flickered in her mother's stunning eyes was nothing but interest in Armanoush's story. Perhaps she was also wondering how much of all this her unruly daughter was willing to translate to the Kazancı women.

"It took Grandma Shushan's elder brother ten full years to track her down. Finally Great Uncle Yervant found her and took her to America to join her relatives," Armanoush added softly.

Auntie Banu tilted her head to one side and started twining the beads of her amber rosary through her bony, never-manicured fingers, all the while murmuring, "*All that is on earth will perish: But will abide (for ever) the Face of thy Lord,—full of Majesty, Bounty and Honor.*"

"But I don't understand," Auntie Feride was the first to raise doubts. "What happened to them? They died because they *walked*?"

Before she translated that, Asya glanced at her mother to see if she should continue translating. Auntie Zeliha raised her eyebrows and nodded.

When the question was asked to her, Armanoush paused briefly and caressed her grandma's Saint Francis of Assisi pendant before she answered. She spotted Petite-Ma sitting at the other end of the table, her sallow complexion carrying the wrinkles of so many years, staring at her with an expression so deeply compassionate that Armanoush could suspect only two possibilities: Either she had not paid attention to the story at all, and was not here with them anymore, or else she had been listening so attentively that she had lived the story, and was not here with them anymore.

"They were denied water and food and rest. They were made to march a long distance on foot. Women, some of them pregnant, and children, the elderly, the sick, and the debilitated . . . " Armanoush's voice now trailed off. "Many starved to death. Some others were executed."

This time Asya translated everything without skipping a word.

"Who did this atrocity?!" Auntie Cevriye exclaimed as if addressing a classroom of ill-disciplined students.

Auntie Banu joined in her sister's reaction, although hers was inclined more toward disbelief than anger. Her eyes wide open, she tugged the ends of her head scarf as she always did in times of stress, and then heaved a prayer, as she always did when tugging the ends of her head scarf didn't get her anywhere.

"My aunt is asking who did this?" Asya said.

"The Turks did it," Armanoush replied, without paying attention to the implications.

"What a shame, what a sin, are they not human?" Auntie Feride volleyed.

"Of course not, some people are monsters!" Auntie Cevriye declared without comprehending that the repercussions could be far more complex than she would care to acknowledge. Twenty years in her career as a Turkish national history teacher, she was so accustomed to drawing an impermeable boundary between the past and the present, distinguishing the Ottoman Empire from the modern Turkish Republic, that she had actually heard the whole story as grim news from a distant country. The new state in Turkey had been established in 1923 and that was as far as the genesis of this regime could extend. Whatever might or might not have happened preceding this commencement date was the issue of another era—and another people.

Armanoush looked at them one by one, puzzled. She was relieved to see that the family had not taken the story as badly as she feared, but then she couldn't be sure that they had really *taken* it. True, they neither refused to believe her nor attacked with a counterargument. If anything, they listened attentively and they all seemed sorry. But was that the limit of their commiseration? And what exactly had she expected? Armanoush felt slightly disconcerted as she wondered whether it would have been different if she were talking to a group of intellectuals.

Slowly it dawned on Armanoush that perhaps she was waiting for an admission of guilt, if not an apology. And yet that apology had not come, not because they had not felt for her, for it looked as if they had, but because they had seen no connection between themselves and the perpetrators of the crimes. She, as an Armenian, embodied the spirits of her people generations and generations earlier, whereas the average Turk had no such notion of continuity with his or her ancestors. The Armenians and the Turks lived in different time frames. For the Armenians, time was a cycle in which the past incarnated in the present and the present birthed the future. For the Turks, time was a multihyphenated line, where the past ended at some definite point and the present started anew from scratch, and there was nothing but rupture in between.

"But you haven't eaten anything. Come on, my child, you came a long way, eat now," Auntie Banu said, shifting the topic to food, one of the two cures she knew for sorrow.

"It's very good, thank you." Armanoush grabbed her fork. She noticed they had cooked the rice exactly the way her grandmother did, with butter and sautéed pine nuts.

"Good, good! Eat, eat!" Auntie Banu nodded as vigorously as she could manage.

With a sinking heart Asya had watched Armanoush politely accept the offer and grab her fork to go back to her *kaburga*. She lowered her head, losing her appetite. Not that she was hearing the story of the deportation of the Armenians for the first time. She had heard things before, some pro and most con. But it was quite a different experience to hear an account from an actual person. Never before had Asya met someone so young with a memory so old.

It wouldn't take the nihilist in her too long, however, to chuck out the distress. She shrugged. Whatever! The world sucked anyway. Past and future, here and there . . . it was all the same. The same misery everywhere. God either did not exist, or was simply too aloof to see the wretchedness into which he had thrust us all. Life was mean and cruel, and a lot of other things she had long been tired of knowing. Her hazy gaze slid toward the screen where the Turkish Donald Trump was now grilling the three most culpable members of the losing group. The uniforms they'd designed for the soccer team had turned out to be so awful that even the most easygoing athletes had refused to wear them. Now somebody had to be fired. As if a button had been pushed, all three contestants started insulting one another to avoid being the one eliminated.

Withdrawn, Asya lapsed into a disdainful smile. This was the world we lived in. History, politics, religion, society, competition, marketing, free market, power struggle, at one another's throats for another morsel of triumph. . . . She sure did not need any of these and all that . . .

. . . shit.

Still keeping an eye on the screen, but now having fully regained her appetite, Asya jerked her chair forward and started filling her plate. She took a large piece of *kaburga* and began to eat. When she lifted her head, she met her mother's piercing gaze, and quickly looked away.

After dinner Armanoush retreated to the girls' room to make two phone calls. First she called San Francisco. She stood face-to-face with a Johnny Cash poster on the wall directly above the desk.

"Grandma, it's me!" she exclaimed excitedly, but instantly stopped. "What is that noise in the background?"

"Oh, it is nothing, honey," came the answer. "They are repairing the pipes in the bathroom. It turns out your Uncle Dikran messed them up the other day. We had to call a plumber. Tell me how you have been doing?"

Anticipating this question, Armanoush talked about her daily routine in Arizona. Though she felt awful about the deception, she tried to assuage her discomfort by thinking it was for the best. How could she tell her, "I am not in Arizona. I am in the city where you were born!"?

After she hung up, she waited a few minutes. Pensively, she took a deep breath, mustered her courage, and made her second call. She decided to stay calm and not to sound frustrated—a promise she found hard to keep upon hearing her mother's edgy voice.

"Amy, honey, why didn't you call before? How are you? How is the weather in San Francisco? Are they treating you well?"

"Yes, Mom. I'm OK. The weather is"—Armanoush regretted

not having checked the weather in San Francisco on the Internet—
"fine, a bit windy, as always—"

"Yeah," Rose interjected, "I have called you over and over but
your cell phone was dead. Oh, I've been so worried!"

"Mom, please listen," Armanoush said, surprised at the note of
determination in her own voice. "I feel uncomfortable when you
keep calling me at my grandma's house. Let's make a deal, OK? Let
me call you and do not call me. Please."

"Are they making you say this?" Rose asked suspiciously.

"No Ma, of course not. For God's sake. I'm the one who's asking you this."

Though reluctant, Rose accepted the terms. She complained
about not having any time for herself, her days being divided between home and work. But then she cheered up as she told how
there was a sale at Home Depot and she and Mustafa had agreed to
get new kitchen cabinets.

"Tell me your opinion," Rose enthused. "What do you think
about cherry wood? Do you think it would look good in our
kitchen?"

"Yeah, I guess so . . ."

"I think so too. But how about the dark oak? It's a bit more expensive but it has class written all over it. Which one do you think
would be better?"

"I dunno, Mom, the dark oak sounds good too."

"Yeah, but you see, you're not helping me much." Rose
sighed.

When she hung up Armanoush looked around her and felt a
deep estrangement. The Turkish rugs, the old-fashioned bedside
lamps, the unfamiliar furniture, books and newspapers that spoke
another language. . . . Suddenly she felt a panic that she hadn't felt
since she was a small child.

When Armanoush was six years old, she and her mother had
once run out of gas in the middle of nowhere in Arizona. They'd

had to wait almost an hour before another vehicle passed by them. Rose stuck her thumb out and a truck stopped to pick them up. Inside there were two rough-looking, brawny men, scary, sullen fellows. They didn't say a word and drove them to the next gas station. Once they were dropped off and the truck disappeared, Rose hugged Armanoush with a quivering lip, weeping in panic. "Oh God, what if they had been bad people? They could have kidnapped, raped, and killed us, and nobody would have found our bodies. How could I have taken this risk?"

Though not quite that dramatic, Armanoush had a similar feeling right now. Here she was in Istanbul staying at the house of strangers without anyone in her family knowing about it. How could she have acted so impulsively?

What if they were bad people?

NINE

Orange Peels

The next day Asya Kazancı and Armanoush Tchakhmakhchian left the *konak* early in the morning to search for the house where Grandma Shushan had been born. They found the neighborhood easily—a charming, posh borough in the European side of the city. But the house wasn't there anymore. A modern, five-story apartment building had been erected in its place. The entire first floor was a classy-looking fish restaurant. Before going in, Asya checked her reflection in the glass, adjusting her hair while discontentedly eyeing her breasts.

As it was still too early for dinner, there was no one inside except for a handful of waiters sweeping the traces of the previous night off the floor and a rosy-cheeked, stout cook in the kitchen preparing the *mezes* and the main courses for the evening under a cloud of mouth-watering smells. Asya talked to each of them, asking questions about the building's past. But the waiters had arrived in the city only recently, migrating from a Kurdish village in the southeast, and the cook, though he had lived longer in Istanbul, did not have any memory of the street's history.

"Of the long-standing Istanbulite families, only a few have remained on their soil of birth," the cook explained with an air of authority, as he started gutting and cleaning a huge mackerel.

"This city was so cosmopolitan once," the cook continued, breaking the mackerel's backbone first above its tail, then below its head. "We had Jewish neighbors, lots of them. We also had Greek neighbors, and Armenian neighbors. . . . As a boy I used to buy fish from Greek fishermen. My mother's tailor was Armenian. My father's boss was Jewish. You know, we were all intermingled."

"Ask him why things have changed," Armanoush turned to Asya.

"Because Istanbul is not a city," the cook remarked, his face lighting up with the importance of the statement he was about to make. "It looks like a city but it is not. It is a city-boat. We live in a vessel!"

With that he held the fish by its head and started moving the backbone right and left. For a second Armanoush imagined the mackerel to be made of porcelain, fearing it would shatter to pieces in the cook's hands. But in a few seconds the man had managed to take the whole bone out. Pleased with himself, he continued. "We are all passengers here, we come and go in clusters, Jews go, Russians come, my brother's neighborhood is full of Moldovans. . . . Tomorrow they will go, others will arrive. That's how it is. . . ."

They thanked the cook and shot a last glance at the mackerel waiting to be stuffed, its mouth still open.

Asya disappointed, Armanoush distressed, they walked out of the restaurant into an exquisite Bosphorus landscape sparkling under the late winter sun. They put their hands over their eyes to block the sun. Both took a deep breath and knew instantly that spring was in the air.

Having no better plans, they strolled through the neighborhood, buying something from almost every street vendor they came upon: boiled sweet corn, stuffed mussels, semolina halvah, and finally, a large package of sunflower seeds. With each new treat, they launched on a new topic, talking about many things, except the three customary untouchables between young women who were still strangers to one another: sex, men, and fathers.

"I like your family," Armanoush said. "They are so full of life."

"Yeah, sure, tell me about it," Asya countered, and jingled her many bracelets. She was wearing a long, sage green hippie skirt with a maroon flower print, a patchwork bag, and lots of jewelry—glass bead necklaces, bracelets, and silver rings on almost every finger. Next to her Armanoush felt a bit underdressed in her jeans and tweed jacket.

"There's a downside," Asya said. "It is so demanding to be born into a house full of women, where everyone loves you so overwhelmingly that they end up suffocating with their love; a house where you, as the only child, have to be more mature than all the adults around. I'm grateful that I was sent to a first-rate school and probably given the best education possible in this country. But the problem is that they want me to become everything they themselves couldn't accomplish in life. You know what I mean?"

Armanoush feared she did.

"As a result, I had to work my butt off to fulfill all their dreams at the same time. I started learning English at six, which was okay if only they could have stopped there, you know? The next year I had a private teacher to teach me French. When I was nine, I was made to study the violin the whole year, although it was obvious that I had absolutely no interest and no talent in it. After that a skating rink was opened near our house and my aunts decided I should become a skater. They dreamed of me in sparkly dresses pirouetting gracefully to the tune of our national anthem. I'd be the Turkish Katarina Witt! Soon there I was spiraling on ice, falling on my rear again and again while trying to pirouette! The sound of skates scraping on ice still sends shivers down my spine."

Out of courtesy Armanoush managed not to laugh, though she

found the image of Asya pirouetting in an international competition hard to resist.

"Then came a time when they expected me to develop into a long-distance runner. If I trained hard enough, I could be this wondrous athlete and represent Turkey in the Olympic Games! Can you imagine me competing in the women's marathon with such big breasts, for Allah's sake!"

Armanoush didn't hold back her laughter this time.

"All those women athletes, I don't know how they do it, but they all have chests as flat as marble, you know. They must be taking male hormones to deflate their tits. But women like me are not created to become athletes; it is against the most basic laws of physics. The body moves forward gaining speed in accordance with the law of acceleration. The amount of change in your speed is proportional to the amount of force impressed upon the body, and in that direction. Then what happens? The boobies accelerate too, even though they move with a completely dissonant rhythm of their own, up and down, eventually slowing your wind. The law of inertia plus the law of universal gravitation! You cannot possibly win. Oh, it was so embarrassing!" Asya exclaimed excitedly. "Thank God that stage was quickly over. After that, I took painting classes and alas, they even made me take ballet until Ma recently found out I had been skipping the classes and gave up on me."

Armanoush nodded with the familiarity of someone identifying fragments of her personal story in the story of another. She could relate to such *overwhelming love* from her own aunts but didn't feel comfortable talking about it. Instead, she asked:

"There's something I couldn't understand. The lady you came to the airport with, the lady with the nose ring." Armanoush giggled but instantly composed herself. "Zeliha. . . . She is your mom, right? But you don't call her *mom* . . . am I right?"

"You're right. It's a bit confusing. I myself get confused sometimes," Asya said as she lit her first cigarette of the day. By now she

had sensed Armanoush's distaste for cigarettes. Though still working on her new friend's profile, Asya classified Armanoush as a
"well-mannered girl." If a cigarette stood out as a blasphemy within
this decently sterile lifestyle of hers, Asya figured, Armanoush would
never be able to accept what other bad habits she had. She blew the
smoke in the opposite direction, as far away from Armanoush as she
could, except that the wind brought it directly back at them.

"I don't even remember when exactly I started calling my mother
'auntie,' at what age. Perhaps from the start, you know, the very
start," Asya replied.

Asya's voice was little more than a whisper but her eyes were
ardent. "You see, I grew up with all these aunts playing the role of
the mother. My tragedy is that I was in a way the only child of four
women. Auntie Feride, as you might have noticed, is a bit of a
cuckoo, and she never got married. She has held numerous jobs on
and off. She was a terrific saleswoman when she was in her manic
stage. Auntie Cevriye was happily married once but then she lost
her husband and her joy in life. After that she dedicated herself to
teaching national history. Between you and me, I think she doesn't
like sex and finds the needs of the human body revolting! Then
there is the eldest, Auntie Banu. She is the salt of the earth. She is
still married on paper but seldom sees her husband. Her marriage
was so tragic. She had two lovely sons, but they died. The men of
this family are cursed, you know. They don't survive."

Armanoush sighed wearily, not knowing how to interpret this
remark.

"You see, I can understand Auntie Banu's need to seek refuge
in Allah," Asya added, stroking the beads of her necklace. "Anyway, the point is, when I was born I found myself surrounded by
four auntie-moms or mommy-aunties. Either I had to call them all
'mom,' or else I had to call my mother 'Auntie Zeliha.' That proved
easier in a way."

"But wasn't she offended?"

Asya's face perked up as she noticed a rust-colored cargo ship sailing on the open sea. She liked to watch the vessels gliding along the Bosphorus, daydreaming what the crew on board was like, trying to see the city from the eyes of a sailor constantly on the move, a sailor with neither a port to disembark at nor the need to do so.

"Offended? No! You see, she was only nineteen when she became pregnant with me. Odd as it might sound, my not calling her 'mom' must have come as a relief to her. They were all my 'aunties,' and somehow that title rendered my mother's sin less visible in the eyes of society. There was no sinful mother to point a finger at. As a matter of fact, I suspect I might have been encouraged to call her 'auntie,' at least for a while, and after that, it was hard to break the habit."

"I liked her," Armanoush said, but then she paused, confused. "What sin are you talking about?"

"Oh, giving birth to an illegitimate child. My mom is"—Asya crinkled her nose hunting for the right word—"she is . . . the black sheep of the family, you know. The warrior rebel who gave birth to a child out of wedlock."

A Russian tanker passed by, sending small waves to the shore. It was a big vessel, carrying petroleum.

"I'd noticed there was no father around, but I thought he might be dead or something," Armanoush stammered. "I'm sorry."

"You're sorry that my father is *not* dead." Asya chuckled. She gave a flickering glance at Armanoush, who had flushed crimson.

"But you are right, you know," Asya said, with a glint of rage in her eyes. "I feel the same way. I mean, if my father were deceased, this vagueness would be over once and for all. That's what infuriates me most. I can't help thinking he could be anyone. When you have absolutely no idea what kind of a man your father is, your imagination fills in the void. Perhaps I watch him on TV or hear his voice on the radio every day, without knowing it's him. Or I might have come face-to-face with him sometime, someplace. I imagine I might have taken the same bus with him; perhaps he is the professor I talk to after class, the photographer whose exhibition I go to see, or this street vendor here. . . . . You never know."

The subject of their attention was a pencil-mustached, wiry man between forty and fifty. In the window case in front of him were dozens of jumbo jars with pickles of all sizes, which he, with the help of an automatic juice machine, turned into fresh pickle juice. Noticing the two young women eyeing him, the man broke into a grin. Armanoush instantly turned her face away while Asya frowned at him.

"You mean your mom hasn't told you who your father is?" asked Armanoush, delicately.

"My mom is a unique species! She won't tell me anything unless she wants to. She is the most stubborn, the most iron-willed woman you could ever chance upon. I don't think the others know my father's identity either. I doubt if my mom has told anyone. Anyway, even if they know something about it, the family wouldn't share it with me. Nobody tells me anything. I am an outcast in that house, eternally exiled from dreadful family secrets. In the name of protecting me, they have separated me from them." Asya bit into a sunflower seed and spat out the shell. "And after a while it became a reciprocal game—they separate themselves from me, I separate myself from them."

In that same moment they both slowed down. There, half a mile away from them out on the sea, was a man standing up in a small motorboat with several other passengers, holding a newly lit cigarette in one hand and in the other a fantastic tree of balloons in glowing yellows, oranges, and purples. Perhaps he was a fatigued balloon vendor, the father of many children, taking a shortcut from one coast to another on his way back from work, without knowing how breathtaking a pose he struck, as he dragged along a rain of colors and a plume of smoke over the blue waves.

Caught utterly unprepared by the exquisiteness of the scene, Armanoush and Asya stood silently watching the motorboat until all the balloons had disappeared into the horizon.

"Let's sit somewhere, shall we?" Asya asked, as if tired out by what she had just seen.

There was a shabby, open-air café nearby.

"So tell me, what kind of music do you like?" Asya asked, as soon as they had found an empty seat and ordered their drinks—Asya, tea with lemon, Armanoush, Diet Coke with ice. The question was a manifest attempt to become better acquainted, since music happened to be Asya's main connection with the entire world.

"Classical music, ethnic music, Armenian music, and jazz," Armanoush replied. "How about you?"

"A bit different." Asya blushed though she didn't know why. "For a while I listened to harsh stuff—you know, alternative music, punk, postpunk, industrial metal, death metal, darkwave, psychedelic, also a bit of third-wave ska and a bit of gothic, that sort of stuff."

Accustomed to regarding "that sort of stuff" as a lost genre shared by decadent teenagers or directionless adults with more fury than character, Armanoush asked, "Really?"

"Yeah, but then some time ago I got hooked on Johnny Cash. And that was it. Ever since then I stopped listening to anything else. I like Cash. He depresses me so deeply, I am not depressed anymore."

"But don't you listen to anything local? Like Turkish music . . . Turkish pop . . ."

"Turkish pop!!! No way!" Asya flapped her hands in panic as if trying to wave away a pushy street vendor.

Sensing her limits, Armanoush did not press the question any further. Self-hatred, she deduced, could be something the Turks went through.

But Asya tossed back her tea, and added, "Auntie Feride likes that kind of stuff. Though, to be perfectly honest, I sometimes can't tell if it's the music or the singers' hairstyles that she is most interested in."

Halfway through her second Diet Coke, Armanoush asked

Asya what kind of books she read, since fiction was her main connection with the entire world.

"Books. Oh yeah, they saved my life, you know. I love reading, but not fiction. . . ."

A boisterous group of boys and girls materialized in the café, and they were ushered to the table across from Asya and Armanoush. As soon as they sat down, they started to scoff at everyone and everything. They laughed at the plastic burgundy chairs, the glass cases displaying a modest selection of refreshments, the errors in the English translations of the items listed on the menu, and the I LOVE ISTANBUL T-shirts the waiters wore. Asya and Armanoush yanked their chairs forward.

"I read philosophy, political philosophy especially, you know, Benjamin, Adorno, Gramsci, a bit of Žižek . . . especially Deleuze. That kind of stuff. I like them. I like abstractions, I guess, philosophy—I love philosophy. Especially existential philosophy." Asya lit another cigarette and asked through the smoke, "How about you?"

Armanoush named an elongated list of fiction writers, mostly Russian and Eastern European.

"You see?" Asya turned both palms up, as if to indicate the situation made by the two of them. "When it comes to your favorite occupation in life, you too are less regional in your choices. . . . Your reading list doesn't sound very Armenian to me."

Armanoush's eyebrow slightly rose. "Literature needs freedom to thrive," she said as she wagged her head. "We didn't have much of that to expand and enlarge Armenian literature, did we?"

Sensing her limits, Asya did not press the question any further. Self-pity, she deduced, could be something the Armenians went through.

The teenagers behind started to play a game of charades. Each chosen player was assigned a movie title by the rival team, which he then had to convey to his fellow team members. A freckled, ginger-haired girl started to mimic the assigned movie title, and each time she came up with a gesture, the others broke into raucous laughter. It was odd to see how a game based on the principle of silence could cause so much clamor.

Perhaps because of the noise in the background, whatever spirit had guided Armanoush not to trespass her limits had now departed. "The music you listen to is so Western. Why don't you listen to your Middle Eastern roots?"

"What do you mean?" Asya sounded perplexed. "We *are* Western."

"No, you are not Western. Turks are Middle Eastern but somehow in constant denial. And if you had let us stay in our homes, we too could still be Middle Easterners instead of turning into a diaspora people," Armanoush retorted, and instantly felt discomfited for she hadn't meant to sound so harsh.

Asya gnawed the insides of her mouth, but when she had finished, all she said was, "What do you mean?"

"What do I mean? I mean, Sultan Hamid's Pan-Turkish and Pan-Islamic yoke. I mean, the 1909 Adana massacres or the 1915 deportations. . . . Do those ring a bell? Did you not hear anything about the Armenian genocide?"

"I'm only nineteen." Asya shrugged.

The teenagers behind cheered as the freckled girl failed to accomplish her task in time and was replaced by a new player, a lanky, handsome boy whose Adam's apple jutted out from his neck with each mimic. The boy lifted three fingers, indicating that the movie's title consisted of three words. He proceeded into the third and last word directly. Raising both hands into the air, he clutched an imaginary, round thing between his palms, smelled and squeezed it. While his team members failed to understand what that meant, the rival team snickered.

"Is that an excuse?" Armanoush looked Asya in the eye. "How can you be so impervious?"

Not knowing the meaning of *impervious,* Asya saw no problem in personifying the word until she had found an English-Turkish dictionary and looked it up. Savoring the brief reappearance of the sun from behind thick clouds, she remained quiet for what felt like a long time. Then she murmured, "You're fascinated with history."

"And you aren't?" drawled Armanoush, her voice conveying both disbelief and scorn.

"What's the use of it?" was Asya's curt answer. "Why should I know anything about the past? Memories are too much of a burden."

Armanoush turned her head, and her gaze involuntarily settled on the teenagers. Narrowing her eyes, she concentrated on the boy's gestures. Asya too turned around, observed the game, and before she knew it blurted out the answer: "Orange!"

The teenagers burst into laughter, all looking at the young women at the next table. Asya flushed crimson, Armanoush smiled. They paid the bill quickly and were out on the street again.

"What movie has 'orange' in its name?" Armanoush asked once they had reached the path along the seaside.

"*A Clockwork Orange* . . . I guess."

"Oh yeah!" Armanoush conceded with a nod. "Listen, about the fascination with history," she said, marshaling her thoughts. "You have to understand, despite all the grief that it embodies, history is what keeps us alive and united."

"Well, I say that's a privilege."

"What do you mean?"

"This sense of continuity is a privilege. It makes you part of a group where there is a great feeling of solidarity," Asya replied. "Don't get me wrong, I can see how tragic the past was for your family, and I respect your wish to keep the memories alive come what may so that the sorrow of your ancestors is not forgotten. But that is precisely where our paths diverge. Yours is a crusade for re-membrance, whereas if it were me, I'd rather be just like Petite-Ma, with no capacity for reminiscence whatsoever."

"Why does the past frighten you so?"

Asya demurred. "It doesn't!" As the capricious to and fro of the Istanbul wind fluttered her long skirt and cigarette smoke every which way, she paused briefly. "I just don't want to have anything to do with it, that's all."

"That doesn't make sense," Armanoush insisted.

"Perhaps it doesn't. But in all honesty, someone like me can never be past-oriented. . . . You know why?" Asya asked after a long pause. "Not because I find my past poignant or that I don't care. It's because I don't know anything about it. I think it's better to have the knowledge of past events than not to know anything at all."

An expression of puzzlement passed over Armanoush's face. "But you also said you didn't want to know your past. Now you sound different."

"I do?" Asya asked. "Well, let's put it this way, I have conflicting voices inside me with respect to this issue." She gave her companion a glance full of mischief but then her voice became more serious. "All I know about my past is that something wasn't right, and I can't attain that information. For me history starts today, you see? There is no continuity in time. You can't feel attached to ancestors if you can't even trace your own father. Maybe I will never be able to learn my father's name. If I keep thinking about it, I'll go nuts. So I say to myself, why do you want to unearth the secrets? Don't you see that the past is a vicious circle? It is a loop. It sucks us in and makes us run like a hamster on a wheel. Then we start to repeat ourselves, again and again."

As they walked up and down on the undulating streets, every neighborhood looked so different that Armanoush began to think Istanbul was an urban maze, cities within a city. She wondered if James Baldwin had felt the same way when he was here.

At three o'clock in the afternoon, exhausted and hungry, they entered a restaurant, which Asya said was a *must,* since it was here that one could find the best chicken *döner* in town. They each got a *döner* and a large glass of frothy yogurt drink.

"I have to confess," Armanoush muttered after a lull. "Istanbul is a bit different from what I expected. It's more modern and less conservative than I feared."

"Well, you should tell that to my Auntie Cevriye sometime. She'd be thrilled. She'll give me a medallion for having represented my country so well!"

They laughed together for the first time since they'd met.

"There's a place I want to take you to sometime," Asya said. "It is this little café where we regularly meet. Café Kundera."

"Really? He's one of my favorite authors!" Armanoush exclaimed in delight. "Why is it called that?"

"Well, that's an endless debate. Actually, every day we develop a new theory."

On the way back to the *konak,* Armanoush grabbed Asya's hand and squeezed it as she said, "You remind me of a friend of mine."

For a while she looked at Asya like she knew something but couldn't tell. But then she remarked, "I have never seen anyone so perceptive and so . . . so empathetic be so stringent and so . . . so confrontational at the same time. Except one person! You remind me of my most unusual friend: Baron Baghdassarian. You two are so alike in many ways, you could well be soul mates."

"Oh yeah?" Asya asked, the name intriguing her. "What is it? Tell me why you're laughing."

"I'm sorry, I couldn't help laughing at the twist of fate," Armanoush said. "It's just that among all my acquaintances Baron Baghdassarian happens to be the most—*most* anti-Turk!

That night when all the Kazancı women had gone to sleep, Armanoush slipped out of her bed in pajamas, turned on the frail desk lamp, and doing her very best not to make any noise, turned on her laptop. Never before had she realized how distressingly noisy it could be to get online. She dialed the telephone number, found the network node, and typed in her password to log on to Café Constantinopolis.

Where have U been? We were so sick worried! How R U?

Questions began to come in from everyone.

I'm okay, wrote Madame My–Exiled–Soul. But I've not been able to find grandma's house. In its place there is an ugly modern building. It's gone. No traces left behind . . . There are no traces, no records, no reminiscences of the Armenian family who lived in that building at the beginning of the century.

I am so sorry dear, Lady Peacock/Siramark wrote. When R U coming back?

I'll stay till the end of the week, Madame My–Exiled–Soul replied. It is quite an adventure here. The city is beautiful. It resembles San Francisco in some ways, the hilly streets, the constant fog and sea breeze, and the bohemian faces in places least expected. It is an urban maze here. More than one single city, it is like cities within a city. By the way, the cuisine is fantastic. Every Armenian would be in heaven here.

Armanoush halted, realizing in panic what she had just written. I mean, in terms of food, she added quickly.

Yo Madame My-Exiled-Soul, you were our war reporter and now you sound like a Turk! You have not been Turkified, have you? It was Anti–Khavurma.

Armanoush took a deep breath.

The opposite. I have never felt more Armenian in my life. You see, for me to fully experience my Armenianness, I had to come to Turkey and meet the Turks.

The family I am living with is quite interesting, a bit crazy but perhaps all families are. But there is something surreal here. Irrationality is part of the everyday rationale. I feel like I am in a Gabriel García Márquez novel. One of the sisters is a tattoo artist; another sister is a clairvoyant; one other is a national history teacher; and the fourth is an eccentric wallflower, or a full-time cuckoo, as Asya would say.

Who is Asya? Lady Peacock/Siramark typed instantly.

She is the daughter of the household. A young woman with four mothers and no father. Quite a character—full of rage, satire, and wit. She'd make a good Dostoyevski character.

Armanoush wondered where on earth Baron Baghdassarian was.

Madame My-Exiled-Soul, have you talked about the genocide with anyone? Miserable-Coexistence wanted to know.

Yes, several times, but it is so difficult. The women in the house listened to my family's history with sincere interest and sorrow but that is as far as they could get. The past is another country for the Turks.

If even the women stop there, I cannot possibly be hopeful about their men. . . , the Daughter of Sappho cut in.

Actually, I haven't yet found the chance to talk to any Turkish men, Madame My-Exiled-Soul wrote back, only just now realizing this. But one of these days Asya will take me to this café where they meet regularly. There I will get to know at least some men, I guess.

Be careful if you drink with them. Alcohol brings out the worst in people, you know. That was Alex the Stoic.

I don't think Asya drinks. They're Muslims! But she sure smokes like a chimney.

Lady Peacock/Siramark wrote, In Armenia people smoke a lot too. I revisited Yerevan recently. Cigarettes are killing the nation.

Armanoush fidgeted in her chair. Where was he? Why wasn't he writing? Was he angry or cross at her? Had he been thinking about her at all? . . . She would have gone on torturing herself with questions, if it hadn't been for the next line that appeared on the shimmering screen.

Tell us, Madame My-Exiled-Soul, since you have been to Turkey, have you pondered the Janissary's Paradox?

It was him! Him! Him! Armanoush reread the two lines, after which she typed: Yes, I have. But then she didn't know what else to write. As if he had sensed her hesitation, Baron Baghdassarian continued.

It's very nice of you to get along with that family so well. And I believe you when you say they are good-hearted people, interesting in their own way. But don't you see? You are their friend only insofar as you deny your own identity. That's how it has been with the Turks all through history.

Armanoush pursed her lips, saddened. At the other end of the room, Asya tossed and turned in her bed, in the throes of what looked like a nightmare, and murmured something incomprehensible. Whatever she was saying, she repeated it many times.

All we Armenians ask for is the recognition of our loss and pain, which is the most fundamental requirement for genuine human relationships to flourish. This is what we say to the Turks: Look, we are mourning, we have been mourning for almost a century now, because we lost our loved ones, we were driven out of our homes, banished from our land; we were treated like animals and butchered like sheep. We have been denied even a decent death. Even the pain inflicted on our grandparents is not as agonizing as the systematic denial that followed.

If you say this, what will be the Turks' response? Nothing! There is only one single way of becoming friends with the Turks: to be just as uninformed and forgetful.

Since they won't join us in our recognition of the past, we are expected to join them in their ignorance of the past.

All of a sudden there was a light knock on the door, and then there were too many knocks. Armanoush slumped in her chair, her heart leaped into her throat. She impulsively turned off the computer screen. "Yes," she whispered.

The door opened gently and Auntie Banu's head popped in. She had a rosy, loosely tied scarf on her head now and a long, pasty nightgown. Awake at this hour for prayer, she had noticed the light coming from the girls' room.

With the discomfort of all the words she lacked in English etched on her face, Auntie Banu made a series of gestures, as if she too were playing charades. She shook her head, furrowed her brows, and then smilingly wagged a finger—all of which Armanoush interpreted as: "You study a lot. Don't tire yourself too much."

After that Auntie Banu shoved forward the plate in her hand

and mimicked an eating effect, both too obvious to need any interpretation. She smiled, patted Armanoush's shoulder, put the plate next to the laptop, and then left, closing the door softly behind her. On the plate were two oranges, peeled and sliced.

Turning on the screen again, Armanoush bit into a slice of orange, as she contemplated what to write back to Baron Baghdassarian.

TEN

Almonds

By the fifth day of her stay, Armanoush had discovered the morning routine of the Kazancı *konak*. Every weekday the breakfast was laid out as early as six and stayed on the table until nine thirty. During that time, the samovar continuously boiled and a new pot of tea was made every hour. Instead of everyone sitting at the table at once, different members of the family came at different intervals, depending on their work or mood or schedule. Thus, unlike dinner, which was an entirely synchronized event, breakfast on weekdays resembled a morning train that stopped at sundry stations, each time with new passengers getting on and others getting off.

Almost always it was Auntie Banu who set the table, the first to wake up, ready for the dawn prayer. She slipped out of her bed, muttering, "Indeed, it is," while the *muezzin* from the nearest mosque blared for the second time: "Prayer is better than sleep." Auntie Banu then went to the bathroom to prepare herself for prayer, washing her face, washing her arms to the elbows and feet to the ankles. The water would be chilly sometimes, but she didn't mind. *The soul needs to shiver to wake up,* she said to herself. *The soul needs to shiver.* Neither did she mind the rest of her family being fast asleep. She prayed twice as hard so that they too would be pardoned.

Thus, this morning when the *muezzin* echoed, "Allah is most great, Allah is most great," Auntie Banu, in bed, had already opened her eyes and was reaching out for her nightgown and head scarf. But unlike any other day, her body felt heavy, very heavy. The *muezzin* called: "I bear witness that there is no god but Allah." Still Auntie Banu couldn't stand up. Even when she heard, "Come to prayer," and then, "Come to the good," she could not pull half of her body out of bed. It felt as if the blood had been drained out of that part of her body, leaving behind a weighty, sluggish sack.

Prayer is better than sleep. Prayer is better than sleep.

"What is wrong with you guys, why don't you let me move?" Auntie Banu asked in a tone tinged with frustration.

The two *djinn* sitting one on each shoulder glanced at each other. "Don't ask me, ask him. He is the one who is causing mischief," said Mrs. Sweet from her right shoulder.

As the name suggests, Mrs. Sweet was a good *djinni*—one of the righteous ones. She had a kind, gleaming face, a corona around her head in the hues of plum, pink, and purple, a thin, elegant neck, and nothing other than a wisp of smoke where her neck ended and, technically, her torso had to start. Having no body, she looked like a head on a pedestal, which was perfectly all right with her. Unlike female human beings, the *djinn* women were not expected to have proportionate features.

Auntie Banu trusted Mrs. Sweet enormously, for she was not one of those renegades but a kindhearted, devout *djinni* who had converted to Islam from atheism—a malady which ran rampant among many a *djinni*. Mrs. Sweet visited mosques and shrines frequently, and was highly knowledgeable in the Holy Qur'an. Over the years she and Auntie Banu had grown very close. That, how-

ELIF SHAFAK

ever, was not the case at all with Mr. Bitter, who was created from an entirely different mold and had come from places where the wind never stopped howling. Mr. Bitter was very old, even in terms of *djinn* years. Consequently, he was far more powerful than he often made it sound, for as everybody knows too well, the older they are the more potent the *djinn* become.

The only reason Mr. Bitter was staying at the Kazancı domicile was because Auntie Banu had bound him years ago, on the last morning of her forty days of penitence. Ever since then she had had him under her control, having never taken off the talisman that held him captive. To tie up a *djinni* was no easy thing. It first and foremost required knowing his name, guessing it right—a lethal game indeed, given that if the *djinni* figured out your name before you discovered his, he would become the master and you the slave. Even when you guessed the name right and had the *djinni* under your control, you couldn't take your authority for granted, since that would be a most foolish delusion. Throughout human history, only the great Solomon had been able to surely defeat the *djinn,* armies of them, but even he had needed an extra hand from a magic iron ring. Since no one else could match the great Solomon, only a narcissistic fool could take pride in capturing a *djinni,* and Auntie Banu was anything but. Though Mr. Bitter had been serving her for more than six years now, she regarded their rapport as a temporary contract that had to be renewed every so often. Never had she treated him callously or condescendingly, for she knew that *djinn,* unlike human beings, had everlasting memories of wrong done to them. They would never forget any injustice. Like a dedicated clerk jotting down every incident to the most infinitesimal aspect, the memories of the *djinn* recorded everything, only to be evoked someday. Accordingly, Auntie Banu had always respected her captive's rights and never exploited her power.

Still, she could have used her authority in an entirely different way, asking for material gains, such as money, jewels, or fame. She hadn't. All these, she knew, were nothing but illusions, and the *djinn* happened to be particularly good in creating illusions. Besides, every sudden wealth one acquired was necessarily a wealth stolen from someone else, since there is no such thing in nature as a pure vacuum and the fates of human beings are interrelated like stitches in a latticework. Hence, all these years Auntie Banu had prudently refrained from asking for any material gains. Instead there was only one thing she had demanded from Mr. Bitter: knowledge.

Knowledge about forgotten events, unidentified individuals, property disputes, family conflicts, unburied secrets, unsolved mysteries—the basics she needed to be able to help her many clients. If a certain family had a valuable document long lost, they would come to Auntie Banu to learn its whereabouts. Or a woman who suspected being put under a vicious spell would come to her to inquire about the perpetrator of the wrongdoing. Once they had brought in a pregnant woman who had suddenly fallen ill and was getting frighteningly worse by the day. After consulting with her *djinn,* Auntie Banu told the pregnant woman to go to the fruitless lemon tree in her own garden, where she would find, in a black velvet purse, a bar of olive soap with her own fingernails jabbed into it—a spell cast by a jealous neighbor. Auntie Banu did not tell her the name of that neighbor, though, so that there would be no further grudge. In a few days news arrived that the pregnant woman had quickly recovered and was doing well. Subsequently, it was along these lines that Auntie Banu used Mr. Bitter's service to this day. Except on one occasion. Only once had she asked him a personal favor, just for herself, a most confidential question: Who was Asya's father?

Mr. Bitter gave her an answer, *the* answer, but she had indignantly, indefatigably refused to believe him, although she knew perfectly well that an enslaved *djinni* could never lie to his master. She refused to believe until her heart one day simply stopped defying what her mind had long recognized. After that Auntie Banu had never been the same. Time and again she still wondered if it would have been better for her not to know, since knowledge in this case had only brought her suffering and sorrow, the curse of the sage. And today, years after that incident, Auntie Banu was reconsidering asking another personal favor from Mr. Bitter. That was why she was so debilitated this morning; the contradictory thoughts churning inside her mind had weakened her vis-à-vis her slave, who, with each dilemma of his master, weighed heavier and heavier on her left shoulder.

Should she ask Mr. Bitter another personal question now, though she had so much regretted doing it that last time? Or perhaps it was time to end this game and take off the talisman, thus releasing the *djinni* once and for all? She could go on performing her duties as a clairvoyant with the help of Mrs. Sweet. Her powers would be somewhat lessened but so be it. Was this much not enough? One side of her warned Auntie Banu against the curse of the sage, recoiling from the harrowing agony that comes with too much knowledge. The other side of her, however, was dying to know more, ever curious, conscientious. Mr. Bitter was well aware of her dilemma and he seemed to be enjoying it, pressing her left shoulder harder with each doubt, doubling the weight of her ruminations.

"Get down from my shoulder," Auntie Banu decreed and uttered a prayer that the Qur'an advised to voice every time one had to face a dodgy *djinni*. All of a sudden compliant, Mr. Bitter jumped aside and let her stand up.

"Are you going to release me?" Mr. Bitter asked, having read her mind. "Or are you going to use my powers for some specific information?"

A whispered word escaped Auntie Banu's slightly parted lips but rather than a "yes" or "no," it sounded like a moan. She felt so small amid the cavernous vastness of earth, sky, and stars and the quandary that pulverized her soul.

"You can ask me the question you have been dying to find out ever since the American girl told you all those sad things about her family. Don't you want to learn if it is true or not? Don't you want to help her find out the truth? Or do you reserve your powers for your clients alone?" Mr. Bitter challenged, his charcoal, bulging eyes feverishly triumphant. Then he added, suddenly placid, "I can tell you, I am old enough to know. I was there."

"Stop it!" Auntie Banu exclaimed, almost shrieking. She felt her stomach lurch and the burn of sour bile in her throat as she snapped, "I don't want to learn. I am not curious. I regret the day I asked you about Asya's father. Oh God, I wish I hadn't. What is knowledge good for if you cannot change anything? It is venom that handicaps you forever. You can't vomit it up and you can't die. I don't want that to happen again. . . . Besides, what do you know?"

Why she had blurted out that last question, she couldn't fathom. For she knew too well that if she wanted to learn about Armanoush's past, Mr. Bitter would be the right one to ask, since he was a *gulyabani,* the most treacherous among all the *djinn,* yet also the most knowledgeable when it came to traumatic ends.

Ill-omened soldiers, ambushed and massacred miles away from their home, wanderers frozen to death in the mountains, plague victims exiled deep into the desert, travelers robbed and slaughtered by bandits, explorers lost in the middle of nowhere, convicted felons shipped to meet their death on some remote island . . . the *gulyabani* had seen them all. They were there when entire battalions were exterminated in bloody battlefields, villages were doomed to starve or caravans reduced to ashes by enemy fire. Likewise, they were there when the Byzantine emperor Heraclius's huge army was crushed by the Muslims at the Battle of Yarmuk; or when Berber Tarik thundered to his soldiers, "Behind you is the sea, before you, the enemy! Oh my warriors, whither would you flee?" and with that they invaded Visigothic Spain, killing everyone on their way; or when Charles, thereafter named Martel, slew 300,000 Arabs in the Battle of Tours; or when the Assassins, intoxicated with hashish, killed the illustrious vizier Nizam-al-Mulk and spawned terror until the Mongolian Hulagu destroyed their fortress, along with everything else. The *gulyabani* had witnessed firsthand each and every one of these calamities. They were particularly notorious for stalking those lost in the desert with no food and water. Whenever, wherever someone died leaving no gravestone behind, they appeared beside the corpse. Should they feel the need, they could disguise themselves as plants, rocks, or animals, particularly vultures. They would spy on calamities, observing the scene from the side or above, though it is also known that occasionally they would haunt caravans, steal whatever food the destitute might need to survive, scare the pilgrims on their holy journey, attack processions, or whisper a terrifying tune of death into the ears of those sentenced to the galleys or those forced to walk a death march. They were the spectators of those moments in time in which humans had no testimony, no written record left behind.

The *gulyabani* were the ugly witnesses of the ugliness human beings were capable of inflicting on one another. Consequently, Auntie Banu reasoned, if Armanoush's family had really been forced on a death march in 1915, as she claimed, Mr. Bitter would surely know about it.

"Aren't you going to ask me anything?" Mr. Bitter mouthed as he sat on the edge of the bed, fully enjoying Auntie Banu's quandary. "I was a vulture," he continued bitterly, the only tone in which he knew to talk. "I saw it all. I watched them as they walked and walked and walked, women and children. I flew over them, drawing circles in the blue sky, waiting for them to fall on their knees."

"Shut up!" Auntie Banu bawled. "Shut up! I don't want to know. Don't forget who the master is."

"Yes, master." Mr. Bitter shrank back. "Your wish is my command and thus it shall be as long as you wear that talisman. But should you want to learn what happened to that girl's family in 1915, just let me know. My memory can be yours, master."

Auntie Banu sat straight up in her bed, biting her lips hard to look adamant, having no intentions of showing weakness to Mr.

Bitter. As she tried to be resilient, the air started to reek of dust and mold, as if the room had fallen into a state of putrefaction. Either the present moment was quickly decaying into a residue of time or the decay of the past was seeping into the present. The inner gates of time awaited being unbolted. To preserve them locked and everything in its place, Auntie Banu took out the Holy Qur'an, which she kept inside a pearly cover in a drawer in her bedside table. She opened a page randomly and read: "I am closer to you than your jugular vein" (50:16).

"Allah." She sighed. "You are closer to me than my jugular vein. Help me out of this dilemma. Either grant me the bliss of the ignorant or give me the strength to bear the knowledge. Whichever you choose shall make me grateful, but please don't make me powerless and knowledgeable at the same time."

On that prayer Auntie Banu slipped out of bed, put on her nightgown, and with soft, swift steps tiptoed to the bathroom to get ready for her morning prayer. She checked the clock on the buffet inside, seven forty-five. Had she been in bed so long, arguing with Mr. Bitter, arguing with her conscience? Hurriedly she washed her face, hands, and feet, walked back to her room wearing her gauzy prayer head scarf, spread her little rug, and stood to pray.

If Auntie Banu had been late to set the breakfast table this morning, Armanoush would be one of the last to realize it. Having remained online till late, she had overslept, and would have liked to have slept in more. She tossed, turned, pulled the blanket up and down over her chest, doing her best to sink back into sleep. She opened one droopy eye and saw Asya at her desk reading a book and listening to music with her headphones on.

"What are you listening to?" Armanoush asked loudly.

"Huh?" Asya shouted, "Johnny Cash!"

"Oh, sure! What are you reading?"

"Irrational Man: A Study in Existential Philosophy," the same loud, steady voice replied.

"Isn't that a bit irrational too? How can you listen to music and concentrate on existential philosophy at the same time?"

"They square perfectly," Asya remarked. "Johnny Cash and existential philosophy, they both probe the human soul to see what's inside, and unhappy with their findings, they both leave it open!"

Before Armanoush could ruminate on that, someone knocked on the door calling both girls to catch the last train to breakfast.

They found the table set just for the two of them, everyone else having already finished their breakfast. Grandma and Petite-Ma had gone to visit a relative, Auntie Cevriye to school, Auntie Zeliha to the tattoo parlor, and Auntie Feride was in the bathroom dyeing her hair ginger. And the only auntie in the living room now looked strangely grumpy.

"What's the problem, have your *djinn* dumped you?" Asya asked.

Instead of answering, Auntie Banu headed to the kitchen. In the following two hours, she reorganized the cereal jars lined on the shelves, mopped the floors, baked raisin-walnut cookies, washed the plastic fruits on the counter, and painstakingly sponged an ossified mustard stain at the corner of the stove. When she finally came back to the living room, she found the two girls still at the breakfast table, scoffing at every single scene in *The Malediction of the Ivy of Infatuation*—the longest-running soap opera in Turkish TV history. But instead of feeling resentful for seeing them mock something she valued, Auntie Banu was only surprised—surprised to realize that she had completely forgotten about it, missing her favorite program for the first time in years. The only other time she had missed it was years ago during her period of penitence. Even then, may Allah forgive her, she had thought about *The Malediction of the Ivy of Infatuation*, wondering what was happening in the show while she repented. But now that there was no reason to miss it, how could she? Was her mind so preoccupied? Wouldn't she know if she were so confused?

Suddenly, Auntie Banu noticed the two girls eyeing her from their chairs, and felt uncomfortable, perhaps because she also realized that with the soap opera now over, they could be rummaging around for some new targets of ridicule.

But Asya seemed to have something else in mind. "Armanoush was wondering if you could read the tarot cards for her?"

"Why would she want that?" Auntie Banu said quietly. "Tell her she is a beautiful, intelligent young woman with a bright future. Only those who don't have a future need to learn about their future."

"Then read some roasted hazelnuts for her," Asya insisted, skipping the translation.

"I don't do that anymore," said Auntie Banu, contritely. "It didn't prove such a good method after all."

"You see, my aunt is a positivistic psychic. She scientifically measures the margin of error in each divination," Asya said to Armanoush in English but then switched back to a serious tone in Turkish. "Well then, read our coffee cups."

"Now that's another thing," Auntie Banu agreed, incapable of saying no to coffee cups. "*Those* I can read anytime."

Coffees were made, Armanoush's with no sugar and Asya's with plenty, although the latter did not want to have her cup read. It was caffeine that she was after, not her fate. When Armanoush finished her coffee, the saucer was placed on top of the coffee cup, held tight, and moved around in three horizontal circles; the coffee cup was then turned upside down over the saucer, letting the coffee grinds slowly descend to form patterns. When the bottom of the cup had cooled off, it was flipped over and Auntie Banu started to read the patterns left in the coffee cup, moving her gaze clockwise.

"I can see a very worried woman here."

"It must be my mother." Armanoush sighed.

"She is deeply worried. She thinks about you all the time, loves you very much, but her soul is stressed. Then there is a city with red bridges. There is water, sea, wind, and . . . mist. There I see a family, many heads—look at this, lots of people, lots of love and caring, lots of food too. . . ."

Armanoush nodded, a little embarrassed at being found out like this.

"Then . . ." Auntie Banu said, skipping the bad news settled at the bottom of the cup—flowers soon to be scattered on a grave, far far away. She rotated the coffee cup between her plump fingers. Her next words came out louder than she intended, startling them all. "Oh, there is a young man who cares deeply for you. But why is he behind a veil? . . . Something like a veil."

Armanoush's heart skipped a beat.

"Can that be a computer screen?" Asya asked mischievously as Sultan the Fifth hopped onto her lap.

"I don't see computers in my coffee grounds," Auntie Banu objected. She didn't like to incorporate technology in her psychic universe.

Auntie Banu solemnly paused, turned the cup an inch, and then paused again. Her face looked troubled now. "I see a girl your age. She has curly hair, black, pure black . . . an ample bosom. . . ."

"Thanks, auntie, I got the message." Asya chuckled. "But you don't have to place your relatives in every cup you read, that's called nepotism."

Auntie Banu blinked, completely deadpan.

"There is a rope here, a thick, strong rope with a noose at one end, like a lasso. You two girls are going to be attached to each other with a strong bond. . . . I see a spiritual bond. . . ."

To the girls' disappointment Auntie Banu said nothing further. She stopped reading, put the coffee cup on the saucer, and filled it with cold water so that the patterns jumbled and vanished before anyone else, good or bad, had a chance to peek inside. That was the

THE BASTARD OF ISTANBUL

one good thing about coffee-cup reading: Unlike the fate written by Allah, that written by coffee could always be washed away.

On the way to Café Kundera, they took the ferry so that Armanoush could see the city in all its vastness and splendor. Like the ferry itself, its passengers too had an air of lassitude, which was quickly swept away by the sudden wind when the huge vessel veered into the azure sea. The hum of the crowd inside amplified for a full minute, and then it dwindled to a monotonous drone to accompany other sounds: the clatter of the outboard motor, the splash of the waves, the shrieks of the seagulls. Armanoush noticed with delight that the lazy seagulls on the shore were coming with them. Almost everyone on the ferry was feeding them with morsels of *simit*—sesame-seed ring breads being a treat these carnivorous birds found irresistible.

A classically dressed, portly woman and her teenage son sat on the bench across from them, side by side but worlds apart. From her face Armanoush could tell the woman was no big fan of public transportation, despising the masses, and if possible would have thrown all of the poorly dressed passengers into the sea. Hidden behind thick-rimmed glasses, the son looked half embarrassed by his mother's standoffish ways. *They are like Flannery O'Connor characters,* Armanoush thought to herself.

"Tell me more about this Baron," Asya said out of the blue. "What does he look like? How old is he?"

Armanoush blushed. Within the vivid light of the winter sun glowing from among thick clouds, her face was that of an enamored young woman. "I don't know. I've never met him in person. We're cyber friends, you see. I admire his intellect and passion, I guess."

"Don't you want to meet him someday?"

"Yes and no," Armanoush confessed after purchasing a *simit* from the small but crowded buffet inside. She ripped a piece off and with the morsel in her hand leaned against the rail surrounding the deck, waiting for a seagull to approach.

"You don't have to wait for them to appear." Asya smiled. "Just toss a piece up in the air and a seagull will catch it instantly."

Armanoush did as told. A seagull materialized from the empty sky and bolted the treat down.

"I am dying to learn more about him, and yet deep down, I don't want to meet him ever. When you date someone the magic perishes. I couldn't bear for that to happen with him. He's too important to me. Dating and sex are just another story, so knotty. . . ."

Now they were entering that murky zone guarded by the three untouchables. A good sign indeed, indicating that they were drawing closer to each other.

"Magic!" Asya said. "Who needs magic? The tales of Layla and Majnun, Yusuf and Zulaykha, the Moth and the Candle, or the Nightingale and the Rose. . . . Ways of loving from a distance, mating without even touching—*Amor platonicus*! The ladder of love one is expected to climb higher and higher, elating the Self and the Other. Plato clearly regards any actual physical contact as corrupt and ignoble because he thinks the true goal of Eros is beauty. Is there no beauty in sex? Not according to Plato. He is after 'more sublime pursuits.' But if you ask me, I think Plato's problem, like those of many others, was that he never got splendidly laid."

Armanoush looked at her friend, amazed. "I thought you liked philosophy . . . " she stammered without quite knowing why she'd said it.

"I admire philosophy," Asya conceded. "But that doesn't necessarily mean I agree with the philosophers."

"So should I assume you are not a big fan of *Amor platonicus*?!"

Now *that* was a piece of information Asya preferred to keep to herself, not because the question itself was unanswerable, but because she was afraid of the implications of her answer. Armanoush being so polite and proper, Asya did not want to intimidate her. How on earth could she now tell Armanoush that, though only nineteen, she had known many men's hands and did not feel a speck of guilt for it? Besides, how could she ever reveal the truth without giving the wrong impression to an outsider about "the chastity of Turkish girls"?

This kind of "national responsibility" was utterly foreign to Asya Kazancı. Never before had she felt part of a collectivity and she had no intention of being so now or in the future. Yet here she was accomplishing a pretty good impersonation of someone else, someone who had gotten patriotic overnight. How could she now step outside her national identity and be her pure, sinning self? Could she tell Armanoush that deep in her heart she believed only when you had sex with a man, could you really be sure that he was the right person for you; that only in bed did people's most imperceptible, innate complexes surface; and that no matter what people assumed all the time, sex was in fact far more sensual than physical. How could she reveal she had had numerous relations in the past, way too many, as if to take revenge on men, but the revenge of what, she still couldn't tell. She had had many boyfriends, sometimes simultaneously, polygamous affairs that had always ended in heartbreak, accumulating a heap of secrets she had neatly kept away from the frontiers of the Kazancı domicile. Could she divulge these? Would Armanoush understand without being judgmental; could she really, truly see into Asya's soul from the echelons of that sterile tower of hers?

Could Asya confess to her that once she had tried to commit suicide, a nasty experience from which she had derived two basic lessons: that swallowing your lunatic aunt's pills was not the right way to go about doing this and that if you wanted to kill yourself you'd better have a rationale ready in hand in case you survived, since "WHY?" would be the one question you would hear from all sides. Could she further confess that to this day she hadn't been able to fathom the answer to that question, other than recalling being too young too foolish too furious too intense for the universe in which she lived? Would any of this make sense to Armanoush?

Could she then disclose that recently she had made some progress toward stability and tranquillity, since she now had a monogamous relationship, except that it was with a married man twice her age whom she met every now and then to share sex, a joint, and refuge from loneliness? How could she tell Armanoush that, if truth be told, she was a bit of a disaster?

Thus, instead of replying, Asya pulled a Walkman out of her knapsack and asked permission to listen to a song, just one song. A dose of Cash was what she needed right now. She offered one of the headphones to Armanoush. Armanoush accepted the headphone warily and asked: "Which Johnny Cash song are we going to listen to?"

" 'Dirty Old Egg-Suckin' Dog!' "

"Is that the name of the song? I don't know that one."

"Yup," Asya said gravely. "Here it comes. Listen . . ."

And the song started, first a listless prelude, then country melodies fusing with seagull shrieks and Turkish vocalizations in the background.

As she listened, Armanoush was too stunned by the dissonance between the lyrics and the surrounding setting to enjoy the song. It dawned on her that this song was just like Asya—full of contradictions and temper, utterly disharmonious with her surroundings; sensitive, reactive, and ready to explode at any time. As she leaned back, the murmur in the background dwindled into a tedious humming, pieces of *simit* disappeared in the air, a touch of enchantment wafted with the breeze, the ferry glided smoothly, and the ghosts of all the fish that had once lived in these waters swam with them in a sea of dense, viscous azure.

When the song was over they had already reached the shore. Some of the passengers jumped off before the ferry reached the dock. Armanoush watched this acrobatic performance with amazement, admiring the many talents the Istanbulites had acquired to cope with the pace of the city.

Fifteen minutes later the shaky, wooden door of Café Kundera opened with a strident tinkle and in walked Asya Kazancı, wearing a mauve hippie dress, with her guest, in a pair of jeans and a plain sweater. Asya found the usual group sitting in its usual place with its usual attitude.

"Hello, everyone!" Asya chirped. "This is Amy, a friend from America."

"Hello, Amy!" they greeted in unison. "Welcome to Istanbul!"

"Is this your first time here?" someone asked. And then the others started to inquire: "Do you like the city? Do you like the food? How long will you stay? Are you planning to come back? . . ."

Though they welcomed her warmly, they were also quick to go back to their standard posture of unremitting languor, since nothing could upset the sluggish rhythm that prevailed in Café Kundera. Those in need of speed and variation could simply go out, for there was plenty of that on the streets. Here it was about mandatory indolence and eternal recurrence. This place was about fixations, repetitions, and obsessions; it was for those who didn't want to have anything to do with the bigger picture, if there indeed was such a thing.

During the brief pauses between questions, Armanoush scrutinized the place and the people, intuiting where the name of the café came from. The constant tension between vulgar reality and treacherous fantasy, the notion of the *outside people* versus *us people inside,* the dreamlike quality of the place, and finally, the sullen expression on the men's faces, as if they were desperately ruminating on what to choose—either to carry the weight of disheveled love affairs or become half real with lightness—everything evoked a scene out of a Kundera novel. They, however, didn't and couldn't know this, being too enveloped, too much a part of it, like fish that couldn't possibly comprehend the immensity of the ocean in which they swam from the blurry lens of the waters surrounding them.

Likening the café to a Kundera scene only doubled Armanoush's interest. She noticed many other things, including the fact that everyone at the table spoke English, although with an accent and grammatical flaws. Overall they seemed to have no trouble switching from Turkish to English. At first Armanoush attributed such ease to their self-confidence, but by the end of the day she suspected that the facilitating factor might be less their confidence in their English than their lack of confidence in any language whatsoever. They acted and talked as if no matter what they said or how they said it, one could not really fully express the innermost self and, in the end, language was only a reeking carcass of hollow words long rotten inside.

Armanoush also noticed that the overwhelming majority of the framed road pictures on the walls depicted either Western countries or exotic places; few had anything to do with what might fall in between. Having made this observation, she didn't quite know how to interpret it. Perhaps the flight of the imagination here was oriented toward either moving to the West or fleeing into an exotic land far away.

A swarthy, slim street vendor sneaked in, almost hiding himself from the waiters, who might have chased him away. The man carried a huge tray of unpeeled yellow almonds on cubes of ice.

"Almonds!" he exclaimed, as if it were somebody's name he was desperately looking for.

"Over here!" the Dipsomaniac Cartoonist exclaimed, as if responding to his name. Almonds would go perfectly with what he was drinking at the moment: beer. By this time he had already openly quit Alcoholics Anonymous, less on grounds of addiction than on grounds of earnestness, seeing no reason why he should call himself an alcoholic when he wasn't one. It didn't sound sincere to him. Instead, he had decided to become his own supervisor. Today, for instance, he'd drink only three beers. Having already guzzled down one beer, there were two more to go. After that, he'd stop. Yes, he assured everyone, he could manage such discipline without someone's pitiful professional guidance. With that kind of decisiveness, he bought four ladlefuls of almonds and piled them in the middle of the table so that everyone could easily reach them.

Armanoush's thoughts, in the meantime, were busy. She watched the lanky, lost-looking waiter take everyone's orders and was somewhat surprised to see so many people drinking. She remembered her blanket comment the other night on Muslims and alcohol. Should she now mention the Turks' fondness for alcohol to her pals in the Café Constantinopolis? How much of what was happening here should she reveal to them?

A few minutes later, the waiter returned with a large glass of frothy beer for the Dipsomaniac Cartoonist and a carafe of dry red wine for everyone else. As he poured the dark crimson liquid into elegant wine glasses, Armanoush took the opportunity to observe the people around the table. She figured that the edgy woman sitting next to and yet miles away from the bulky man with the bulbous nose must be his wife. One by one she examined the Dipsomaniac Cartoonist's wife and the Dipsomaniac Cartoonist, as well as the Closeted-Gay Columnist, the Exceptionally Untalented Poet, the Nonnationalist Scenarist of Ultranationalist Movies, and . . . she couldn't help staring a bit longer at the young, sexy brunette across from her, who didn't look like part of the group but seemed, if anything, awkwardly attached to it. Definitely a cell phone person, the brunette kept toying with her pink, glittery phone, flipping it open for no apparent reason, pressing on this button or that, sending an SMS or receiving one, absorbed by the small device. From time to time, she inched toward the bearded man next to her and nuzzled his ear. Evidently, she was the *new* girlfriend of the Nonnationalist Scenarist of Ultranationalist Movies.

"I had a tattoo done yesterday."

The words were so out of context that Armanoush could not instantly grasp if they were addressed to anyone, let alone to her. Yet, either out of sheer boredom or in an attempt to befriend the only other recent addition to the group, the new girlfriend of the

Nonnationalist Scenarist of Ultranationalist Movies was talking to her: "Would you like to see it?"

It was a wild orchid, as red as hell, snaking around her belly button.

"That's cool," Armanoush said.

The woman grinned, pleased. "Thank you," she said as she patted her lips with a napkin even though she hadn't eaten anything.

In the meantime, Asya too had been observing the woman, albeit with a far more disapproving gaze. Having met a new female, as usual, she could do one of two things: either wait to see when she would start hating her or take the shortcut and hate her right away. She chose the latter.

Asya leaned backward and picked up her glass between thumb and forefinger, observing the red liquid. Even when she started to talk she didn't remove her gaze from the glass.

"In point of fact, when we come to recall how long-standing the practice of tattooing is . . . " Asya said, but didn't finish her sentence. Instead she started a new one. "At the beginning of the 1990s, explorers found a well-preserved body in the Italian Alps. It was more than five thousand years old. It had fifty-seven tattoos on its body. The world's oldest tattoos!"

"Really?" Armanoush asked. "I wonder what kinds of tattoos were done back then?"

"Often they tattooed animals, the ones that were their totems . . . probably donkeys, deer, owls, mountain rams—and snakes, of course, I'm sure snakes were always on demand."

"Wow, more than five thousand years old!" the new girlfriend of the Nonnationalist Scenarist of Ultranationalist Movies enthused.

"But I guess he didn't have a tattoo on his belly button!" he cooed back to her. And they laughed together, followed by a kiss and a cuddle.

There were a few tables scattered outside on the sidewalk. A grim couple settled themselves at one of them, and then another couple, with stressed-out, serious urban faces. Armanoush watched their gestures with curiosity, likening them to characters from a Fitzgerald novel.

"We somehow tend to associate tattoos with originality, inventiveness, and even modernism. In point of fact, having tattoos around your belly button is one of the oldest customs in world history. Let me remind you that by the end of the nineteenth century a mummified body was discovered by a group of Western archaeologists. It belonged to an Egyptian princess. Her name was Amunet. And guess what? She had a tattoo. Guess where?" Now Asya turned toward the scenarist and looked him directly in the eye. "On her belly button!"

The scenarist blinked, puzzled by so much information. His new girlfriend seemed just as impressed when she asked: "How do you know all this?"

"Her mother operates a tattoo parlor," interjected the Dipsomaniac Cartoonist without tearing his eyes from Asya. He sank into his chair, resisting the urge to kiss her angry lips, resisting the urge to ask for another beer without ado, resisting the urge to stop impersonating the man he was not.

His mood went unnoticed by all but one. Armanoush detected the warmth in his eyes when he looked at Asya and sensed he might be in love with her.

Asya meanwhile seemed to be in an entirely different state of mind, getting ready to launch another attack on the new girlfriend of the Nonnationalist Scenarist of Ultranationalist Movies. Leaning forward with a hard look on her face, she said: "Tattoos can be very dangerous though."

Asya waited a few seconds for the word *dangerous* to sink in. "The instruments used in the process should be thoroughly disinfected, but the truth is you can never be a hundred percent sure about the risk of contamination, which, of course, is a serious issue given that the most common technique of tattooing is inserting ink into the skin via needles. . . ."

She had uttered the word *needles* in such a menacing way that everyone at the table felt the chill. Only the Dipsomaniac Cartoonist watched her with an impish sparkle in his eyes, fully enjoying the show.

"The needle is repeatedly driven in and out of the skin with a rhythm that approximates three thousand times a minute," Asya continued. She took out a cigarette from her pack, repeatedly pushing it back and forth as if illustrating the act, until she finally lighted it. The new girlfriend of the Nonnationalist Scenarist of Ultranationalist Movies tried to smile at the overtly sexual gesture, but something in Asya's eyes stopped her halfway through.

"Blood poisoning and hepatitis are only two of the many fatal diseases you can contract at a tattoo parlor. The artist needs to break open a new sterile package each time and wash his hands with hot water and soap, and on top of that use sanitizing liquids and wear latex gloves. . . . Theoretically, of course. I mean, come on, who would bother with all that fuss?"

"He did all that. The needles were new and his hands were clean," the new girlfriend remarked in Turkish with a tinge of panic.

Asya did not yield, continuing in English. "Yeah, good. Unfortunately that's not enough. How about the ink? Did you know that not only the needles but the ink has to be renewed each time? You have to use fresh ink for each session, for each customer."

"The ink . . ." Now the new girlfriend looked really concerned.

"Right, the ink!" Asya decreed with certitude. "There are many infections that can surface after a tattoo operation just because of the ink. One of the most common ones is *Staphylococcus aureus,* which sadly"—she frowned—"is known to cause serious cardiac damage."

Though she tried not to lose her cool, upon hearing this piece of information the color drained from the face of the new girlfriend of the Nonnationalist Scenarist of Ultranationalist Movies. Her cell phone beeped just then but she didn't even look at it.

"Had you consulted a physician before getting it done?" Asya asked with a concerned expression that she hoped would prove persuasive.

"No, I didn't," the new girlfriend of the Nonnationalist Scenarist of Ultranationalist Movies said. Her face now turned grave, etching new lines around her lips and eyes.

"Oh, really? Well, never mind, don't worry." Asya flung up her hands. "Almost certainly nothing bad will happen."

And with that she leaned back. The Dipsomaniac Cartoonist and Armanoush smiled, but none of the others reacted in any way.

Deciding to join the game, the Dipsomaniac Cartoonist turned to Asya with sly amusement and asked, "But she can have it removed if she wanted to, right? It is possible to have it removed, isn't it?"

"It's possible," Asya instantly replied. "However, the entire process is painful and daunting at best. You can choose one of three methods: surgery, laser treatment, or skin peeling."

With that Asya took an almond from the pile and peeled off the skin. Everyone at the table, even Armanoush, couldn't help but stare at the almond with horror. Pleased with her audience's reaction, Asya tossed the peeled almond into her mouth and chewed heartily. The eyes of the new girlfriend of the Nonnationalist Scenarist of Ultranationalist Movies grew wide as she watched Asya chew the almond.

"I personally would never recommend the third. Not that the others are any better. You need to find a good—a *very* good—dermatologist or cosmetic surgeon. It costs a lot, but what can you do? Each visit is a ton of money and you need to pay for several visits. Even when the tattoo is removed, there will be a visible scar left behind, not to mention skin discoloration. If you want to get rid of that, you'll need another cosmetic surgery. Even then there is no hundred-percent guarantee."

Armanoush pinched herself not to laugh.

"Well, why don't we drink?" the Dipsomaniac Cartoonist's

wife broke in with a tired smile. "And what better reason do we have to drink than Mr. Tiptoe? What was his name? . . . Cecche?"

"Cecchetti," Asya corrected her, still lamenting the day she had been intoxicated enough to give the group a speech on ballet history.

"Yes, yes, Cecchetti." The Exceptionally Untalented Poet chuckled and explained to Armanoush, "If it weren't for him, ballet dancers wouldn't have to tire themselves out walking on their toes, you know?"

"What was he thinking?" someone added, and then everybody laughed.

"So tell us, Amy, where do you come from?" the Exceptionally Untalented Poet now asked Armanoush over the customary muttering in the café.

"Actually, Amy is short for Armanoush," Asya interjected, still in a provocative mood. "She is Armenian American!"

Now the word *Armenian* wouldn't surprise anyone at Café Kundera, but *Armenian American* was a different story. *Armenian Armenian* was no problem—similar culture, similar problems—but *Armenian American* meant someone who despised the Turks. All heads turned toward Armanoush now. Their stares revealed interest tainted with alarm, as if she were a flamboyant gift box with unknown content. Inside the box there could be a present as exquisite as the outside, or there could be a bomb. Armanoush squared her shoulders as if steeling herself against a blow, but, being regulars at Café Kundera for so many years, the group had too deeply absorbed the sluggish characteristic of the place to get excited for long.

Asya, however, did not let the excitement wane. "Did you know that Armanoush's family was Istanbulite?" she said in between chomping on two almonds.

"They were made to suffer all sorts of pain in 1915. Many died during the deportations—died of hunger, fatigue, brutality. . . ."

Pure silence. No comment. Asya pulled the strings a bit tighter under the concerned gaze of the Dipsomaniac Cartoonist.

THE BASTARD OF ISTANBUL

"But her great-grandfather was killed before all that, mainly because"—Asya turned to face Armanoush, though her next statement was directed less at her than at the members of the group—"he was an intellectual!" She sipped her wine slowly. "The thing is, the Armenian intelligentsia were the first to be executed so that the community would be left without its leading brains."

It didn't take long for the silence to be broken.

"That didn't happen." The Nonnationalist Scenarist of Ultranationalist Movies shook his head vigorously. "We never heard of anything like that." He took a puff on his pipe and amid the swirling smoke looked Armanoush in the eye, his voice now dwindling into a compassionate whisper. "Look, I am very sorry for your family, I offer you my condolences. But you have to understand it was a time of war. People died on both sides. Do you have any idea how many Turks have died in the hands of Armenian rebels? Did you ever think about the other side of the story? I'll bet you didn't! How about the suffering of the Turkish families? It is all tragic but we need to understand that 1915 was not 2005. Times were different back then. It was not even a Turkish state back then, it was the Ottoman Empire, for God's sake. The premodern era and its premodern tragedies."

Armanoush pressed her lips together so hard that they paled. She had so many counterarguments, she didn't quite know where to begin. How she wished Baron Baghdassarian were here and could hear all this.

Armanoush's pause was instantly filled by Asya's interruption: "Oh yeah? I thought you weren't nationalist!"

"I'm not!" the Nonnationalist Scenarist of Ultranationalist Movies exclaimed, raising his voice a couple of octaves. To keep his temper, he began to stroke his beard. "But I do respect historical truths."

"People have been brainwashed," his new girlfriend rallied in an attempt to both support her lover and take revenge for the tattoo discussion.

Asya and Armanoush now exchanged looks. Within that fleeting moment the waiter appeared again and replaced the empty carafe of wine with a new one.

"Well, how do you know? Maybe you too have been brainwashed," Armanoush said slowly.

"Yeah, what do you know?" Asya echoed. "What do we know about 1915? How many books have you read on this topic? How many controversial standpoints did you compare and contrast? What research, which literature? . . . I bet you've read nothing! But you are so convinced. Aren't we just swallowing what's given to us? Capsules of information, capsules of misinformation. Every day we swallow a handful."

"I agree, the capitalist system nullifies our feelings and curtails our imagination," the Exceptionally Untalented Poet broke in. "This system is responsible for the disenchantment of the world. Only poetry can save us."

"Look," the Nonnationalist Scenarist of Ultranationalist Movies replied. "Unlike many other people in Turkey, I have done a lot of research on this issue due to my job. I write scenarios for historical movies. I read history all the time. So I talk like this not because I have heard it elsewhere or because I have been misinformed. Quite the opposite! I talk as someone who has done meticulous research on the topic." He paused to take a sip of his wine. "The claims of the Armenians are based on exaggeration and distortion. Come on, some go as far as claiming that we killed two million Armenians. No historian in his right mind would take that seriously."

"Even one is too many," Asya snapped back.

The waiter rematerialized with a new carafe in his hand and a concerned expression on his face. He made a gesture to the Dipsomaniac Cartoonist: "Do you want to keep ordering?" In return he was given the thumbs-up. Having long finished his three beers and loyal to his decision to have only that amount, the Dipsomaniac Cartoonist had by this time switched to wine.

"Let me tell you something, Asya," the Nonnationalist Scenarist of Ultranationalist Movies said while refilling his glass. "You know about the infamous Salem witch trials, don't you? The interesting thing is that almost all the women accused of witchcraft had made similar confessions, shown common symptoms, including fainting at the same time. . . . Were they lying? No! Were they pretending? No! They were suffering from collective hysteria."

"What does that mean?" Armanoush asked, barely able to control her anger.

"Yeah, what the hell does that mean?" Asya chimed in, without controlling her anger.

The scenarist allowed a tired smile to cross his grim features. "There is such a thing as collective hysteria. I'm not saying that the Armenians are hysterical or anything, don't get me wrong. It is a scientifically known fact that collectivities are capable of manipulating their individual members' beliefs, thoughts, and even bodily reactions. You keep hearing a certain story over and over again, and the next thing you know you have internalized the narrative. From that moment on it ceases to be someone else's story. It is not even a story anymore, but reality, *your* reality!"

"It's like being under a spell," remarked the Exceptionally Untalented Poet.

Running a hand through her hair, Asya slouched back in her chair, puffed some smoke, and said, "Let me tell you what hysteria is. All those scripts you've penned thus far, the whole series of *Timur the Lionheart*—the muscular, herculean Turk running from one adventure to another against the idiot Byzantine. That's what I call hysteria. And once you make it into a TV show and make millions *internalize* your awful message, it becomes collective hysteria."

This time it was the Closeted-Gay Columnist who broke in. "Yes, all those vulgarly macho Turkish heroes you created to ridicule the effeminacy of the enemy are signs of authoritarianism."

"What's wrong with you people?" the Nonnationalist Scenarist of Ultranationalist Movies asked, his lower lip quivering in rage.

"You guys know so well I do not believe in that crap. You know those shows are just for entertainment."

Armanoush did her very best to change the mood. Though she knew Baron Baghdassarian would strongly disagree, she believed increasing the tension did not help the recognition of the genocide. "That frame over there," she pointed to the wall. "You know that carroty-framed road picture over there is from Arizona. That's a road my mom and I used to take many times when I was a kid."

"Arizona," the Exceptionally Untalented Poet muttered, and sighed as if the name implied a utopialand for him, some sort of Shangri-la.

But Asya was not going to let it go. "But that's the thing," she said. "What you have been doing is even worse. If you believed in what you were doing, if you had the foggiest faith in those movies, I would still question your standpoint, but at least not your sincerity. You write those screenplays for the masses. You write and sell and earn huge amounts of money. And then you come here, take cover in this intellectual café, and join us to mock those movies. Hypocrisy!"

Color drained from the scenarist's face, leaving his expression hard and his eyes almost glacial. "Who do you think you are to tell me about hypocrisy, Miss Bastard? Why don't you go and rummage around for your *papa* instead of plaguing me here?"

He reached for his wine glass but there actually was no need since by this time a glass of wine was reaching out for him: The Dipsomaniac Cartoonist jumped to his feet, grabbed a wine glass, and threw it at the scenarist, just missing. The glass hit a frame on the wall, spilling wine all over, but surprisingly it did not break. Having failed to hit his target, the Dipsomaniac Cartoonist rolled up his sleeves.

Though barely half the Dipsomaniac Cartoonist's size, and just as drunk, the Nonnationalist Scenarist of Ultranationalist Movies managed to dodge the first blow. He then quickly retreated to a corner, keeping an eye on the exit.

He didn't see it coming. The Closeted-Gay Columnist bolted from his chair and darted to the corner with the carafe in his hand. In next to no time the scenarist was on the floor with blood oozing from his forehead. Pressing a bloody napkin to his head like a war casualty, he stared first at the columnist, next at the cartoonist, and then at an oblique angle.

But after all, Café Kundera is a comfy, dreary intellectual café where the rhythm of life is, for better or worse, never disrupted. This is no place for a drunken brawl. Even before the scenarist's forehead stopped bleeding, everyone else at the café had gone back to what they were doing before the interruption—some grimacing, some chatting over wine or coffee, and some others drifting into the framed photos on the walls.

ELEVEN

Dried Apricots

I t is almost dawn, a short step away from that uncanny threshold between nighttime and daylight. It is the only time in which it is still possible to find solace in dreams and yet too late to build them anew.

If there is an eye in the seventh sky, a Celestial Gaze watching each and every one from way up high, He would have had to keep Istanbul under surveillance for quite some time to get a sense of who did what behind closed doors and who, if any, uttered profanities. To the one in the skies, this city must look like a scintillating pattern of speckled glows in all directions, like a firecracker going off amid thick darkness. Right now the urban pattern glowing here is in the hues of orange, ginger, and ochre. It is a configuration of sparkles, each dot a light lit by someone awake at this hour. From where the Celestial Gaze is situated, from that high above, all these sporadically lit bulbs must seem in perfect harmony, constantly flickering, as if coding a cryptic message to God.

Apart from the scattered twinkles, it is still densely dark in Istanbul. Whether along the grimy, narrow streets snaking the oldest quarters, in the modern apartment buildings cramming the newly built districts, or throughout the fancy suburbs, people are fast asleep. All but some.

Some Istanbulites have, as usual, awakened earlier than others. The *imams* all around the city, for instance; the young and the old, the mellow-voiced and the not-so-mellow-voiced, the *imams* of the copious mosques are the first ones to wake up, ready to call the believers to morning prayer. Then there are the *simit* vendors. They too are awake, headed to their respective bakeries to pick up the crispy sesame bagels they will be selling all day long. Accordingly, the bakers are awake too. Most of them get only a few hours of sleep before they start work, while others never sleep at night. Every day without exception, the bakers heat their ovens in the middle of the night, so that before dawn, the bakeries in the city are thick with the delicious smell of bread.

The cleaning ladies are also awake. These women, of all ages, get up early to take at least two or three different buses to arrive at the houses of the well-off, where they will scrub, clean, and polish all day long. It is a different world here. The wealthy women always wear makeup and never show their age. Unlike the husbands of the cleaning ladies, the husbands in suburbia are always busy, surprisingly polite, and somewhat effeminate. Time is not a scarce commodity in suburbia. People use it as lavishly and freely as hot water.

It is dawn now. The city is a gummy, almost gelatinous entity at this moment, an amorphous shape half-liquid, half-solid.

To the Celestial Gaze up in the sky, the Kazancı domicile must seem like a glittering sphere of sullied sparklers amid the shadows of the night. Most of its rooms are dark and quiet now, but a few are lit.

One of the Kazancı residents awake at this hour is Armanoush. She woke up early and instantly went online, eager to tell the members of the Café Constantinopolis about the shocking incident of the day before. She told them about the bohemian circles in Istanbul and then about the quarrel, summarizing every character and detail she took in at Café Kundera. Now she is giving them a full description of the Dipsomaniac Cartoonist, adding how he had found a new function for the wine at the table.

That cartoonist sounds fun, writes Anti-Khavurma. So you are saying he might go to prison for drawing the prime minister as a wolf? Humor is serious biz in Turkey!

Yeah, the guy seems cool, Lady Peacock/Siramark agrees. Tell us more about him.

But apparently someone has an entirely dissimilar interpretation of the incident.

Come on, guys, there is nothing cool or that interesting either in him or in any other character at that dingy cafe. Don't you see, they are all faces and names from the bohemian, avant-gardist, arty-farty side of Istanbul. Typical third world country elite who hate themselves more than anything else in the world.

Armanoush winced at this sharp message from Baron Baghdassarian and looked around.

Asya is asleep on the other side of the room with Sultan the Fifth curled up on her chest, a pair of headphones on her head, and an open book in her hand: *Totality and Infinity: An Essay on Exteriority*, by Emmanuel Levinas. There is also a CD case next to Asya's bed—Johnny Cash dressed from head to toe in black, erect against a gray, gloomy sky with a dog on one side of him and a cat on the other, staring dourly at something far beyond the frame. Asya has slept with the Walkman set on constant replay. She is her mother's daughter in this respect as well, perfectly capable of battling all sorts of voices but unable to cope with silence.

Armanoush cannot make out the lyrics from where she is, but she can hear the rhythm spinning round. She enjoys hearing Cash's baritone voice pour into the room from the headphones, just as she enjoys listening to the various sounds circulating inside and outside: the morning prayers echoing from the distant mosques; the clatter of the milkman as he leaves milk bottles in front of the grocery store across the street; the surprisingly cadenced breathing of Sultan the Fifth and Asya, a whistlelike fusion of snores and purrs, though it is not always easy to tell who does which; and the sound of Armanoush's fingertips as they move on the keyboard searching for the best response to give to Baron Baghdassarian. It is almost morning, and although Armanoush hasn't had enough sleep, she feels elated, with the sense of triumph that comes after defeating sleep.

Downstairs is Grandma Gülsüm's room. She could indeed have been Ivan the Terrible in another life but the harshness of her persona is not without reason. Like many who end up bitter in life, Grandma too has her story. Growing up in a little town on the Aegean Coast where life was idyllic yet deprived; getting married into the Kazancıs, a family much wealthier, much more urbane than hers, but certainly more ill-fated; the uneasiness of being a young, rural bride to the only son of a debonair, disaster-prone lineage; the burden of being assigned to give birth to sons, the more the merrier, for you never knew how long they would survive, yet giving birth to one girl after another; enduring the anguish of seeing her husband drift further away from her with each birth.

Levent Kazancı was a troubled man who didn't hesitate to use his belt to discipline his wife and children; *a boy, if only Allah had bestowed a boy, everything would have been all right.* Three girls in a row, and then the dream, the fourth baby, finally a boy. Hoping their fate had changed, they tried again, a fifth baby, but it was a girl again. Still, Mustafa was enough, he was all they needed to continue the family line. There was Mustafa, pampered, mollycoddled, spoiled, always favored over the girls, his every whim catered to . . . then the melody ceased and darkness and despair set into the dream: Mustafa left for the United States never to return.

Grandma Gülsüm was a woman who had never been reciprocally loved; one of those women who aged not gradually but in a hurry, leaping from virginity to wrinkles, never given the chance to dwell in the middle. She had fully dedicated herself to her only son and valued him often at the expense of her daughters, trying to find solace in him for everything that life had taken from her. Yet, once in Arizona, the boy's existence had been reduced to postcards and letters. He had never returned to Istanbul to visit his family. Grandma Gülsüm buried a deep pain of being rejected. In time, she became more and more hard-hearted. Today she bore the look of someone who had willingly accomplished austerity and meant to keep it that way.

At the right corner of the first floor, Petite-Ma is deeply asleep, cheeks flushed, mouth agape, snoring peacefully. Next to her bed there is a cherry cabinet and on it rests the Holy Qur'an, a book on Muslim saints, and a gorgeous lamp radiating soft sage green light. Beside the book lies an ochre rosary with an amber stone dangling from its end, and a half-full glass containing her false teeth.

Time for her has long lost its linear command; there are no regulatory signs, no warning lights, and no directions along the highway of history anymore. She is free to move in any direction, or change lanes. Or, she can stop right in the middle of the road, refusing to move, refusing the obligation to proceed, since there is no such thing as "progress" in her life, but only a perpetual recurrence of isolated moments.

Certain childhood recollections are coming back to her these days, as vivid as if they were happening here and now. There she is as an eight-year-old blue-eyed, blond girl in Thessaloníki with her mom, as both silently weep after her dad's death in the Balkan Wars; then she sees herself in Istanbul, it is late October, the proclamation of the modern Turkish Republic. Flags. She sees lots of flags, red and white, crescent and star, fluttering in the wind like newly washed clothes. Behind the flags looms Rıza Selim's face, his thick beard and full, somber eyes. Then she sees herself as a young woman sitting at her Bentley piano, playing jovial tunes to well-groomed guests.

In the small room right above Petite-Ma's sleeps Auntie Cevriye. She is having the nightmare she has had countless times over the last years. She is a student in a classroom again, wearing an ugly, ash gray uniform. The headmaster calls her to the front of the room to take an oral quiz. She breaks into sweat as she wobbles there unsteadily, her feet heavy. None of the questions asked make any sense. Auntie Cevriye discovers she hasn't really graduated from high school. There has been a mistake somewhere in the records and now she has to pass this one course in order to graduate and become a teacher. Every time, she wakes up at exactly the same scene. The headmaster pulls out the class grade sheet and a fountain pen with crimson ink, and then writes a huge red zero right where the name *Cevriye* is inscribed.

This is the nightmare she has had for the last ten years, ever since she lost her husband. He was in prison for bribery—a charge Auntie Cevriye always refused to believe. And only one month before his release he died watching a brawl, taken by a stupid live electrical cable. In her dreams Auntie Cevriye saw this scene over and over and envisioned the offender (there *had* to be an offender) who put the cable there and killed her husband. She dreamed of waiting at the prison gates. The rest of the scenario changed each time. Sometimes she was there to spit on the killer's face as soon as he was released from jail, sometimes she watched him from a distance, and at other times she shot him as he walked out into the sunlight.

After losing her husband, Auntie Cevriye sold her house and joined the other daughters who had come to accept living under the same roof. In her first months there, all she did was shed tears. She started the day sifting through her late husband's photographs, talking to them, sobbing over each one, only to end the day tired from so much sorrow. Her eyes swollen like two puffy bags of red distress, her nose peeling from too much wiping—this had been her state until one morning she had come home from the cemetery to find all the old photos gone.

"What did you do with his pictures?" Auntie Cevriye exclaimed, knowing too well whom to accuse. "Give them back to me!"

"No," Grandma Gülsüm answered, stern and dry. "The pictures are available. You will not spend your days crying over them. For the heart to heal, the eyes need not see them for a while."

Nothing healed. If anything, she got used to envisioning him without looking at his pictures. From time to time she found herself redesigning his face, furnishing him with a grizzled mustache or some more tufts of hair here and there. The disappearance of the photographs coincided with Auntie Cevriye's evolution into a staunch teacher of Turkish national history.

In the room across from her sleeps Auntie Feride. She is a clever and creative woman, a collage woman. If only she could hold the pieces together. It is unusual to be so sensitive, it is fabulous to be so sensitive, it is frightening to be so sensitive. Since anything can happen at any time, she can never be sure of the ground beneath her feet. There is no sense of safety or continuity. Everything comes in bits and pieces that beg to be united and yet defy any notion of wholeness. Now and again Auntie Feride dreams of having a lover. She wants a love that will absorb her in her entirety, even to the point of embracing her multiple anxieties, eccentricities, and abnormalities. A beloved who will adore everything about her. Auntie Feride doesn't want a love that is good to her good side but shuns her dark side. She needs someone who can stand with her through thick and thin, sanity and insanity. *Perhaps that is why lunatics have a harder time dating*, she thinks—*not because they are off the wall but because it is hard to find someone who is willing to date so many people in one person.*

But those are only daydreams. In real dreams Auntie Feride doesn't see lovers but abstract collages. At nighttime she creates patchworks with stunning colors and manifold geometrical shapes. The wind blows hard, the oceanic currents slide along, and the world becomes an orb of endless possibilities. Everything constructed can be deconstructed at the same time. The doctors have told Auntie Feride to take it easy, to use her pills regularly. But they know little about this dialectic. Make and destroy make and destroy make and destroy. Auntie Feride's mind is an excellent collage artist.

Next to Auntie Feride's room there is the bathroom and next to that, Auntie Zeliha's. She is awake. She is sitting straight up in her bed, eyeing her room as if it belonged to someone else, as if she were memorizing the details to feel closer to the stranger who belongs there.

She looks at her clothes, the dozens of skirts, all of them short, all of them flamboyant, her own way of protesting the moral codes she was born into. On the walls there are pictures and posters of tattoos. Auntie Zeliha is a woman in her late thirties but her room in many ways resembles that of a teenager. Perhaps she will never grow up and lose the anger within, the anger she has unintentionally passed on to her daughter. To her way of thinking, anyone who can't rise up and rebel, anyone devoid of the ability to dissent, cannot really be said to be alive. In resistance lies the key to life. The rest of the people fall into two camps: the vegetables, who are fine with everything, and the tea glasses, who, though not fine with numerous things, lack the strength to confront. It is the latter that are the worse of the two. Auntie Zeliha crafted a rule about them, back when she used to make rules.

The Iron Rule of Prudence for an Istanbulite Woman: If you are as fragile as a tea glass, either find a way to never encounter burning water and hope to marry an ideal husband or get yourself laid and broken as soon as possible. Alternatively, stop being a tea-glass woman!

She had opted for the third choice. Auntie Zeliha abhorred fragility. To this day, she was the only one among all the Kazancı females capable of getting infuriated at tea glasses when they cracked under pressure.

Auntie Zeliha reaches out for the pack of Marlboro Lights on the bedstand and lights a cigarette. Aging has not changed her smoking habits at all. She knows her daughter is a smoker too. It all sounds like a tawdry passage from a brochure by the Ministry of Health: *Children of parents addicted to smoking are three times as likely to become smokers themselves.* Auntie Zeliha is worried about Asya's wellbeing and yet she is wise enough to sense that if she intervenes too much, showing signs of mistrust, it will only generate a backlash. It's difficult to pretend not to look concerned, just like it's difficult to be called "auntie" by your own child. It kills her. Nonetheless, she still believes this might be better for them both. It has somehow freed the child and the mother; the two had to be detached nominally so that they could be attached physically and spiritually. Allah is her only witness; the only problem is, she doesn't believe He exists.

She inhales a thoughtful drag, holds it for a moment, and exhales an angry puff. Provided that Allah exists and knows so much, why didn't He do anything with that knowledge of His? Why does He let things happen the way they do? No, Auntie Zeliha is resolute, there is no way she'll give in to religion. She lived as an agnostic, and she will die as one. Sincere and pure in her blasphemy. If Allah really exists somewhere, He should appreciate this heartfelt denunciation of hers, germane to only a select few, rather than being sweet-talked by the self-absorbed pleas of the religious fanatics, who are everywhere.

In the room at the other end of the second floor is Auntie Banu. She too is awake at this hour. The third person awake in the Kazancı domicile. There is something unusual about her this morning. Her face is pale and her large, fawn eyes flicker with worry. Across from her is a mirror. She looks at herself and sees a woman aged before her time. For the first time in years she misses her husband—the husband she walked out on, but never fully abandoned.

He is a good man who deserves a better wife. Never has he treated her badly or said a mean word, but after losing her two sons, Auntie Banu couldn't stand living with him anymore. Every now and then, she goes to her old house, like a stranger who knows every detail of a place from déjà vu. She always buys dried apricots on the way, his favorite. Once there she does some cleaning, sews on a few buttons, cooks a few dishes, always his favorites, and tidies up the place. Not that there is too much to tidy up because he is a man who keeps the house in order. While Auntie Banu works, he watches her from close by.

At the end of the day he always asks: "Will you stay?"

Her response to that never changes: "Not today."

Before she leaves the house she adds: "There is food in the fridge, don't forget to heat the soup, finish the *pilaki* in two days or it'll go bad. Don't forget to water the violets, I changed their place next to the window."

He nods and mutters softly, as if talking to himself: "Don't worry. I know how to take care of myself. And thanks for the apricots. . . ."

After that Auntie Banu returns to the Kazancı domicile. That is how it has been, day after day, year after year.

The woman in the mirror looks old tonight. Auntie Banu always thought aging swiftly was the price she had to pay for her profession. The overwhelming majority of human beings age year by year, but not the clairvoyants: They age story by story. If only she had wanted to, Auntie Banu could have asked for compensation. Just as she has not asked her *djinn* for any material gains, she has not asked for physical beauty either. Maybe she will some day. So far Allah has given her the strength to carry on without asking for more. But today Auntie Banu is going to request something extra.

Allah, give me knowledge, for I cannot resist the urge to know, but also give me the strength to bear that knowledge. Amin.

From a drawer she produces a jade rosary and strokes the beads. "All right then, I'm ready, let's start. May Allah help me!"

Dangling from the bookshelf where the gas lamp stands, Mrs. Sweet grimaces, unhappy with the role of observer she has all of a sudden found herself in, unhappy with the things she is about to witness shortly in this room. Meanwhile, Mr. Bitter smiles bitterly, the only way he knows how to smile. He is content. Finally, Auntie Banu is convinced. It wasn't Mr. Bitter's *djinnish* command that convinced her but her own mortal curiosity. She couldn't resist the urge to learn. That antediluvian urge for more knowledge. . . . Who could resist it, after all?

Now, Auntie Banu and Mr. Bitter will together travel back in time. From 2005 to 1915. It looks like a long trip, but it is only a matter of steps in terms of *gulyabani* years.

In front of the mirror, between the *djinn* and the master stands a silver bowl of consecrated water from Mecca. Inside the silver bowl there is silvered water and inside the water there is a story, similarly silvered.

TWELVE

Pomegranate Seeds

Hovhannes Stamboulian stroked the hand-carved walnut desk he had been sitting at since early afternoon and felt the smooth, glossy surface glide under his fingers. The Jewish antique dealer who sold it to him had said such pieces were quite rare because they had been so hard to manufacture. Carved from walnut trees on the Aegean Islands, then adorned with tiny drawers and secret compartments like a fine piece of embroidery. Despite the delicacy of its adornment, the desk was so durable it could last several lifetimes.

"This desk will outlive you and even your children!" The dealer had guffawed, as if his merchandise outliving his customers was a standing joke with him. "Isn't it sublime that a piece of wood lives longer than us?"

Though he knew the remark was meant to demonstrate the quality of the merchandise, Hovhannes Stamboulian had felt a pang of sadness.

Even so, he had bought the desk. Along with it, he had also purchased a brooch from the same store—a graceful brooch in the shape of a pomegranate, delicately smothered with gold threads all over, slightly cracked in the middle, with seeds of red rubies glowing from within. It was a deftly crafted piece by an Armenian artisan in Sivas, he had been told. Hovhannes Stamboulian bought the piece as a present for his wife. He was planning to give it to her tonight, after dinner, or perhaps better, before, as soon as he was done with this chapter.

Of all the chapters he had written, this was the most demanding. Had he known it was going to be this grueling, he might have abandoned the entire project. But he was up to his neck in the book, and the only way out was to keep at it. Hovhannes Stamboulian, a renowned poet and columnist, was secretly writing a book entirely outside his main field. He could be rejected, ridiculed, or reviled at the end. At a time when the entire Ottoman Empire was sated with grandiose undertakings, revolutionary movements, and nationalist divisions, at a time when the Armenian community was pregnant with innovative ideologies and ardent debates, he in the privacy of his house was writing a children's book.

Writing a children's book in Armenian was something never done before, almost inconceivable. Why was there not a single piece of literature in this field? Was it because the Armenian minority had become a society unable to consider its children as children? Was childhood a futility, if not a luxury, denied to a minority in need of growing up as quickly as it could? Or was it because the literati in Istanbul had been cut off from the oral traditions faithfully ferried by Armenian grandmothers to their grandchildren?

The book was titled *The Little Lost Pigeon and the Blissful Country*. It was about a pigeon lost up there in the blue skies while flying with his family and friends over a blissful country. The pigeon would stop at numerous villages, towns, and cities, searching for his loved ones, and at each stop he would listen to a new story.

In this manner, Hovhannes Stamboulian gathered in the book old Armenian folktales, most of which had been transmitted from generation to generation, others long forgotten. Throughout the book he remained loyal to the authenticity of each tale, hardly changing a word. But now he planned to end the book with a story of his own. When done, the book would be published in Istanbul and then distributed in the major cities, like Adana, Harput, Van, Trabzon, and Sivas, where Armenians lived in large numbers. Even though the Muslims had started using the printing press about two centuries ago, the Armenian minority had been printing its own books and texts long before then.

Hovhannes Stamboulian wanted Armenian parents to read these stories to their children before they went to bed each night. It was ironic that this book had taken so much of his time over the past eighteen months that he himself hadn't been able to spend much time with his own children. Every afternoon he would come into this room, sit at his desk, and write for however long it took him. Each night when he emerged from the room his children would already be in their beds, asleep. The urge to write had cast a spell over everything and everyone in his life. But fortunately he was about to finish. This was the last chapter he was writing this evening, the most demanding of all. When he was finished he would go downstairs, bundle up the whole text with a ribbon, hide the golden brooch inside the knot, and hand the package to his wife. *The Little Lost Pigeon and the Blissful Country* was dedicated to her.

"Read it, please," he was planning to say. "If it is not good enough, I want you to burn it. All of it. I promise I won't even ask you why. But if you think it is good, I mean, good enough to be published and distributed, then please take it to Garabed Effendi at Dawn Publishers."

Hovhannes Stamboulian respected his wife's opinion like no one else's. She had sophisticated taste in literature and fine art. Thanks to her hospitality, this chalky *konak* along the Bosphorus had for years been a center for intellectuals and artists, visited by countless men of letters, some eminent writers, some aspiring to be. They would come to eat, drink, read, contemplate, and fervently discuss one another's works, and even more fervently, their own.

After flying too long the Little Lost Pigeon felt tired and thirsty and perched on a snowbound branch, which belonged to a pomegranate tree ready to blossom. He filled his little beak with some snow and having thus quenched his thirst, started to shed tears for his parents.

"Don't cry, little pigeon," said the pomegranate tree. "Let me tell you a story. The story of a little lost pigeon."

Hovhannes Stamboulian paused without quite understanding what exactly disturbed his concentration. He let out a sigh of exasperation, much to his own surprise. For the last hour or so his mind had been a free-for-all of gloomy thoughts. He had a hard time understanding why he was so worried deep inside, as if his mind had been operating on its own, contemplating nameless worries. Whatever the reason behind such uneasiness he had to get rid of the torpor. This was the last chapter, the last story. It had to be good. He pursed his lips and went back to writing.

"But that's me you are talking about. I am that pigeon!" chirped the Little Lost Pigeon in surprise.

"Oh really?" asked the pomegranate tree, but didn't sound the least surprised. "Then listen to your story. . . . Don't you want to learn about your future?"

"Only if it's a happy one," said the Little Lost Pigeon. "I don't want to learn about it if it's sad."

Suddenly the still air was pierced by the smashing of glass. Hovhannes Stamboulian flinched in his chair, stopped writing, and instinctively turned toward the window, all ears, frozen. For a long while he heard nothing but the howling of the wind. Oddly enough he found the silence more ominous than that eerie sound. The night was thick with a ghostly stillness while the wind outside roared as if it ferried the wrath of God, fuming for a reason unknown to mortals. In contrast to the wind whipping the walls outside, here in the house it was exceptionally silent. Hovhannes Stamboulian felt so deeply unnerved by this unusual quiet that he was almost relieved when he heard some sounds coming from downstairs. Someone scurried from one end of the house to the other, and then all the way back; panicky, abrasive footsteps in a rush as if running away from someone or something.

That must be Yervant, he thought, as a new concern crept into his eyes, a look of pensiveness and apprehension. His eldest son, Yervant, had always been naughty and boisterous, but recently the boy's waywardness had soared beyond limits. In truth, Hovhannes Stamboulian felt a pang of guilt for not spending as much time with him as he should have. Obviously the boy longed for his father. Compared to him his three other children, two boys and a girl, were so docile it was as if their eldest brother's frenzied energy had a soporific effect on them. The two younger boys were three years apart but equally compliant. And then came the youngest sibling, the only girl in the family, little Shushan.

"Don't you worry, little bird," the pomegranate tree smiled and shook the snow on her branches. *"The story that I'm going to tell you is a happy one."*

Downstairs in the corridor footsteps multiplied alarmingly. Now it sounded as if there were dozens of Yervants disobediently running from one end to the other, stomping and crushing the floor underneath. But amid the scuttle, all of a sudden, he *thought* he heard a voice, so unexpected and curt it was hard to be sure—stern and husky, cracking for a split second. That was it. After that it was silence again, as if it all had been a figment of his imagination.

Ordinarily, he would have run out of his room to check if everything was all right. But tonight was no ordinary night. He didn't want to be disturbed, not now, not when he was about to finish the work of eighteen months. Hovhannes wriggled in angst like a diver who, after having submerged too deep, could not bring his body to swim its way back to the surface. The whirl of writing was cavernous and encapsulating but also distinctively enticing. Words jumped to and fro on the parched paper, begging him to bring this last story to a close and to shepherd them to their long-awaited destiny.

> *"All right, then," the Little Lost Pigeon chirped. "Tell me the story of the Little Lost Pigeon. But I warn you, if I hear anything sad, I will take wing and fly away."*

Hovhannes Stamboulian knew what the pomegranate tree was going to say in return and how the last story started, but before he could put it down on paper, something somewhere fell on the floor and smashed into pieces. Amid the burst he picked up a snuffle; though it was muffled and short he instantly recognized his wife's sob. He jumped to his feet, now entirely flushed out of the abyss of his writing, and popped up to the surface like a dead fish.

As he darted toward the staircase, Hovhannes Stamboulian recalled his quarrel that very morning with Kirkor Hagopian, an eminent lawyer and member of the Ottoman Parliament.

"The times are bad, very bad. Get ready for the worst," was the first thing Kirkor muttered when they ran into each other at the barber's shop. "First they conscripted Armenian men. 'Aren't we all equal, aren't we all Ottomans?' they declared. 'Muslims and non-

THE BASTARD OF ISTANBUL

Muslims, we will fight the enemy together!' But then they dis-
armed all the Armenian soldiers as if they were the enemy. Next
they gathered Armenian men in labor battalions. And now, my
friend, there are rumors. . . . Some say the worst is coming."

Though sincerely concerned, Hovhannes Stamboulian had not
been particularly shaken by the news. He himself was too old to be
recruited and his boys too young. The only one in the family within
the range of conscription age was his wife's younger brother, Levon.
But he had avoided military service during the Balkan Wars thanks to
receiving the badge of "the unguarded" during the selection process.
Men who were the sole providers of their families were spared military duty. That old Ottoman rule, however, might be changing.
Nowadays one could never be completely sure. At the beginning of
the First World War, they had announced they would solely recruit
those in their early twenties, but once the war had gathered speed,
those in their thirties and even forties had also been conscripted.

Combat was not for Hovhannes Stamboulian. Neither was hard
manual work. He loved poetry. He loved words, feeling each individual letter of the Armenian alphabet upon his tongue and lips.
After ample reflection he had deduced that what the Armenian
minority needed most was not arms, as some revolutionaries posed,
but books, more and more books. Though new schools were
founded after the Tanzimat, they were in dire need of more open-
minded and cultivated teachers and better books. Some additional
progress had been made after the revolution in 1908. The Armenian population had supported the Young Turks in the hope that
their treatment of non-Muslims would be fair and decent. The
Young Turks had stated it in their proclamation:

> Every citizen will enjoy complete liberty and equality, regardless of
> nationality or religion, and be submitted to the same obligations. All
> Ottomans, being equal before the law as regards rights and duties
> relative to the State, are eligible for government posts, according to
> their individual capacity and their education.

True, they had not stuck to their promise, abandoning multinational Ottomanism for Turkism, but the European powers watched the empire carefully; they would surely intervene if something grim were to take place. Hovhannes Stamboulian believed that under the present circumstances Ottomanism was the best option for Armenians, not radical ideas. Turks and Greeks and Armenians and Jews had lived together for centuries and still could find a way to coexist under one umbrella.

"You don't understand a thing, do you?" Kirkor Hagopian snapped furiously. "You live in your fairy tales!"

Hovhannes Stamboulian had never seen him so unnerved and confrontational. Still, he didn't go along with him. "I don't think zealousness is going to help us," he said, barely getting his voice above a whisper. It was his belief that nationalist zeal would solely serve to replace one misery for another, inevitably working against the deprived and the dispossessed. In the end minorities tore themselves apart from the larger entity at a great cost, only to create their own oppressors. Nationalism was no more than a replenishment of oppressors. Instead of being oppressed by someone of a different ethnicity, you ended up being oppressed by someone of your own.

"Zealousness!" Kirkor Hagopian's face scrunched into a mask of gloom. "There is news pouring in from numerous towns in Anatolia. Have you not heard about the incidents in Adana? They enter into Armenian houses with the pretext of searching for guns, and then plunder. Don't you understand? All the Armenians are going to be exiled. All of us! And here you are betraying your own people."

Hovhannes Stamboulian remained quiet for a while, chewing the ends of his mustache. Then he muttered slowly but surely, "We need to work together, Jews and Christians and Muslims. Centuries and centuries under the same imperial roof. We have been living together all this time, albeit on unequal ground. Now we can make it fair and just for all, transform this empire together."

It was then that Kirkor Hagopian uttered those gloomy words, his face already closing up: "My friend, wake up, there is no together anymore. Once a pomegranate breaks and all its seeds scatter in different directions, you cannot put it back together."

Now as he stood still at the top of the staircase, listening to the eerie silence in the house, Hovhannes Stamboulian couldn't help seeing that image in his mind's eye: a broken pomegranate, red and sad. With visible panic he called out to his wife: "Armanoush! Armanoush, where are you?"

They must all be in the kitchen, he thought to himself, and hurried down to the first floor.

Following the commencement of the First World War, a general mobilization had been declared. Though everyone in Istanbul talked about this, it was in the small towns where its effects had been mostly felt. They had beaten the drums in the streets, echoing again and again: *Seferberliktir! Seferberliktir!* That was when many Armenian young men were drafted into the army. More than three hundred thousand. At the outset all these soldiers were given arms, just like their Muslim peers. After a short time, however, they were all asked to return those arms. Unlike the Muslim soldiers, the Armenians were taken into special labor battalions. Rumors ran amok that Enver Pasha was the one behind this decision: "We need working hands to construct the roads for the soldiers to cross," he had announced.

But then there came dour news, this time about the labor battalions themselves. People said all the Armenians were employed in hard labor for the road construction although some had paid their *bedel* and should have been exempt. They said the battalions were taken to dig roads, but that was just a pretext; in actual fact they were made to dig pits, deep and wide enough to . . . They said Armenians were buried in the same pits that they had been made to dig.

"The Turkish authorities have announced that the Armenians are going to dye their Easter eggs with their own blood!" That was what Kirkor Hagopian stated before he left the barbershop.

Hovhannes Stamboulian didn't give those rumors much credit. Yet he acknowledged that the times were bad.

Downstairs on the first floor he called his wife's name once again and sighed upon hearing no answer. As he stepped outside onto the patio and walked past the long cherry table where they had their breakfast when the weather was mild, a new scene from the Little Lost Pigeon crossed his mind.

"Listen to your story, then," said the pomegranate tree as it fluttered a few branches, shaking off specks of snow. "Once there was; once there wasn't. God's creatures were as plentiful as grains and talking too much was a sin."

"But why?" chirped the Little Lost Pigeon. "Why was it a sin to talk too much?"

The kitchen door was shut. It was strange given the hour of the day; Armanoush would be working in there with Marie, their maid of five years, while the children clustered around them. They never shut the door.

Hovhannes Stamboulian reached for the handle but before he could turn it, the old, wood door was opened from inside and he stood face-to-face with a Turkish soldier, a sergeant. Both men were so shocked to run into each other like this that for a full minute they stood staring at each other blankly. It was the sergeant who first shed his stupor. He took a step back and eyed the other from head to toe. He was a tawny man who would have had a smooth, youthful face had it not been for the harshness of his stare.

"What is going on here?!" Hovhannes Stamboulian exclaimed. He spotted his wife and kids and Marie lined against the kitchen wall at the back, standing side by side like penalized children.

"We have orders to search the house," the sergeant said. There was no discernible hostility in his voice but no empathy either. He sounded as if he was tired, and whatever the reason he was here for, he wanted to be done as fast as possible and be gone. "Could you please show us the way to your study?"

They went to the back of the house and trudged up the great curved staircase; Hovhannes Stamboulian in front, the sergeant and the soldiers following behind. Once upstairs in the study, the soldiers moved around, each poring over some article of furniture, like honey-sucking bumblebees in a field of wildflowers. They searched the cupboards, the drawers, and every single shelf of the wall-to-wall bookcase. They leafed through hundreds of books seeking documents hidden among the pages; they looked over his favorite literature, from Baudelaire's *The Flowers of Evil* and Gerard de Nerval's *Les Chimères* to Alfred de Musset's *Les Nuits* and Hugo's *Les Miserables* and *The Hunchback of Notre-Dame*. While a brawny soldier with beady eyes suspiciously scanned through Rousseau's *Social Contract,* Hovhannes Stamboulian couldn't help but ponder the passages the man was staring at without really seeing:

> *Man is born free but everywhere is in chains. In reality, the difference is that the savage lives within himself while social man lives outside himself and can only live in the opinion of others, so that he seems to receive the feeling of his own existence only from the judgment of others concerning him.*

When done with the books, they started to sift through the many drawers of the walnut desk. It was then that one of the soldiers spotted the gold brooch on the desk. He handed it to the sergeant, who picked up the miniature pomegranate, weighed it in his palm, rotated it in the air to better see the rubies inside, and then gave it to Hovhannes Stamboulian with a smile.

"You should not leave such a precious gem in the open. Here, take it," the sergeant said with an air of placid courteousness.

"Yes, thank you. It is a present for my wife," Hovhannes Stamboulian said quietly.

The sergeant gave him a confiding man-to-man smile. But rapidly his face turned from cordiality to sulk, and when he spoke again his voice didn't have the same mild tone anymore.

"Tell me what it says here," the sergeant said as he pointed to a bunch of papers he had found in a drawer, all written in the Armenian alphabet.

Hovhannes Stamboulian immediately recognized the poem he had penned at a time when he had fallen ill with a high fever. It had been sometime last fall. He had been in bed for three days straight without being able to move, shivering and sweating at the same time as if his entire body had become a barrel of water that was full of holes and constantly oozing. Throughout Armanoush had stayed beside his bed, putting vinegar-soaked cold towels on his forehead and rubbing his chest with ice cubes. Then, at the end of the third day, when the fever had finally diminished, a poem had come to Hovhannes Stamboulian, and he had welcomed it as a compensation for his suffering. Though not a religious man at all, he was a firm believer in divine compensations, which he thought operated less in large-scale manifestations than through small signs and gifts such as this.

"Read it!" The sergeant nudged the papers.

Hovhannes Stamboulian put on his glasses and with a trembling voice read the first lines aloud:

> *The child weeps in his sleep without knowing why,*
> *A hushed yet unending sob of longing*
> *Impossible to console*
> *That's how I long for thee,...*

"This is *poetry*," the sergeant barged in, stressing the last word with an intonation that sounded like disappointment.

"Yes." Hovhannes Stamboulian nodded, though not sure if this was good or bad.

But the sparkle he saw in the sergeant's eyes did not seem *that* hostile. Perhaps he had liked it. Perhaps he would leave now, taking his soldiers with him.

"Hov-han-nes Stam-bou-li-an," the sergeant muttered, slurring the words. "You are an erudite man, a man of knowledge. You are well known and well respected. Why would a sophisticated man like you conspire with a bunch of ignoble insurgents?"

Hovhannes Stamboulian raised his dark eyes from the paper and blinked absentmindedly. He didn't know what to say in his defense since he had no idea what he was being accused of.

"The Armenian insurgents. . . . They read your poems and then rebel against the Ottoman Sultanate," the sergeant said, creasing his forehead in thought. "You goad them into mutiny."

All of a sudden Hovhannes Stamboulian grasped what he was being accused of and the gravity of the charge. "Officer," he said, fixedly staring at the sergeant who fixedly stared back at him, afraid that if he broke eye contact the only bridge of interchange between them would forever disintegrate. "You are an educated man yourself and you'll understand the difficulty of my situation. My poems are the echo of my imagination. I write and publish them, but I cannot possibly control who reads them and with what particular intention."

Looking pensive, the sergeant cracked his knuckles one by one. He then cleared his throat as if to accentuate the importance of what he was about to say. "I perfectly understand that dilemma. However, you can control your own words. You are the one who writes them. You are the poet. . . ."

In a desperate effort to diminish what was quickly becoming real panic, Hovhannes Stamboulian scanned the room until he came eye to eye with his eldest son, standing by the door, peeking inside. When had he sneaked out of the kitchen? How long had he been watching them? The boy's cheeks were rosy with the intensity of his fury against the soldiers. But something in his expression contained far more than that. Yervant's young face looked oddly unflustered and somehow *wise*. Hovhannes Stamboulian smiled at his son, trying to convince him that things were OK, and then gestured for him to go back to his mother. But Yervant didn't move.

"I am afraid you need to come with us," the sergeant said.

"I can't," Hovhannes Stamboulian said inadvertently, but he realized how miserable was the excuse he was about to give. *Tonight I need to finish my book. . . . It is the last chapter. . . .* Instead he asked permission to speak to his wife.

Before they took him away, the very last thing ingrained in his memory was his wife's expression, her pupils dilated and her lips pallid. But Armanoush was neither crying nor did she look shocked. If anything she looked extremely tired, as if standing there in the doorway had drained her of all her strength. How he wished he could hold her hands now, embrace her tightly, and whisper to her to be strong, always strong, for the sake of their children and the one on the way. Armanoush was four months pregnant.

Only when nudged through the outside door onto the dark street with soldiers on both sides did Hovhannes Stamboulian remember having forgotten to give his wife her present. He thrust his hands into his pockets and was relieved not to feel the golden pomegranate on the tips of his fingers. He had left it at home, in a drawer in the desk. He softly smiled at the thought of how Armanoush would be pleased when she found it there.

———

As soon as the soldiers left, there were quick footsteps echoing on the doorstep. It was the Turkish neighbor next door. A sweet-tempered plump woman, always jolly, except that right now she was anything but. Seeing the terrified expression on her neighbor's face helped Armanoush to emerge from her trance and allow herself to be frightened. She pulled Yervant toward her and with quivering lips whispered, "Go my son, go to your uncle Levon's house. . . . Tell him to come here right away. Tell him what happened."

Uncle Levon's house was nearby, around the corner of the market square. He lived on his own in a modest, two-story house, the first floor of which was his workshop. Having been refused the hand of a beautiful Armenian woman he had loved in his youth and perhaps still did, he had chosen not to marry anyone and thereafter had spent his years working hard in his workshop, which was famous for the quality of its products. Uncle Levon was a cauldron maker and he crafted the best cauldrons in the entire empire.

Once outside on the street Yervant walked a few steps toward Uncle Levon's house, but then he stopped abruptly and turned in the opposite direction, the direction his father had been taken, and started to run. But even when he had covered the street from one end to the other, there was no sign of his father. Nothing. No one. It was as if the Turkish soldiers and his father had altogether vanished.

He reached Uncle Levon's house shortly after, yet there was no one upstairs. He knocked on the door of the workshop, hoping he might be there. It wasn't unusual for Uncle Levon to work late hours at his store. But the door was opened by his apprentice, Rıza Selim—a quiet, diligent Turkish teenager with skin as white as porcelain and raven hair curling wildly above and around his head.

"Where is my uncle?" Yervant asked.

"Master Levon is gone," Rıza Selim said with a strangled voice that he could hardly push out of his throat. "The soldiers came and took him away this afternoon."

As soon as he uttered these ominous words, Rıza Selim let go of the tears he had been holding back. The boy was an orphan and Uncle Levon had been like a father to him for the last six years. "I don't know what to do," he said. "I am waiting. . . ."

On the way back to his house Yervant ran the snaky, steep streets east and west, searching for something, *anything,* that could be an auspicious sign. He passed by empty coffeehouses, grubby plazas, ramshackle houses from which wafted the smells of *türlü* and the cries of babies. The only sign of life was a tan kitten painfully meowing next to a filthy gutter, licking its tiny belly where the flesh was cut open and the blood had caked around a deep, swollen wound.

Years later when he thought about his father, Yervant would remember that kitten all alone on the dark, empty street. Even in Sivas, in the small Catholic Armenian village of Pirkinik where

ELIF SHAFAK

they went next to seek shelter with Grandpa and Grandma, only to be expelled one night by soldiers breaking into the house; even when he found himself walking amid thousands of drained, famished, beaten Armenians guarded by soldiers on horseback; even when he trudged through a long, thick carpet of mud, vomit, blood, and excrement; even when he didn't know how to stop the cries of his little sister, Shushan, and then one day, amid an ensuing turmoil, let go of her hand for a split second and lost sight of her; even when he watched his mother's feet swell into two blue pillows of pain covered with purple veins and blood; even when she died, quiet and light as a dry willow leaf swirling in the gusting breeze; even when he saw swollen and stinking corpses along the road, stables filled with smoke and fire; even when upon having nothing left to eat, he and his brothers grazed on grass like sheep in the Syrian desert; even when they were saved by a group of American missionaries dedicated to collecting the Armenian orphans lost hither and thither along the road of exile; even when they were brought all the way back to the American College in Sivas that operated as a sanctuary, and from there sent to America; even when years later he was finally able to find his little sister, Shushan, in Istanbul and bring her to San Francisco; and even after many happy suppers surrounded by his children and grandchildren, that kitten remained ingrained in his mind.

"That's enough," Auntie Banu exclaimed, flinching. She untied her head scarf and covered the silver bowl with it. "I don't want to see this anymore. I learned what I had wanted to learn. . . ."

"But you have not seen it all," Mr. Bitter objected with a rasping voice. "I haven't told you about the lice yet."

"The li- . . . li-ce?" Auntie Banu stuttered. Whatever spirit had moved her to put an end to this session seemed to have passed now. She picked up her head scarf and peeped into the bowl again.

"Oh yeah, the lice, my master, is an important detail," Mr. Bitter said. "Remember the part when little Shushan let go of her elder brother's hand and all of a sudden got lost in the crowd? She got the lice from a family whom she had approached in the hope of getting some food. The family had little to consume themselves, and they pushed her away. A few days later little Shushan was aflame with a roaring fever: typhus!"

Auntie Banu let out a loud, prolonged sigh.

"I was there. I saw it all. Shushan dropped to her knees. Nobody in that convoy of people was in any condition to help her. They left her there on the ground, her forehead covered with sweat and her hair full of lice!"

"Enough!" Auntie Banu rose to her feet.

"But aren't you going to listen to the best part? Don't you want to learn what happened to little Shushan?" Mr. Bitter asked, sounding offended. "You wanted to learn about your guest's family, didn't you? Well, that little Shushan in my story is your guest's grandmother."

"Yes," Auntie Banu replied. "I had figured that out. Continue!"

"All right!" Mr. Bitter enthused, savoring his triumph. "After she was left half-dead on the road and after the convoy had disappeared on the horizon, little Shushan was discovered by two women from a nearby Turkish village. They were a mother and a daughter. They took the sick girl back home with them and bathed her with chunks of daphne soap and washed off the lice in her hair with potions concocted from the herbs in the valley. They fed and cured her. Three weeks later when a high-ranking officer stopped by the village with his men and interrogated the villagers to learn if they had chanced upon any Armenian orphans in the area, this Turkish mother hid Shushan inside her daughter's dowry chest to save her from harm. A month later the little girl was on her feet again, except she didn't talk much and cried in her sleep at nights."

"I thought you said she was brought to Istanbul. . . ."

"Eventually she was. During the following six months this

mother and daughter looked after her as if she were one of their own family, and would probably have kept doing so. But then a horde of bandits arrived, searching and plundering the houses. They stopped and ransacked every Turkish and Kurdish village in the region. It didn't take them long to find out that there was a little Armenian girl there. Despite the wails of the mother and daughter, they took Shushan away from them. They had heard about the orders to deliver all Armenian orphans below the age of twelve to the orphanages around the country. So before long Shushan was in an orphanage in Aleppo, and when there was no room there, in a school in Istanbul under the care of several *hocahanım,* some benevolent and caring, others cold and strict. Like all of the children there she was dressed in a white robe and a buttonless, black coat. There were both boys and girls. The boys were circumcised and all the children were renamed. So was Shushan. Everyone called her Shermin now. She was also given a surname: 626."

"Enough is enough," Auntie Banu put her head scarf back over the silver bowl and gave her *djinni* a long, piercing stare.

"Yes, master, as you wish," Mr. Bitter muttered. "However, you skipped the most important part of the story. Should you wish to listen to that part too, just let me know because we *gulyabani* know everything. We were there. I told you the past of Shushan, once a little girl, now the grandmother of Armanoush. I told you things that your guest doesn't know. Will you tell her? Don't you think she has a right to know?"

Auntie Banu stood silent. Would she ever narrate for Armanoush the story she had learned tonight? Even if she wanted to, how could she tell her she had seen the story of her family in a silver bowl of water shown by a *gulyabani,* the worst kind of *djinn?* Would Armanoush believe her? Besides, even if she *did* believe her, wasn't it better that the girl never learned about all of these sorrowful details?

Auntie Banu turned toward Mrs. Sweet for solace. But instead of an answer all she got from her benevolent *djinni* was a bashful

smile and a sudden shimmer of the corona around her head, flickering in shades of plum, pink, and purple. Together with the *djinni*'s
corona, a thorny question flared up: Was it really better for human
beings to discover more of their past? And then more and more . . . ?
Or was it simply better to know as little of the past as possible and
even to forget what small amount was remembered?

It is past dawn now. A short step away from that uncanny threshold
between nighttime and daylight. The only time of the day when it
is early enough to harbor hopes of realizing one's dreams but far too
late to actually dream, the land of Morpheus now flung far away.

Allah's eye is omnipotent and omniscient; it is an eye that never
closes, or even blinks. But still no one can tell for sure if the earth
is equally omniobservable. If this is a stage wherein spectacle after
spectacle is displayed for the Celestial Gaze, there might be times in
between when the curtains are down and a gauzy head scarf covers
the surface of a silver bowl.

Istanbul is a hodgepodge of ten million lives. It is an open book
of ten million scrambled stories. Istanbul is waking up from its perturbed sleep, ready for the chaos of the rush hour. From now on
there are too many prayers to answer, too many profanities to note,
and too many sinners, as well as too many innocents, to keep an
eye on.

Already it is morning in Istanbul.

THIRTEEN

Dried Figs

Through the range of the months of the year, every month knows the particular season it belongs to and behaves accordingly, every month but one: March.

March is most unbalanced in Istanbul, both psychologically and physically. March might decide she belongs to the spring season, warm and fragrant, only to change her mind the very next day, turning into winter, sending chilly winds and sleet all around. Today, March nineteenth, was an unusually sunny Saturday, far above the average temperature for this time of the year. Asya and Armanoush took their sweaters off as they walked the wide, windswept road from Ortaköy toward Taksim Square. Asya was wearing a long batik dress, hand painted in tones of beige and caramel brown. Every step she took, tiers of necklaces and bracelets jingled. Armanoush, in turn, was loyal to her style: a pair of blue jeans and on top of it a loose UNIVERSITY OF ARIZONA sweatshirt, pasty pink as a ballet slipper. They were on their way to visit the tattoo parlor.

"I'm so glad you will finally meet Aram." Asya beamed as she shifted her canvas bag from one shoulder to the other. "He is such a nice person."

"I heard you mention his name before, but I have no idea who he is."

"Oh, he is . . ." Asya paused, searching for the right word in English. *Boyfriend* sounded too light for the situation, *husband* was technically wrong, *husband-to-be* didn't look plausible. *Fiancé* seemed to suit better, but the truth is they had never been formally engaged. "He is Auntie Zeliha's significant other."

Across the road, under an elegantly carved Ottoman archway, they caught a glimpse of two Gypsy boys, one of them plucking cans from garbage bins and then piling them on a dilapidated cart. The other boy sat on the edge of the cart sorting the cans, doing his best imitation of working hard while basking in the sun. *That could be such an idyllic life*, Asya thought to herself. She would give anything to switch places with that boy on the cart. First, she would go and buy the most lackadaisical horse she could find. Then every day she would ride her horse cart up and down along the steep streets of Istanbul, collecting things. She would wholeheartedly gather the most unattractive artifacts of human life, embracing the debris rotting underneath its polished surface. Asya had a feeling that a garbage collector in Istanbul probably led a far less stressful life than she and her friends at Café Kundera did.

If she became a garbage collector, she would wander the city whistling Johnny Cash songs, while a balmy breeze caressed her hair and the sun warmed her bones. Should anyone dare to disturb such blissful harmony, she would scare the hell out of him with the threat of her mammoth Gypsy clan in which probably everyone was convicted of a felony of some sort. Despite the problem of poverty, Asya concluded, as long as it was not wintertime, it must be fun to be a garbage collector. She made a mental note to herself to remember this in case she couldn't come up with a better profession after graduating from college. On that note she started to whistle; only when she reached the end of the couplet did Asya notice that Armanoush was still waiting for a more detailed response to the question she had asked her a few minutes ago.

"Well, yeah, Auntie Zeliha and Aram have been seeing each other for Allah knows how long. He is like my step-dad, I guess, or for the sake of consistency, I should call him step-uncle. . . . Whatever."

"Why don't they get married?"

"Married?" Asya spat out the word as if it were food between her teeth. They were now passing the can collectors, and upon closer inspection of her role models, Asya realized that they were not boys but girls. This she liked even more. To blur the gender boundaries was one more reason to become a garbage collector. She put a cigarette between her lips, but instead of lighting it, she sucked the end for a moment as if it were one of those cigarette-shaped chocolate sticks wrapped in edible paper. She then revealed an inner thought: "Actually, I am sure Aram wouldn't mind getting married, but Auntie Zeliha would never have any of that."

"But why not?" Armanoush wanted to know.

The breeze shifted direction just then, and Armanoush caught a pungent whiff of the sea. This city was a jumble of aromas, some of them strong and rancid, others sweet and stimulating. Almost every smell made Armanoush recall some sort of food, so much so that she had started to perceive Istanbul as something edible. She had been here for eight days now and the longer she stayed, the more twisted and multifaceted Istanbul grew to be. Perhaps she was getting used to being a foreigner in this city, if not getting used to the city itself.

"My guess is it's all because of Auntie Zeliha's experience with my dad, whoever that was," Asya continued. "That must be why she is so against marriage. I think she has a trust issue with men."

"Well, I can understand that," Armanoush said.

"But don't you think there is a huge difference between the two sexes when it comes to recovery after an affair? I mean, when women

survive an awful marriage or love affair, and all that shit, they generally avoid another relationship for quite some time. With men, however, it is just the opposite; the moment they finish a catastrophe they
start looking for another one. Men are incapable of being alone."

Armanoush gave a curt nod of acknowledgment, although the
pattern did not quite fit her parents' situation. It was her mother
who had remarried after her divorce while her father had remained
single to this day. Armanoush then asked:

"This Aram . . . where is he from?"

"He's from around here, just like us." Asya shrugged, but then
in a flash she understood what was being asked. Surprised at her
own ignorance, she lit the cigarette she had been sucking on and
took a puff. How could she have failed to make the connection?
Aram came from an Armenian family in Istanbul. He was, theoretically, Armenian.

And yet there was a sense in which Aram could *not* be Armenian or Turk or any other nationality. Aram could only be Aram,
entirely sui generis. He was a unique member of a unique species.
He was a charmer, a colossal romantic, a political science professor
who often confessed to being more inclined to live the life of a
fisherman in a seedy village on the Mediterranean. He was a fragile
heart, a gullible soul, and a walking slice of chaos; a sanguine uto-
pian and an irresponsible promiser; an outstandingly messy and
quick-witted and honorable man. He was one of a kind and conse-
quentially Asya had never associated him with any collective identity. Tempted as she was to say something in this vein, she simply
replied: "Actually, he is Armenian."

"I thought so." Armanoush smiled faintly.

Five minutes later they were at the tattoo parlor.

"Welcome!" Auntie Zeliha exclaimed in her slightly husky
drawl as she heartily hugged them both. Whatever her perfume
was, it was strong—a combination of spice and wood and jasmine.
Her dark hair fell on her shoulders in dazzling curls, some of which
she had highlighted with a substance so glittery that whenever she

made a move under the halogen lights, her hair shimmered. Armanoush looked at her agape, for the first time sympathizing with the fright and admiration that she imagined Asya must have felt toward her mother since she was a child.

Inside it was like a little museum. Across from the entrance there was a huge framed photograph of a woman of uncertain nationality, her back turned toward the viewer to better expose the intricately detailed tattoo on her body. It was an Ottoman miniature. It looked like a scene from a banquet, with an acrobat above the diners walking a tightrope from one shoulder to the other. Such a traditional miniature tattooed on the back of a modern woman was startling. Below was a phrase in English: A TATTOO IS A MESSAGE SENT FROM BEYOND TIME!

There were showcases all over the store in which hundreds of tattoo designs and piercing jewelry were displayed. The tattoo designs were clustered under several titles: "Roses & Thorns," "Bleeding Hearts," "Stabbed Hearts," "The Way of the Shaman," "Creepy Hairy Creatures," "Non-Hairy but Equally Creepy Dragons," "Patriotic Motifs," "Names & Numbers," "Simurg and the Bird Family," and finally "Sufi Symbols."

Armanoush couldn't remember ever seeing so few people in one room making so much noise. Besides Auntie Zeliha, there was an eccentric man with orange hair and a needle in his hand, a teenager and his mother (who couldn't seem to decide whether to stay or leave), and two longhaired, long-unshaven men who looked completely out of space and time, like drugged-out rock musicians from the 1970s just now recovering from a bad trip. One of the latter was sitting in a large comfortable chair, noisily chewing bubble gum while chatting with his friend and having a purple mosquito tattooed on his ankle. The man with the needle turned out to be Auntie Zeliha's assistant and a talented artist in his own right. While he worked, Armanoush stared at him, surprised at how much sound a tattoo needle was capable of producing.

"Don't worry. The sound is more dramatic than the pain," Auntie Zeliha remarked, reading her mind. Then she added with a wink, "Besides, that customer is used to it. This must be his twentieth. Tattoo is an addiction sometimes. One is never enough. With every new tattoo you will discover the urge to get another one. I wonder why addiction recovery centers have not included this in their programs yet."

Armanoush was silent for a long moment, studying the outlandish rock musician out of the corner of her eye. If the man felt any pain, he showed no signs of it. "Why would anyone want a purple mosquito tattooed on his ankle?"

Auntie Zeliha chuckled knowingly. "*Why?* That is one question we never ask here. You see, in this store we refuse to accept the *tyranny of normalcy*. Whichever design a customer asks for, I am sure there must be a reason, one that even he might not know himself. I never ask *why*."

"How about the piercings?"

"The same," Auntie Zeliha said, pointing to her nose piercing and smiling. "You know, this one is nineteen years old. I did it when I was Asya's age."

"Really?"

"Yes, I went to the bathroom, I used a baby carrot, a sterilized needle, ice cubes to anesthetize, and also, lots of rage. I had so much rage against everything but mostly against my own family. I said to myself I am gonna do this and I pierced my nose. My hands shook in my nervousness, so I pierced it wrong the first time and hit the septum. It bled a lot. But then I got the technique and the next time pierced it right on the nostril."

"Really?" Armanoush said again, only this time she sounded perplexed at the turn the conversation was taking.

"Yup!" Auntie Zeliha patted her nose with pride. "I screwed a ring there and just walked out of the bathroom like that. Back then I used to enjoy driving my mom crazy."

Hearing these last words from where she stood, Asya gave her mother an amused glance.

"But what I am trying to say is, I pierced my nose because it was forbidden. You know what I mean? It was out of the question for a Turkish girl from a traditional family to have a piercing, so I went ahead and did it on my own. But times have changed now. That's what we're here for. In this store we give advice to our customers, and sometimes we even refuse some people, but we never judge them. We never ask *why*. That is one thing I learned early in life. If you judge people, they'll go and do it anyway."

Just then the teenager slid his gaze from the showcases toward Auntie Zeliha and asked, "Can you make this dragon's tail longer so that it can cover my whole arm? I want it to extend from my elbow to my wrist—you know, as if it were crawling down my arm."

Before Auntie Zeliha could answer that, however, it was the mother who piped in. "Are you crazy? No way! We had agreed to have something small and simple, like a bird or a ladybug. Never did I give you permission for dragons' tails. . . ."

For two hours Asya and Armanoush watched the action in the parlor as customers came and went. Five high school students came in saying they each wanted to have an eyebrow pierced, but as soon as the sterilized needle went through the eyebrow of the first, the others changed their minds. Then a soccer fan walked in who wanted to have the emblem of his favorite team on his chest. After that came an ultranationalist who asked to have the Turkish flag on his fingertip so that when he wagged his finger at other people he would be waving the flag. And finally, there was an impressive blond transvestite singer who wanted to have the name of her lover tattooed on the knuckles of her hands.

Then a middle-aged man came in who looked abnormally *normal* among the usual clientele in the tattoo parlor. It was Aram Martirossian.

Aram was a tall, slightly stout, good-looking man who had a kind but weary face, dark beard, rather hoary hair, and deep dimples that materialized each time he broke into a smile. His eyes glittered with intellect behind his thick-rimmed glasses. From the way he looked at Auntie Zeliha, one could instantly see love. Love and respect and synchronization. When he talked she completed his gestures, when she gestured he completed her words. They were two complicated individuals who seemed to have achieved a miraculous harmony together.

When she started to converse with him, Armanoush switched to her English-as-a-second-language English, the way she did each time she met someone new in Istanbul. Thus she introduced herself as unhurriedly as possible in a slow-moving, rhythmic, almost child-like English. She was surprised to hear Aram's English flow fluently, with a subtle British accent.

"Your English is so good!" Armanoush couldn't help but remark. "How did you pick up a British accent, may I ask?"

"Thank you," Aram said. "I went to college in London, both undergrad and grad. But we can speak Armenian if you'd like."

"I can't." Armanoush shook her head. "As a child I learned some from my grandma but because my parents were separated, I didn't stay in one place for too long and there were always disruptions. Then every summer when I was between ten and thirteen, I went to an Armenian youth camp. That was fun and my Armenian improved there, but afterward, it deteriorated again."

"I learned Armenian from my grandmother too." Aram smiled. "To tell the truth, both Mom and Grandma thought I should be raised bilingual, except they disagreed about what the second language had to be. Mom thought it would be better for me to speak Turkish at school and English at home, since when I grew up, I was destined to leave this country anyway. But Grandma proved resolute. She wanted Turkish at school, Armenian at home."

Armanoush was intrigued by Aram's aura, but she was even

ELIF SHAFAK

more fascinated by his humbleness. They talked about Armenian grandmothers for a while—those in the diaspora, those in Turkey, and those in Armenia.

At six thirty p.m. Auntie Zeliha handed the store over to her assistant and the four of them headed to a tavern nearby.

"Before you leave Istanbul, Aram and Auntie Zeliha want to take us to a tavern so that you can see a typical evening of drinking," Asya had explained to Armanoush.

On the way, as they passed through a poorly lit street, they came across an apartment building from whose windows transvestite prostitutes eyed the passersby. The two on the first floor were so close that Armanoush was able to glimpse the details of their heavily made-up faces. One of them, a hefty woman with thick lips and hair as glowing red as fireworks in the dark, laughingly said something in Turkish.

"What did she say?" Armanoush asked Asya.

"She said my bracelets are gorgeous and far too many for me!"

To Armanoush's surprise, Asya took off one of her beaded bracelets and gave it to the red-haired transvestite. The latter joyously accepted the gift, put it on, and with perfectly manicured, crimson-nailed fingers raised a can of Diet Coke, as if offering a toast to Asya.

Watching the scene with marveling eyes, Armanoush wondered what Jean Genet would make of it. That Cherry-Vanilla Diet Coke, bead bracelets, the tart odor of semen, and childish joy could all coexist on a seamy street in Istanbul?

The tavern was a stylish but convivial place near the Flower Passage. As soon as they sat, two waiters appeared with a cart of *mezes*.

"Armanoush, why don't you surprise us again with your culinary vocabulary?" Auntie Zeliha requested.

"Well, let's see, there is *yalanci sarma, tourshi, patlijan, topik, enginar* . . ." Armanoush started naming the dishes the waiters were leaving on the table.

Customers kept arriving in couples or groups, and in no more than twenty minutes the tavern was full. Amid all these equally unfamiliar faces and sounds and smells, Armanoush lost her sense of place. She felt like she could be in Europe or in the Middle East or in Russia. Auntie Zeliha and Aram drank *rakı,* Asya and Armanoush had white wine. Auntie Zeliha smoked cigarettes, Aram puffed on cigars, while Asya, apparently avoiding the use of tobacco in front of her mother, chewed the insides of her mouth instead.

"You're not smoking this evening," Armanoush said to Asya, sitting next to her.

"Yeah, tell me about it." Asya sighed. Then she dropped her voice to a whisper. "Hush! Auntie Zeliha doesn't know that I smoke."

Armanoush was surprised that Asya rebelliously, almost sadistically, took pleasure in infuriating her mother at every opportunity, but when it came to smoking cigarettes in front of her, she was a docile daughter.

During the following hour they chatted idly while waiters brought one dish after another. First they served the *mezes*—the cold dishes—followed by lukewarm dishes, the hot dishes, and desserts and coffee. *This must be the style here,* Armanoush figured out, *instead of choosing from a menu, the whole menu comes to you.*

When both the noise and the smoke inside intensified, Armanoush inched closer toward Aram, having finally summoned the courage to ask him the question that had been tugging at the edges of her mind for some time:

"Aram, I understand you like Istanbul, but didn't you ever consider coming to America? I mean, you could come to California, for instance. There's a large Armenian community there, you know. . . ."

Aram stared at her for a full minute, as if taking in every detail, until he slumped back in his chair and gave a puzzling laugh. Armanoush was rather perturbed by this laughter, which she felt somehow shut her out. Not convinced that she had been understood correctly, she leaned forward and tried to offer a better explanation: "If they are oppressing you here, you can always come to America. There are many Armenian communities there who would be more than happy to help you and your family."

Aram did not laugh this time. Instead he gave her a warm smile, warm but somewhat tired.

"Why would I want to do that, dear Armanoush? This city is my city. I was born and raised in Istanbul. My family's history in this city goes back at least five hundred years. Armenian Istanbulites belong to Istanbul, just like the Turkish, Kurdish, Greek, and Jewish Istanbulites do. We have first managed and then badly failed to live together. We cannot fail again."

Just then the waiter materialized again, this time serving fried calamari and fried mussels and fried pastries.

"I know every single street in this town," Aram continued, taking another sip of *rakı*. "And I love strolling these streets in the mornings, in the evenings, and then at night when I am merry and tipsy. I love to have breakfasts with my friends along the Bosphorus on Sundays, I love to walk alone amid the crowds. I am in love with the chaotic beauty of this city, the ferries, the music, the tales, the sadness, the colors, and the black humor. . . ."

They fell into an awkward silence, taking a rare distant glimpse into each other's positions, realizing there could be more than geographical distance between them—he suspecting she was too Americanized, she construing he was too Turkified. The mordant gap between the children of those who had managed to stay and the children of those who had to leave.

"Look, the Armenians in the diaspora have no Turkish friends. Their only acquaintance with the Turks is through the stories they heard from their grandparents or else from one another. And those stories are so terribly heartbreaking. But believe me, just like in every nation, in Turkey too there are good-hearted people and bad people. It is as simple as that. I have Turkish friends who are closer to me than my flesh-and-blood brother. And then there is, of course"—he lifted his glass and signaled toward Auntie Zeliha—"this crazy love of mine."

Auntie Zeliha must have sensed her name being mentioned for she gave them a wink, lifted her glass of *rakı,* and toasted: "*Şerefe!*" They all followed suit and clinked their glasses as they echoed: "*Şerefe!*" This word, as it would soon turn out, was some sort of a refrain that was repeated every ten or fifteen minutes. Another hour and seven *Şerefe*s later, Armanoush's eyes were glowing with alcohol. With amusement she watched an albino waiter bring in the hot dishes—broiled striped bass on a bed of green peppers, basil-marinated catfish with creamy spinach, charbroiled salmon with field greens, and stir-fried shrimp in spicy garlic sauce.

Armanoush giggled tipsily before she turned toward Aram and asked, "Tell us, you must have some tattoos too. Auntie Zeliha must have tattooed you."

"No way," Aram said behind the veil of wispy smoke curling up from his cigar. "She doesn't let me have one."

"Yeah," Asya added. "She won't permit him to have a tattoo."

"Really?" Armanoush said in surprise as she turned to Auntie Zeliha. "I thought you were fond of tattoos."

"I am, indeed," Auntie Zeliha replied. "It is not the tattooing part that I am opposing but the design he asks for."

Aram smiled. "The tattoo that I would like to have is a gorgeous fig tree. But, unlike other trees, this one is upside down. My fig tree has all its roots up in the air. Instead of the earth, it is rooted in the sky. It is displaced but not placeless."

They were all silent for a few seconds, watching the flickering light of the candle at the table.

"It's just that the fig tree . . ." Auntie Zeliha lit the last cigarette in her pack and unintentionally blew smoke in the direction of Asya. "The fig tree is an ominous sign. It does not bring good luck. I am fine with Aram's wish to have his roots up in the air, but it is the fig tree that I object to. Should he choose it to be a cherry tree,

for instance, or an oak tree, still with its roots up in the air, I'd tattoo him right away!"

It was then that four Gypsy musicians, all dressed in silky white
shirts and black trousers, entered the tavern with their instruments—
an *ud,* a clarinet, a *kanun,* and a *darbuka.* There was a general excitement among the customers who, having eaten and drunk their fill,
were more than ready to sing.

When the musicians materialized by their side, Armanoush felt
a pang of shyness. But to her relief they didn't force her to sing.
It turned out that Asya wasn't much of a singer either. They listened to Auntie Zeliha accompany the musicians with a mellow
contralto—a voice that sounded nothing like her usual cigarette-
tainted, husky tone. Armanoush noticed that Asya glanced in her
mother's direction with a look of inquisitiveness.

When the leader of the band asked if there was a particular song
they would now like to request, Auntie Zeliha elbowed Aram flir-
tatiously, and exclaimed, "Come on, ask for a song. Sing, my nightingale!"

Blushing, Aram leaned forward, coughed, and then whispered
something in the leading musician's ear. Once the band had embarked on the requested melody, much to Armanoush's surprise,
Aram started to sing along—not in Turkish, not in English, but in
Armenian.

> *Every morning at dawn*
> *Ah . . . I say to my love,*
> *Where are you going?*

It flowed slowly, forlornly, while the tempo picked up with a
distinctive rise of the clarinet and the hard-to-contain *darbuka* in the
background. Aram's voice soared and then fell in mellow waves.
Initially his voice was diffident, yet it became increasingly assertive
in its tone.

She's the golden chain
Of my memories,
She's the pathway to
The story of my life.

Armanoush held her breath, failing to understand all the words but feeling mourning deep in her heart. When she raised her head, she was intrigued by Auntie Zeliha's expression. It was a look that embodied the fear of happiness that only those who had unexpectedly, unguardedly fallen in love could wear.

When the song was over and the musicians had moved to the next table, Armanoush thought Auntie Zeliha would give Aram a kiss. But instead she tenderly squeezed Asya's hand, as if acknowledging that her love for a man had allowed her to better comprehend her love for her daughter. "Sweetheart," she murmured, a hint of anguish creeping into her tone. But if Auntie Zeliha was planning to say something to her daughter, she was quick to beat the urge. Instead, she took out a new pack of cigarettes and offered her one.

Seeing her mother have sentiments so near the surface was far more surprising for Asya than being offered a cigarette by her. She lit hers and then her mom's. As the smoke slowly coiled between them, daughter and mother smiled at each other awkwardly. They looked startlingly similar from this angle and light, two faces molded by a past that one knew nothing about and the other chose not to remember.

It was precisely then that Armanoush felt the pulse of the city for the first time since she had arrived in Istanbul. It had just hit her why and how people could fall in love with Istanbul, in spite of all the sorrow it might cause them. It would not be easy to fall out of love with a city this heartbreakingly beautiful.

With this recognition she raised her glass in a toast: "*Şerefe!*"

FOURTEEN

Water

"Shall I go inside and tell them to quiet down?" Auntie Feride asked. She was standing in front of the girls' room, her gaze fixated on the knob.

"Oh, leave them alone!" Auntie Zeliha exclaimed from the couch where she had collapsed. "They're a bit tipsy and when you're a bit tipsy you listen to music loud." To make a point she then exclaimed: "*LOUD!*"

"Tipsy!" bellowed Grandma Gülsüm. "Mind you, why are they *tipsy*? Is it not enough that you always bring disgrace to this family? Look at that skirt you are wearing. The dish towels in the kitchen are longer than your skirts! You are a single mother, a divorcée. Hear me well! I have never seen a divorcée with a ring in her nose. You should be ashamed of yourself, Zeliha!"

Auntie Zeliha raised her head from the cushion she had been hugging. "Ma, for me to be a *divorcée,* I would have had to have gotten married first. Don't distort the facts. I cannot be called a *di-*

THE BASTARD OF ISTANBUL

vorcée or a *grass widow* or any of those sticky terms you have in reserve in your glossary for unfortunate women. This daughter of yours is a sinner who wears miniskirts and she loves her nostril ring and she loves the child she gave birth to out of wedlock. Like it or not!"

"Is it not enough that you spoiled your daughter and forced her to drink? Why did you also have to make the poor guest drink? She's Mustafa's responsibility; she is your brother's guest in this house. How dare you spoil the girl!"

"My brother's responsibility! Yeah, right!" Auntie Zeliha laughed morosely, and she closed her eyes.

Inside the girls' room, meanwhile, Johnny Cash was playing full blast. The two girls were sitting side by side at the desk staring at the computer screen, with Sultan the Fifth curled between them, his eyes half-closed. The girls were so absorbed in the Internet that neither of them heard the argument outside their door. Armanoush had just logged on to the Café Constantinopolis, determined to take Asya with her this time.

Hello everyone! Haven't you missed Madame My-Exiled-Soul? she typed.

Our reporter from Istanbul is back. Where were you? Did the Turks gobble you up? wrote Anti-Khavurma.

Well, one of the gobblers is with me right now. I want to introduce you all to a Turkish friend of mine.

There followed a pause.

She has a nickname, of course: A Girl Named Turk.

What was that? Alex the Stoic couldn't help asking.

It's a reinterpretation of the title of this Johnny Cash song. Anyway, you can ask her yourself. Here she is. Dear Café Constantinopolis meet A Girl Named Turk. A Girl Named Turk meet Café Constantinopolis.

Hello! Greetings from Istanbul, Asya wrote.

There was no response.

I hope the next time you too will come to Istanbul with Arman . . .

Asya realized her mistake only when Armanoush slapped her hand . . . with Madame My-Exiled-Soul.

Oh, thanks. But frankly, I am in no mood for a touristy tour to a country that has caused so much suffering for all my family. It was Anti-Khavurma again.

Now it was Asya's turn to pause.

Look, don't get us wrong, we don't have anything against you, OK? joined in Miserable-Coexistence. I am sure the city is nice and scenic, but the truth is we don't trust the Turks. Mesrop would turn in his grave if, Aramazt forbid, I would forget my past just like that.

"Who is Mesrop?" Asya asked Armanoush in a voice barely above a whisper, as if they could hear her.

All right. Let's start with the basics. The facts. If we can make it thru the facts we can then talk about other things, decreed Lady Peacock/ Siramark. Let's start with this touristy Istanbul trip. These magnificent mosques you show to tourists today, who was the architect behind them? Sinan! He designed palaces, hospitals, inns, aqueducts. . . . You exploit Sinan's intelligence and then deny he was Armenian.

I didn't know he was, Asya wrote puzzled. But Sinan is a Turkish name.

Well, U R good at Turkifying the names of the minorities, replied Anti-Khavurma.

OK, I see what you are saying. True, Turkish national history is based on censorship, but so is every national history. Nation-states create their own myths and then believe in them. Asya lifted her head and squared her shoulders and continued to type. In Turkey there are Turks, Kurds, Circassians, Georgians, Pontians, Jews, Abazas, Greeks. . . . I find it too oversimplistic and far too dangerous to make generalizations of this sort. We are not brutal barbarians. Besides, many scholars who have studied the Ottoman culture will tell you it was a great culture in many ways. The 1910s were a particularly difficult time. But things are not the same as they were 100 years ago.

Lady Peacock/Siramark countered instantly. I don't believe the Turks have changed at all. If they *had*, they would have recognized the genocide.

Genocide is a heavily loaded term, wrote back A Girl Named Turk. It implies a systematic, well-organized, and philosophized extermination. Honestly, I am not sure the Ottoman state at the time was of such a nature. But I do recognize the injustice that was done to the Armenians. I am not a historian. My knowledge is limited and tainted, but so is yours.

You see, here's the difference. The oppressor has no use for the past. The oppressed has nothing but the past, commented Daughter of Sappho.

Without knowing your father's story, how can you expect to create your own story? Lady Peacock/Siramark joined in.

Armanoush smiled to herself. So far everything had gone just like she had imagined. Except Baron Baghdassarian. He had not responded to anything yet.

In the meantime, Asya, still fixated on the screen, typed, I do recognize your loss and grief. I do not deny the atrocities committed. It's just *my* past that I am recoiling from. I don't know who my father is or what his story was like. If I had a chance to know more about my past, even if it were sad, would I choose to know it or not? The dilemma of my life.

You are full of contradictions, replied Anti-Khavurma.

Johnny Cash wouldn't mind that! interjected Madame My-Exiled-Soul.

Tell me, what can I as an ordinary Turk in this day and age do to ease your pain?

Now this was a question hitherto no Turk had asked the Armenians in the Café Constantinopolis. In the past, they had had Turkish visitors twice, both heatedly nationalist young men who had popped up out of nowhere, apparently with the intention to prove that the Turks had done nothing wrong to the Armenians, and if anything, it was the Armenians who had rebelled against the Ottoman regime and killed the Turks. One of them had gone so far as to argue that if the Ottoman regime had really been as genocidal as claimed, today there would be no Armenians left to talk about this. The fact that there were so many Armenians lashing against the Turks was a clear indication that the Ottomans had not persecuted them.

Until today the Café Constantinopolis's encounter with the Turks had basically been a fuming exchange of slander and soliloquy. This time the tone was radically different.

Your state can apologize, answered Miserable-Coexistence.

My state? I've got nothing to do with the state, Asya wrote as she thought about the Dipsomaniac Cartoonist prosecuted for drawing the prime minister as a wolf. Look, I am a nihilist! She stopped short of mentioning her Personal Manifesto of Nihilism.

Then *you yourself* can apologize, barged in Anti-Khavurma.

You want me to apologize for something I personally had nothing to do with?

So you say, Lady Peacock/Siramark wrote. We R all born into continuity in time and the past continues to live within the present. We come from a family line, a culture, a nation. Are you gonna say let bygones be bygones?

As Asya's eyes raked the screen she looked baffled, as if in the midst of a presentation she had forgotten her lines. She stroked Sultan the Fifth's head absently a few times before her fingers went back to the keyboard again.

Am I responsible for my father's crime? A Girl Named Turk asked.

You are responsible for recognizing your father's crime, Anti-Khavurma replied.

Asya seemed confused by the bluntness of the statement, briefly irritated but also intrigued. Within the glow radiating from the computer, her face was pale and still. She had always tried to distance her past as far as possible from the future she hoped to attain. In the hope that, whatever the memories of times past entailed, no matter how dark or depressing, the past would not consume her. The truth is, as much as she hated to admit it, she knew the past *did* live within the present.

All my life I wanted to be pastless. Being a bastard is less about having no father than having no past . . . and now here you are asking me to own the past and apologize for a mythical father!

There came no answer, but Asya didn't seem to be waiting for one. She kept typing as if her fingers acted on their own, as if she were navigating with eyes closed.

Yet, perhaps it is exactly my being without a past that will eventually help me to sympathize with your attachment to history. I can recognize the significance of continuity in human memory. I can do that . . . and I do apologize for all the sufferings my ancestors have caused your ancestors.

Anti-Khavurma wasn't content. It really doesn't mean much if you apologize to us, he cut in. Apologize aloud in front of the Turkish state.

Oh come on! all of a sudden Armanoush had pulled the keyboard toward her and wrote, unable to resist the temptation to interject. It's Madame My-Exiled-Soul, here. What is that gonna do other than get her into trouble?"

She has to go thru that trouble if she is sincere! Anti-Khavurma blew up.

But before anyone could respond to that came a most unexpected comment.

Well, the truth is, dear Madame My-Exiled-Soul and dear A Girl Named Turk . . . some among the Armenians in the diaspora would never want the Turks to recognize the genocide. If they do so, they'll pull the rug out from under our feet and take the strongest bond that unites us. Just like the Turks have been in the habit of denying their wrongdoing, the Armenians have been in the habit of savoring the cocoon of victimhood. Apparently, there are some old habits that need to be changed on both sides.

It was Baron Baghdassarian.

"They still aren't sleeping," Auntie Feride paced left and right outside the girls' room. "Is there something wrong?"

The older women had gone to sleep, and so had Auntie Cevriye, as a disciplined teacher. Auntie Zeliha had passed out on the couch.

"Why don't you go to sleep, sister, and let me guard their door to make sure they are all right." Auntie Banu squeezed her sister's shoulder. Now and then, whenever her illness escalated, Auntie Feride panicked about the possible harm that might come from anyone or anything in the outside world.

"Let me take the night shift," Auntie Banu smiled. "You go to bed and sleep. Don't forget that your mind is a stranger at nights. Don't talk to strangers."

"Yes." Auntie Feride nodded, and for a moment she seemed like a little girl stirred by a tale. Now visibly relaxed, she shuffled toward her room.

As soon as they had logged off Armanoush checked her watch. It was time to give her mother a call. This week she had called her every day at the same time, and each time Rose had scolded her for not calling more often. Trying not to be distressed about this unvarying pattern, she dialed the number and waited for her mom to pick up.

"Amy!!!" Rose's voice escalated into a shriek. "Honey, is it you?"

"Yes, Mom. How are you doing?"

"How am I doing? How am I doing?!" Rose repeated, now sounding bewildered and her voice muffled. "I need to hang up now, but you promise, you promise me, you will call me back in ten . . . no, no, ten isn't enough, in fifteen minutes exactly. I need to hang up and collect my thoughts now and then I will wait for your call. Promise me, promise me," Rose echoed hysterically.

"Okay, Mom, I promise," Armanoush stammered. "Mom, are you all right? What's happening?" But Rose had already gone.

Stunned, pale, and desolately holding the phone, Armanoush looked at Asya. "My mother asked me to call back later instead of asking me why I hadn't called before. It's so unlike her. This is so not her."

"Please relax." Asya shifted in her bed, popping her head up from under the blanket. "Maybe she was driving or something and couldn't talk on the phone."

But Armanoush shook her head, a fretful shadow crossing her face. "Oh God, there's something wrong. Something's very wrong."

***

Her eyes swollen from crying, her nose miserably red, Rose reached out for a paper towel as she broke into tears. She always bought the same paper towels from the same store: strong, absorbent Sparkle. The company produced these in different styles and Rose's favorite was called *My Destination*. Printed on the towels were pictures of seashells, fish, and boats, all in blue, and among them swam the following words: I CAN'T CHANGE THE DIRECTION OF THE WIND, BUT I CAN ADJUST MY SAILS TO ALWAYS REACH MY DESTINATION.

Rose liked this slogan. Besides, the azure tint of the printed images perfectly matched the color of the tiles in her kitchen, the part of the house she was particularly proud of. Despite her initial fondness, once they had purchased the house, Rose had lost no time in remodeling the kitchen, adding pull-out shelves, placing a thirty-six-bottle lacquered-top wine rack in the corner—though neither she nor Mustafa were drinkers—and decorating the entire room with oak swivel stools. Now as she felt a surge of panic, it was onto one of those stools that she dropped her body.

"Oh my God, we've got fifteen minutes. What are we gonna tell her? We've only got fifteen minutes to decide," she cried to Mustafa.

"Rose, darling, will you please calm down," Mustafa said as he rose from his chair. He didn't like the stools and instead kept two solid-wood honey pine dining chairs in the kitchen, one for him and the other for him too. He approached his wife and held her hand, in the hope of laying her worries to rest. "You will be calm, very calm, you understand? And you will calmly ask her where she is right now. This is the first thing you need to ask her, OK?"

"What if she doesn't tell me?" Rose said.

"She will. You ask her nicely, she'll tell you nicely." Mustafa spoke slowly. "But no scolding. You need to keep your cool. Here, have some water."

Rose took the glass with trembling hands. "Is that possible? My little girl has lied to me! How stupid of me to trust her. All this time I think she's in San Francisco with her grandma and then it turns out she's lied to everyone . . . and now her grandma . . . oh, God, how am I gonna tell her?"

The day before when they were both in the kitchen, she making pancakes, he reading the *Arizona Daily Star,* the phone rang. Rose picked up the phone with the spatula in her hand. The call was from San Francisco. Her ex-husband, Barsam Tchakhmakhchian, was on the line.

How many years had they spent without exchanging a word? After their divorce they had been forced to communicate often concerning their baby girl. But then, as Armanoush had grown up, their talks had become rare and then ceased entirely. Of their brief marriage, only two things remained: mutual resentment and a daughter.

"I am sorry to disturb you, Rose," Barsam said with a smooth yet drained voice. "But it is an emergency. I need to talk to my daughter."

"*Our* daughter," Rose corrected tartly, and as soon as the words had come out of her mouth she instantly regretted her bitterness.

"Rose, please, I need to give Armanoush some bad news. Will you please call her to the phone? She is not answering her cell phone. I had to call her here."

"Wait . . . wait—isn't she *there*?"

"What do you mean?"

"Isn't she there in San Francisco with you?" Rose's lips quivered with panic.

Barsam wondered if his ex-wife was playing games. He tried

not to sound irritated. "No, Rose, she decided to go back to Arizona. She is spending the spring break there."

"Oh my God!! But she is not here! Where is my baby?! Where is she?!" Rose started to sob, falling into one of those anxiety attacks she thought she had long ago left in the past.

"Rose, will you please calm down? I don't know what's going on, but I am sure there is an explanation. I trust Armanoush with all my heart. She won't do anything wrong. When did you last speak with her?"

"Yesterday, she calls every day—from San Francisco!"

Barsam paused. He didn't tell her that Armanoush had been calling him too, although from *Arizona*. "That's good, it means she is fine. We need to trust her. She is an intelligent, dependable girl, you know that. Next time she calls just tell her to give me a call. Tell her it is urgent. You got that, Rose? Will you do that?"

"Oh my God!" Rose started to cry louder. But then all of a sudden it occurred to her to ask: "Barsam, you said there was bad news. What is it?"

"Oh . . ." A heavy pause. "It's my mom . . ." He could not finish his sentence.

"Just tell Armanoush that Grandma Shushan has died in her sleep. She did not wake up this morning."

Fifteen minutes had never passed so slowly. Armanoush paced the room under the worried gaze of Asya. Finally, it was time to give her mom another call. This time Rose picked up the phone instantly.

"Amy, I will ask you just one question and you will tell me the truth; you promise you'll tell me the truth."

Armanoush felt a wave of worry well up in her stomach.

"Where are you?" Rose rasped, her voice breaking. "You lied to us! You are not in San Francisco, you are not in Arizona, where are you?"

Armanoush swallowed hard. "Mom, I'm in Istanbul."

"What?!"

"Mom, I'll tell you everything but please calm down."

Rose's eyes sparkled with pure indignation. How she hated to hear everyone telling her to calm down.

"Mother, I am terribly sorry for worrying you so much. I should never have done this. I am so sorry, but there is nothing to worry about, believe me."

Rose put her hand over the phone. "My baby is in Istanbul!" she said to her husband with a hint of a reprimand as if this were his fault. Then she yelled into the receiver: "What the hell are you doing there?"

"Actually, I am staying at your mother-in-law's house. It is a wonderful family."

Flabbergasted, Rose turned again to Mustafa and this time scolded harder: "She is staying with *your* family."

Then, before an ashen and alarmed Mustafa Kazancı could put in a word, she said, "We are coming there. Don't disappear anywhere. We are coming. And don't you ever turn off your cell phone again!" With that she hung up.

"What the hell are you talking about?" Mustafa squeezed his wife's arm, harder than he intended. "I am not going anywhere."

"Yes, you are going," Rose said. "*We* are going. My only daughter is in *Istanbul*!!!" she screamed, as if it meant Armanoush had been taken hostage.

"I cannot leave my job now."

"You can take a few days off. And if you don't, I will go alone," Rose, or someone who looked like Rose, snapped. "We will go there, make sure she is safe, pick her up, and bring her back home."

Late that night when they were about to go to sleep the Kazancıs' phone rang.

"*Inshallah* it is nothing bad," Petite-Ma whispered from her bed, a rosary in her hand, a shadow of anxiety on her face. She reached out for the glass of water with her false teeth inside and, still praying, took a sip. Only water could quell fear.

Still awake, it was Auntie Feride who picked up the phone. More than anyone else in the family, she was the most talkative and communicative when it came to phone conversations.

"Alo?"

"Hi, Feride, is it you?" the receiver asked in a male voice. And without waiting for an answer, he added, "It is me . . . from America . . . Mustafa. . . ."

Thrilled to hear her brother's voice, Auntie Feride grinned. "Why don't you call us more often? How are you? When are you coming to see us?"

"Listen, dear, please. Is Amy—Armanoush there?"

"Yes yes, of course, you sent her to stay here with us. We love her very much." Auntie Feride beamed. "Why didn't you come with her, you and your wife?"

Mustafa stayed put, his forehead buckled with discomfort. Behind him in the window lay the Arizona soil, always dependable, always secretive. In time he had learned to appreciate the desert, its infinity soothing his fear of looking back, its tranquillity easing his fear of death. At times like this he remembered, as if his body reminisced on its own, the fate awaiting all the men in his family. At times like this he felt close to committing suicide. Finding death before death found him. He had lived two very different lives. Mustafa and Mostapha. And sometimes the only way to bridge the gap between the two names seemed to silence them simultaneously—to bring both of his lives to an abrupt end. He shunned the thought. A sound similar to sighing. Perhaps it was him. Perhaps it was just the desert.

"I think we are. We will come for a few days to pick Amy up and to see you. . . . We are coming."

These words seemed to come effortlessly, as if time was not a sequence of ruptures but an uninterrupted continuity, easily bendable even when fractured. Mustafa would visit as if it had not been almost twenty years since he had been home.

FIFTEEN

Golden Raisins

The miraculous news that Mustafa was coming to visit them
with his American wife instantly instigated a series of reactions
in the Kazancı domicile. The first and foremost one involved deter-
gents, washing powder, and soap flakes. In two days the whole house
had been thoroughly cleaned from top to bottom, windows scoured
and buffed up, shelves dusted, curtains washed and ironed, every tile
on all the three floors scrubbed and mopped. One by one Auntie
Cevriye wiped the leaves of every houseplant in the living room,
the geranium and the bellflower, the rosemary and the sweet wood-
ruff. She even wiped the leaves of the touch-me-not. Meanwhile
Auntie Feride surprised everyone by taking out the most precious
latticework in her dowry. But it was no doubt Grandma Gülsüm
who was most thrilled with the news. At first she refused to believe
her only son was coming to visit them after all these years, and
when she finally was convinced of the news, she incarcerated
herself in the kitchen amid the dishware, cutlery, and ingredients,
cooking the favorite dishes of her favorite child. Now the air inside

the kitchen was heavy with the scents of freshly baked pastries. She had already oven-baked two different types of *börek*—spinach and feta cheese—and simmered lentil soup, stewed lamb chops, and prepared the *köfte* mixture to be fried upon the guests' arrival. Though she was determined to make ready half a dozen more dishes before the end of the day, undoubtedly the most important item on Grandma Gülsüm's menu was going to be the dessert: *ashure*.

All throughout his childhood and teens, Mustafa Kazancı had relished *ashure* more than any other sweet, and if those terrible American fast-food products had not messed up his culinary habits, Grandma Gülsüm hoped, he would be delighted to encounter bowls of his favorite dessert in the fridge, waiting for him, as if life here were still the same and he could pick up from where he had left off.

Ashure was the symbol of continuity and stability, the epitome of the good days to come after each storm, no matter how frightening the storm had been.

Grandma had soaked the ingredients the day before and was now getting ready to begin cooking. She opened a cupboard and took out a huge cauldron. One always needed a cauldron to cook *ashure*.

Ingredients
1/2 cup garbanzo beans
1 cup whole hulled wheat
1 cup white rice
1-1/2 cups sugar
1/2 cup roasted hazelnuts, chopped
1/2 cup pistachios
1/2 cup pine nuts
1 teaspoon vanilla
1/3 cup golden raisins
1/3 cup dried figs
1/3 cup dried apricots
1/2 cup orange peels
2 tablespoons rosewater

Garnishes

2 tablespoons cinnamon
1/2 cup blanched and slivered almonds
1/2 cup pomegranate seeds

Preparation

Most of the ingredients should be soaked in separate bowls the day before as follows:

In one bowl, cover the beans with cold water and soak them overnight. The wheat and rice should be rinsed carefully and then covered with water in a different bowl. Soak the figs and apricots and orange peels in hot water for 1/2 hour, then drain and reserve the soaking water; chop them, mix them with the golden raisins, and set aside.

Cooking

Cover the beans with 1 gallon of cold water. Bring to a boil and cook over medium heat until the beans are just tender, about an hour. While the beans are cooking, boil 2-1/2 quarts of water, stir in the wheat and rice, and simmer over low heat, stirring frequently, until the wheat and rice mixture is tender, about an hour. Combine.

Add the reserved soaking water, the sugar, chopped hazelnuts, pistachios, and pine nuts to the pot and bring it all to a boil over medium heat, stirring constantly. Simmer and stir for 30 minutes or more. Allow the mixture to thicken slightly until it resembles a thick soup. Add the vanilla, raisins, figs, apricots, and orange peels and cook for another 20 minutes, stirring constantly. Turn off the heat and blend in the rosewater. Let the *ashure* stand at room temperature for an hour or more. Sprinkle with cinnamon and garnish with slivered almonds and pomegranate seeds.

Inside the girls' room, Armanoush had been quiet and pensive since early morning. She didn't feel like going out or doing anything.

Asya stayed indoors with her playing *tavla* and listening to Johnny Cash.

"Six six! You lucky thing!"

But Armanoush showed no trace of pleasure about the dice she had rolled. Instead, she broodingly pouted at her checkers as if hoping to move them by the force of her gaze.

"I have this awful feeling something bad has happened and my mother isn't telling me."

"Please don't worry," Asya said, chewing the end of her pencil, craving nicotine. "You've talked with your mom and she sounded all right. Thanks to you they will now visit Istanbul. They'll come and meet you here and soon you will be back in your house. . . ." Though Asya had meant to soothe, the words had oddly come out as an objection. The truth is, it saddened her that Armanoush would be leaving so soon.

"I don't know. It's just this feeling I can't get rid of." Armanoush sighed. "My mom doesn't travel anywhere, not even to Kentucky. That she is flying to Istanbul is mind-boggling. But then again, it is so typical of her. She cannot stand not being in control of my life. She would fly around the globe to keep me under her eye."

While she waited for Armanoush to decide where to move which checker, Asya drew her legs under her, working on yet another article of her Personal Manifesto of Nihilism.

Article Ten: If you find a dear friend, make sure you don't get so accustomed to her as to forget that in the end, each one of us is existentially lonely and that sooner or later the everlasting solitude will overtake any fortuitous friendships.

Distressed though she might be, Armanoush's playing skills were surely unaffected by her mood. With the "six six," she rammed into Asya's home board, and trounced her opponent by crushing all three of her checkers at once. Triumph!

Asya sunk her teeth deeper into the pencil.

Article Eleven: Even if you have found a dear friend whom you have gotten so accustomed to as to forget Article Ten, never overlook the fact that she can still give you a drubbing in other spheres of life. On the *tavla* board, just as in birth and death, each one of us is alone.

Having three checkers waiting on the bar, and with only two gates still open in the opposing home board, Asya now had to roll either a "five five" or a "three three." There was no other roll that could save her from defeat. She spat in her palms for good luck and heaved a prayer to the *tavla djinni,* whom she had always envisaged as a half-black, half-white ogre with madly rotating dice as eyeballs. She then rolled the dice: "three two." Damn! Unable to play, she clasped her hands and grumbled.

"Poor thing!" Armanoush exclaimed.

Asya put the awaiting black checkers on the bar as she listened to a street vendor outside yelling at the top of his voice: *"Raisins! I've got golden raisins. For kiddos and toothless grannies, golden raisins are for everyone!"* When she spoke again she raised her voice over the vendor's.

"I'm sure your mom is fine. Think about it, if she weren't fine how could she make this trip all the way from Arizona to Istanbul?"

"I guess you're right." Armanoush nodded and rolled the dice. "Six six" again!

"Yo, are you gonna keep rolling six six forever? Are those loaded dice or what?" Asya volleyed suspiciously. "Are you cheating, miss?"

Armanoush chuckled. "Oh yeah, if only I knew how to!"

But right when she was about to move another pair of white checkers into the open space, Armanoush paused abruptly, pale and drawn.

"Oh my God, how could I not see this?!" Armanoush exclaimed in anguish. "It's not my mother, you see, it's my *father*. This is exactly how Mom would react if something bad happened to my father . . . or to dad's family. . . . Oh God, something has happened to my father!"

"But now you're speculating." Asya tried to soothe her without success. "When did you last speak with your father?"

"Two days ago," Armanoush said. "I called him from Arizona and he was OK, everything sounded normal."

"Wait, wait, wait! What do you mean you called him from *Arizona*?"

Armanoush blushed. "I lied." Then she shrugged, as if to savor the satisfaction of having done something wrong for a change. "I lied to almost everyone in my family to be able to take this trip. If I'd revealed I was going to Istanbul on my own, everyone would have been so alarmed they wouldn't have let me travel *anywhere*. So I thought, I'll go to Istanbul and tell them about the whole thing when I get back. My father thinks I'm in Arizona with my mom while Mom thinks I'm in San Francisco with Dad. I mean, she *used* to think, at least until yesterday."

Asya stared at Armanoush with a disbelief that soon vanished, replaced by something closer to reverence. Perhaps Armanoush was not the immaculate, well-behaved girl that Asya had suspected she was. Perhaps somewhere in her luminous universe there was room for darkness, dirt, and deviance. The confession, far from upsetting Asya, had only served to increase her esteem of Armanoush. She closed the *tavla* board and stuck it under her armpit, a symbol of accepted defeat, though Armanoush had no way of knowing this cultural gesture. "I don't think anything is wrong . . . but come on, why don't you give your dad a call?" Asya asked.

As if waiting for these words to take action, Armanoush reached out to the phone. Given the time difference, it was early morning in San Francisco.

It was answered after one ring, not by Grandma Shushan as usual, but by her dad.

"Sweetheart." Barsam Tchakhmakhchian heaved a sigh of intense endearment as soon as he heard his daughter's voice. There was an eerie clatter in the phone connection, which made them both aware of the geographical distance in between. "I was going to call you in the morning. I know you are in Istanbul; your mom called to tell me."

A brief, prickly silence ensued but Barsam Tchakhmakhchian did not comment on it, nor did he scold her. "Your mom and I were so worried about you. Rose is flying to Istanbul with your stepfather. . . . They are coming there to get you. They will be in Istanbul tomorrow by noon."

Now Armanoush stood frozen. Something was wrong. Something was so very wrong. That her father and her mother were talking to each other, and what's more, updating each other, was a surefire sign of apocalypse.

"Dad, has something happened?"

Barsam Tchakhmakhchian paused, stricken with sorrow from the weight of a childhood memory that had appeared out of nowhere.

When he was a boy, every year a man with a dark pointed hood and black cape would visit their neighborhood, going door to door with the deacon of the local church. He was a priest from the old country looking for young, bright boys to take back to Armenia to train them to be priests.

"Dad, are you all right? What is going on?"

"I'm all right sweetheart. I missed you," was all he could say.

Barsam was fascinated by religion at a young age, the best student in Sunday school. Consequently, the man with the black hood visited their house often, talking to Shushan about the boy's future. One day, as Barsam, his mother, and the priest were sitting in the kitchen sipping hot tea, the priest had said if a decision was to be made, this was the time to do it.

Barsam Tchakhmakhchian would never forget the flash of fear in his mother's eyes. As much as she respected the holy priest, as much as she'd have been delighted to see her son as a grown-up man in pastoral garb, as much as she wanted her only son to serve the Lord, Shushan could not help but recoil with fright, as if faced with a kidnapper who wanted to take her son away from her. She had flinched with such force and fear that the cup in her hand had shaken, spilling some tea on her dress. The priest had softly, amiably nodded, detecting the shadow of a dark story secreted in her past. He had patted her hand and blessed her. Then he had left the house, never to come back with the same request again.

That day Barsam Tchakhmakhchian had sensed something he hadn't felt before and wasn't going to feel ever again. A spiky, creepy premonition. Only a mother who had already lost a child would react with such profound fear in the face of the danger of losing another one. Shushan might have had another son at some point who had become separated from her.

Now as he mourned his mother's death, he couldn't find the heart to tell his daughter.

"Dad, talk to me," Armanoush said urgently.

Just like his mother, his father came from a family deported from Turkey in 1915. Sarkis Tchakhmakhchian and Shushan Stamboulian shared something in common, something their children could only sense but never fully grasp. So many silences were scattered among their words. When coming to America they had left another life in another country, and they knew that no matter how often and how truthfully you evoked the past, some things could never be told.

Barsam remembered his father dancing around his mother to a *Hale*, drawing circles within circles with his arms raised like a soaring bird; the music starting out slow, becoming faster and faster, this Middle Eastern swirl that the children could only watch with admiration from the side. Music was the most vivid trace left from his upbringing. For years Barsam had played the clarinet in an Armenian band and danced in traditional costume, black bloomers and a yellow shirt. He remembered leaving his house in those costumes while all the other kids in their non-Armenian neighborhood watched him with mocking eyes. Each time he would hope the kids would forget what they had seen or simply wouldn't bother to poke fun at him. Each time he was wrong.

While being enrolled in one Armenian activity after another, all he really wanted was to be like them, nothing more, nothing less, to be American and to get rid of this Armenian dark skin. Even years later, his mother would reproach him every now and then, explaining how as a little boy he had asked the Dutch American tenants upstairs what particular soap they used to wash themselves, because he wanted to be just as white as them. Now as the memories of his childhood gushed back to him with the loss of his mother, Barsam Tchakhmakhchian couldn't help but feel guilty for rapidly unlearning what little Armenian he had learned as a child. He now felt sorry for not having learned more from his mother, and not having taught more to his daughter.

"Dad, why are you silent?" Armanoush asked, her voice filled with fright.

"Do you remember the youth camp you went to as a teenager?"

"Yes, of course," Armanoush answered.

"Were you ever angry at me for not sending you there anymore?"

"Dad, it was *me* who didn't want to go there anymore, did you forget? It was fun at the beginning but then I decided I was too mature for it. I'm the one who asked you not to send me there the next year. . . ."

"Right," Barsam said tentatively. "But still I could have looked for a different camp for Armenian teenagers your age."

"Dad, why are you questioning this now?" Armanoush felt on the verge of tears.

He did not have the heart to tell her. Not like this, not over the phone. He did not want her to learn about her grandmother's death while all alone and thousands of miles away. As he tried to mutter a few words of distraction, his voice rose softly over a hum that broke out in the background. The droning hum of a gathering. It sounded like the entire family was there, relatives and friends and neighbors under the same roof, which, as Armanoush was wise enough to know, could be the sign of only two things: either someone had gotten married or someone had died.

"What's wrong? Where is Grandma Shushan?" Armanoush said softly. "I want to talk to Grandma."

That is when Barsam Tchakhmakhchian brought himself to tell her.

Since late evening Auntie Zeliha had been pacing her room with a brisk energy she didn't know how to contain. She couldn't confide in anyone at home how bad she felt, and the more she buried her feelings, the worse she felt. First she thought of brewing herself some soothing herbal tea in the kitchen, but the heavy smell of all the cooking almost made her throw up. Then she went into the living room to watch TV, but finding two of her sisters in there frantically engaged in cleaning while chatting excitedly about the next day, she instantly changed her mind.

Once back in her room again, Auntie Zeliha closed her door, lit a cigarette, and took out the companion she kept under her mattress for such trying days: a bottle of vodka. She hurriedly, but then with increasing sluggishness, imbibed one third of the bottle. Now, after four cigarettes and six shots, she didn't feel anxious anymore; actually, she didn't feel anything, except hunger. All she had to snack on in her room was a package of golden raisins she had bought from a rake-thin street vendor yelling in front of the house earlier in the evening.

Halfway through the bottle and with only a handful of raisins left, her cell phone rang. It was Aram.

"I don't want you to stay in that house tonight," was the first thing he uttered. "Or tomorrow, or the day after that. As a matter of fact, I don't want you to spend a day away from me for the rest of my life."

In response, Auntie Zeliha snickered.

"Please my love, come and stay with me. Leave that house right now. I got you a toothbrush. I even have a clean towel!" Aram attempted to make a joke but stopped halfway. "Stay with me until he's gone."

"How are we going to explain my sudden absence to my dear family, then?" Auntie Zeliha grumbled.

"You don't need to explain anything," Aram said imploringly. "Look, this must be the one benefit of being the maverick in a traditional family. Whatever you do, I'm sure nobody will be shocked. Come. Please stay with me."

"What am I going to tell Asya?"

"Nothing, you don't have to say anything. . . . You know that."

Holding the phone tightly, Auntie Zeliha curled up in a fetal position. She shut her eyes, ready to sleep, but then mustered the energy to ask: "Aram, when is it going to end? This compulsory amnesia. This perpetual forgetfulness. Say nothing, remember nothing, reveal nothing, not to them, not to yourself. . . . Is it ever going to come to an end?"

"Don't think about that now," Aram tried to soothe her. "Give yourself a break. You're being too hard on yourself. Come here first thing tomorrow morning."

"Oh my love . . . how I wish I could. . . ." Auntie Zeliha turned away her anguished face, as if he could monitor her via the receiver. "They expect me to go to the airport to welcome them. I am the only one who can drive in this family, remember?"

Aram remained silent, conceding this.

"Don't worry," Auntie Zeliha whispered. "I love you . . . I love you so. . . . Let's sleep now."

As soon as she hung up, Auntie Zeliha began to slip into a deep slumber. How she turned off the cell phone, put the vodka bottle aside, stubbed the cigarette into the ashtray, turned off the light, and slid under the covers she would have no recollection of the next morning, when she woke up with an excruciating headache and one of her blankets missing.

"Is it chilly in Istanbul? Should I have brought warmer clothes?" Rose asked, despite the fact that there were three main reasons not to: because she had asked this question before, because she had already packed her luggage, and because just now they were on their way to the Tucson Airport and it was too late to wonder anyway.

Tempted as he was to remind his wife of these three reasons, Mustafa Kazancı kept his eyes fixed on the road and shook his head.

On the day of their flight, Rose and Mustafa left the house at four p.m. to drive to the airport. They had two flights awaiting them: one short, the other quite long. They would first fly from Tucson to San Francisco, then from San Francisco to Istanbul. This being her very first trip to a country where English wasn't the primary language and people did not eat maple syrup–soaked pancakes in the morning, Rose found herself simultaneously excited and distressed. The truth is, she had never been the explorer type, and if it weren't for that much-wished-for but never-actualized dream trip to Bangkok, she and Mustafa wouldn't even have had passports. The closest she had gotten to international travel was to watch their six DVD *Discovering Europe* collection. From it she had a sense of what Turkey was like—a far more coherent sense than the scraps of information Mustafa had let slip every now and then during their many years of marriage. The problem, however, was that because Rose had watched all six disks in one sitting, and because the "Traveling Turkey" episode happened to be at the very end, after the episodes about the British Isles, France, Spain, Portugal, Germany, Austria, Switzerland, Italy, Greece, and Israel, she couldn't help but doubt if the scenes that popped into her mind now were from Turkey or from some other country. *Discovering Europe* DVDs were indeed handy for educational purposes, especially for American families with no time, means, or desire to travel overseas, but the producers should have put a notice on the collection urging the viewers not to watch the six disks uninterrupted, not to "travel" to more than one country in one sitting.

At the Tucson International Airport, they visited every store, which meant one kiosk and one souvenir stand. Despite the ostentatious INTERNATIONAL AIRPORT sign (a name bestowed because of its out-of-country flights to Mexico, which was only an hour by car), the airport was so modest that it resembled a local bus terminal, and even Starbucks didn't care to open a branch there. All the same, once inside the souvenir store, Rose was able to find numerous gifts for Mustafa's family. Despite the impromptu nature of this trip and her constant worry about how her daughter was doing there, not to mention her concern about how to tell her about her grandmother's death, as the time of departure neared, Rose had lapsed into a kind of tourist daze. Aspiring to get a special present for every member of Mustafa's all-female family, she carefully pored over the merchandise on every shelf, though there weren't many options. Cactus-shaped notebooks, cactus-shaped key chains, cactus-shaped magnets, tequila glasses with pictures of cacti—a bunch of tchotchkes and trinkets with images of, if not cactus, either lizards or coyotes painted on them. In the end, Rose got each Kazancı woman a gift—exactly the same to be fair—composed of a multi-colored I LOVE ARIZONA pencil curved into the shape of a cactus, a white T-shirt with the Arizona map printed on the front, a calendar with photos of the Grand Canyon, a mammoth BUT IT'S A DRY HEAT mug, and a refrigerator magnet with a real baby cactus in it. She also purchased two pairs of floral shorts like the kind she was wearing at the moment, in case someone would like to try them on in Istanbul.

After having lived in Tucson for more than twenty years, Rose, once a Kentucky girl, had *Arizona* written all over her. It wasn't only the customary leisure clothes—light T-shirts, denim shorts, and straw hats—that gave her away, or the sunglasses that stayed glued to her face, but also her body language that radiated the Arizona style. Rose was forty-six this year but carried herself with the sprightly attitude of a retired criminal court clerk who, after having rarely had the chance to don flowery dresses throughout her life, now enjoyed them to the extreme. The truth is there were a number of things Rose deeply regretted not having done by this age, including having more children. How she lamented not giving birth to another child while she was still able. Mustafa had not been particularly eager to have children, and for a long time, Rose had been fine with that, never really suspecting how she might eventually regret the decision. Perhaps it was a professional hazard —being surrounded by fourth graders all day long, she never noticed the lack of children in her own life. That said, she and Mustafa did overall have a happy marriage. Theirs was a marriage characterized more by the solace of mutually developed habits than passionate devotion, but nevertheless a marriage far better than thousands of others claiming to be amorous in essence. It was a twist of fate, when she came to remember that she had started dating Mustafa just to take revenge on the Tchakhmakhchians. But the more she had gotten to know him, the more she had liked and desired him. Though the allure of romantic affairs had from time to time left Rose secretly pining away for a different life with a different man, she had overall been quite content with the one she had.

"Leave the sauce," said Mustafa upon seeing that Rose was considering buying a spicy Mexican sauce in a cactus-shaped bottle. "Believe me, Rose, you are not going to need that in Istanbul."

"Really, is the Turkish cuisine spicy?"

To that, as to many other painfully obvious questions, Mustafa had only tentative answers. After so many years of complete detachment, his familiarity with Turkish culture, like a parchment drawing stripped by the sun and the wind, had been bit by bit rubbed out. Istanbul had imperceptibly become a ghost city for him, one that had no reality except to appear every now and then in dreams. Much as he used to fancy the city's many quarters and characters and culture, ever since he had settled in the United States he had gradually become numb toward Istanbul and almost everything associated with it.

Yet it was one thing to move away from the city where he was born, and another to be so far removed from his own flesh and blood. Mustafa Kazancı did not so much mind taking refuge in America forever as if he had no native soil to return to, or even living life always forward with no memories to recall, but to turn into a foreigner with no ancestors, a man with no boyhood, troubled him. Throughout the years, there were times when he had been tempted, in his own way, to go back to see his family and face the person he once had been, but Mustafa had discovered that this was not easy and did not become any easier with age. Finding himself more and more distanced from his past, he had eventually cut all ties to it. It was better this way. Both for him and the ones he had once badly hurt. America was his home now. Yet, if truth be told, more than Arizona or any other place, it was the future that he had chosen to settle in and call his home—a home with its backdoor closed to the past.

Mustafa was visibly contemplative and withdrawn on the plane. As they took off, he sat very still, and barely changed his position even after they had reached cruising altitude. He felt fatigued, exhausted by this mandatory journey that was only just starting.

Rose, on the contrary, was full of nervous excitement. She sipped cup after cup of bad airplane coffee, munched the meager pretzels they served, skimmed through the complimentary magazine, watched *Bridget Jones: The Edge of Reason,* though she had seen the movie before, engaged in a long prattle with the old lady sitting next to her (she was going to San Francisco to visit her elder daughter and see her newborn grandchild), and when the latter fell asleep, dedicated herself to attempting to answer the history trivia questions on the video screen in front of her.

Who suffered the most casualties in World War II?

a. Japan
b. Great Britain
c. France
d. Soviet Union

What was the name of the leading character in George Orwell's 1984?

a. Winston Smith
b. Akaky Akakievich
c. Sir Francis Drake
d. Gregor Samsa

For the first question Rose confidently answered B, but having no idea whatsoever about the second, she simply guessed A. She would soon be surprised to learn she had the first response wrong and the second one right. If Amy were here next to her, she would have answered *both* correctly, and certainly not by accident. Her heart ached when she thought about her daughter. For all their conflicts and quarrels, for all her personal failures as a mother, Rose was still confident that she had a good relationship with Amy. As confident as believing Great Britain suffered the most casualties in the Second World War.

Then they landed in San Francisco.

Once inside the airport, Rose was swept away by another shopping urge: goodies for the road. So miserable had she been with the crumbs served on the first flight that she now took matters into her own hands. Though Mustafa tried hard to explain to her that Turkish Airlines, unlike the domestic flights in America, would serve a whole bunch of delicacies, she wanted to be on the safe side before embarking on the twelve-hour flight.

Rose purchased a package of Planters peanuts, cheese crackers, chocolate-chip cookies, two packages of BBQ potato chips, a bunch of honey-and-almond granola bars, and sticks of bubblegum. Long gone was the idea of carb watching just for the sheer *possibility* of being watchful of something, *anything*. That was back in the days when she was young and determined enough to prove to the Tchakhmakhchian family that this woman they had stamped as *odar*, and never seen as one of them, was in fact a very nice and even enviable person. Now, twenty years later, she only smiled at the resentful young woman she once had been.

Although her bitterness toward her first husband and his family had never really subsided, in time Rose had learned to make peace with her flaws and incapacities, including her widened hips and belly. She had been on diets for such a long time, on and off, she didn't even remember when exactly she had stopped dieting once and for all. Whatever the timing, Rose had managed to discard, though not the pounds, at least the *need* to shed the pounds. The urge had simply ceased. Mustafa liked her the way she was. He never criticized her looks.

The announcement for boarding came when they were standing in line at Wendy's, waiting for two Big Bacon Classic combos and a sour cream–and–chive baked potato to be ready, just in case the food they served on Turkish Airlines turned out to be inedible. They grabbed their orders just in time and headed to the gate, where they would have to go through an extra security check reserved for those on intercontinental flights, particularly those heading to the Middle East. Rose watched with worried eyes as a polite but sullen officer searched through the presents she had bought in

Tucson. The officer plucked a cactus-shaped pencil into the air and waved it to and fro as if wagging a finger at some wrong she was about to commit.

Once aboard the plane, however, Rose swiftly relaxed, enjoying every detail of the experience—the tiny, chic travel kits they distributed, the matching pillows, blankets, and eye blinds, the continuous service of beverages interrupted by complimentary turkey sandwiches. Before long, the dinner service commenced, rice and oven-roasted chicken with a small salad and stir-fried vegetables. THERE ARE NO PORK PRODUCTS IN OUR FOODS, it stated on a piece of paper that came with the tray. Rose couldn't help but feel guilty about the Wendy's combos.

"You were right about the food. It's good," she said, giving her husband a shy smile and rotating a bowl of dessert in her hand. "And what's this?"

"*Ashure,*" Mustafa said, his voice oddly constricted as he looked at the golden raisins decorating the small bowl. "It used to be my favorite dessert. I'm sure my mother cooked a big pot of it when she heard I was coming."

Much as he tried to refrain from remembering such details, Mustafa couldn't erase the sight of dozens of glass bowls of *ashure* lined on the shelves inside the refrigerator, ready to be distributed to the neighbors. Unlike other desserts, *ashure* was always cooked as much for others as for one's own family. Accordingly, it had to be cooked abundantly, each bowl an epitome of survival, solidarity, and cornucopia. Mustafa's fascination with the dessert had become apparent when at the age of seven he was caught wolfing down the bowls he had been entrusted to dole out door to door.

He still remembered waiting there in the stillness of the apartment building next to their *konak* with the tray in his hand. There were half a dozen bowls on the tray, each for a different neighbor. First he had nibbled the golden raisins sprinkled on each bowl, confident that if he ate just those nobody would notice. But then he went on to the pomegranate seeds and the slivered almonds used for decoration, and before he knew it, he had eaten everything, consuming six bowls at one sitting. He had hidden the empty bowls in the garden. The neighbors often kept the bowls until they would return them with some other food that they had cooked, oftentimes another *ashure*. Thus, it had taken the Kazancı family some time to discover Mustafa's misdeed. And when they had, though visibly embarrassed by his greediness, his mother had not scolded him, but from then on she had kept extra bowls of *ashure* in the fridge, ready for him and him alone.

"What would you like to drink, sir?" asked the stewardess in Turkish, half bent toward him. She had eyes of sapphire blue and wore a vest of exactly the same color, on the back of which were printed puffy, pasty clouds.

For a split second Mustafa hesitated, not because he didn't know what he would like to drink but because he didn't know which language to reply in. After so many years he felt much more comfortable expressing himself in English than in Turkish. And yet, it seemed equally unnatural, if not arrogant, to speak in English to another Turk. Consequently, Mustafa Kazancı had up till now solved this personal quandary by avoiding communicating with Turks in the United States. His aloofness toward his fellow countrymen and countrywomen became painfully blatant at ordinary encounters like this one, however. He glanced around, as if searching for an exit, and having failed to find one nearby, finally answered, in Turkish: "Tomato juice, please."

"I don't have tomato juice." The stewardess gave him a sprightly smile, as if finding great humor in this. She was one of those devoted employees who never lost their faith in the institutions they worked for, capable of saying no regularly with the same cheery face. "Would you care for a Bloody Mary mix?"

He took the thick, scarlet mixture and leaned back, his forehead broodingly creased, his hazel eyes blurred. Only then did he notice

Rose staring at him, scrutinizing his moves carefully, apprehensively. Her expression darkened when she asked, "What is it, honey? You look nervous. Is it because we're going to see your family?"

Having already discussed this trip exhaustively, there wasn't much to say now. Rose knew Mustafa had no desire to go to Istanbul and was simply yielding to her adamant request to go there together. Though she appreciated that, it is hard to say she felt grateful. *A wife of nineteen years has the right to ask her husband for an act of kindness once in a blue moon,* she thought to herself, as she held Mustafa's hand and squeezed it tenderly.

This gesture caught Mustafa off guard. An immense melancholy surged over him as he inched closer to his wife. From her he had learned two fundamental things about love: first, that unlike what the romantics so pompously argued, love was more a gradual course than a sudden blossoming at first sight, and second, that he was capable of loving.

Over the years he had grown used to loving her and had found in her a measure of tranquillity. Rose, though highly demanding and difficult at times, was always true to her essence, decipherable and predictable; she was a straightforward chart of energies, every possible reaction of which he was familiar with. She never challenged him, just as she never truly confronted life, and she had a natural talent for adapting to her surroundings. Rose was an amalgam of clashing forces that effortlessly operated on their own, purely out of time, and thereby, out of family genealogies. After meeting her, the family torments that festered inside him had been transformed into a plodding but easygoing love, which was perhaps the closest he could get to real love. Rose might not have been a perfect wife in her first marriage, where she had failed to adapt to an extended Armenian family, but for exactly the same reason she was the ideal haven for a man like him, a man trying to flee his extended Turkish family.

"Are you OK?" Rose repeated with a slight edge to her tone this time.

And in this same moment, a wave of anxiety washed over Mustafa Kazancı. He paled as if he couldn't get enough air. He shouldn't be on this plane. He shouldn't go to Istanbul. Rose should go there alone and pick up her daughter and return home . . . *home*. How he longed to be back in Arizona now, where everything was canopied by the smooth flow of familiarity.

"I think I should walk a little," Mustafa said, handing his drink to Rose and standing up to control what was quickly turning into a panic attack. "It's no good sitting still for hours on end."

As he walked toward the back of the plane down the narrow aisle, he glanced at the passengers in each row, some Turkish, some American, some of other nationalities. Businessmen, journalists, photographers, diplomats, travel writers, students, mothers with newborn babies, complete strangers with whom you shared the same space and could even share the same fate. Some of them were reading books or newspapers, some watching King Arthur slay his enemies on an in-flight video game, while others were immersed in crossword puzzles. A woman ten rows back, a tanned brunette in her midthirties, looked at him intently. Mustafa averted his eyes. He was still a good-looking man, not so much for his tall, burly body, sharp features, and raven hair as for his genteel manners and style of chic dressing. Even though he had attracted the attention of numerous women throughout his life, he had never cheated on his wife. The irony was that the more he steered clear of other women, the more they had been attracted to him.

While passing the brunette's row, Mustafa noticed uneasily that the woman wore a brashly short skirt and had crossed her legs in such a way that you could easily be fooled into thinking that you might catch a glimpse of her underwear. He didn't like the disconcerting feeling the miniskirt brought on him; heavy, thorny memories he wished he could jettison once and for all; the sight of his younger sister, Zeliha, who had always been fond of such skirts, scurrying on the cobblestones of Istanbul in painfully hurried steps as if to escape her own shadow. As he lurched ahead, Mustafa's eyeballs darted to the other side so as to avoid looking where he shouldn't. Now that he had reached middle age, he sometimes wondered if he had ever liked women at all. Other than Rose, of course. But then again, Rose was not a woman. Rose was Rose.

Overall he had been a good stepfather to Rose's daughter. Though he truly loved Armanoush, he himself had not wanted to have any children. No kids for him. Nobody knew that deep inside his heart he believed he didn't deserve to have them. He wasn't sure he'd make a good father. Whom was he kidding? He would make a terrible father. Even worse than his own father.

He recalled the day he and Rose met, not a very romantic encounter perhaps, in a supermarket aisle as he stood with a can of garbanzo beans in each hand. Over the years, they had talked about that day so many times, making fun of every detail they could recollect. Still they had quite different memories of it: Rose always evoked his shyness and nervousness, while he recalled her glowing blond hair and intrepidness, which initially had intimidated him. Never again had he felt intimidated by Rose. On the contrary, to be with Rose was like abandoning himself to a serene stream, knowing that it would never pull him down, an imperturbable flow with no surprises along the way. It hadn't taken him a long time to start loving her.

In the mornings Mustafa would watch Rose toil in the kitchen. They both loved the kitchen, although for completely different reasons. Rose loved it because she loved cooking, and it made her feel at home. As for Mustafa, he simply liked to watch her amid the multiple ordinary details, the paper towels that matched the tiles, the mugs sufficient for a garrison, the puddle of chocolate fudge sauce hardening on the counter. He particularly liked to observe her hands as they sliced, stirred, minced, and chopped. Watching her make pancakes was one of the most soothing sights life had ever bestowed upon him.

At first, his mother and elder sisters kept writing to him, asking him how he was doing, when he was coming to visit them. They asked questions he busily ran away from and kept sending letters and gifts, his mother more than anyone else. Throughout these twenty years he met his mother again only once, not in Istanbul but in Germany. While on a visit to Frankfurt for a conference of geologists and gemologists, he had asked her to fly there to join him. So they met in Germany, mother and son, just as political refugees who couldn't go back to Turkey had been doing for many years.

By that time his mother had been so desperate to see him that she hadn't even questioned why he didn't come to Istanbul. It was astounding how quickly people managed to get used to such abnormal circumstances.

When he reached the rear of the plane, Mustafa Kazancı stopped in front of the toilets, right behind two men in line. He heaved a sigh as he thought about the evening before. Rose didn't know that on the way home from work, he had stopped by a corner in Tucson he had secretly been visiting every now and then for the last ten years. The shrine of El Tiradito.

It was a modest, out-of-the-way place in downtown Tucson, the only shrine in America dedicated to the soul of a sinner, reported the historical plaque there. The soul of an excommunicate, a *tiradito,* an outcast. Today nobody knew much about the details of the story, which went back to the mid-nineteenth century; who exactly the sinner was, what exactly his sin was, and more significantly, how he had ended up with a shrine dedicated to his immoral name. Mexican immigrants knew more about him than others, but then again, they were inclined to share less with outsiders. But Mustafa Kazancı wasn't interested in investigating historical details. Suffice it to know that El Tiradito was a good man, at least no worse than the rest of us, and yet he had committed awful deeds in the past, mistakes base enough to turn him into a sinner. Yet he had been spared and given what many a mortal lacked, a shrine.

So last night Mustafa had visited the shrine again, tormented by thoughts. Though small, Tucson was large when it came to holy places and he could have gone to a mosque if he desired. The truth is, he wasn't a religious man, and never had been. He needed no temples or holy books. He did not go to the El Tiradito to worship. He went there because that was the one holy place that didn't compel him to change into someone else in order to welcome him. He went there because he liked the feeling of the place, unpretentious and yet imposing and gothic at the same time. The mixture of Mexican spirits with American mores, the dozens of candles and *milagros* placed by different people, perhaps sinners themselves, the folded papers in the walls where visitors confessed and hid their sins—all appealed to him in his present mood.

"Are you all right, sir?" It was the stewardess with the sapphire eyes.

He gave a curt nod and answered, this time in English.

"Yes, thank you. I'm OK. Just a bit airsick. . . ."

Under the velvety light of a streetlamp penetrating the curtains, Auntie Zeliha lay slumped with the cell phone still in her hand, the vodka bottle leaning against her chin, and the cigarette still lit in her other hand.

Auntie Banu tiptoed into her room. Briskly she smothered the smoldering blanket and stubbed the cigarette butt out in the ashtray. She grabbed the cell phone and placed it on the cupboard, took the vodka bottle and hid it under the bed, then tucked her sister under the bedsheet and turned off the lamp.

She opened the windows. The air was crisp with the salty tang of a sea breeze. As the smoke and smell inside the room wafted out, Auntie Banu looked at her youngest sister's pale face, tired beyond her age. In the dim, yellowish light filtering in from the outside, Zeliha's face had grown incandescent, as if alcohol and sorrow had given her a radiance rarely encountered in nature. Auntie Banu softly kissed her on her forehead, compassion welling in her eyes. She then glanced left and right at her two *djinn* who had been carefully watching her every move from their usual places on her shoulders.

"What are you gonna do, master?" asked Mr. Bitter, a tinge of gloating in his voice. He did not bother to hide his delight in seeing his master so helpless and distressed. It always amused him to see the powerlessness of the mighty.

Auntie Banu wore just a hint of a frown. She gave no response.

Mr. Bitter then jumped aside and sat by the bed, dangerously close to Auntie Zeliha in deep sleep. His eyes brightened with the idea that had just crossed his mind. He harshly grabbed the end of the bedsheet, almost waking Auntie Zeliha, and tied the sheet on his head like a head scarf.

"Let me tell you something," Mr. Bitter declared, arms akimbo, voice thinned to a feminine tone, imitating someone. "There are things in this world . . ."

Auntie Banu instantly recognized whom he mimicked and felt her spine tingle.

"There are things so awful in this world that the good-hearted people, may Allah bless them all, have absolutely no idea of. And that's perfectly fine, I tell you; it is all right that they know nothing about such things because it proves what good-hearted people they are. Otherwise they wouldn't be good, would they? But if you ever step into a mine of malice, it won't be one of these people you will ask help from."

Auntie Banu stared at Mr. Bitter with awe but the latter now pulled the bedsheet off his head, jumped back to his previous position, facing the place where he had spoken from, ready to depict the second speaker in his imaginary dialogue. To imitate the second speaker he grabbed the remaining golden raisins Zeliha had left last night, and in a flash magically arranged them in the air, making a long necklace and several bracelets. He then put on the necklace and the bracelets and grinned. It wasn't hard to fathom whom he was mimicking now. It wasn't hard to recognize Asya's style.

Suffused with the charm of his narcissistic creativity, Mr. Bitter went on, "And you think, Auntie, I will ask help from a malicious *djinni!*"

Mr. Bitter now took off the necklace and bracelets, leaped back onto the bed, put the bedsheet back over Zeliha, and replied in a thicker tone, "Perhaps you will, dear. Let's just hope you'll never have to."

"Enough! What was all that?" Auntie Banu cut in furiously, though she knew the answer.

"That—" Mr. Bitter hunched forward and bowed like a humble actor encountering with thunderous applause at the end of his performance—"was a moment in time. It was a petite slice of memory."

With venom in his eyes, he then straightened his back and raised his voice: "That was a reminder to you of your very own words, master!"

Auntie Banu felt a fright so strong her entire body shuddered. There was so much malevolence in this creature's gaze, she didn't know how to explain to herself why she didn't tell him to get out of her life once and for all. How could she be drawn to him like this, as if they shared an unpronounceable secret? Never had Auntie Banu been so afraid of her *djinni*.

Never had she been so afraid of the acts she might be capable of committing.

SIXTEEN

Rosewater

"There goes another evil eye. Did you hear that ominous sound? Crack! Oh it echoed in my heart! That was somebody's evil eye, so jealous and malicious. May Allah protect us all!"

Thus exclaimed Petite-Ma Sunday morning at the breakfast table as a samovar boiled in the corner of the room. As Sultan the Fifth purred under the table waiting to be fed another chunk of feta cheese, and the candidate who had been fired on this week's Turkish version of *The Apprentice* appeared on TV in an exclusive interview announcing what had gone wrong and why he shouldn't have been fired, a tea glass cracked in Asya's hands. So unexpectedly did this happened that it gave her a jolt. All she knew was that she had as usual filled up half the tea glass with black, brewed tea, poured hot water to the brim, and then, just when she was about to take a sip, heard a crack. The glass fractured from top to bottom in a zigzag, like an ominous rift appearing on the face of the earth from a violent earthquake. In a flash, the tea inside the glass started to leak out and a dark brown puddle formed on the lacework tablecloth.

"Is there an evil eye on you?" Auntie Feride said, peering at Asya suspiciously.

"Evil eye on me?" Asya laughed bitterly. "I'll bet there is! Isn't everyone in this city jealous of my beauty?"

"There was an article in today's newspaper about an eighteen-year-old who dropped on his knees and died while crossing the street. I think it might have been the evil eye," Auntie Feride said with an air of genuine fear.

"Thanks for the morale boost," Asya said. But her grin quickly turned into a frown when she noticed what her crazy aunt was now gaping at: the snowman and snowwoman shakers. Just yesterday Asya had hidden them in a cupboard with the hope that nobody would find them for at least a month. And there they were on the table again. The ceramic pair was not only shoddy and kitschy—and regrettably durable—but also so alike that it was hard to tell which one was the pepper, which the salt.

"I wish Petite-Ma was feeling better, she could have poured some lead for you," Auntie Banu remarked with as vexed a look as Asya had ever seen on her face. Though indisputably the most experienced in the house with respect to the crepuscular and the paranormal, Auntie Banu was not authorized to pour lead since that required being initiated by a practitioner, a right she had been denied in the past.

Oddly enough, almost ten years ago, when she was still in the earlier stages of Alzheimer's and had decided that the time was ripe to choose the next woman in the family to hand over the secret of lead pouring, Petite-Ma picked out as her successor not Auntie Banu, as everyone had rightly expected, but the all-time champion agnostic Auntie Zeliha—a decision which back then had caused considerable turmoil in the family.

"Are you kidding?" Auntie Zeliha remarked upon hearing the

old woman's decision. "I can't pour lead, I am not even a believer. I'm an agnostic!"

"I don't know what that word means, but I can tell it is no good." Petite-Ma snorted. "You've got the talent. Learn the secret."

"Why me?" Auntie Zeliha asked while forcing herself to consider the possibility. "Why don't you choose my eldest sister? Banu will be more than happy to learn the secret. I am the last person you should teach magic to."

"This has nothing to do with magic. The Qur'an forbids us to practice magic!" Petite-Ma retorted, looking slightly affronted. "You are the right person. You have the determination and spirit and fury."

"Fury? But what do you need fury for? I could have been the perfect candidate if this were about hurling obscenities at obnoxious people, but I doubt I would be of any use when it comes to helping others." Auntie Zeliha broke into a grin.

"Do not underestimate the good in you," Petite-Ma replied.

It was then that Auntie Zeliha unleashed a remark to end the subject once and for all. "I am not the right person for this task. I might be a confused agnostic, but at least I've got the balls to stay one!"

"Wash your mouth out with soap!" Grandma Gülsüm flashed a scowl, overhearing the discussion.

But Auntie Zeliha entirely avoided the subject after that. Half of her family was staunchly secularist Kemalist, the other half, practicing Muslim. While the two sides constantly conflicted but also managed to coexist under the same roof, paranormality, crosscutting ideological divisions, was deemed to be as *normal* in their lives as consuming bread and water on a daily basis. This being the general framework, Auntie Zeliha, for her part, had chosen to spurn both sides equally.

Consequently, after all these years, Petite-Ma remained the one and only lead pourer in the Kazancı domicile. Lately she felt obliged to stop the practice, however, when one day she found herself with a blazing hot pan of melted lead that she didn't know what to do with. "Why are you handing me a boiling pan?" she asked in visible panic. They had gently taken the pan from her and, ever since then, never entrusted her with the task. But now that the topic had come up once again, all heads turned toward the old woman to see if she was following the conversation.

Being the object of all the attention at the breakfast table, Petite-Ma raised her head and looked curiously back at her family, while continuing to chew loudly on a piece of *sucuk*. She gulped down her bite, belched, and just when she seemed to be slipping off into her own world once again, shocked everyone with the clarity of her memory.

"Asya, my dear, I will pour lead for you and crack whatever evil eye might have clustered around you."

"Thank you, Petite-Ma." Asya smiled.

When Asya was a young girl, Petite-Ma had on a regular basis poured melted lead to ward off the evil eye around her. The truth is, given the weedy toddler that she once was, Asya seemed in need of a little boost at the onset of her mortal life. For some reason she used to frequently trip over and fall down, face-first, cutting her bottom lip each time. Suspecting the evil eye, instead of the toddler's yet unbalanced steps, they would hand her to Petite-Ma.

At first the ceremony had been a fun game for Asya, amusing and exciting, and also somewhat gratifying since she was flattered to be at the center of so much attention. She remembered taking great pleasure in every paranormal feat as a child, back when she was still young enough to have faith, not necessarily in magic, but in her family's ability to command destiny. She used to enjoy every detail of the ritual: sitting cross-legged on the prettiest rug in the house while a blanket would be stretched above her head, feeling protected and well hidden inside this peculiar tent, listening to the prayers uttered from all sides, and finally, that sizzling sound, like a shriek, the sound of Petite-Ma pouring melted lead into a pan full of water, as she kept repeating: *"Elemterefiş kem gözlere şiş. Göz edenin gözüne kızgın şiş."*

The lead would quickly solidify into ever-changing shapes. If there happened to be some evil eye in the vicinity, there would always materialize a hole in the lead in the shape of an eye. To this day Asya didn't remember an occasion where there wasn't one.

When all had been said and done, even though Asya had grown up watching Auntie Banu read coffee cups and Petite-Ma ward off the evil eye, she had eventually inherited her mother's skeptical agnosticism. She had deduced that it all boiled down to a matter of *rendition*. If you were looking for purple unicorns, it wouldn't take you long to start seeing them everywhere. In a similar vein, if there ever was a rapport between *divinatory material*—be it coffee cups or poured lead—and the process of interpretation, it ran no deeper than that between the desert and a desert moon. Though the latter needed the former as background scenery, it undoubtedly had an autonomous existence of its own. A desert moon existed outside the desert. Likewise, what the human eye saw in a piece of gray lead could not be reduced to the shape that materialized there. If you looked long and devotedly enough, you could even come across a purple unicorn there.

But despite her lingering disbelief, now that Petite-Ma remembered the routine, Asya did not intend to object. Her affection for Petite-Ma was too profound to turn the offer down. "All right." She shrugged. She was also confident that the old woman would probably forget the issue in a matter of minutes. "After breakfast you will pour lead for me, like in the old days."

The door of the bathroom downstairs opened just then and Armanoush joined them, looking sleepless and worn out, despondency showing in her beautiful eyes. This was a different Armanoush, barely connected with the world around her and somehow older. She walked in slowly and cautiously.

"We are very sorry for the loss of your grandma," Auntie Zeliha

said after a brief silence. "You have our most heartfelt condolences."

"Thank you," Armanoush replied, avoiding everyone's eyes.
She grabbed an empty chair and sat between Asya and Auntie Banu.
Asya poured tea into her glass, while Auntie Banu served her eggs
and cheese and homemade apricot marmalade. They also gave her
the eighth *simit*, not having broken the habit of buying eight *simits*
from a street vendor every Sunday morning.

Yet Armanoush looked at the food indifferently. She stirred her
tea distractedly for a few seconds, and then turned to Auntie Zeliha
and asked, "Can I come to the airport with you to pick up my
mother?"

"Sure, we will go there together," Auntie Zeliha said, and
translated her words to the rest.

"I am coming too," Grandma Gülsüm interjected.

"Okay, Mom, we'll all go there together," Auntie Zeliha said.
Asya blurted out: "I am coming too."

"No, miss, you stay here," Auntie Zeliha responded with a
tone of finality. "You stay and have your lead poured."

Asya stared at her as if to say: *What the hell was that?* Why was
she left out? If there ever was any degree of democracy and freedom
of speech in this house, it was reserved for everyone but her. When
it came to matters about her, the domestic regime automatically
metamorphosed into sheer totalitarianism. Asya sighed with a look
that bordered on despair. Then, without knowing why, but somehow goaded by a sudden urge to put pepper in her food, she grabbed
the ceramic shakers. A fleeting uncertainty crossed her face as she
dismissed the ugly snowman and grabbed the ugly snowwoman,
and with that, sprinkled way too much salt on the last bites of her
scrambled egg.

During the rest of the breakfast Asya remained remote and reserved. Watching her from aside, Auntie Banu rose to her feet after
a while and asked, her voice sopping with compassion, "Why don't

you and I go out shopping, sweetheart? We can leave after breakfast and be back in two hours. It'll be fun!"

"But first—" Auntie Banu perked up in midsentence—"come and help me in the kitchen to dole out the *ashure*."

Asya nodded her head in surrender. *What the hell?* she thought. *What the hell . . . ?*

The kitchen smelled like a popular diner might on a busy weekend afternoon. The scent of cinnamon pungently outweighed all others. Asya took a scoop and started to dole out *ashure* from a huge pot into small glass bowls, one and a half scoops in each. She wondered why Auntie Zeliha didn't want to take her along to the airport. There certainly was room in the car. It crossed her mind that perhaps Auntie Zeliha was trying to keep her away from the visitors. Asya had noticed that her mother was not thrilled with the news of Mustafa's return after twenty years.

"Can I help you?"

When she turned around she spotted Armanoush standing, watching her.

"Sure, why not? Thanks." Asya gave her a bowl of slivered almonds. "Would you sprinkle a few of these into each bowl?"

For the following ten minutes they worked side by side as they exchanged brief, poignant words about Grandma Shushan.

"I came to Istanbul because I thought if I made a journey on my own into my grandmother's city, I could better understand my family heritage and where I stood in life. I guess I wanted to meet Turks to better absorb what it means to be an Armenian. This whole trip was an attempt to connect with my grandma's past. I was going to tell her that we looked for her house . . . and now she's gone. . . ." Armanoush began to cry. "I didn't even have the chance to see her one last time."

Asya gave Armanoush a hug, though clumsily, not being used to showing love and compassion. "I'm so sorry for your loss," she said. "Before you leave Istanbul, you and I can go hunt for other reminiscences from your grandma's past. We can go to that place again and talk to other people, see if we can find anything."

Armanoush shook her head. "I appreciate that, but the truth is, once my mother is here, it'll be hard to go around alone. She's very overprotective."

They got quiet hearing footsteps behind them. It was Auntie Banu, coming to check how they were doing. She watched them decorate the desserts for a while. "Does Armanoush know the tale of the *ashure*?" she asked, smiling, not so much a question as an introduction to a narrative.

As the two young women worked together, cracking pomegranates and sprinkling cinnamon powder and slivered almonds on dozens of *ashure* bowls lined up on the counter, Auntie Banu began.

"Once there was, once there wasn't, in a land not so far away, the ways of the human beings were despicable and the times were bad. After watching this wretchedness for long enough, Allah finally sent a messenger, Noah, to correct the people's ways and to give them a chance to repent. But when Noah opened his mouth to preach the truth, nobody listened to him and his words were interrupted by curses. They called him names: crazy, lunatic, erratic. . . ."

Asya cast an amused look at her aunt, knowing how to get to her: "But more than anyone else it was the betrayal of his wife that devastated Noah, right Auntie? Didn't Noah's wife join the ranks of the pagans?"

"Indeed she did, that she-snake in the grass!" Auntie Banu replied, torn between narrating a religious story fittingly, and peppering it with a few remarks of her own.

"Noah tried hard to convince his wife and his people for eight hundred years. . . . And don't ask me how come it took him that long," Auntie Banu counseled. "Because time is a drop in the ocean, and you cannot measure off one drop against another to see which one is bigger, which one smaller. Just like that, Noah spent eight hundred years praying for his people, trying to bring them to the right path. One day God sent him the Angel Gabriel. 'Build a ship,' the angel whispered, 'and take a pair of each species.' . . ."

Translating a story that needed no translation, Asya's voice dropped a notch, for this happened to be the part she liked least.

"Eventually, in Noah's ark there were good people of all faiths," Auntie Banu continued. "David was there; so were Moses, Solomon, Jesus, and peace be upon him, Mohammed. Thus equipped, they embarked and started to wait.

"Soon the flood came. Allah commanded: 'O sky! Now is the time! Let your water pour down. Do not hold yourself back anymore. Send them your water and wrath!' He then commanded the earth: 'O earth, hold your water, do not absorb it. The water rose so quickly no one outside the arc could survive.' "

Now the translator's voice rose, for this happened to be Asya's favorite part. She liked to visualize the flood in her mind's eye, washing away villages and civilizations, as well as all the unwanted memories of the past.

"For days on end they sailed and sailed, it was all water everywhere. Soon food became scarce. There wasn't food enough to make a meal. So Noah ordered: 'Bring whatever you have.' And they did, animals and humans, insects and birds, people of different faiths, they brought whatever little they had left. They cooked all the ingredients together and thus concocted a huge pot of *ashure*." Auntie Banu proudly smiled at the pot on the stove as if it were the same as the one in the legend. "That is the story of this dessert."

According to Auntie Banu every significant event in world history had taken place on the day of *ashure*. It was on this day that Allah had accepted Adam's repentance. So was Yunus released by the dolphin that had swallowed him, Rumi encountered by Shams, Jesus taken to the heavens, and Moses given the Ten Commandments.

"Ask Armanoush to tell us the most important date for the Armenians," Auntie Banu remarked, thinking there was a good chance it could be this very same day.

As soon as the question was translated, Armanoush replied, "The genocide."

"I don't think that suits your pattern." Asya smiled at her aunt, skipping the translation.

It was then that Auntie Zeliha appeared in the kitchen armed with her purse. "All right airport passengers, it's time to go!"

"I'm coming with you." Asya dropped the scoop on the counter.

"We've talked about this," Auntie Zeliha responded indifferently. It didn't quite sound like her. A husky, scary tinge infiltrated her tone, as if someone else were speaking but using her mouth. "You stay at home, miss," decreed the stranger.

What upset Asya most was the fact that she couldn't read Auntie Zeliha's expression. She must have done something wrong to upset her mother, but she had no idea what it could be, unless, of course, it was her very existence.

"What have I done to her this time?" Asya lifted her hands in despair when Auntie Zeliha and Armanoush had gone.

"Nothing, my dear; she loves you so," Auntie Banu muttered. "You stay with me and the *djinn*. We'll all finish decorating the *ashure* and then go shopping."

But Asya didn't feel like going shopping. With a sigh she grabbed a handful of pomegranate seeds to sprinkle on the still-undecorated bowls to the side. She scattered the seeds evenly, as if leaving behind a trail of marks to guide some star-crossed fable child homeward. It occurred to her that pomegranate seeds could have been tiny, precious rubies in another life.

"Auntie." She turned to her eldest aunt. "What happened to that golden brooch that you had? The pomegranate brooch, remember? Where is it?"

Auntie Banu paled as Mr. Bitter on her left shoulder whispered into her ear: "*When do we remember the things we remember? Why do we ask the things we ask?*"

Noah's flood, terrifying though it was, started gently, inaudibly, with a few drops of rain. Sporadic drops, heralding the catastrophe to come, a message noticed by no one. There were dark, gloomy clouds clustered in the sky, so gray and heavy, as if loaded with molten lead full of evil eyes. Each hole in each cloud was an unblinking celestial eye that shed a tear for each sin committed on earth.

But the day Auntie Zeliha was raped was not a rainy day. As a matter of fact, there was not even a single cloud in the bright blue sky. She remembered the sky on that ill-omened day for years and years to come, not because she had turned her eyes up toward the heavens to pray or beg Allah for help, but because during the struggle there came a time when her head was hanging over the bed, and while unable to budge under his weight, unable to fight him back anymore, her gaze had inadvertently locked on to the sky, only to catch sight of a commercial balloon slowly floating by. The balloon was orange and black, and on it was stenciled in huge letters: KODAK.

Zeliha shivered at the thought of a colossal camera taking pictures of everything happening down here on earth at that moment in time. A Polaroid camera taking a snapshot of a rape inside a room in a *konak* in Istanbul.

She had been alone in her room since late morning, enjoying the solitude, which was a rare occasion in their household. When her father had been alive, he wouldn't permit anyone to close the doors of their rooms. Privacy meant suspicious activity; everything had to be visible, in the open. The only place where you could lock the door was the bathroom, and even there someone would knock on the door if you lingered inside for too long. It was only after her father's death that Zeliha was able to close her door and retreat into herself. Neither her sisters nor her mother recognized her need to shut off from the world. From time to time Zeliha fantasized how fabulous it would be to move out and have a place of her own.

Early this morning the Kazancı women had left home to visit the grave of Levent Kazancı, but Zeliha had excused herself. She didn't want to go to the cemetery with the whole family. She'd rather go there alone, sit on the dusty ground, and ask her father several questions he had left unanswered in his lifetime. Why did he always have to be so harsh and unloving toward his own flesh and blood? Zeliha wanted to know. She also wanted to ask him if he had any idea how much his ghost still haunted them—to this day they couldn't help but lower their voice sometimes during the day, afraid of disturbing Daddy with their presence. Levent Kazancı didn't like noise, especially children's clamor. As toddlers, they had to talk in whispers. Being a Kazancı child first and foremost meant learning the meaning of *dad,* not as in "Daddy" but as in "DAD": Deliberate Ache Deferment. The principle of DAD was applied to every moment of their lives. If a child happened to trip and cut herself in a room next to his, for instance, she would hold in her wail, press her hand tightly on the wound, tiptoe downstairs into the kitchen or into the garden, make sure she was far enough away not to be heard, and only then, only there, let loose a painful cry. Underlying it all was an alluring but never-realized expectation— that if you behaved correctly, Father wouldn't get angry.

Every evening when their father returned from work, the children would assemble in front of the table before dinner, waiting to be inspected. He never asked them directly if they had behaved well during the day. Instead he lined them up like a small regiment, and stared at each of their faces for varying amounts of time: Banu (more worried for her siblings than for herself, always the protective elder sister), Cevriye (biting her lips so as not to cry), Feride (eyes rolling nervously), Mustafa, the only son (hoping to make his way out of this miserable group, still assuming he was his father's favorite), and the youngest, Zeliha (a subtle sourness welling up in her heart). They waited until Father finished his soup, and then gradually asked one or two or three . . . or sometimes, if they were lucky, all of them at the same time to join the table.

Zeliha did not mind her father's repeated scoldings or even his regular spankings as much as she did these predinner inspections. It pained her to wait there by the table to be looked over, as if whatever wrong she might have committed during the day was written on her forehead with ink so invisible only Father could read it. "Why can't you ever get anything right?" Levent Kazancı asked each time he read a misdemeanor on one of the children's foreheads and decided to punish them all for it.

It was almost impossible to correlate this Levent Kazancı with the man he developed into once he stepped outside the house. Anyone who ran into him outside the *konak* would have taken him for an icon of reliability, considerateness, togetherness, and righteousness, the kind of man each one of his daughters' closest friends dreamed of marrying one day. Inside the house, however, his kindness was reserved for strangers alone. Just like he took his shoes off as soon as he entered the house and put on his slippers, just as naturally he transformed from a gentle bureaucrat to an authoritarian father. Petite-Ma once said the reason why he was so strict with his children was because he had suffered as a child, having been abandoned by his own mother.

Sometimes Zeliha couldn't help but think it had been fortunate that her father died so early, like all other males in their ancestry. A man as dominant as Levent Kazancı would have probably not enjoyed his old age, becoming weak and ill and in need of his children's mercy.

If she went to her father's grave, Zeliha knew she would want to talk to him, and if she talked to him, she might cry, cracking like a tea glass under an evil eye. But even the thought of crying in front of others was enough to repel her. Recently she had promised herself she would never become one of those weepy women and that whenever she needed to shed tears, she would do it alone. Hence, on that rainless day twenty years ago, Zeliha had chosen to stay at home.

She had spent most of the day lying in bed, browsing through magazines and daydreaming. Next to the bed stood a razor blade she shaved her legs with and a bottle of rosewater lotion she had applied afterward to soothe her skin. If her mother had seen this, she would have been extremely upset. Mother believed women should wax all their bodily hair but never shave. Shaving was for men only. Waxing was a womanly collective ritual. Twice a month the Kazancı women gathered in the living room to wax their legs. First they melted a clump of wax on the stove, which gave off a sweet smell like candy. Then they all sat on the carpet and applied the hot, sticky substance to their legs, chatting all the while. When the wax stiffened they peeled it off. Sometimes they all went to the local *hamam* and waxed their legs there on the huge marble slab under the steam. Zeliha hated the *hamam,* that all-women space, just as she hated the ritual of waxing. She preferred to shave with a razor; it was quick, simple, and private.

Zeliha dangled her legs over the bed and checked herself in the mirror across the way. She put some more lotion in her palm and as she slowly smeared the lotion on her skin, she studied her body carefully, admiringly. She was cognizant of her beauty and did not try to conceal it. Mother said beautiful women had to be twice as modest and careful with men. Zeliha thought that was sheer claptrap from a woman who had never been beautiful herself.

Languidly, Zeliha walked across the room and put a cassette into the tape player. It was an *alla turca* album by one of her favorite singers, a transsexual with a divine voice. The singer had started her career as a man, playing the hero in melodramatic movies; eventually he had undergone surgery to become a woman. She always wore flamboyant costumes topped with glittery accessories and lots of jewels, and so would Zeliha, if she had that much money. Zeliha adored her and had all of her albums. It was time the singer made a new album but she had recently been banned by the military, which was still controlling the country although it had been three years since the coup d'état. As to why the generals didn't like the idea of a transsexual singer on stage, Zeliha had a theory.

"It's because they feel threatened by her presence." She winked at Pasha the Third, who was curled on the bed like a heavy cushion of pure white fur, watching her with two narrow slits of brilliant green eyes. "Her voice is so celestial and her costumes so ostentatious, I am sure they are worried that when she appears on TV, nobody will listen to the generals with their husky voices and frog green uniforms. Can you imagine? What could be worse than a military takeover? A military takeover that goes unnoticed!"

It was then that there was a knock on the door.

"Are you talking to yourself, silly?" Mustafa exclaimed, poking his head inside. "Turn that awful music down!"

His hazel eyes glittering with the fervor of youth, his dark hair overly brilliantined and combed back, he could be called handsome if it weren't for the tic he had developed Allah knows when. He had the habit of tilting his head to the right when speaking, a brusque, mechanical movement that intensified when he was especially nervous or around strangers. Sometimes others mistook this tic for shyness, but Zeliha thought it was nothing but a sign of sheer insecurity.

Propping herself up on one elbow, she shrugged. "I can listen to whatever I want, the way I want."

But instead of quarreling with her or slamming the door shut behind him, as he had done numerous times before, he paused, as if distracted by a thought. "Why do you wear these short skirts?"

The question was so unexpected Zeliha looked at him stunned, only now detecting the hazy veil in his stare. *This year more than ever,* she thought, *he has been working himself into a jerk.* She uttered the last word aloud: "Jerk!"

Pretending not to hear that, Mustafa scanned the room. "Is that my razor blade over there?"

"Yes," Zeliha confessed. "I was going to put it back."

"What did you do with my razor blade?"

"That's none of your business," she said, although with some hesitation.

"None of my business?" his brow deepened further. "You sneak into my room, steal my razor, shave your legs so that you can show them to all the men in the neighborhood, and then tell me it's none of my business. Well, I'll tell you what. You are damn wrong, miss! It is my business to make sure that you behave."

Zeliha's eyes brightened a little. "Why don't you go and busy yourself with something else? Go and masturbate!" she snapped.

Mustafa blushed. He looked at his sister with venom in his eyes.

It had become clear recently that he had trouble relating to women. Even though he had grown up among women of all age groups and was used to being the center of their attention, his experience with the opposite sex still lagged dramatically behind his male peers. Though twenty by now, Mustafa felt like he was still stuck in that dangerous threshold between boyhood and manhood. He could neither return to the former nor leap into the latter. All he knew about the threshold was that it unnerved him and all he knew about being unnerved was that he didn't like it. He abhorred the carnal cravings of his body, and yet at the same time he was lured to them. In the past he had succeeded in holding his impulses back, unlike the other boys in his class, who would masturbate continually. Between the ages of thirteen and nineteen, he had managed to suppress what he named "it," managed not to masturbate. But last year, after failing his college entrance exam, years of self-castigation and self-loathing had provoked a backlash in him and the urge had come back even stronger, in the form of IT.

IT came upon him everywhere, any time of the day. In the bathroom, in the basement, in the toilet, under the bedsheet, in the living room, and once in a while, when he sneaked into his youngest sister's room when there was no one around, in her bed, on her chair, by her desk. . . . Like a capricious patriarch, IT demanded absolute obedience. No matter how much he obeyed, Mustafa would never use his right hand. The right hand was reserved for clean things, clean and consecrated. It was with his right hand that he'd touch the Qur'an, hold a rosary, and open closed doors. It was with his right hand that he would take the old people's hands to kiss. As blessed as the right hand was, the left hand was reserved for the abominable. He could masturbate with his left hand only.

Once he had a dream where he masturbated in front of his father. There was no expression on his father's face; he just watched from his place at the dinner table.

The last time Mustafa had seen his father stare at him like that he was eight and being circumcised. He remembered that miserable boy, lying in a huge, showy satin bed with presents all around, waiting to *have it cut,* surrounded by relatives and neighbors, some chatting, some eating, some dancing, while others were busy teasing him; seventy people there to celebrate his initiation from boyhood to manhood. It was on that day, right after the circumcision, right when he had let out an awful cry, that Father approached him, kissed him on the cheek, and whispered in his ear: "Did you ever see me cry, my son?" Mustafa shook his head. No, nobody had ever seen Father cry. "Did you ever see your mom cry, my son?" Mustafa nodded heartily. Mom cried all the time. "Good." Levent Kazancı smiled gently at his son. "Now that you are a man, behave like a man."

Whenever he masturbated he would never dare pull his pants down fully, not only out of fear of getting caught by someone in the house, but because he was irritated by the ghost of his father still whispering in his ears that same sentence over and over again. Suddenly in the past year his body had prevailed over not only his will but also his father's inspecting gaze. Like some contagious disease—for he was sure this *had* to be some sort of a disease—he started masturbating at all hours of the day and night. Stop it. Can't stop it. Stop it. Can't stop it. In dreams he would see himself caught by his parents while in the act. They would ram against the door, break it open, and bust him red-handed. Amid screams and wails, Mom would kiss and pat him on the back, while Father would spit on him and spank him hard. Where Father would leave bruises, Mom would rub in a speck of *ashure,* as if the dessert was some sort of an ointment. He woke up disgusted and shivering each time, sweat beaded on his forehead, and to calm down he would masturbate.

Zeliha knew none of this when she scoffed at him.

"You have no shame," Mustafa said. "You don't know how to talk to your elders. You don't care when men whistle at you on the streets. You dress like a whore and then expect respect?"

Zeliha broke into a scornful smile. "What's the matter? Or are you scared of whores?"

Mustafa just looked at her.

A month ago he had discovered *the* most infamous street in Istanbul. He could have gone to other places, where he could have found less inexpensive, less shoddy, and less disgraceful sex, but he deliberately went there—the cruder and the uglier the better. Dingy houses lined side by side, the smells and the stains and the lewd jokes men cracked less because they were humorous than because they needed a laugh; prostitutes in each room on every floor, prostitutes who perhaps never refused your money but all the same would disparage your performance. He had returned from there feeling filthy and weak.

"Are you spying on me?" he asked.

"What?" Zeliha guffawed, only now realizing she had made a discovery without knowing it. "You are so stupid. If you go to prostitutes, that's your problem, I couldn't care less."

Affronted, Mustafa felt a sudden urge to hit her. She had to understand that she could not mock him like that.

Zeliha squinted at him as if trying to read his thoughts. "What I wear and how I live is none of your business," she said. "Who the hell do you think you are? Father is dead and I am not gonna let you replace him like that."

Oddly, as soon as she uttered this line, she recalled having forgotten to pick up her lace dress from the dry cleaner that morning. *Make a mental note to pick it up tomorrow.*

"If Father were alive you couldn't talk like that," Mustafa replied. The hazy look he had a moment ago was gone, replaced by an embittered flicker. "But just because he's gone doesn't mean we have no rules in this house. You have responsibilities toward your family, miss. You cannot bring disgrace to this family's good name."

"Oh shut up. Whatever disgrace I might bring will be nothing compared to those you have caused to this day."

Mustafa paused, looking confused. Had she found out about his gambling or was she bluffing again? He had been betting on sports games, only to screw up bigger each time. If Father were alive he would beat him, no matter his age. The russet leather belt with the brass buckle. Could there be a rationale behind one of the belts hurting more than all the others, or was it simply his imagination concentrating on one particular belt and thereby allowing himself to believe that it wouldn't hurt as much when he chanced upon the others, feeling grateful, even lucky?

But his father was gone now and somebody needed to be reminded of who was in control.

"Now that Dad is dead," Mustafa declared, "I am in charge of this family."

"Are you?" Zeliha laughed. "You know what your problem is? Spoiled, you are too spoiled, precious phallus! Get out of my room."

As if in a dream, out of the corner of her eye she saw his hand rise up in the air to smack her on the face. Still disbelieving that he could hit her, she stared at him blankly and then managed to swing aside at the last instant.

She escaped the slap but that only enraged him. The second attempt burned her cheek. So she hit him back on the cheek, just as hard.

In a minute they were fiercely grappling on the bed like two children, except they had never grappled back when they were kids. Father had never approved of such brawls. For a few seconds Zeliha felt victorious, having hit him really hard, or so she thought. She was a tall, muscular woman and was not accustomed to feeling fragile. Like a champion in the ring, she clutched both hands in the air and saluted her invisible audience, delighted at her triumph: "I gotcha!"

It was then that he twisted her arm behind her back and got on top of her. This time everything was different. He was different. Holding her chest down with one arm, with his other hand he pulled up her skirt.

The very first thing she felt was mortification, and then more mortification. The sense of disgrace was so fervent there was no room inside her for any other feeling. She was instantly debilitated, almost frozen in a bashful kind of way, a way that revealed her up-bringing, the embarrassment of being exposed in her underwear prevailing over everything else.

But then, in an instant, a surge of panic washed the humiliation away. She tried to block him with one hand while with the other she attempted to pull her skirt back down, but in next to no time he had lifted it again. She fought, he fought, she slapped him, he slapped her harder, she bit him, he punched her in the face, one single blow. She heard someone shriek "Stop!" at the top of her voice, shrill and inhuman, like an animal in a slaughterhouse. She did not recognize her own voice, just as she didn't recognize her body, as though it were alien territory, when he entered it.

It was then that Zeliha noticed the KODAK balloon in the clear sky.

She closed her eyes as if it were a childhood game, hoping that if she didn't see, she wouldn't be seen. There were only sounds now, sounds and smells. His breathing got heavier, his hands on her breast and around her neck tightened. Zeliha feared he would strangle her, but the fingers soon loosened and the movement stopped. He made a wounded sound as he collapsed on top of her, his chest pressed against hers. She could hear his heartbeat race. What she couldn't hear was her own. She felt like life had been drained away from her.

She did not open her eyes until he slumped over, now soft inside her. When he stood up, Mustafa could hardly walk. Wobbling, he made it across the room and leaned against the door, gasping for breath. He took in a deep breath and caught a mixed smell—sweat and rosewater. He stood there briefly, his back turned to his sister, before he could bring himself to move again and run out of the room.

As soon as he stepped into the corridor, he heard the outer door being opened, his family now back home. He hurried to the bathroom, locked the door, turned on the shower, but instead of getting in, he collapsed to his knees and threw up.

"Hello!!! Where's everyone?" Banu's voice came from the front room. "Anybody home?"

Zeliha rose to her feet and attempted to smooth down her clothes. Everything had happened so swiftly, perhaps she could convince herself that it hadn't happened at all. But the face she saw in the mirror revealed a different story. There in the frame of her reflection, her left eye looked swollen with a purplish half circle under it. The very first thing Zeliha felt upon seeing her eye was a pang of guilt at her habitual skepticism. All these years she had snickered at cheesy action movies whenever someone got a purple eye, never believing that the human eye could swell that color with one blow.

Her face yes, but her body hadn't been damaged, she concluded. She touched herself to see if she still had feeling. How come she could feel the touch of her fingers but nothing else? If she were hurt or sad, wouldn't her body know? Wouldn't she know?

There was a knock on her door and without waiting for a response, Banu popped her head in. She was about to say something but her mouth opened and closed without words as she stood frozen, staring at her youngest sister.

"What happened to your face?" Banu asked anxiously.

Zeliha knew if there ever was a time to reveal this, it was now. She could either tell it now or hide it forever. "It's not as bad as it looks," she said slowly, the moment already gone and the choice made. "I went out for a walk and then I saw this man beating the hell out of his wife in the middle of the street. I tried to save a battered woman from her husband, but I guess I ended up getting beaten myself."

They believed her. It was something she would do, something that could only happen to her, if it were to ever happen to anyone.

The day Zeliha was raped she was nineteen years old. An age deemed to be a grown-up according to the Turkish laws. At this age she could get married or get a driver's license or cast a vote, once the military permitted free elections to be held again. Likewise, should she need one, she could also get an abortion on her own.

Too many times Zeliha had the same dream. She saw herself walking on the street under a rain of stones. As cobblestones fell one by one from above, digging a hole underneath, digging it deeper, she started to panic, afraid to follow suit, afraid to be swallowed without a trace by the hungry abyss. "Stop!" she cried out as stones kept rolling under her feet. "Stop!" she commanded the vehicles that sped toward her and then ran her over. "Stop!" she begged the pedestrians who shouldered her aside. "Please stop!"

That next month she missed her period. A few weeks later she paid a visit to a newly opened lab near her house. FREE PREGNANCY TEST WITH EACH BLOOD SUGAR TEST! it said on a sign at the entrance. When the results arrived, Zeliha's blood sugar turned out to be normal and she was pregnant.

Once there was; once there wasn't.

In a land far, too far away, there lived an old couple with four children, two daughters and two sons. One daughter was ugly, and the other was beautiful. The younger brother decided to marry the beautiful one. But she did not want to. She washed her silk clothes and went to the water and rinsed them. She rinsed and cried. It was cold. Her hands and feet were freezing. She came home and knocked on the door, but it was locked. She knocked on her mother's window, and her mother answered: "I'll let you in if you will call me mother-in-law." She knocked on her father's window, and he answered: "I'll let you in if you will call me father-in-law." She knocked on her older brother's window, and he answered: "I'll let you in if you will call me brother-in-law." She knocked on her sister's window, and she answered: "I'll let you in if you will call me sister-in-law." She knocked on her younger brother's window, and he let her in. He hugged her and kissed her, and she said: "Let the earth open up and swallow me!"

And the earth opened up and she escaped into an underground kingdom.★

Looking out the kitchen window with a spoon in her hand, Asya sighed as she watched the silver-metallic Alfa Romeo depart.

"You see?" She turned to Sultan the Fifth. "Auntie Zeliha didn't want me to go to the airport with them. She is being mean to me again."

How stupid of her to allow herself to be vulnerable the other night when they had all gone out to drink! How stupid of her to count on finally bridging the barrier between them. It would never entirely disappear. This mother she had auntified would always remain at an unbridgeable distance. *Maternal compassion, filial love, familial camaraderie, she sure needed none of that. . . .* Asya paused and spat out: "*Shit.*"

Article Twelve: Do not try to change your mother, or more precisely, do not try to change your relationship with your mother, since this will only cause frustration. Simply ac-

---

★ Indo-European folk tale, retold from "A Brother Wants to Marry His Sister," Range, *Lithauische Volksmärchen,* no. 28.

**cept and consent. If you cannot simply accept and consent,
go back to Article One.**

"You are not talking to yourself, are you?" said Auntie Feride, just then entering the kitchen.

"Actually, I was." Asya instantly exited her trancelike rage. "I was just telling my cat friend here how strange it is that the last time Uncle Mustafa was here he wasn't even born and Pasha the Third ruled the house. It's been twenty years. Isn't it strange? The man never visits us, and now here I am scooping out his *ashure* because we still welcome him."

"What does the cat say?" Auntie Feride asked.

Asya smiled sardonically. "He says I'm right, this must be a nuthouse. I should lose all hope and work on my manifesto instead."

"Of course we will welcome your uncle. Family is family, whether you like it or not. We are not like the Germans; they kick their children out of the house at the age of fourteen. We have strong family values. We don't meet just once a year to eat turkey. . . ."

"What are you talking about?" Asya asked, puzzled, but before she reached the end of her question, she sort of guessed the answer. "Are you referring to the Americans' Thanksgiving Day?"

"Whatever." Auntie Feride dismissed the information. "My point is that Westerners don't have strong families. We are not like that. If somebody is your father, he is your father forever; if someone is a brother, he will be your brother till the end. Besides, everything in this world is strange enough already," Auntie Feride continued. "That is why I like to read the third pages of the tabloids. I cut and collect them so that we don't forget how crazy and dangerous the world is."

Never having heard her aunt attempt to rationalize her behavior before, Asya couldn't help but look at her with renewed interest. They sat there in the kitchen amid appetizing smells, while the March sun shone through the window.

They sat together until Auntie Feride left after hearing her favorite VJ announce the video clips of a new band, and Asya craved a cigarette. She craved not as much a cigarette as smoking that cigarette with the Dipsomaniac Cartoonist, though it surprised her that she had missed him so much. She had at least two hours until the guests came back from the airport. *Besides, even if she were late, what difference would it make to anyone?* she thought.

A few minutes later, Asya closed the door softly behind her.

Auntie Banu heard the door, but before she could call out, Asya had already stepped out.

"What are you planning to do, master?" Mr. Bitter croaked.

"Nothing," Auntie Banu whispered as she opened a dresser drawer and took out a box. Inside the velvet cover rested the pomegranate brooch.

As the oldest of the Kazancı children, this brooch was given to her, a present from her father, who had inherited it from his mother—not his stepmother, Petite-Ma, but from the mother he never talked about, the mother who had abandoned him when he was a child, the mother he had never forgiven. The brooch was both sublime and heartbreaking, Auntie Banu feared. This nobody knew, but she had once kept the golden pomegranate with ruby seeds in salted water to wash away its sad saga.

Under the watchful gaze of the *djinn,* Auntie Banu caressed the brooch, feeling the glamor of the rubies glowing inside. Until she met Armanoush it had never occurred to her to investigate the story of the pomegranate brooch. Now that she knew the story, however, she couldn't figure out what to do next. Tempted as she was to give the brooch to Armanoush, for she believed it belonged to her more than to anyone else, she hesitated because she wasn't quite sure how to explain why she was giving it to her.

Could she tell Armanoush Tchakhmakhchian that this brooch had once belonged to her grandma Shushan without telling her the rest of the story? How much of her knowledge could she share with those whose stories she learned through magic?

Forty minutes later on the other side of the city, Asya entered through the squeaky, wooden door of Café Kundera.

"Yo, Asya!" the Dipsomaniac Cartoonist called out cheerfully. "Over here! I'm here!"

He hugged her and then, as she drew back from his arms, he exclaimed, "I've got news for you, one piece is good, one is bad, and one is yet to be classified. Which one would you like to hear first?"

"Give me the bad one," Asya said.

"I am going to prison. My drawings of the prime minister as a penguin weren't well received, I guess. I am sentenced to eight months in prison."

Asya stared at him with astonishment that soon widened into alarm.

"Shush, dear," the Dipsomaniac Cartoonist mumbled in a meek voice, putting his finger on her lips. "Don't you want to hear the good news?" Then he beamed with pride. "I decided I need to be true to my heart and get a divorce."

As the shadow of bewilderment that marred her face faded out, it finally occurred to Asya to ask, "And the yet-to-be classified news?"

"Today is my fourth day without a drink. Not even a drop! You know why?"

"I guess because you went to Alcoholics Anonymous again," Asya replied.

"No!" the Dipsomaniac Cartoonist drawled, looking hurt. "Because today was the fourth day since I last saw you and I wanted to be sober the next time we met. You are my one and only incentive in this life to become a better person."

Now he blushed. "Love!" he declared. "I am in love with you, Asya."

Asya's hazel eyes slid toward a frame on the wall, the photo of a rutted road from Camel Trophy 1997 in Mongolia. It would be nice to run into that picture now, she thought, to be traversing the Gobi Desert in a 4x4 Jeep, heavy, dirty boots on her feet, sunglasses on her face, sweating out her troubles as she went, until she'd become as light as a nobody, as light as a dry leaf in a gust, and thus waft into a Buddhist monastery in Mongolia.

"Don't you worry, little bird," the pomegranate tree smiled and shook the snow on her branches. "The story that I'm going to tell you is a happy one."

Hovhannes Stamboulian pursed his lips, as his mind worked feverishly, and the whirl of writing swallowed him up. With each new line added to this last story of his children's book, generations of lessons swirled back to him, some disheartening, others raising his spirits, but all similarly reverberating from another time, a time without beginning or end. Children's stories were the oldest stories in the world, where the ghosts of generations long gone spoke through the words. The urge to finish this book was so instinctive and undeniably riveting as to be irrepressible. The world had been a gloomy place since he had started writing it and now he had to finish without ado, as if its becoming a less heartrending place depended on this.

"All right, then," the Little Lost Pigeon chirped. "Tell me the story of the Little Lost Pigeon. But I warn you, if I hear anything sad, I will take wing and fly away."

After Hovhannes Stamboulian had been taken away by the soldiers, his family did not have the heart to enter his writing room for days. They had been in and out of every room but that one, and kept the door closed as if he were still inside working day and night. But the despondency permeating the house had become too intense and too palpable to pretend that life could return to normal. Soon Armanoush decided they would all be better off in Sivas, where they would stay with her parents for a while. It was only after this decision that they entered Hovhannes Stamboulian's room and found his manuscript, *The Little Lost Pigeon and the Blissful Country*, waiting to be completed. There among the pages they also found the pomegranate brooch.

Shushan Stamboulian saw the pomegranate brooch for the first time there on the walnut desk that belonged to her father. All of the other details of that ominous day faded away, but not that brooch. Perhaps it was the twinkle emanating from the rubies that had mesmerized her, or else seeing the world around her fall apart in a day made this the only thing she could remember. Whatever the reason, Shushan never forgot that pomegranate brooch. Not when she dropped half dead on the road to Aleppo and was left behind; not when the Turkish mother and daughter found her and took her into their house to heal her; not when she was taken by bandits to the orphanage; not when she ceased to be Shushan Stamboulian and became Shermin 626; not when years later Rıza Selim Kazancı would fortuitously chance upon her in the orphanage and, finding out she was the niece of his late master, Levon, decide to take her as his wife; not when she would the next day become Shermin Kazancı; and not when she would learn she was pregnant and would become a mother, as if she wasn't still a child herself.

The Circassian midwife revealed the sex of the baby months before his birth, by observing the shape of her belly and the types of food she craved. Crème brûlée from posh patisseries, apfelstrudel from the bakery opened by White Russians who escaped from Russia, homemade baklava, bonbons, and sweets of all sorts. . . . Not even once during her pregnancy had Shermin Kazancı craved anything sour or salty, the way she would have had she been expecting a girl.

Indeed it was a boy, a boy born into harrowing times.

"May Allah bless my son with longer life than any man in this family has ever had," Rıza Selim Kazancı said when the midwife handed him the baby. He then put his lips to the baby's right ear and announced to him the name he'd carry hereafter: "You will be named Levon."

Honoring the master from whom he had learned the art of cauldron making was not the only incentive behind this nominal choice. By naming their son Levon, he was also hoping it would be a favor to his wife for having converted to Islam.

Thus he chose the name Levon and like a good Muslim repeated it thrice: "Levon! Levon! Levon!"

Shermin Kazancı, in the meantime, remained as silent as a displaced stone.

It wouldn't take long for the triple echo to boomerang back to them in the form of a negative question. "Levon? What kind of a Muslim name is that? No Muslim boy can be named that!" the midwife balked aloud.

"Ours will," Selim Kazancı rasped in return, a defense he would repeat each time. "I made up my mind. Levon it shall be!"

But when the time came to take the baby to the Population Registrar, he softened.

"What is the boy's name?" the lanky, edgy-looking clerk asked without lifting his head from over a mammoth, clothbound notebook with a maroon spine.

"Levon Kazancı."

The officer lifted his reading glasses to the bridge of his nose and took a long look at Rıza Selim Kazancı for the first time. "Kazancı is indeed a fine surname, but what kind of a Muslim name is Levon?"

"It is not a Muslim name; it was a good man's name nevertheless," Rıza Selim Kazancı replied tensely.

"Sir," the officer raised his voice a notch, sounding self-important and knowing it. "I know what an influential family the

Kazancıs are. A name like Levon will not serve you well. If we write down this name, this boy of yours might have problems in the future. Everyone will assume that he is Christian, although he is a hundred percent Muslim. . . . Or am I mistaken? Is he not Muslim?"

"He sure is," Rıza Selim immediately corrected. *"Elhamdülil-lah."* For a fleeting moment it occurred to him to confide in the clerk that the boy's mother was an Armenian orphan converted to Islam and this would be a gesture to her, but something inside told him to keep this information to himself.

"Well, then, with all due respect to the good man you want to name this child after, let's make a slight change. Make it something akin to Levon, if you so wish, but choose a Muslim name this time. How about Levent?" The clerk then added kindly, too kindly for the harshness of the statement he was about to make: "Otherwise, I am afraid I will have to refuse to register him."

And so it was Levent Kazancı; the boy born upon the ashes of a past still smoldering; the boy no one knew his father had once wanted to name Levon; the boy who would one day be abandoned by his mother and grow up sullen and bitter; the boy who would be a terrible father to his own children. . . .

Were it not for the pomegranate brooch, could Shermin Kazancı have ever found the urge to leave her husband and son? It is hard to say. With them she had started a family and a new life with only one direction for it to go in. For her to have a future, she had to become a woman with no past. Her childhood identity was nothing more than morsels of memory, like crumbs of bread she had scattered behind for some bird to nibble on, since she herself would never be able to return the same way back home. Though even the dearest memories of her childhood eventually vanished, the brooch remained vividly ingrained in her mind. And years later when a man from America appeared at her door, it would be this very brooch that helped her to fathom that the stranger was none other than her own brother.

Yervant Stamboulian appeared at her door with dark, bright eyes set off by black, bushy eyebrows, a sharp nose, and a thick mustache that grew to his chin, making him look like he was smiling even when doleful. With a trembling voice and in words that were lacking to him, he announced who he was and then told her, half in Turkish, half in Armenian, that he had come all the way from America to find her. As much as he wanted to hug his sister there and then, he knew she was a married Muslim woman now. He stayed on the doorstep. Around them the Istanbul breeze drew circles and for a second it was as if they were pulled out of time.

At the end of their brief exchange, Yervant Stamboulian gave Shermin Kazancı two things: the golden pomegranate brooch and time to think.

Perplexed and dazed, she closed the door and waited for the revelation to sink in. Beside her on the floor Levent crawled and babbled with unbounded enthusiasm.

She went quickly to her room and hid the brooch inside one of the drawers in her wardrobe. When she came back she found the toddler laughing, having just managed to pull himself up into a standing position. The baby stood like that for a full second, took a step, then another one, and brusquely fell back on his bottom, the delightful fear of his first steps sparkling in his eyes. Suddenly the boy broke into a toothless smile and exclaimed: "Ma-ma!"

The entire house took on a rare, almost ghostly luminosity, as Shermin Kazancı broke out of her daze and repeated to herself: "Ma-ma!" This was the second word that had come out of Levent's mouth, after experimenting with "Da-da" for a while and finally saying "Ba-ba" the day before. Now she realized her son had uttered the word *father* in Turkish but the word *mother* in Armenian. Not only had she herself had to unlearn the language once so dear to her, but now she was obliged to teach the same process to her son. She stared at the toddler, baffled and brooding. She didn't want to correct "Ma-ma" by replacing the word with its equivalent in Turkish. The withdrawn but still vivid profiles of her ancestors surfaced. This new name, religion, nationality, family, and self she had acquired had not succeeded in overtaking her true self. The pomegranate brooch whispered her name and it was in Armenian.

Shermin Kazancı cuddled her son and for three full days managed not to think about the brooch.

But on the third day, as if her mind had been reflecting and her heart aching without her knowing it, she ran to the drawer and held the brooch tightly in her palms, feeling its warmth.

Rubies are distinguished gemstones known by their fiery red color. Yet it is not uncommon for them to alter their color, growing darker and darker inside, especially when their owners are in jeopardy. There exists a particular kind of ruby which the connoisseurs call the "Pigeon's Blood"—a precious blood-red ruby with a hint of blue, as if dimmed deep inside. That ruby was the last surviving reminiscence from *The Little Lost Pigeon and the Blissful Country*.

On the eve of the third day, Shermin Kazancı found a brief moment of solitude after dinner to sneak into her room. Appealing for consolation that no one could grant her, she stared at the Pigeon's Blood.

Only then did she acknowledge what she needed to do.

A week later on a Sunday morning she went to the harbor where her brother awaited her with a pounding heart and two tickets to America. In lieu of a suitcase, Shermin only had a small bag. She left all her possessions behind. As for the pomegranate brooch, she put it in an envelope with a letter explaining her situation and asked her husband two things: to give the brooch to their son as something to remember her by, and to forgive her.

When the plane landed in Istanbul, Rose was exhausted. She moved her swollen feet carefully, fearing they wouldn't fit into her shoes anymore, though she was wearing comfortable orange leather

DKNY footwear. She wondered to herself how on earth these stewardesses with their high heels could stay on their feet through a whole day of flying.

It took Mustafa and Rose half an hour to get their passports stamped, get through customs, pick up their luggage, exchange money, and find a car rental service. Mustafa thought it would be better if they had their own car, rather than using the family car. From a brochure Rose first chose a Grand Cherokee Laredo 4x4, but Mustafa advised something smaller for the crammed streets of Istanbul. They agreed on a Toyota Corolla.

Shortly thereafter, the two of them walked out of the arrivals area, pushing a cart loaded with a matching luggage set. They found a semicircle of strangers waiting outside. Among the group they first spotted Armanoush, smiling and waving; next to her was Grandma Gülsüm, her right hand pressed on her heart, about to faint from excitement. A step behind them stood Auntie Zeliha, tall and aloof, wearing a pair of dark purple-lensed sunglasses.

SEVENTEEN

White Rice

Rose and Mustafa spent their first two days in Istanbul eating. At the table they answered a plethora of questions different members of the Kazancı family asked them from all directions: How was life in America? Was there really a desert in Arizona? Was it true that Americans survived on mammoth portions of fast food, only to go on a diet in TV contests? Was the American version of *The Apprentice* better than the Turkish version? And so on.

Then there followed a series of more personal questions: Why didn't they have children together? Why hadn't they come to Istanbul before? Why didn't they stay longer? WHY?

The questions had opposing effects on the couple. Rose for her part did not seem to mind the interrogation. If anything she enjoyed being in the spotlight. Mustafa, however, steadily drifted into silence, getting smaller and smaller in his body. He spoke little, spending most of his time reading Turkish newspapers, conservative and progressive alike, as if trying to catch up with the country he had left. From time to time he asked questions about this or that politician, questions answered by whoever might know the answer. Though always an avid newspaper reader, he had never been so interested in politics.

"So this conservative party in power seems to be losing blood. What is their chance of winning in the coming elections?"

"Rascals! They are a bunch of liars," growled Grandma Gülsüm, in lieu of an answer. There was a tray in her lap with a pile of uncooked rice, which she sorted through before cooking in case there were any stones or husks. "All they know is to make promises to the people and forget what they said as soon as they get elected."

From his armchair by the window, Mustafa glanced up at his mother over the newspaper in his hand. "What about the party in opposition? The social democrats?"

"Same difference!" came the answer. "They are all a bunch of liars. All politicians are corrupt."

"If we had more women in the parliament everything would be different," Auntie Feride joined in, wearing the I LOVE ARIZONA T-shirt Rose had brought her as a present.

"Mama is right. If you ask me, the only trustworthy institution in this country has always been the army," Auntie Cevriye said. "Thank God we have the Turkish army. If it weren't for them—"

"Yes, but they should let us women serve in the army," interrupted Auntie Feride. "I myself would go immediately."

Asya stopped translating the conversation for Rose and Armanoush, who were sitting alongside her, and chuckled as she said in English, "One of my aunts is a feminist, the other is a staunch militarist! And they get along so well. What a nuthouse!"

Grandma Gülsüm turned to her son, suddenly concerned. "How about you, dear? When are you going to complete your military duty?"

Having a hard time following despite the instantaneous translation, Rose turned to her husband and blinked.

"Don't you worry about me," Mustafa said. "Provided I pay a certain fee, and show them I live and work in America, I do not have to complete full-term military service. I'll be done with only basic training. Just a month, that's all. . . ."

"But isn't there a deadline for that?" someone asked.

"Yes there is," Mustafa replied. "You need to go through this training by age forty-one."

"Well, then you need to do it this year," Grandma Gülsüm said. "You are forty now. . . ."

Sitting at the end of the table painting her nails a shiny cherry, Auntie Zeliha raised her head and darted Mustafa a glance. "What a fateful age," she hissed all of a sudden. "The age your father died, just like his father and his grandfather. . . . You must be pretty nervous now that you are forty, my brother. . . . So close to death. . . ."

The silence that followed was so deadly it made Asya inadvertently recoil.

"How can you talk to him like that?" Grandma Gülsüm rose to her feet, the tray of rice still in her hands.

"I can say whatever I want to whomever I want." Auntie Zeliha shrugged.

"You shame me! Get out, miss," Grandma Gülsüm rasped, her voice low and steely. "Get out of my house right now."

Still having two fingernails unpainted, Auntie Zeliha left the brush in the bottle, pulled back her chair, and walked out of the room.

On the third day of their visit, Mustafa stayed in his room all day long, excusing himself as sick. He had been running a fever, which must have diminished not only his energy but also his ability to talk, for he had grown excessively quiet. His face was drawn, his mouth dry, and his eyes bloodshot, though he was neither boozed up nor had he cried. For hours on end, he stayed in bed lying still and supine, studying indiscernible motifs of dirt and dust up on the ceiling. Meanwhile, Rose and Armanoush and the three aunts walked the streets of Istanbul, particularly the streets around shopping centers.

They went to bed earlier than usual that night.

"Rose, honey," Mustafa whispered to his wife as he caressed her light blond hair. The straightness, the blondness, the smoothness of his wife's hair had always soothed him, canopying him tenderly against his dark-haired family and dark-haired past. She lay against him, her body warm and soft. "Rose, sweetheart. We need to go back. Let's fly back tomorrow."

"Are you crazy? I'm still jet-lagged." Rose yawned, stretching her sore limbs. She was wearing an embroidered satiny nightgown she had bought that day from the Grand Bazaar, and looked pale and tired, less from the jet lag than from the shopping frenzy. "Why are you so antsy? Can't you bear to see your own family for a few days?" She pulled the soft covers up to her chin and in the warmth of the bed pressed her breasts against him. Then she patted his hand as if sweet-talking a boy and she kissed his neck gingerly, soothingly, but when she tried to pull away he wanted more, hungry for passion.

"Everything's fine," Rose said as her body tensed up and her breath quickened only to rapidly dwindle. "I am so tired, sorry honey. . . . Five more days and then we'll go home." With that she turned off the lamp by her side and it only took her a few seconds to fall asleep.

Mustafa lay there in the dim light, distracted from his erection, looking disappointed and taut. Though heavy-eyed he couldn't possibly sleep. He lay still there for a long time until he heard a knock on the door. "Yes?"

The door opened a crack and a second later Auntie Banu's head peeked into the room. "Can I come in?" she asked in a hushed, hesitant voice. Upon hearing a plausibly affirmative noise, she cautiously stole across the room with her bare feet buried in the high pile carpet, and then stopped. Her red head scarf glowed as if lit by a mysterious light and the dark bags under her eyes made her look ghostly. "You haven't come downstairs all day long. I just wanted to check on you," she whispered while eyeing Rose, asleep on the other side of the bed, her arms wrapped around her pillow.

"I wasn't feeling well." Mustafa looked at her, and then quickly glanced away.

"Here, my brother," Banu said as she handed him a bowl of *ashure*, decorated with pomegranate seeds. "You know, Mom has cooked a huge pot of *ashure* for you." Her serious face broke into a smile. "I must say, she is the cook but I am the one who decorated the bowls."

"Oh thank you, you are so kind," Mustafa stuttered as he felt a chill run down his spine. He had always feared his eldest sister. Whatever voice he possessed deserted him the moment he felt Banu's gaze inspecting him. Though she had made it a habit to scrutinize others, she herself remained inscrutable. Banu was the exact opposite of Rose: transparency was not among her virtues. If anything, she resembled a cryptic book written in an arcane alphabet. No matter how hard Mustafa tried to read her intentions, he could not for the life of him unravel her shadowy expression. Nevertheless, he did his best to look appreciative as he took the bowl of *ashure*.

The silence that followed was heavy and unfathomable. No silence had ever felt so cruel to Mustafa. As if disturbed by it, Rose turned in her sleep, but she did not wake up.

There had been many times in his life when Mustafa had been swept away with a sudden urge to confess to his wife that what she saw in him was not the whole of him. Yet at other times he had been satisfied impersonating a man without a past, a man with a cultivated denial. This amnesia of his was deliberate, though not calculated. On the one hand, there was somewhere inside his brain a gate that wouldn't close no matter what; some memories always escaped. On the other hand was the urge to dredge up what the mind had neatly expunged. These twin currents had accompanied him all throughout his life. Now, back in his childhood house and under the penetrating gaze of his eldest sister, he knew one of the currents was bound to lose its strength. He knew if he stayed here any longer, he would start to remember. And every memory would trigger yet another one. The moment he had stepped into his childhood home, the spell that had shielded him all these years against his own memory had been shattered. How could he take refuge in his manufactured amnesia any longer?

"I need to ask you something," Mustafa gasped, his gasp almost that of a boy's in between a spanking.

A leather belt with a copper buckle. As a boy Mustafa prided himself on never crying, not even a tear, when Daddy would take the leather belt out. As much as he had learned to control his tears, he had never managed to suppress the gasp. How he hated this gasp. Struggling for breath. Struggling for space. Struggling for affection.

He paused briefly as if to gather his thoughts. "There's something that has been nagging at me for quite some time now. . . ." There was just the slightest hint of fear in his otherwise tranquil voice. Moonlight penetrated the curtains and made a tiny circle on the rich Turkish carpet. He focused on that circle as he unleashed the question: "Where is Asya's father?"

Mustafa turned to his eldest sister in time to catch her grimace, but Banu was quick to restore her composure.

"When we met in Germany, Mom told me Zeliha had a baby from a man she had been engaged to briefly. But, she said, he had left her."

"Mom has lied to you," Banu interrupted. "But what difference does it make anymore? Asya grew up without seeing her father. She doesn't know who he is. The family doesn't know who he is either," she added hastily. "Other than Zeliha, of course."

"Including you?" Mustafa asked incredulously. "I heard you were a genuine soothsayer. Feride says you have enslaved some bad *djinni* to get all the information you need. You seem to have customers from everywhere. Now are you trying to tell me that you lack the knowledge of something this crucial? Haven't your *djinn* revealed anything to you?"

"They have, actually," Banu confided. "I wish I didn't know the things I know."

Mustafa's heart beat faster as he absorbed the words. Petrified, he closed his eyes. But even behind closed eyes he could see Banu's piercing gaze. And another pair of eyes portentously glittering in the dark, so hollow and bloodcurdling. Was that her evil *djinni*? But all of this must have been a dream, for when Mustafa Kazancı opened his eyes again, he was alone with his wife in the room.

Yet right beside his side of the bed there was a bowl of *ashure* waiting for him. He stared at it and suddenly he knew why it was placed there and what exactly he was asked to do. The choice belonged to him . . . to his left hand.

He looked at his left hand, now waiting next to the bowl. He smiled at his hand's power. Now his hand could either grab this bowl or just push it aside. If he chose the second option, he would wake up tomorrow to just another day in Istanbul. He would see Banu at the breakfast table. They wouldn't talk about the exchange they had the night before. They would pretend this bowl of *ashure* was never concocted and never served. If he chose the first option, however, things would come full circle. But having reached the age limits for a Kazancı man, death was close anyway, one day more or less would not make much difference at this point in his life. At the back of his mind echoed an old story—the story of a man who had escaped to the ends of the earth hoping to avoid the Angel of Death, only to run into him where they were originally destined to meet.

It was a choice less between life and death than between self-controlled death and sudden death. With such a family heritage he was sure he would die soon anyway. Now his left hand, his guilty hand, could choose when and how.

He remembered the little piece of paper he had stuck in the

stone wall at the shrine of El Tradito. "Forgive me," he had written there. "For me to exist, the past had to be erased."

Now, he felt like the past was returning. And for it to exist, he had to be erased. . . .

All these years, a harrowing remorse had been gnawing him inside, little by little, without disrupting his outer facade. But perhaps the fight between amnesia and remembering was finally over. Like a sea plain stretching as far as the eye could see after the tide went out, memories of a troubled past surfaced hither and thither from the ebbing waters. He reached out to the *ashure*. Knowingly and willfully, he started to eat it, little by little, savoring each and every ingredient with every mouthful.

It felt so relieving to walk out on his past and his future at once. It felt so good to walk out on life.

Seconds after he finished the *ashure*, he was seized with an abdominal cramp so sharp he couldn't breathe. Two minutes later his breathing stopped completely.

That is how Mustafa Kazancı died at the age of forty and three-quarters.

EIGHTEEN

Potassium Cyanide

The body was cleansed with a bar of daphne soap, as fragrant and pure and green as the pastures in paradise are said to be. It was scrubbed, swabbed, rinsed, and then left to dry naked on the flat stone in the mosque-yard before being wrapped in a three-piece cotton shroud, placed in a coffin, and, despite the adamant counsel of the elderly to bury it on the same day, loaded in a hearse to be driven directly back to the Kazancı domicile.

"You cannot take him home!" exclaimed the scrawny dead-washer as he blocked the exit of the mosque-yard and frowned at each and every one involved. "The man is going to stink, for Al-lah's sake! You are embarrassing him."

Somewhere between the "you" and "him" it started to drizzle; sparse, reluctant drops, as if the rain too wanted to play a role in all this but just hadn't taken sides yet. This Tuesday, in the month of March, no doubt the most unbalanced and unbalancing month in Istanbul, seemed to have changed its mind yet again, deciding it in fact belonged to the winter season.

"But dead-washer brother"—Auntie Feride sniffed, instantly integrating the nervous man into her engulfing and egalitarian cosmos of hebephrenic schizophrenia—"we will take him back to his house so that everyone can see him one last time. You see, my brother had been abroad for so many years, we had almost forgotten his face. After twenty years, he finally returns to Istanbul and on his third day here, he breathes his last breath. His death was so unexpected, neighbors and distant relatives will not believe he has passed away if they don't have a chance to see him dead."

"Woman, are you out of your mind? There is no such thing in our religion!" the dead-washer snapped, hoping this would stop whatever she might be planning to say next. "We Muslims do not exhibit our deceased in a showcase." His face visibly hardened as he added, "If your neighbors want to see him, they'll have to visit his gravestone in the cemetery."

While Auntie Feride paused to ponder this suggestion, Auntie Cevriye, standing next to her, stared at the man with a raised eyebrow, the way she looked at her students in an oral quiz when she wanted them to realize, by themselves, how illogical was the answer they had just given.

"But dead-washer brother," Auntie Feride continued, now catching up. "How can they *see* him when he is in a grave six feet down?"

The dead-washer's thick eyebrows shot up in frustration, but he preferred not to answer, finally sensing the futility of discussing anything with these women.

Auntie Feride had dyed her hair black that morning. This was her mourning hair. She shook her head with determination and then added: "Don't you worry. You can rest assured that we are not going to display him like the Christians do in the movies."

Pouting at Auntie Feride's relentlessly moving eyeballs and fluttering hands, the dead-washer stood dead still for an awful minute, now looking less annoyed than distressed, as if he had suddenly realized she was the craziest person he had ever come across. His ferrety eyes looked around for help. Having found none, they then slid toward the corpse patiently waiting for them to reach a decision about its fate, and finally back to both aunts again, but if there was a message secreted somewhere in this back-and-forth chilly glance, none of them could decode the meaning.

Instead, Auntie Cevriye tipped him, generously.

So the dead-washer took his tip and the Kazancıs their dead.

In a flash, they formed a convoy of four vehicles. Leading the procession was a hearse, sage green as a Muslim hearse is dictated to be, the color black being reserved for the funerals of the minorities, Armenians and Jews and Greeks alike. The coffin lay at the back of the three-sided truck, and since somebody had to go with the dead, Asya volunteered. Armanoush, her face full of confusion, was tightly gripping Asya's hand so that it looked like the two had volunteered together.

"I am not having any women sitting in front of a hearse," remarked the driver who startlingly looked very much like the dead-washer. Maybe they were brothers; one of them washed while the other carried the dead, and perhaps there was a third brother working in the cemetery, in charge of burying them.

"Well, you have to because there aren't any more men left in our family," Auntie Zeliha chided from behind, in a voice so icy the man grew quiet. Perhaps it had occurred to him that if there truly were no men to escort the dead in the hearse, it was better that these two girls accompanied him rather than this intimidating woman with her miniskirt and nose ring.

So the man stopped complaining and soon the hearse lumbered off.

Right behind them was Rose's Toyota Corolla. Her panic was almost palpable from the way the car lurched and halted, moving inch by inch, as if she were either convulsed by rhythmic hiccups or intimidated by the wild traffic.

Given her steadily increasing trepidation, it was now hardly possible to imagine Rose at the wheel of a five-door, ultramarine Grand Cherokee Limited 4x4, equipped with an 8.0 cylinder engine. The woman who roared down the wide boulevards of Arizona had turned into a different driver on the snaky, crowded streets of Istanbul. Truth be told, Rose was completely astounded at the moment, her bafflement and disorientation almost outweighing her grief. In no more than seventy-two hours after their arrival, she felt like she had accidentally fallen through a wormhole in the cosmos and stumbled into another dimension, a strange land where nothing seemed normal, and even death was smothered by surrealness.

Grandma Gülsüm sat next to her, unable to communicate with this American daughter-in-law she hadn't seen all her life, but also feeling concern and pity for her now that she had lost her husband, though not as much concern and pity as she felt for herself, now that she had lost her son.

In the back seat was Petite-Ma. Today she wore a teal outdoor head scarf trimmed with inky black on the edges. On her first day in Istanbul, Rose had spent a great deal of time trying to unravel the essential criteria that would illuminate once and for all why some women in Turkey wore the head scarf and others did not. Before long, however, she had given up, failing to solve the puzzle even at the local level, or even within the household. Why on earth ageless Petite-Ma wore the head scarf while her daughter-in-law Gülsüm did not, and why one of the aunties wore the head scarf while her three sisters did not, was simply beyond her.

Right behind the Toyota was Auntie Zeliha's metallic silver Alfa Romeo, with her three sisters crammed inside and Sultan the Fifth curled in a basket on Auntie Cevriye's lap, startlingly tranquil today, as if human death had a soothing effect on his feline ferocity.

Alongside the Alfa Romeo whooshed a yellow Volkswagen Beetle driven by Aram. Having a hard time understanding why the Kazancı women were taking their dead home but wise enough to know that nothing so tires a person as to attempt an objection to the aunties, especially when they came in a cluster like that, he had chosen not to ask. Hence he simply tagged along, trying to make sure his sweetheart was doing okay amid all this commotion.

At the jam-packed traffic lights at Shishli, only blocks away from the Muslim cemetery the dead-washer had tried to direct them to, by chance they all lined up side by side, like the leading regiment of an indomitable army with all the zeal to fight but no common cause. Auntie Feride popped her head out of the window and waved left and right, apparently thrilled by the happenstance of them all being lined up like this, acting in unison for the first time, even if it were for the sake of some mechanical red light. Rose ignored the gesture, Grandma Gülsüm the gesturer.

At the next red light, sitting between Armanoush and the driver of the hearse, Asya scrutinized the surrounding cars again, but luckily they had lost sight of one another. She felt a sudden, shameless relief to spot no Kazancı relatives of hers within eye range, except the one lying in the coffin in the back, of course, but then again that might not be included in her eye range as long as she did not turn around. As they drifted along in the jellylike traffic, so thick and congealed, slit here and there by unpredicted openings, in front of them materialized a bright red Coca-Cola van.

When the light turned green and they were moving again, in the lane to their right a fleet of cars with soccer fans appeared. They had caps and scarves and flags and banners and bandannas, and some had the colors of their team in their hair: red and yellow. Frustrated with the slow-moving traffic, most of the fans had momentarily sunk into lethargy, idly chattering among themselves, and once in a while waving a bandanna or two from the open windows.

As the traffic began lurching forward again, however, they resumed their chants and shouts with renewed vigor. Before long, a yellow cab with dozens of bumper stickers on it recklessly boxed itself into the tiny bit of space between the hearse and the Coca-Cola van ahead. The driver next to Asya cursed angrily as he slowed down. While he growled some more and Armanoush watched the cab in front with increasing wonder, Asya struggled to decode the writing on the bumper stickers. There, among many others, she spotted an iridescent sticker that claimed: DON'T CALL ME WRETCHED. THE WRETCHED TOO HAVE A HEART.

The driver of the cab in front was a rough-looking, swarthy man who had a gray Zapata mustache and who looked to be at least sixty, too old to get involved in such a soccer hullabaloo. There was a sharp mismatch between the man's utterly traditional look and the frenzy with which he drove. Even more interesting than him, however, were the customers—or else, friends—in his cab. The man next to the cabdriver had his face painted half yellow, half red. This Asya could clearly see from the hearse behind because this man had popped his head out the open window, waving a yellow and red banner with one hand, while loosely holding on to the front seat with the other. The upper part of his body jerking outside, and the lower part hidden inside the car, he looked like someone cut in two by a magician. Even from a distance Asya could see that the man's nose was so alcohol crimson that it upset the symmetry of half yellow and half red on his face, tipping the balance on behalf of the red. Just as she was pondering which particular drink—beer or *rakı* or both—could endow a human being's nose with this particular shade, the window behind his was rolled down and another fan raised a drum in the air with one hand and held on to the interior of the car with the other. In perfect unison, the two hooligans sprouted half their bodies out of the windows, like the pruned branches of a yellow cab tree.

Then the man in the front seat pulled out a stick and started beating the drum the other held in the air. The impossibility of the task must have energized them, for they soon supplemented the banging and thumping with an anthem. Several pedestrians on the sidewalks stood stunned, but a good number applauded and joined the duo, mouthing the lyrics in an ever-increasing fervor:

Let earth, sky, water listen to our voice
Let the whole world shake with our heavy steps.

"What are they saying?" Armanoush elbowed Asya, but Asya was slow to translate mainly because her attention had been fixed on a pedestrian. It was a lanky lad in rags, inhaling glue from a plastic bag while stomping his naked, blackened feet in time to the rhythm of the anthem. Every few seconds the boy stopped inhaling and mouthed the words of the anthem, but behind the rest of them, like an eerie echo: ". . . with our heavy steps. . . ."

In the meantime the other partyers also started to wave flags and bandannas out of their car windows, as they jovially joined in the song. Now and then the drummer stopped and used his stick to draw imaginary snakes in the air at the pedestrians and the street vendors on the sidewalk, as if directing them all, orchestrating the whole city's hubbub.

When the first half of the song was over, a brief confusion ensued since few in this motley chorus seemed to know the lyrics of the second half. Not letting this bothersome detail shatter their solidarity, they started singing right from the beginning once again, this time more feistily than before.

Let earth, sky, water listen to our voice
Let the whole world shake with our heavy steps.

Thus they all flowed along the avenue in a flood of red and yellow, amid chaos and clamor. Inside the hearse Armanoush and Asya and the driver silently watched, their eyes fixed on the yellow cab ahead. They tailgated so dangerously close to the vehicle that Asya could see empty cans of beer rolling around in the back window.

"Look at them! Is this how grown-up men should behave?!" the driver of the hearse exploded. "Now and again it happens. A fanatic dies, and his family or his madcap friends want to wrap his coffin with the flag of this or that soccer team. Then they shame-lessly expect me to transport these sacrilegious coffins to the ceme-tery! If you ask me, all this is sheer blasphemy! There should be a law prohibiting such nonsense. Only the green prayer mantle should be allowed, I say. Nothing else. What do these people think they are doing? Aren't they Muslim or what? You are dead for Allah's sake, what do you need a soccer flag for? Has Allah built a stadium up there in the sky? Are there tournaments in heaven?"

Not knowing how to answer this last question, Asya fidgeted uncomfortably in her seat, but then the driver's attention was drawn toward the yellow cab again. A mechanical melody rang out from the cell phone of the fanatic leaning out the front window. Still holding on to the cab with one hand, still conducting the city with his other hand, the portly hooligan made an attempt to answer his phone, forgetting he had no other hand for the task. He lost his balance, and along with it he lost two other things: first the drum-stick, then the cell phone. Both fell onto the road, right in front of the hearse.

The yellow cab abruptly stopped and the hearse came to a halt just when the rift between the two cars had shrunk to a hair. Asya and Armanoush lurched forward with the sudden stop, and then both simultaneously checked the coffin in the back. It was safe and sound.

In a flash the owner of the dropped items jumped down, still smiling and singing, his half-yellow, half-red face glowing with fer-vor. He stared back as if apologizing to the traffic behind for halting them all. Only then did he notice it was no ordinary vehicle that had been tailgating them but a sage green hearse, the symbol of death tagging along like an ominous shadow. For a long, prickly minute the man stood there in the middle of the traffic, looking perplexed. Finally, when yet another carful of fans whisked past him singing the anthem and his buddy impatiently banged the drum with his hand, it occurred to him to grab his cell phone and stick

ELIF SHAFAK

from the road. After giving the coffin in the hearse one last look he
turned around and climbed back into the cab. This time he did not
pop out the window again, but remained inside, subdued.

Armanoush and Asya couldn't help but smile.

"You must hold the most revered profession in this city," Asya
proclaimed to the driver, who had been watching the whole scene
with them. "Your shadow can terrify even the most hot-blooded
rabid fan."

"No," the driver said. "It pays so little, you have no coverage,
no health insurance, no right to go on strike, no nothing. I used to
drive large lorries in the past, long-distance transportation, you
know. Coal, petroleum, butane gas, industrial water . . . you name
it. I transported them all."

"Was that better than this?"

"Are you kidding? Of course it was better! You load the cargo
in Istanbul and head to another city. No boss to butter up, no supervisor to bootlick! You are your own master. If you feel like it,
you can linger on the road provided the boss does not ask you to
deliver the cargo too fast. In that case, you gotta drive with no
sleep. Other than that, it was a clean job. Clean and dignified. You
didn't have to bow to anyone."

The traffic began to accelerate and the driver shifted gears. Before long the soccer fleet veered right toward the stadium.

"Then why did you quit that job?" Asya wanted to know.

"I fell asleep at the wheel. One moment I am speeding down
the road. The next moment there is a terrible blast, like it is Judgment Day and Allah is summoning us all. When I open my eyes, I
find myself inside the kitchen of this shanty house by the road."

"What is he saying?" Armanoush whispered.

"Believe me, you wouldn't want to know," Asya whispered
back.

"Well, ask him how many dead he carries in his hearse
per day?"

When the question was translated, the driver shook his head:

"It depends on the season. Spring is the worst time of all; not many people die in spring. But then comes the summer, the busiest season. If it is above eighty degrees, it gets pretty hectic for us, especially the old. . . . They die like flies. . . . In the summer Istanbulites die in droves!"

He paused broodingly, leaving Asya with the semantic burden of the very last sentence he had constructed. Then he glanced at a pedestrian in a tuxedo shouting orders into his cell phone and exclaimed:

"All these rich people! Huh! They stockpile money all through their life, what for? How foolish! Do shrouds have pockets? It's a cotton shroud that we are all going to wear in the end. That's it. No chic clothes. No jewelry. Can you wear a tuxedo to the grave or a ball gown? Who holds the skies for these people?"

Asya had no answer to offer, so she didn't attempt one.

"If nobody's holding it how could we possibly live under this sky? I see no celestial columns, do you? How can one play soccer in these stadiums if Allah says 'I am not holding the sky up anymore'?"

With that question still hovering in the air, they turned the corner and finally reached the Kazancı domicile.

Auntie Zeliha was waiting for them in front of the house. She exchanged a few words with the driver and tipped him.

The Volkswagen, the silver metallic Alfa Romeo, and the Toyota Corolla were lined up in front of the house. It looked like everyone had arrived before them. The house was full of guests, all waiting for the coffin to be unloaded.

Upon entering the house Asya and Armanoush encountered a jam-packed, all-female space. Though the majority of the guests were clustered in the living room on the first floor, some were momentarily dispersed to the other rooms, either to change a baby's diapers or to scold a child, to gossip a bit or to pray, now that it was time for the afternoon prayer. With no bedroom to retreat into, the girls headed to the kitchen, only to find all the aunts there whispering about the tragedy that had befallen them, as they prepared trays of *ashure* to be served.

"Poor Mama is devastated. Who would have thought all the *ashure* she had cooked for Mustafa would be served to his mourners?" Auntie Cevriye said, standing near the stove.

"Yeah, the American bride is devastated too," Auntie Feride remarked, without lifting her gaze from a mysterious stain on the floor. "Poor thing. She comes to Istanbul for the first time in her life and loses her husband. How creepy."

Sitting at the table, listening to her sisters while smoking a cigarette, Auntie Zeliha said softly, "Well, I suppose she will go back to America now and remarry there. You know Allah's share is three. If she married for a second time, she has to marry for a third time. But I wonder, after one Armenian and one Turkish husband, what will her third choice be?"

"The woman is mourning, how can you say such things?" asked Auntie Cevriye.

"Mourning is like virginity." Auntie Zeliha heaved a sigh. "You should give it to the one who deserves it most."

Aghast at what they had just heard, the two aunts flinched in stupefied amazement. It was in that instant Asya and Armanoush entered the room, followed by Sultan the Fifth, meowing in hunger.

"Come on, sisters, let's give the cat something to eat before he devours all the *ashure*," Auntie Zeliha said.

Just then Auntie Banu, who had for the last twenty minutes or so been working at the counter, brewing tea, slicing lemons, and listening to the ongoing debate without ever interjecting, turned toward her youngest sister and decreed: "We've got more urgent things to do."

Auntie Banu opened a drawer, pulled out a huge, shiny knife, grabbed an onion lying on the counter, and cut it in half. She then cupped one half of the onion and pushed it toward Auntie Zeliha's nose.

"What are you doing?" Auntie Zeliha jumped in her chair.

"I am helping you to cry, my dear." Auntie Banu shook her head. "You wouldn't want the guests inside to see you like this, would you? As much of a free spirit as you might be, even you need to shed a tear or two in the house of the dead."

With the onion under her nose, Auntie Zeliha closed her eyes, looking like an avant-garde statue that had no chance of being exhibited in a mainstream museum: *The Woman Who Couldn't Cry and the Onion*.

Auntie Zeliha opened her jade green eyes and sniffed a tear. The onion had worked.

"Good!" Auntie Banu nodded. "Come on, everyone, we need to go into the living room. The guests must be wondering where their hosts are, leaving their dead alone!"

So said the sister who once used to play "mom" to Auntie Zeliha, singing her half-made-up lullabies, feeding her cookies on cardboard boxes turned into imaginary tables, narrating stories that always ended with the pretty girl getting married to the prince, cuddling and tickling her, the sister who made her laugh like no one else.

"All right!" Auntie Zeliha agreed. "Let's go, then."

So they ambled into the living room, the four aunts in the front, Armanoush and Asya following behind. In harmonized steps, they entered the room full of guests, the room where the body was.

Sitting in the corner on a floor cushion, her light blond hair covered with a scarf, her eyes puffy from crying, her plump body squeezed in among strangers, was Rose. She instantly gestured to Armanoush, calling her to her side.

"Amy, where were you?" Rose asked, but before waiting for the answer, she hurled other questions at her: "I have no idea what's going on here. Could you find out what they're going to do with his body? When are they planning to bury him?"

Having barely any answers herself, Armanoush inched closer toward her mother and held her hand. "Mom, I'm sure they know what they're doing."

"But I'm his wi-fe," Rose faltered over the last word, as if she were starting to doubt that.

They had laid him on the divan. His hands were placed with the two thumbs tied together on his chest, where a heavy blade of steel lay so that the corpse would not swell up. Two large coins of darkened silver were placed on his eyelids so that they wouldn't flip open. On his mouth they'd poured a few spoonfuls of water from Holy Mecca. Beside his head, in a copper plate, bits of sandalwood incense were burned. Though no windows were open, not even slightly ajar, the smoke in the room revived every few minutes as if fanned by an undetectable breeze sneaking in from somewhere behind the walls. When it perked up like that the smoke zigzagged around the divan, dissolving finally into a grayish whiff. But now and then the smoke followed a distinct route, descending closer and closer to the corpse in circles within circles, like a marauder bird going after its prey down on earth. The smell of sandalwood, as sour and sharp as it was, became so intense that everyone's eyes watered. Most didn't mind; they were crying anyway.

There was a crippled *imam* squeezed into a corner. In utter absorption he swayed the upper part of his body as he read the Qur'an aloud. There was a rhythm to his recitation, a beat that went up and up and then suddenly came to a halt. Armanoush tried not to pay any attention to the stark disparity between the *imam*'s diminutive body and the stoutness of the women surrounding him. She tried equally hard not to eye the void where the man's fingers were supposed to be. On each hand the *imam* had only one and a half fingers. It was impossible not to wonder what had happened. Was he born like that, or had they been chopped off? Whatever the story, the incompleteness of his body was one reason why all these women were so at ease next to him. In his imperfection resided the key to his perfection, in his lack of wholeness the secret of his holiness. He was a soul of thresholds, and like all souls of thresholds, had something eerie about him. He was both a man and yet so holy you could not possibly regard him as one. He was a holy man and yet so crippled you could not possibly disregard how mortal he was. No matter what, the crippled *imam* was in no need of fingers to turn the pages of the Holy Qur'an in his mind. He had it all stored in his memory, every verse of it.

At the end of the specified verses, the *imam* halted for a split second or two, swallowing the taste left behind in his mouth from all those sacrosanct words. Then he started reciting again. It was precisely this undulating rhythm that touched the female mourners' hearts; none of them understood a word of Arabic. Even when they broke down and sobbed, the women were always careful not to cry loud enough to overpower the *imam*'s voice. Never did they weep too softly either, by no means forgetting, not even for a moment, that this place they were all jammed in was an *ölüevi*.

Next to the *imam,* in the second most respected place, sat Petite-Ma, her diminutive body looking like a dry prune left in the sun, shrunk and wrinkled. Every newcomer kissed her hand and expressed their condolences, but it was hard to know if she really heard them. For the most part, to every one who kissed her hand, Petite-Ma eyed them in return. But now and again, to this guest or that, she responded with a set of questions. "Who are you, my dear?" she inquired of relatives or lifelong friends. "Where have you been all this time?" "Don't go anywhere, you naughty girl!" she scolded complete strangers. And then, in between her remarkable silences and silencing remarks, her face retreated into complete blankness and she blinked in furtive panic. At those moments she failed to grasp why all these people were here in their living room and why they cried so much.

The divan was still; the women were in constant motion. The divan was white; the women wore mostly black. The divan was soundless; the women were all voice—as if doing the exact opposite of the dead was a requisite of living. In a little while, each and every woman jumped to her feet and bowed her head obediently. Their faces alert with grief and reverence but also nosiness, they watched the crippled *imam* leave the room. As she walked him outside, Auntie Banu kissed his hands and thanked him many times, after which she tipped him.

As soon as the *imam* left, a piercing shriek ripped the air apart. It was emitted by a chubby woman nobody had ever seen before. Her cry escalated in piercing decibels, and in next to no time her face was crimson, her voice grating, and her whole body shaking. So miserable was her state and so palpable her pain that the others watched her in awe. The woman was a performer, paid beforehand to come and cry at the house of the dead, wailing for people she'd not even seen once. Her wail was so touching that the other women couldn't help but break down.

Thus finding herself surrounded by a swarm of mourning strangers (even her mother looked like a stranger at this point), Armanoush Tchakhmakhchian watched the swirl of women shift and part. In complete harmony and unfaltering shifts, guests exchanged seats with newcomers. Like birds of a feather they perched on the armchairs, the couch, and the floor cushions, so close that their shoulders touched. They wordlessly greeted and stridently cried; all these women who could be so quiet on their own yet so loud when they grieved collectively. By now Armanoush had detected some of the rules of the rite of mourning: There was no more cooking in the house, for instance. Instead, every guest came with a tray of food; the kitchen was jammed with casseroles and saucepans. There was no salt, no meat, no liquor in sight, and no appetizing smells of baked goods. Just like smells, sounds too were controlled. Music was not allowed; no TV, no radio. Thinking of Johnny Cash, Armanoush looked around for Asya.

She spotted her sitting on the couch with a bunch of neighbors, her head held high, distractedly tugging at a curl while looking at the dead body. Just when she was going to make a move toward her, Armanoush saw Auntie Zeliha sit next to her daughter, and with an unreadable expression say something into her ear.

So there was the dead body, lying on the divan.

And among a group of ceaselessly wailing and weeping women, Asya was sitting quietly, the color draining from her face.

"I don't believe you," Asya said without looking directly at her mother.

"You don't have to," Auntie Zeliha muttered. "But I finally realized, I owed you an explanation. And if I don't make it now, there will be no other time. He's dead."

Asya slowly rose to her feet and looked at the body. She looked hard and intently so as not to forget that this body washed with green daphne soap and wrapped in a three-piece cotton shroud, this body now lying motionless under a blade of steel and two coins of darkened silver, this body given holy water from Mecca and scented with sandalwood incense, was her father.

Her uncle . . . her father . . . her uncle . . . her father. . . .

She lifted her gaze and combed the room until she saw Auntie Zeliha, now sitting at the back with an unresponsiveness that even freshly cut onions could not touch. As Asya gaped at her mother, it dawned on her why she hadn't objected to her daughter calling her "auntie."

Her aunt . . . her mother . . . her aunt . . . her mother. . . .

Asya took a step toward her dead father. One step and then another, closer. The smoke intensified in tandem. Somewhere in the room Rose wailed in pain. So did all the women in an endless chain. All were interconnected in a sequence of reaction and rhythm, each and every story woven into those of others, whether their owners recognized it or not. There was a lull in every wail— or perhaps, in every communal grief there was someone who could not mourn with others.

"*Baba* . . ." Asya murmured.

In the beginning there was the word, says Islam, preceding any and every existence. Be that as it may, with her father it was just the opposite. In the beginning was the absence of the word, preceding existence.

Once there was; once there wasn't.

A long, long time ago, in a land not so far away, when the sieve was inside the straw, the donkey was the town crier, and the camel was the barber . . . when I was older than my father so that I rocked his cradle upon hearing his cry . . . when the world was upside down and time was a cycle that turned around and around so that the future was older than the past and the past was as pristine as newly sowed fields . . .

Once there was; once there wasn't. God's creatures were as plentiful as grains and talking too much was a sin, for you could tell what you shouldn't remember and you could remember what you shouldn't tell.

Potassium cyanide is a colorless compound, the salt of potassium and hydrogen cyanide. It looks like sugar and is highly soluble in water. Unlike some other toxic compounds it has a noticeable smell.

It smells like almonds. Bitter almonds.

Should a bowl of *ashure* be decorated with pomegranate seeds and drops of potassium cyanide, it would be hard to detect the presence of the latter for almonds are among the many ingredients.

"What have you done, master?" Mr. Bitter croaked as he broke into a sulky grin, as was expected of him. "You intervened in the way of the world!"

Auntie Banu tightened her lips. "I did," she said, tears running down her cheeks. "True, I gave him the *ashure,* but he is the one who chose to eat it. We both decided it was better this way, far more dignified than to survive with the burden of the past. It was better than not to do anything with this knowledge. Allah will never forgive me. I am ostracized forever from the world of the virtuous. I will never go to heaven. I will be thrown directly into the flames of hell. But Allah knows there is little regret in my heart."

"Perhaps purgatory will be your abode forever." Mrs. Sweet tried to offer some solace, feeling helpless as she witnessed the master cry. "How about the Armenian girl? Are you going to tell her about her grandmother's secret?"

"I can't. It is too much. Besides, she wouldn't believe me."

"Life is coincidence, master." It was Mr. Bitter again.

"I cannot tell her the story. But I will give her this." Auntie Banu opened a drawer and took out a golden pomegranate brooch with seeds of rubies buried inside.

Grandma Shushan, once the owner of this brooch, was one of those expatriate souls destined to adopt one name after another, only to abandon each at every new stage of her life. Born as Shushan Stamboulian, she then became Shermin 626. Next she was Shermin Kazancı, and after that, Shushan Tchakhmakhchian. With every name acquired something was also lost in her forever.

Rıza Selim Kazancı was a shrewd businessman, a dedicated citizen, and also a good husband in his own way. He had been astute enough to switch from cauldron making to flag making at the beginning of the Republican era, right at a time when the nation needed more and more flags to adorn the entire motherland. That is how he became one of the wealthiest businessmen in Istanbul. His visit to the orphanage took place sometime around then, as he intended to see the headmaster for potential business arrangements. There in the dimly lit corridor, he saw a converted Armenian girl, only fourteen. It wouldn't take him long to find out she was the niece of the man he most adored in this world: master Levon—the man who had taught him the art of cauldron making and who had taken care of the needy boy that he once was. Now it was his turn to help master Levon's family, he thought. And yet, when after numerous visits he would finally propose to her, it wasn't kindness that guided him but love.

He was convinced that she could and eventually would forget. He was convinced that if he treated her nicely and dotingly, and gave her a child and a magnificent home, she would bit by bit forget her past and her wound would ultimately heal. It was just a matter of time. Women cannot keep carrying the burden of their childhood once they themselves give birth to a child, he reasoned. Thus, when the news arrived that his wife had abandoned him to go with her brother to America, he at first refused to believe it, and then ostracized her. Shushan disappeared from the annals of the Kazancı family, including from the memories of her own son.

Being named Levon or Levent made little difference to Shushan's son. Either way, he grew up to be a dour man. As gentle and polite as he was outside his house, he was cruel to his own children, four girls and a boy.

Family stories intermingle in such ways that what happened generations ago can have an impact on seemingly irrelevant developments of the present day. The past is anything but bygone. If Levent Kazancı hadn't grown up to be such a bitter and abusive man, would his only son, Mustafa, have ended up being a different person? If generations ago in 1915 Shushan hadn't been left an orphan, would Asya today still be a bastard?

Life is coincidence, though sometimes it takes a *djinni* to fathom that.

Late in the afternoon, Auntie Zeliha stepped outside into the garden. Not wanting to enter the house, Aram had been waiting there for hours, having long since finished smoking all his cigars.

"I brought you tea," she said. The spring breeze caressed their faces, carrying from far and wide the sundry smells of the sea, growing grass, and the yet-to-blossom almond flowers of Istanbul.

"Thank you, my love," Aram replied. "What a lovely tea glass."

"Do you like it?" Auntie Zeliha rotated the tea glass in her hand as her face brightened with recognition. "This is so bizarre. You know what I've realized just now? I bought this set twenty years ago. So strange!"

"What is so strange?" Aram asked, feeling at that moment a drop of rain.

"Nothing," Auntie Zeliha said, her voice lowering. "It's just that I never believed they could survive this long. I always feared they would break so easily, but I guess they live to tell the tale, after all. Even tea glasses do!"

In a few minutes, Sultan the Fifth slowly padded out of the house, his stomach full, his eyes drowsy. He drew a circle around them before curling up next to Auntie Zeliha. For a while he seemed immersed in meticulously licking a claw, but then he stopped, looking around in alarm to ascertain what might possibly have disturbed the serenity. In lieu of an answer, a lukewarm drop fell on his nose. Then followed another drop, this time on his head. The cat rose slowly with deep discontent, and stretched his limbs before heading back into the house. Another drop. He quickened his pace.

Maybe he didn't know the rules. He just didn't know that whatever falls from the sky shall not be cursed.

And that includes the rain.

ACKNOWLEDGMENTS

This novel was written while commuting between Arizona, New York, and Istanbul. My gratitude goes to numerous Armenian and Turkish families who have welcomed me, hosted me in their houses, cooked for me, and shared their personal stories with me, despite the difficulty of remembering a painful past. I am particularly indebted to Armenian and Turkish grandmothers, who have an almost natural ability to transcend the very boundaries that nationalists on each side take for granted.

Much gratitude to Marly Rusoff and Michael Radulescu, my literary agents and dear friends, for their matchless support, work, and amity. Thank you to Paul Slovak for his editorial guidance, faith, and encouragement. Thanks to Muge Gocek, Anne Betteridge, Andrew Wedel, and Diane Higgins for their generous contribution.

Between the Turkish edition and the English edition of this novel in 2006, I was put on trial for "denigrating Turkishness" under Article 301 of the Turkish Penal Code. The charges that were brought against me were due to the words that some of the Armenian characters spoke in the novel; I could have been given up to a three-year prison sentence, but the charges were eventually dropped. During this time, I have been fortunate enough to receive enormous support from so many people, friends, and strangers alike, of such different nationalities and religions. I owe them more than I can say.

And finally, as ever, I thank Eyup, for his patience and love . . . for just being himself. . . .

Dreaming in English

'Why do you write your novels in English when Turkish is your mother tongue?'

It is a question I hear often. Each time, I need to pause for a split second. How can I explain? I try to offer a compact, rational answer. Yet I also know deep down that my urge to write stories in a language other than my native tongue was an irrational choice, if it was a choice at all. I did not exactly decide to write in English. Rather than a logical resolution, it was an animal instinct that brought me to the shores of the English language. Perhaps I escaped into this new continent. I sent myself into perpetual exile, carving an additional zone of existence, building a new home, brick by brick, in this other land.

Being a foreigner and an outsider in the English language intimidates me sometimes. My children make fun of my accent: they find it fascinating, an odd blend of unlikely ingredients. It is a challenge to write in English, both intellectually and spiritually. Yet the joy and the pleasure I derive from the experience are so much greater than the fear. And whatever pain there is, it is certainly less than the pain of feeling like a stranger in my motherland. Somehow, that is heavier.

I started learning English at the age of ten when I became a student at a British School in Madrid, Spain. It was the flexibility of its anatomy and the versatility and openness of its vocabulary that struck me most. Soon I was scribbling secret poems and stories in English.

When I took the step of writing my novels in English first, about fourteen years ago, I was already an established author in Turkey. Immediately there was a negative reaction in my motherland. They accused me of betraying my nation, an allegation I had heard before. They claimed I was 'forsaking' my inherited language for the language of Western Imperialism. 'How can she be one of us now?' declared a critic. 'If she writes in English she is not a Turkish author any more.'

I have never understood this either/or mentality. All I know is the more they want me to fit in, the more my soul resists. I refuse to make a choice between English and Turkish: in truth, it is the commute back and forth between the two that fascinates me to this day. As a nomad, I pay extra attention to those words that cannot be ferried from one continent to the other. I am more aware: of idioms, colloquialisms and street slang; meanings and nuances; linguistic cracks, gaps and silences. Languages shape us while we are busy thinking we are in charge of them.

I write my novels in English first. The English is translated into Turkish by professional translators (whose work I admire and respect), and I then take the new Turkish version and rewrite it with my rhythm, my energy, my vocabulary. I love using old Ottoman words, many coming from Arabic and Persian, which have been plucked out of the Turkish language by a modernist nationalist elite in the name of 'purity'. Critical of this linguistic xenophobia, I use both old and new words while writing in Turkish.

Separation can be a form of connection. Writing in English creates a cognitive distance between me and the culture I come from; paradoxically, this enables me to take a closer look at Turkey and Turkishness. *The Bastard of Istanbul* is a novel that concentrates on an Armenian and a Turkish family and the unspoken atrocities of the past. Had I written this in Turkish, it might have been a different book: more cautious, more apprehensive. But writing the story in English first freed me from the cultural and psychological constraints I internalize unconsciously in Turkish. Sometimes, absence is actually a bond and distance can help you to look closer.

I respect novelists and poets who see their mother tongue as their primary source of identity but I sincerely believe my own homeland is none other than Storyland: a vast expanse where static identity is replaced by multiple belongings and the boundary between dream and reality is fluid. This is what keeps me going despite my broken accent and enduring foreignness. I believe that if we can dream in more than one language then, yes, we can also write in more than one language.

He just wanted a decent book to read ...

Not too much to ask, is it? It was in 1935 when Allen Lane, Managing Director of Bodley Head Publishers, stood on a platform at Exeter railway station looking for something good to read on his journey back to London. His choice was limited to popular magazines and poor-quality paperbacks – the same choice faced every day by the vast majority of readers, few of whom could afford hardbacks. Lane's disappointment and subsequent anger at the range of books generally available led him to found a company – and change the world.

'We believed in the existence in this country of a vast reading public for intelligent books at a low price, and staked everything on it'
Sir Allen Lane, 1902–1970, founder of Penguin Books

The quality paperback had arrived – and not just in bookshops. Lane was adamant that his Penguins should appear in chain stores and tobacconists, and should cost no more than a packet of cigarettes.

Reading habits (and cigarette prices) have changed since 1935, but Penguin still believes in publishing the best books for everybody to enjoy. We still believe that good design costs no more than bad design, and we still believe that quality books published passionately and responsibly make the world a better place.

So wherever you see the little bird – whether it's on a piece of prize-winning literary fiction or a celebrity autobiography, political tour de force or historical masterpiece, a serial-killer thriller, reference book, world classic or a piece of pure escapism – you can bet that it represents the very best that the genre has to offer.

Whatever you like to read – trust Penguin.